The Healer

LISA FOUGÈRE

ISBN: 978-0-578-67717-0

To Bruce, Leyna, Luke and Maggie.
My whole world

THANK YOU

Most thanks go to my indefatigable and ever-supporting husband, Bruce. I so appreciate you always believing in me, and doing all the tech stuff that makes me insane.

Serendipitous:
Occurring or discovered by chance in a happy or beneficial way.

PROLOGUE:

"Metaphysical." The word entered the air around me with a fizzling and crackling sensation that abruptly broke me from my daydream. I had been sitting and waiting for my father to finish his meeting for what felt like ages, so I turned my attention to the soft velvet of the chair beneath me. It was a mystical green blue like the picture of the deep ocean on my "old-fashioned" map of the world picture book. I was probably too old for the book now, really, but held on to it because the drawings were so beautiful. Most of the pictures had rough outlines of the continents, surrounded by swirling water capped with white. There were ships at sea with their sails filled with wind, as though in the midst of a storm. I liked to imagine they were pirate ships. Dirty, wrinkled pirates with missing teeth and greasy hair in long knots. Yelling curses into the wind as they tried against all odds to keep the ship from succumbing to the violence of the storm. Many of them would, sadly, get tossed into the churning sea. Even if the pirates succeeded in outwitting the weather, they would most certainly be eaten by the tentacled sea monsters of bright pink or purple peppered throughout the water. The monsters were drawn to appear twice the size of the poor ships. And even though I know I'm supposed to despise pirates as despicable, drunken criminals, I can't help but root for their escape from the sea beasts that hunt them. A triumph of pure human effort.

I was imagining an epic pirate-ship-and-sea-beast battle while running my hand over the velvet chair. When I swiped one way, the color was lightened, and the fabric was smooth under my fingers, like our cat Frisco. It felt safer, like the shallow end of the ocean where I can see my feet. But when

I moved my hand in the opposite direction, the color darkened, like the deep and unknown parts of the ocean. Where you feel you could be snatched up from below at any moment. This made the velvet feel coarser, as though it were unhappy with the change. Even Frisco hated being petted the "wrong way." It was the only time he would take a swipe at me - if I petted him "up" instead of "down." I moved my hand back and forth, passing between safety and danger.

I had left the conversation between my father and this man for the depths of the sea, so didn't pay attention to what they were discussing. But then the man spoke that word: "metaphysical." He did so as though it was nothing important. My head turned sharply to stare at the mouth where it originated, alarmed by the shift in the air.

I have always loved words. Words that had physical feelings, like *effervescent*, or words like *persnickety* that sounded like a bird's song. And while my eight-year old brain couldn't understand what such a powerful word like *metaphysical* might mean, the reaction in my body was startling. My arms were covered in goosebumps, like when the first cold breeze of fall hits you and you're still in your summer tank top. I felt a vibration emanate from the top of my head through my whole body down to my toes. My eyes wide and alert, my pirate battle forgotten, I concentrated on the man's lips, desperate for him to say it again. "Metaphysical." It felt like a window to a magical, and maybe scary, place had been opened. I looked at my father, but he was acting like nothing had changed.

Suddenly, I was self-conscious about my physical reaction. Maybe, because the grown-ups didn't notice anything, my reaction wasn't normal. Maybe I was having a "fit" like the women in those daytime shows my mom used to watch when I was home sick from school.

Now I worried my father or the man he was with would notice what was happening to me and decide I needed to go to the hospital. Decide I was unwell and should be seen. But how could I explain the terrifying thrill of that word? I decided to say nothing at all, even though the vibration had grown to a pulse behind my eyes, and I was sure my whole head was growing and shrinking. I tried calming my breath like my mom does when I know I'm annoying her and she's "trying not to yell so much." Count to four with each inhale, hold for a two count, and count for six with the exhale. I shut my eyes to concentrate on the counting: One… two…three…four… hold…six…five…four…three…two…one. Slowly, the pulsing pushed out from behind my eyes and the vibration reversed its course from my toes up to the top of my head. Then it was over, and only a shadow of the sensation lingered in my body. I opened my eyes. My father and the man were standing and shaking hands. Then my father turned to me and smiled.

"Ready to go, kiddo?"

I nodded quickly and kept my eyes on his feet as I followed him out of the house and into our car.

When we got home, I ran up to my room and shut the door. Grabbing the big, blue Oxford English dictionary my aunt Mary Ann gave me for my birthday a few months earlier, I sprawled out on my bed. My friends at the time wrinkled their noses and wondered aloud why she would get me such a boring gift. But I was overjoyed. My aunt understood my excitement over words because she felt it, too. She was always telling me about whatever book she was currently "smitten with." And if she found an author using a word like "great" or "fine" instead of something more inspirational like "exceptional" and "sublime," she would wrinkle her nose and call the book basic. Though I wasn't really sure what that meant, I would shake my head in commiseration. I thought Mary Ann was the best.

The corners of the dictionary's cover were already showing little signs of wear, betraying how much time I actually spent poring over the tiny type. Each night, I let my fingers slowly hover over the little half-moon indentations that led me to a letter. The anticipation of what word I might find when I landed on a page was exciting; last night I opened the pages between “open air” and “opossum.” Open air, open-armed, open book…I read through the words. I laughed at “open sesame,” which only had “see SESAME” listed after it.

My favorite word that night was “Ophicleide: An obsolete usu. Bass brass wind instrument with keys, developed from the serpent.” I pictured a winding scaly beast with piano keys along its torso that, when played, made the poor creature sing a low, deep melody.

Tonight, however, my fingers immediately found the L/MN halfmoon and threw the book open. Suddenly, I realized I didn’t know how to spell it. I said the word out loud a few times and figured it must start with M-E-T-A. I had no luck with M-E-T-A-F, but then I remembered that “PH” can make the “F” sound too. I found the page starting with “metaphase” and scanned down the type until I saw it a quarter of the way down. “Metaphysical.”

I hesitated. All of a sudden, I was nervous. What if it didn’t mean anything exciting. What if it meant something normal, like a type of toe infection or a sandwich spread? Then my reaction earlier on the velvet chair would make no sense at all. Maybe it would mean I actually *was* having a fit. I took a deep breath and looked at the definition.

Metaphysical: 1. Of or relating to metaphysics. 2. Based on abstract general reasoning. 3. Excessively subtle or theoretical…

What good was any of this? I didn’t even understand what these definitions meant. Why did grown-up books have to be so confusing? Why couldn’t they just say plainly what it means instead of trying to make it sound all important and serious? I felt myself getting angry when I turned back to the definition to read further.

...4. Incorporeal. 5. Supernatural. 6. Visionary.

The vibration was suddenly back at the top of my head. I didn't know what these other words meant, but I knew they were important based on my body's reaction. Careful to keep my finger holding the page, I quickly flipped to the "I" section.

Incorporeal: 1. Not composed of matter. 2. Of immaterial beings. 3. LA: Having no physical existence.

My heart was beating so fast I felt like it might fly right out of my chest. The pulse was back behind my eyes, and I felt a little lightheaded. With another finger, I held the second page and flipped to the back of the "S" section. Super - Supersede... supercomputer... superheterodyne... superintendent...How many words starting with *super* are there?! Finally, I found it and read:

Supernatural: Attributed to or thought to reveal some force above the laws of nature; magical; occult; mystical.

As suddenly as my physical symptoms began, they were replaced with an overwhelming sense of calm and peace.

Swullocking:
(British) Hot, humid oppressive weather.

CHAPTER 1

I didn't like the feeling of sweat as it beaded on my forehead and neck. Strands of hair were sticking to the side of my face, and I stopped running to carefully gather them back up into my ponytail. I got a haircut the week before school started, and now slightly regretted my decision to start the fourth grade by making my long, dark waist-length hair into a shoulder-grazing bob. New starts, new look. The beginning of a school year always filled me with a sense of hope and determination. Whatever tests I didn't do well on, trouble I had with friends, or embarrassing things I did the year before were pretty much erased during the three months of summer break. Not erased from my mind, of course, but from the minds of the teachers and classmates who I so desperately wanted to like me. Still, when my mom and I were loading up the cart with black and white composition notebooks and unsharpened #2 pencils last Saturday, I felt inspired. Why couldn't this year be better? Why *shouldn't* this year be better? I could be a straight A student, no problem!

I even convinced my mom to buy me a planner. One with a pink, glittery, hard cardboard cover and the quote, "Seize the Day!" in bubbly white print. Inside were columns for each day of the week, and I could just picture all my daily homework assignments neatly printed in the slim rows. An example of organization and preparedness that would help me calmly sit and do my homework, my "Seize the Day" planner cheering me on.

Mom was happy to encourage the excitement. I could tell she had been worried about me and knew I was anxious about the start of school. If I was being honest, third grade was pretty rough. Two of my closest friends moved away (job transfer, divorce), and at the end of the year I got a stomach bug and ended up throwing up all over Mrs. Jameson's desk. I was teased mercilessly when I returned to class, so that the end of school was a relief. Summer turned out to be long and quiet, despite my parents' urgings to call other friends and invite them to the pool, or to the movies…or to anything. I did hang out with my neighbor Isaac a few times. Our moms are best friends and he's just a couple doors down on the same street. He was always really nice and we had fun, but Isaac is a doer. And between summer camps and sports he was rarely home.

When I seemed excited that afternoon while getting school supplies, my mom was encouraged. In an effort to keep me feeling positive, she suggested a trip to her salon as a treat. Normally, I get my hair cut by whichever place is the cheapest and has availability to do it *that day*. But as luck would have it, my mom already had a hair appointment scheduled for herself that afternoon. Instead, she offered it to me. I loved the shampooing seat—it felt so good to have my head rubbed like that. I guess all those happy vibes made me a little adventurous. So when the stylist asked me what I'd like, I told her to make it short. Short and cute. My mom raised her eyebrows and said, "How short are we talking here?" I put my hand up just above my shoulder and smiled. When the stylist finished, I looked in the mirror and burst into tears. It wasn't that it looked that terrible, it's just that I didn't look like myself anymore. It was unsettling. My mom took me for ice cream and told me she thought it was really chic…and that it would grow back, and I would get used to it. That was three weeks ago now, and I guess my mom was right, because I don't mind it so much. It didn't hurt that on the first day of school about three people came up to me telling me how cool it looked.

But now it was driving me crazy. I didn't think about being able to still get it into a ponytail. A bunch of hair on the bottom just won't reach and is now sticking to the sweat on my neck. Why was it so hot out here anyway? Weren't we almost in the middle of September? Dad said we were having a heat wave—a last gasp of summer. All I knew was that it was the wrong weather to be having a running unit outside for P.E.

Once my hair was mostly back in place, I looked out over the woods to the north of the school. The trees were still mainly green, but some of the leaves had begun browning on the edges. A shock of orange leaves on one branch in an otherwise green tree made a beautiful color contrast, and I lingered to look at it.

"Leah—you haven't finished your laps. Stop daydreaming and get it done!" called out Mrs. Hopmeyer, the P.E. teacher. She had somehow come up close to me and the bark of her voice made me jump. She was a short, squat person who reminded me of a dust ball. All round and dusty brown-colored. Her short, light brown hair was under a tan baseball cap that, curiously, had no writing or emblem or picture on it of any kind. Strands stuck out at random angles like they were trying to escape. She wore a darker tan t-shirt over dark brown basketball shorts and her head, arms, torso and calves were all round in the middle like a ball. You can bet Mrs. Hopmeyer hadn't run four laps in a *long* time.

"Okay, sorry, Mrs. Hopmeyer," I said and started my painful lope around the soccer fields. "How many times around do we have to go, again?" I asked, hoping somehow, I had heard wrong the first time.

"Four *full* times around the fields, Leah. And you only did one so far, so get going!" It's not that Mrs. Hopmeyer was mean, she just wasn't very nice. No one could accuse her of being "warm and cuddly," that's for sure. I nodded and jogged along.

As I got halfway around the fields—and halfway away from Mrs. Hopmeyer—I saw my friend Ella walking ahead. She was swaying a little, not moving in a straight line. I caught up to her and slowed down. Ella did not look good. She had one hand on her head and the other at her stomach, and she was staring down at her feet as though concentrating on how they were supposed to work. Sweat dripped down her temple and had made a dark pink blob on the collar of her light pink t-shirt.

"Ella, are you okay?" I asked, bowing my head so I could see her face.

She looked up at me. "Hey Leah, yeah, I'm just feeling a little dizzy all of a sudden. Kind of, like, light-headed, you know?"

Ella was a star athlete. She played soccer in the spring, field hockey in the fall, and ice skated all winter. She was the kind of girl who always seemed to need to be moving. When she sat, her knee would be bouncing up and down or her pencil flicking back and forth between her fingers. The Ella in front of me was not looking so great. I knew she had been out sick with some cold or virus earlier in the week, so I figured she was probably still not fully recovered.

"You're probably still not feeling normal because you were sick. And it's so hot and humid! My dad said it was supposed to get in the nineties today! We should *not* be running out here. I'll walk you over to Mrs. Hopmeyer—I think you should sit down."

We turned to cut across the soccer fields. Ella seemed to wobble a bit, so I reached out to steady her. The moment I touched her I felt a little jolt of what I can only describe as electricity. An image of crisscrossing light blue lines appeared in my mind all running into a central section where they gathered and pulsed. The image flashed and then it was gone. *Well…that was strange.* We continued walking and a few moments later it happened again. It was as though my normal vision was shut off for a brief moment. Gone was the green of the field with its orange and white lines dividing up the playing areas. Gone was the running track with the woods beyond. For a split second, it was all replaced with black, striated with those blue electric lines weaving to the pulsing center, and then it was gone again. This time, however, when it went away, I suddenly understood what it meant. It was like some part of my brain could interpret those little lines and whispered to me softly, "It's in her heart." I looked at Ella, still making her way slowly across the field.

"Ella? Do you have anything wrong with your heart?" I asked, timidly.

"What do you mean?" she asked.

"Like, has the doctor ever told you there is something different about your heart?" I replied.

"No," she said, "my heart is okay. Why?"

At that moment, Mrs. Hopmeyer saw us approaching and walked over to meet us. "What's going on, girls? Why did you stop your laps?" she demanded.

"Ella is feeling dizzy and faint," I answered. "I thought she should maybe sit down for a bit, so I walked her over to you."

Mrs. Hopmeyer looked down at Ella and frowned. "Ella, what's the problem? I saw you run the first lap without any trouble."

"I know, I'm not sure what happened. All of a sudden, I was light-headed. It's not as bad now, though." In the short walk across the field, she had straightened up and seemed to be almost back to normal. "I started to feel better as we were walking over here. I am just a little tired now, but not dizzy or anything."

I looked at Ella. It was true, she seemed way better than she was just moments ago. Her face had gained some color back, and she was standing up straighter. Now I was confused. I was *sure* the blue lines were telling me something was wrong with Ella's heart. I didn't know how I knew, but I *knew*.

"Mrs. Hopmeyer, I think Ella should go to the nurse. She was really bad when I ran by her, she could barely walk, and her face had turned all white." I said. Then I added, much more quietly, "I think something might be wrong with her heart."

Mrs. Hopmeyer and Ella regarded me. "What makes you think something's wrong with her heart?" Mrs. Hopmeyer responded, in a voice laced with suspicion.

I could feel heat rising in my cheeks and the backs of my ears. What *did* make me think it was her heart? How was I supposed to explain seeing the blue electric lines and the pulse, and then just *knowing*? I looked down and tugged at the damp edge of my t-shirt.

"I don't know exactly…I just have a, sort of, like…a feeling. You know? Like…a strong feeling that it's something wrong with her heart." I stammered, my voice getting quieter and quieter as I spoke.

"But I told her my heart is fine," said Ella, not unkindly. "No doctor or anything has ever said I had a problem. And you know I played summer league soccer this year, which was, like, two hours a day of running. I'm pretty sure my heart is okay!" She laughed a little as she finished talking. "Besides, I'm feeling much better now. I think it was like you said first, Leah. I'm just still a little sick from my virus. I'm good to keep running, Mrs. Hopmeyer."

Now I was almost panicked. What if I was wrong? What the heck were blue lines anyway? How did I know this meant anything at all? Here she was telling me she was fine, and she looked completely returned to normal. Ella's right. If there was something wrong with her heart, she would not have been able to do the summer soccer practices, right? What I was feeling was so confusing.

Mrs. Hopmeyer said, "Great. Then get back to your laps, Ella." I looked up. Ella turned to me.

"Thanks for your help, Leah! I really am feeling better now!" She took off running down the track. Mrs. Hopmeyer glared down at me. It took every ounce of courage I had to speak.

"Mrs. Hopmeyer, I really think Ella should go see the nurse. Just to make sure she's really okay." It had come out as barely a squeak, and Mrs. Hopmeyer's eyes bored into mine. She put her hands on her hips and scowled.

"Look at her running. You heard her say, herself, that she's fine. You, on the other hand, seemed to find several excuses to get out of *your* laps. No more about Ella. Stop trying to get out of running and get on the track!" I was about to protest that I wasn't trying to get out of anything—I was trying to help my friend—but Mrs. Hopmeyer put her hand in front of my face in a silencing gesture, then pointed to the track. I turned away and started jogging.

Thankfully P.E. was almost at the end of the day, so I only had to sit through reading club. When I packed up my backpack to leave, I saw raw skin around my nails and felt the sharpness of torn cuticles for the first time. I hadn't even realized I was picking at my nailbeds, and I managed to almost make them bleed. I didn't linger on the playground, but kept my head down and went straight home. Ella was not in my regular class, so I didn't get to see how she was the hour before school let out. I couldn't concentrate on anything else, though. If what I was feeling wasn't real, and Ella was fine, why did I feel it so strongly? Like a stone sitting in my belly; the uncertainty that I might know something terrible, or I might be a complete fool.

At dinner, I could barely eat. My mom and dad exchanged looks across the table. "Leah, you okay, love?" asked my mom. "Did something happen at school today?"

I put my hands on my eyes, something I did sometimes when I didn't feel like facing reality. "Mrs. Hopmeyer thought I was trying to get out of running laps today." *Do I say anything more?* I thought. "She thought I was cheating or something. But I was just trying to help Ella. Ella was feeling dizzy and stuff." *Should I say that when I put my hands on her everything changed? Will they think I'm crazy?*

"I…I told Mrs. Hopmeyer I thought Ella should see the nurse."

"Did she?" asked my dad.

"No…at least not during P.E. When we got over to Mrs. Hopmeyer, Ella started feeling better. She said she didn't need the nurse and went off running to finish her laps," I responded.

"She must have been okay if she could keep running," said my mom.

"I know…she did seem okay. But I said she should see the nurse anyway. Mrs. Hopmeyer said I should get back to my own laps, that Ella was fine…but I'm not sure she is," I said, working through the event out loud. Suddenly the frustration of the afternoon welled up in me. "I wish she had just gone to the nurse…just to check…to make sure!" I balled my fists on the table and nearly yelled, surprising my parents by my sudden change of tone.

"Leah, why are you so upset? If Ella was running and said she was feeling better, why do you think she should have gone to the nurse anyway?" my dad asked in a soothing voice.

I let out all the air I hadn't realized I was holding in a big sigh and unclenched my hands. I looked at my parents, all attentive and concerned. Of anyone, they'd be the ones to at least *try* to understand what I experienced. I looked down at my hands, now on my lap. Frisco, who had been sitting on the dining chair next to mine, and who never misses an opportunity for pets, noticed my attention shift and slowly crawled over to sit on my legs.

"Something happened when I went to help Ella—something I'm not sure how to explain." I kept my eyes down and petted Frisco, nervous how this would all sound. "I put my hands on her to, like, help her walk because she was feeling so dizzy. When I touched her, I saw…I mean I didn't really *see* so much as I felt…I mean, it was like it was in my head but not in, like the world around me." I gestured with my hands out as to indicate the space around me and bopped Frisco in the nose. He hopped down and trotted away, indignant. It was then that I looked up and saw my mom and dad watching me with confused expressions. "I mean I saw it in my mind, you know?" I said.

"Like daydreaming?" asked my mom.

"Yes! More like that. So, like I said, I put my hands on Ella and the whole picture in my mind changed immediately. It got sort of black, I guess, with all these little blue crisscrossing lines…like lightning but small, and a ton of them. And they all led into this one ball of blue light kind of in the middle." A thought occurred to me, "They felt kind of alive, you know? Like not really moving around but…I don't know…not staying still either. Like they were alive." It was the only way I could think to explain it. "I don't know how…but at that moment I just *knew* it meant the problem was in Ella's heart."

Suddenly, I remembered a discussion my mom and I had over the summer, when I told her I wanted to start walking the short three blocks to and from school alone when fourth grade began. She wasn't against the idea—there was only one real street with lights to cross, and there was always a crossing guard, but she spent a lot of the next hour talking about personal safety and how not everyone is a great person. There had been an uptick in muggings and car jackings in the news over the previous few months, and though there was hardly any chance that anything would happen in the short distance between our house and the school, surrounded by kids and parents all walking to the same place, she just wanted me to be informed. What came to me now was the part about trusting your gut if you feel something's not right. I looked at my mom.

"It's like you said this summer…about intuition. About trusting your feelings about a situation even if your eyes don't tell you everything. I had the strongest intuition I've ever had when I touched Ella and saw the blue lines. I just knew it was a problem with her heart. I don't know how, and I can't think of any other way to explain it." I was eager now. Eager to see if *they* would believe me.

"Did you see Ella after P.E. at all? See if she was still okay?" asked my dad.

"No," I sighed. "And I've been freaking out about it all day. What if she really does have a big problem with her heart and I didn't help her?" I could feel my eyes burn with the promise of tears to come. I tried to blink them away.

"You know," started my mom, slowly, "your great-grandma Luisa, Grammy-Lou, claimed to have 'visions' when she was young—that's what she called it. She said she could tell what was wrong with a person just by touching them. Aunt Emilia, her younger sister, told me the story of when she was a girl. Grammy-Lou lifted her up into her high chair—because of course, Aunt Emilia was almost 13 years younger than Grammy-Lou—and Grammy-Lou suddenly shouted out, nearly dropping her, crying that Aunt Emilia's foot was hurt. Aunt Emilia hadn't been crying or acting hurt at the time, and when they looked all they could see was a little cut or blister or something on the bottom of her foot. Certainly, nothing to worry about. But in the middle of the night she was screaming. And when they got her out of her bed, her foot was purple. It turns out there was an infection that had gotten into that cut on her heel and was spreading up her foot. I don't remember exactly what it was, but your Aunt Emilia had to have her foot amputated at the ankle because of it. "

I was staring hard at my mom while she spoke. The top of my head began vibrating. I remembered this feeling…my body was alert and the back of my neck had goosebumps. Could I have the same "vision" that Grammy-Lou had? I never actually met my Grammy-Lou, I had only seen pictures of her. She died before I was born.

"It's only through Aunt Emilia I knew anything about it. Something happened when she was in high school, and she almost never mentioned her ‘visions’ again. I’m not sure if she stopped having them or if she chose not to talk about them. Aunt Emilia didn’t seem to know, either. And she didn’t tell me that story until after Grammy-Lou had already passed away.”

“I remember Emilia talking about that! It was mostly considered a coincidence, though, right? I don’t think anyone took her very seriously, did they?” my dad asked.

My mom nodded. “That’s the way Emilia remembers it, yes.”

“Maybe I have what Grammy-Lou had! It was totally like a vision! Mom, we have to do something! What if Ella’s in trouble?!” My voice came out like a shriek, and there was a gentle pulsing now around my eyes. I could tell my mom was trying to concentrate on what to do. Her forehead scrunched down, and she started biting on the inside of her lip.

“You know, I don’t know if you have what Grammy-Lou had, or really even *what* Grammy-Lou’s experience was, but I think we should check on Ella at home just to see how she’s doing.” Having made that decision, she got up from the table and went into the kitchen to find the school directory. I followed at her heels, feeling equally anxious and excited. Just fretting about Ella all day and not doing anything felt torturous. At least now there was *something* to do. My mom found the number for Ella’s mom and made the call. I held my breath waiting for her to answer the phone, but after several rings I could hear the voicemail message click on.

“Hi Ginny…this is Marisa, Leah’s mom from school. Leah said that Ella wasn’t feeling so well during P.E. today, and we just wanted to check on her, see how she’s doing. When you get a chance, can you give me a call back? Thanks, Ginny! Bye!” My mom put her phone down on the kitchen counter and looked up at me. “Sorry love, no answer. I’m sure everything is fine, and you’ll see Ella running around the track tomorrow at school. If her mom calls back tonight, I'll let you know. Even if you're already asleep, okay?" My mom placed her hands lightly on my shoulders. I suddenly felt exhausted. The buzzing in my body gone. All the emotion from the day had caught up with me, and I let my shoulders sag.

"Okay," I said. I knew there wasn't much more my mom could do, but I felt defeated.

"Come on," said my dad. "I'll give you a piggy upstairs." He turned his back to me so I could hop on. Then he bounced me up to shift my weight to the right place, and I let my head fall on his back as he carried me up the stairs.

As I lay in my bed in the dark, I thought about my Grammy-Lou's visions. Why did she stop talking about them? I rolled over onto my side and faced the windows across my room. I had left the blinds up on purpose tonight. I wanted to see the sky, even though there was too much light around here to have good stars. Sometimes, just looking at the inky blue was calming. I scrunched my pillow to make it fatter under my head. What if I was right? What if Ella wasn't okay? I sighed. I tried to think about what my Dad said right before kissing me goodnight. He'd sat on the edge of my bed and gently brushed the hair off my forehead.

"You know, kiddo, if Ella was able to run around for the rest of P.E., then she's probably fine. I know you're worried but think of how she looked when you last saw her today. She was full of energy, right? Focus on that for now." He kissed my nose, turned off my light and gently closed the door. So I tried to picture Ella sprinting away in P.E., smiling at me and yelling, "Thanks, Leah!" I must have drifted off to sleep because when I opened my eyes next, the early sunlight of the day was threading its way across my bed.

Maeror:

(Latin) Grief, sorrow, sadness, mourning.

CHAPTER 2

When I got to school, everything seemed completely normal. Kids were running around, getting to their homerooms, and joking in the halls. In fact, the first hour or so of the day continued in this way. But as we were about to start our math unit, there was an announcement over the speakers for all fourth grade classes to make their way to the auditorium. Half the class cheered as this meant math was interrupted, but I only felt apprehension. I looked at our teacher, trying to shepherd us out the door in something that resembled an orderly fashion. Did she look more worried than usual? She glanced up and caught my eye, then quickly turned away. Why did she do that?

We finally made it to the auditorium. Principal Bacarro and Assistant Principal Copeland were standing at the front of the stage. All our teachers were lined up against the left wall, whispering to each other. All except Mrs. Hopmeyer. She stood a little apart and was staring down at the ground. Principal Bacarro raised up his hands and waited for the noise to die down, then he looked at all the kids assembled at his feet.

"Thank you all for quieting down," he began gently. "I'm afraid I called you here because I received some bad news this morning, and it affects all of you in fourth grade the most."

I felt nauseous, and there wasn't enough air around me.

"It seems our dear friend Ella Richards collapsed at her house yesterday afternoon." He paused for just a moment and it looked as though he was concentrating very hard on how to proceed. He certainly had the group's attention, now, though. Ella was friends with just about everyone. Principal Bacarro cleared his throat, "I'm terribly sad to tell you all this, but Ella passed away last night." His voice faltered just slightly, and I could see his eyes glistening in the auditorium lights. Half of the kids gasped and exclaimed, but the other half seemed confused.

"Mr. Bacarro, what does that mean? Passed away…" asked Jasmine with a timid voice.

"Oh, I'm so sorry, children. Passed away means…it means that Ella died from her collapse yesterday. She died at…at the hospital." He looked right at Jasmine with the softest most comforting expression on his face. I wanted him to look at me like that. To make me feel better. Ella had died? Some kids around me started to cry and I could see Mrs. Copeland standing next to Mr. Bacarro, dabbing at her eyes with a tissue.

"But I don't understand!" cried Isabel. "I just saw her yesterday, and she was fine!"

"Yes, that's true, Isabel," Mr. Bacarro replied, turning his steady gaze to her scared face. "It turns out that Ella had something called hypertrophic cardiomyopathy. It is a very rare problem with the heart that she had since she was a baby. Though it's very serious, it doesn't give any signal that there's a problem…until…until it makes the heart stop. Ella and her parents didn't know she had any trouble with her heart…but she was born with it, kids. The heart gets worse over time, but Ella didn't feel any pain. The virus she had recently weakened her and…it just made her heart stop beating." He took a deep breath and began again. "Ella was a wonderful, joyful girl who always had a smile for everyone. We are as heartbroken as you are, and as her family is, that this happened. But there was nothing they could do, there was no warning that there was a problem with her heart."

Yes, there was. I knew. I knew it was her heart. I *felt* it. Why didn't Mrs. Hopmeyer listen to me? I looked over to her, rage boiling in my stomach—My fists balled up at my sides. She had her head in her hands and her shoulders were shaking like she was crying. Like she was weeping.

Principal Bacarro dismissed us and said that counselors would be coming around to our classrooms to talk with us. That our normally scheduled classes would be canceled. He said something about how it's okay to cry and normal to be confused…all I felt at the moment was fury. I could've saved Ella! If only that horrible Mrs. Hopmeyer had listened to me! The teachers gathered their students to go back to class. Some were hugging, some talking together wide-eyed, and others walking with their mouths agape and staring at the ground as though trying to understand. As my class was leaving the auditorium, we passed Mrs. Hopmeyer walking with her co-teacher back to the office. The co-teacher had his arm around her shoulders and was leaned in like he was trying to comfort her. I couldn't stand to see her upset. I was too angry. She didn't deserve to be comforted.

I ran over and stood directly in front of her so she had to stop. "I *told* you! I *told* you it was her heart!" I shouted. "Why couldn't you have just listened to me!? I *told* you she should go to the nurse! Why didn't you send her?! She died. She *died*, and we could have saved her!" I was screaming now, and my face wet with tears.

Mrs. Hopmeyer looked at me with wild eyes and yelled back, "She was *fine*! She finished her laps…she was okay…she told me she was fine!" Her voice caught and she covered her mouth with her hand, pushed past me, and ran off into the office.

Principal Bacarro heard the commotion and came running over, kneeling down in front of me. "Leah, what's happened? Why are you yelling at Mrs. Hopmeyer?" His voice urgent. At this point I was sobbing so hard I could barely breathe.

My reply came out as a whisper, "I told her…I told her it was Ella's heart. She wouldn't listen. I want to go home. I just want to go home. Please. Can I just go home?" I opened my eyes and looked at him pleadingly.

"Why not come into the office for a few minutes and we can talk with Mr. Grey?" he softly suggested.

I stepped back from him. "No! I don't want the counselor…I want to go home! I need to go home! Please call my mom or dad…they'll come get me I promise. Just let me go home!"

He looked at me intently for a moment, and then gave just a slight nod. "Okay, Leah. Let's go call home." He held my hand and walked me back into his office to wait for my parents.

I stayed home for the rest of that week, barely getting out of bed. I just felt sick with guilt and anger and sadness. My mom and dad tried to convince me that it wasn't my fault. But I couldn't shake the feeling that somehow it was. At the funeral, it seemed like the entire town showed up. Most of the women were crying and holding tissues to their faces…hugging each other and saying things like, "I just can't believe it." Or more quietly, "That poor family." Meanwhile, the dads looked sad and serious and mostly just shook their heads at each other. All the kids in my school seemed to be there, too. I held my mom's hand and kept my eyes down most of the time, staring at the worn wooden floor below our pew while the priest talked about heaven and love and loss. Though I tried to focus on what he was saying, I could hear the whispers all around me… "She said she *knew* what was wrong with Ella…" "…How could she possibly know anything like that…?" Whenever I got brave enough to raise my head, I found people staring at me.

Only Isaac actually tried to speak to me, though. As we were walking out to the car he and his parents came over. He asked if I was okay while his mom and mine were hugging. I just weakly shrugged my shoulders and said, "Not really."

He replied, looking at me with kindness, "Yeah, I figured."

Then we went our separate ways, and ordered pizza for dinner because my mom just "couldn't face it."

When Ella's parents learned I had told Mrs. Hopmeyer I thought something was wrong with Ella's heart, and that she could have potentially been treated sooner, they lost their minds. Principal Bacarro tried to explain how Ella, herself, had told Mrs. Hopmeyer she felt fine as she went off running. That there was really no just cause for Mrs. Hopmeyer to be concerned about Ella that day, and that they supported her decision to let Ella continue her run based on the information at hand. It came down to me, though. Even though I couldn't explain why I thought Ella's heart was the issue (they didn't really seem to get my "blue lines" answer), Ella's parents believed I should have been listened to, and that Ella should have at the very least been sent to the nurse for checking. Of course, their actions were guided by their grief and not necessarily by the most logical conclusions, but no one was about to point that out. Two weeks after Ella's death, Mrs. Hopmeyer was asked to resign as our P.E. teacher.

I can't say I was over my anger at her, but I did feel bad that she lost her job. Still, almost no one talked to me at school. Even my teacher seemed to be avoiding me, asking other kids to relay messages or pass me things. I guess they either thought I had powers that I couldn't explain and that was scary, or they thought I was making it all up and got Mrs. Hopmeyer fired. Either way, I was someone to avoid. It was okay with me. In truth, I was scared. I wanted to face what I had seen with the blue lines and try to understand it better, but I couldn't make it happen again. I tried with my mom and dad and our cat Frisco, but I didn't see anything. I knew I had been sure at the time, but as the weeks passed, doubt crept in. Maybe I was just hallucinating, and the heat had gotten to me, too. I settled into my new, lonely existence, and the year went on.

Gapeseed:
(British) Something that causes people to stare gapingly; An unusual or remarkable thing to be gaped at.

CHAPTER 3

"Move it." I was shoved from behind as Eric and his cronies filed past me. "Careful, you don't want to touch her…might get some disease," said the short, overweight one on his left…Jerry or Jake or something boring and predictable like that. Like I cared what their names were. "Don't you know witches' bodies are covered in warts and boils? She probably worships the devil at night," quipped another one. They all snickered.

This was nothing new for me at the lovely, well-regarded Cranston Middle School. You'd think by eighth grade people could have gotten over something that happened so long ago. Too bad high test scores and rich parents didn't mean anything when it came to creating decent human beings. I was used to being ridiculed and this was a minor affront. Still, my cheeks burned from the humiliation of being called out in public. I could feel the eyes of bystanders turn and look at us to see what would happen. Stay quiet or respond? This was always my debate. It's not that I'm afraid of them. It's just that, being the weird one at school, it was usually me who got in trouble when I fought back. No matter who said what, I ended up the troublemaker.

If only I hadn't petted that dog at the start of sixth grade. People were beginning to forget a little. Forget about what happened with Ella and Mrs. Hopmeyer. Forget that they once believed I was responsible. But then that adorable puppy bounded towards me on the sidewalk. The boy walking it, a kid from school, wasn't in control and the puppy broke free from his leash. It was so sweet; all fluffy and excited. But when I knelt to pet it, the blue lines appeared. It was the first time it happened to me since touching Ella. I was startled and jumped back exclaiming, "Oh! You're sick!" The boy had caught up to us in time to hear me, and wanted to know what I meant. I mumbled I meant nothing at all, and hurried off home. But the little puppy died the next morning. An infection in his brain. The boy told everyone at school I killed his dog. My fate as a pariah was sealed.

My parents transferred me to Cranston a short while later, hoping to save me from what had become a toxic environment, and give me a fresh start. That's not the way rumors work, however, and by the end of the year everyone there knew, too.

I didn't care as much by then, though. By then my parents were dead. And very little mattered to me anymore.

It didn't mean that I liked being the weird one at school, though. It was, in fact, exhausting. Now at the end of my last year here people usually just left me alone. Like I was invisible. I preferred that to any altercation like the one I sensed was about to take place. Eric stepped directly in my path so I had to stop walking. I looked up. "She's nothing but a fraud," he spit as he looked me up and down with disgust. "She can't do anything, she just wants people to think she can. It's a mind game. She's a pathetic loser like every other pathetic loser at this school."

I met his stare. My humiliation was replaced with anger. I could handle the teasing, the names, people messing with me. But I couldn't stand it when someone accused me of wanting this kind of attention. Of creating this situation for myself intentionally. Who in hell would choose this? *Breathe, Leah, breathe.* I tried to calm myself down. *He isn't worth your time, none of them are. They don't understand. Hell, you don't understand it yourself.* I looked at Eric's hard stare, daring me to do something. It would be so easy to hit him. I knew how strong I was. I might get hurt, too, but it would be worth it to see him bleed. *Jesus, Leah, you're falling right into his trap.* I exhaled, then softened my gaze and gave him a small smile. Fine, if I'm a fraud, I'll give him a show. I started chanting nonsense, quietly like a whisper, and slowly at first.

"What the hell are you saying, freak?" Eric snorted.

I made my chants faster and raised my hands in front of me, close to his face. His eyes got wide, and he backed away from me just a bit.

"You're nuts. Get out of my face!" he yelled as I started swirling my hands. I could tell I was making him nervous. Ha! So he did believe at least some of the rumors. This little show would serve him right. Maybe I could get him to run away scared in front of his stupid friends. Make him feel some of the embarrassment he'd doled out to me over the last year. Of course, because I was making it up as I went along, I didn't really know what I should do next. Should I writhe on the ground with spit coming out of my mouth? They did say I'm a devil-worshipper, right? Maybe I should just pretend to faint and see if any of them even try to help me…these cowards.

All of a sudden, I felt the vibrations beginning. Like always, they started at the top of my head and made their way down my body, pulsing around my eyes. I'd felt the vibrations a handful of times over the last few years, so that now I recognized it meant something was about to happen. I took in a sharp breath as I looked at my hands. Ever so lightly, there arose a pink glow in the air between and around them. I thought at first my eyes were playing tricks on me, but Eric saw it, too.

"What the hell is that?" he said.

I stopped moving and chanting and looked at my hands held in front of my chest. The pink glow, like a fine mist, floated gently through my fingers and around my palms.

"Dude, what's the problem?" Eric's friends hadn't seen the pink mist, hadn't noticed that something remarkable had happened. Then it disappeared. Eric stared at my hands, the glow now gone, then back at me. His face, no longer hard, looked confused and frightened.

"Freak!" he spit at me as he turned to rejoin his group. "Let's go," he said to them.

"You aren't gonna do anything?" the short one goaded.

"I said, let's go," Eric growled at him.

Taking a step back and bringing his hands up defensively, his short friend said, "Okay, okay, man. We're going." Then he shot a quizzical look at me before yelling, "Freak!" Just for good measure.

I kept eyeing my hands where the mist had been. How did I do that? I was just speaking nonsense —there wasn't any pattern or reason to it. Maybe it was the hand movements that made it appear? I started swirling them around again, trying to mimic my previous actions. It was just random though. It's not like I knew what I was doing. Isaac rushed over, grabbed my hands and held them down by my side.

"What the hell are you doing? You look like a crazy person waving around like that!" he hissed.

Finally, I looked around. Groups of kids were staring and laughing or furrowing their brows at me. I turned back to Isaac.

"Did you see it, though? Did you see the pink?" I asked him.

"All I saw was you waving your hands around here in the middle of the courtyard. Don't you have enough trouble? C'mon, time to go home." He turned to the crowds still staring, "Show's over people, I gotta get this girl some food, she's gone delirious with hunger."

I looked at him. Shit. I'd embarrassed him. All the things he'd been through with me, he'd never actually seemed embarrassed to be my friend…until now. Shit. I couldn't lose Isaac. I couldn't.

"I was just trying to freak out Eric and his idiot friends. You know, make them think I was the witch they always accuse me of." I could hear my voice get higher as I desperately tried to explain myself. *Please, Isaac, you have to stay by me!*

"All I saw was you, alone, waving your hands in the air and staring at them like you'd never seen anything so amazing before. You looked completely insane. Eric wasn't anywhere near you," Isaac replied without turning to look at me.

"But he was! He had just left! Look, I saw this pink glow, like pink air around my hands when I messed with him the first time. He must have seen it too because he got scared, and they left, and I was just trying to see if I could make it happen again."

Isaac walked fast and I was having a hard time keeping up. He had grown about six inches since the beginning of last year when we were pretty much at eye level. Now he towered over my still five-foot, five-inch frame. Having grown so fast he was super skinny and self-consciously rounded his shoulders forward. With his wavy mop of dirty blond hair he looked like a surfer dude. I took two steps for every one of his long strides. We left the school grounds and started to cross to Adams Street.

Isaac and I had lived on the same street since as long as I could remember. We didn't spend much time together until fourth grade. Then he pretty much became my closest friend. At first, I wasn't sure if his parents forced him to hang out with me or not, but it didn't take long to find out that we actually had fun together. Once middle school started, we didn't spend as much time together, even though he ended up getting sent to Cranston, too. (The public school couldn't compete with Cranston's advanced science lab and lacrosse program.) His friends started teasing him about his "girlfriend," and I could feel a distance grow between us. Not outside school, though. We could still spend hours just talking and playing darts or listening to music. It was only since the middle of eighth grade that I felt him shift a little around me. I blamed Brenna.

He actually asked her out on a date and everything. The whole week following the date, Isaac had been weird around me. Short tempered and quiet. I asked him if he was planning on seeing Brenna again; if they were now dating. But he just shrugged and said no. Come to find out she had asked him about me that night. She demanded to know how he could he be my friend, and why didn't he think I was strange and a loser. Things like that. So Isaac decided not to date her, this girl he'd been wanting to date all year, for me. To stay loyal as my friend. Though he decided this on his own, he had changed toward me in the weeks that followed. Like he was more aware of my behavior or how I might be perceived. It wasn't so easy for me. I felt like I needed to watch my actions and words around him…I think it was starting to make me depressed.

But he was still Isaac. He was there for me when I had no one else. I was staying at his house when I found out about my parents' accident. It was supposed to be a quick vacation to a friend's lake house in Michigan. Four days of "couple time" as my dad had called it. They never found the car that forced them off the road—just my parents' car upended, three-quarters down the embankment of the country lane.

It was the second night when the call came. Isaac's mom came into the rec room where we were playing video games. We could tell by the cautious way she entered, how she lingered before speaking, looking back and forth at us, that something important was happening. She could barely get the words out. The next several days she was as distraught as if she'd lost her own sister, as she kept whispering to the air around her, "She was my sister, my best friend."

My aunt Mary Ann, my mom's only sibling, lived several states away. She and my mom were close, and I loved her immensely. She was a professional artist and yoga instructor, and a few other things I could never remember. She dressed in bright colors and flowing fabrics and looked right at you when she spoke. She didn't have the same thick, dark hair and curvy body my mom had—and I inherited. (My mom called them her "Latina curves".) Instead she was long and willowy like their dad, the English/German side of the family, and her hair was light brown and wavy. She was married once, but when I asked my mom about it, she just said, "Grown-up love is a complicated business."

It turns out Mary Ann was teaching at a yoga retreat in Costa Rica when my parents got run off the road. It took nearly two days to track her down, then nearly two days for her to get to me. In the weeks that followed she uprooted her life and moved into my house, becoming my sole guardian.

Isaac had been my only real friend in the two years since then. I couldn't bear the thought of him being ashamed of me. I caught up with him at the corner as he waited for a break in traffic to cross. We didn't speak, and after a minute he let out a sigh and his shoulders collapsed forward even further. We crossed and as we passed his house, he turned to look at me.

"Leah, I'm worried about you, okay?" I wasn't sure what to say at that, and I hoped he would continue, but he didn't. "Never mind, I gotta go. Maybe I'll see you tomorrow." And with that he turned down his driveway and into his house.

I stood there watching the door for a minute, not really wanting to move. Slowly, I turned toward my own house and closed myself in my room. It took me a while to fall asleep that night, but eventually I drifted off.

Guarish:
(Old English) To heal or cure.

CHAPTER 4

***

I was dressed in a white sheath that draped across one shoulder and reached to my ankles. A crown of horns set around a disk was balanced on my head. I sat in a smooth marble throne in front of crowds of people, and in my hand, I held a pink stone. It was cool to the touch and completely smooth, about the size of a grapefruit. There were thin veins of milky white woven into the pink, and one line of faint blue that cut a jagged path on the stone's underside. A woman approached me with a baby in her arms—a little boy who was wrapped in an animal skin, but was otherwise naked. The woman, his mother, had tears falling down her cheeks and didn't speak. She held out the boy before me, dropping her eyes to the floor. His ribs protruded slightly, and his limbs were thin. Like most who came to me for healing, he was malnourished. His eyes were closed, and his chest barely moved; I could sense he was dying. My heart ached for the young mother. On his abdomen, I noticed a sore; It was darker red in the middle and spread out in a circle of diminishing pink. I placed the stone ever so gently above the sore and closed my eyes. I calmed my breath and focused my attention to the infinite space behind my eyes—the mind's eye. Suddenly, I could see blue lines crossing around the wound, and the notion of a scorpion flashed. A scorpion bite, then, I thought to myself. Keeping my eyes closed, I placed my index finger softly between the baby boy's eyes, just above the nose. I felt the connection between his energy and mine flowing back and forth. Yes, I thought with relief, he can still be saved. I removed my finger and opened my palm to the sky. I could now "see" soft white bands of light moving around where my hand lay open. Using my mind's eye, I pulled one of the light bands gently into my fingers and guided it to the scorpion bite. The light entered his small body and seemed to diffuse into every part of him.

After two more ribbons of light, I moved my finger back to the space where our minds' eyes could connect. Good—the transfer of energy had worked, and I could feel he was strengthening. The stone had grown warm during the healing, and I gently pulled it away and opened my eyes. Looking at the baby, I saw the flutter of his eyelids, and his chest expanded in a full inhale. His mother was still looking down and had not watched the ritual. I gently placed my hand on her arm, still holding out her little boy. She started a little at the touch, and slowly, fearfully raised her head. I told her to gaze on her son, now renewed with the energy of life. She cried out as she saw him open his eyes and laughed through tears of joy as he began wailing the cry of a hungry baby. She bowed to my feet and thanked me repeatedly as she backed out of the room, all the while crying and hugging her sweet child.

Next, an old man approached, led by a young boy. He was coated in dust and dirt, with a scrap of linen wrapped around his eyes. As he shuffled toward me, however, my attention was pulled toward noise at the back of the room. Though I couldn't clearly see what was happening, it looked as though someone was pushing their way through the throngs of people waiting, with a force that sent the sick and injured falling to the ground. I stood and strained my neck forward, trying to get a better view, but there were too many people. Finally, a man broke through the crowd and stood facing me, only ten feet away. Gasping, I recognized the figure of my brother and enemy before me. His energy radiated hatred. He said nothing but charged at me, plunging a spear deep into my abdomen. I cried out as pain erupted in my lower belly.

***

I woke up grasping at my stomach in the dark, my hands pulling at the fabric of my t-shirt, searching for a spear or wound. I was confused when I found neither. The line between dreaming and waking was difficult to cross, but finally I shook awake enough to realize that I was in my room and my own bed. Breathing that information in, my thoughts went back to my dream. It had felt so real, and so intense. I hadn't dreamed vividly like that since the weeks after my parents died, when I dreaded bedtime for the nightmares that plagued me. Most mornings I woke and had no sense of having dreamed at all. But this was very alive. So much so that I could remember feeling the cool stone's polished surface in my palm. In the dark, my breath began to slow. Suddenly, I felt a deep ache in my lower belly that wrapped around to my back. It felt like I was being squeezed around my pelvis. Quickly shifting my weight up to sitting, I felt something wet between my thighs. I reached across my bed, turned on my bedside light and threw back my covers. A small circle of deep red covered the sheet where I was sitting.

The next morning, when I told Mary Ann that I'd started my period, she clapped her hands and congratulated me. We spent the next half hour with her telling me what to expect, and me dying from embarrassment. When she was done, she looked at me lovingly and said, "Oh Leah, your mom would be so proud of the woman you're becoming." We sat in silence for a couple seconds until she jumped up from her seat, scaring me half to death.

"I know!" she exclaimed while running to her bedroom and grabbing her wallet. "Here's $20. Run to Sloane's bakery and pick out some goodies…we'll have *period* pastries! Oh wait," she laughed. "Let's not call them that! That's awful!" Her face wrinkled in a look of mock disgust. "Just pick out some treats for us to celebrate *you*!"

I laughed. "Okay—you want the poppy seed one?" I asked, getting my shoes on.

"Always!!" she chimed back, walking toward the kitchen. "I'm going to put some coffee on—for me, of course—do you want some tea ready for when you get back?"

"Sounds good! Be right back!" I yelled in as I was closing the door behind me. Sloane's was only about four blocks from our house, and they had the most amazing assortment of pastries, pies, cookies and breads. Mary Ann's favorite was a poppy-seed strudel kind of thing, and I loved the chocolate croissants. It seemed quiet out for a Saturday morning. The green of early spring was everywhere, and I took a deep breath of air rich with the scent of soil and grass. There was a line at Sloane's, as usual, but finally I got our pastries and headed back toward the house.

As I was leaving, however, a bike sped by me. I reflexively stepped back just as the rider whipped his head around to look back at me. Shit, it was Eric, and he'd seen me. I decided to quickly turn onto Morningside Street. I would take a roundabout way to avoid Eric if I could. Picking up my pace I looked behind me but didn't see him. Maybe, just maybe, he wouldn't think I was worth his time. I rounded off Morningside and onto Walter Street. From there I would only be about two and a half blocks from the house, but Walter Street. was smaller with fewer houses. As I passed a dense line of tall hedges bordering the sidewalk, my heart sank. Eric was almost upon me with his bike. He stopped right in front of me and let the bike fall to the ground.

"Look who I found…" he said as he walked toward me, making me retreat back toward the hedges. "What the hell were you trying to pull yesterday? Trying to make me look like an idiot? Huh, freak?" He kept closing the distance between us.

"Back off, Eric!" I yelled, but he kept moving toward me so that my back hit the hedge and I had no more room.

"Tell me how you did it!" he hissed. "Tell me how you made that light!" He put his hands on my shoulders and shoved me a little to the right, while putting his face right up to mine.

I was scared now. I looked around but couldn't see any other person on the street. There was a gap in the hedges where different plants connected. *Maybe I could duck through it and get away from him*, I thought as he yelled at me. The front door of the house on the other side wasn't far if I could just short cut through the hedge…Maybe someone would be home to help me.

"Did you hear me? I said tell me how you did it!" Eric grabbed at my shirt and pulled me slightly toward him.

"I don't know how I did it!" I yelled. "I was as freaked out as you, okay? It never happened before!"

"Liar—you stupid liar!" He shoved me hard. Suddenly I was falling back through the opening in the hedge. I tried to regain my balance, but something caught my feet on the other side. The last thing I remember was flailing my arms trying futilely to grab at the weak branches as I fell backwards into empty space.

I woke up in a light blue room with blue pictures on the walls and a light blue blanket over my chest. I was alone, and next to me were all these machines with blinking lights. My brain registered that I was in a hospital bed, but I was at a complete loss as to how I got there. *Think, Leah, think!* Maybe if my head hadn't been pounding it would have been easier. The pastry shop…Eric…falling. Just then the door opened and a man in blue scrubs walked in.

"You're awake!" he exclaimed. "I'm so glad to see it—how are you feeling? How's the pain?" He looked at me earnestly and then walked over to peer at the machines. What was he checking me for? Did I have any pain? I brought my attention to my body. I could move my fingers and arms without problem.

"My head hurts," I said, "and it hurts when I breathe."

"That's from the broken ribs, sweetie. It's going to take a little while, but they'll heal," he replied.

"Broken ribs?" I asked, feeling rising panic. "Why are my ribs broken? Where am I? I don't know how I got here!" I squeaked, looking frantically around the room for some clue. Just then the door opened and Aunt Mary Ann walked through it.

"Oh, Leah! Thank God!" she cried as she ran over to my bedside. "I've been dying of worry! My sweet girl…thank God!" she repeated, grabbing my hand and kissing it. "How do you feel?"

"I don't know anything…why am I here? What happened to me?" I could feel tears welling up and my breathing got faster, which hurt my apparently broken ribs.

"Of course, Leah, of course, my sweet girl. You poor thing—you must be so confused!" she replied. "You were out buying the pastries at Sloane's, remember? That was this morning. I thought you were taking an awfully long time when Isaac called. He got you in an ambulance and I raced to the hospital to meet you. That other boy, Eric, was here, too, blubbering and carrying on. He said that he pushed you—Lord, he felt so guilty—and you fell through a break in the hedges on the corner house on Walter Street. You landed on some cement blocks on the ground behind the hedges. Completely blacked out! Eric panicked when he couldn't wake you up. The people at the house weren't home, so he ran to Isaac's house, the only person he knew in the area. Isaac called the ambulance… and here we are." She let out a huge sigh. "God, Leah. You were unconscious for four hours!" The stress of the day seeped through her composure. "I just don't know what I'd do without you my girl." She tried to smile at me, but the corners of her mouth fought to stay down. She let my hand go and got up to grab a tissue from the table in the corner. Getting herself calmed down, she returned to my side. "So, are you in pain?" she asked, letting her gaze drift from my toes up to my head. "The doctors say you have two broken ribs and a moderate concussion but should heal up fine. Now that you're awake, that is."

I tried to take in what she was telling me. I could remember Eric pushing me and yelling at me…and how I fell backwards through the hedge. I felt a rush of anger that made the ache in my head turn to a throb.

"That jerk was pushing me—shouting! I tried to get away from him…he probably wanted this to happen! He kept pushing me, he wouldn't leave me alone!" I turned to Mary Ann, who knew all that I'd gone through with the visions, and fell apart. "He did this because of my vision, Mary Ann! I'm cursed! I hate it! I wish I never got it from Grammy-Lou! It just ruins everything! People hate me…I have no friends! Even Isaac is starting to pull away from me." I tried to keep from crying because it hurt so much, but I couldn't help it. I felt so tired. Tired of worrying, tired of feeling like an outcast. Tired of not knowing what was happening to me. It was the most exhausted I'd ever felt. Mary Ann put her arms around me and held me until I stopped.

"There you go," she said when I was finally done. "You needed to get all that sadness out, sweet girl. It's been sitting in you far too long." She sat by my side and looked thoughtful for a moment.

"Maybe you're looking at this backwards." She spoke slowly, choosing her words carefully and turning her soft gaze to me. "Just because you don't fully understand it doesn't mean it has to be a curse. I believe we simply don't have the full story yet. I don't believe what's happening to you is inherently bad or scary, but it's being turned against you because it makes you different. Remember, Leah, you have done nothing wrong throughout all of this. The world just hasn't treated you very fairly. I like to think there's some wonderful, greater purpose for you having this ability. And when it's finally revealed, all this trouble and sadness will be pushed away for good." She gave me a small smile as she finished.

Mary Ann stayed with me for the next few hours. When I wasn't sleeping, I told her about my interaction with Eric at school and about the pink light that swirled in my hands. She couldn't recall hearing about Grammy-Lou having any experience like that. She told me how Eric seemed devastated by what had happened, knew it was his fault, and that he regretted his actions terribly. I wasn't sure I wanted to forgive him. When the doctor suggested I needed rest, she headed home with the promise of returning first thing with the pastries we didn't get to share the day before. Alone in the room, I laid in the hospital bed staring at the ceiling, trying to piece together some understanding. I was feeling dizzy, and there was a scab where the concrete block and my head collided. It was strange not to have any memory of what happened after that. I tried to picture how Eric would have seen me, lying there unresponsive. What he must have thought when he saw the pink mist surrounding my hands the day before. I remembered the feeling of the vibration in my head. Like every nerve in my body was at attention, waiting for something to happen. It wasn't a scary feeling at all, even though seeing the pink mist was startling. The vibration and pulsing were kind of pleasant, actually. And…maybe even comforting in a way, like they were familiar and natural.

Mary Ann's words played in my head. Maybe I *was* looking at this the wrong way. I mean, if someone had listened to me with Ella maybe she could've been helped. Maybe if I wasn't afraid of telling that boy about his dog, they could have taken it to a veterinarian. What would happen if I embraced it—tried to learn how to use it? These thoughts kept me company as I drifted off to sleep.

***

I was in blackness. Surrounding me were three oval shaped beings of soft white light. I knew intuitively that they were beings, even though they were made of light that diffused into the blackness at the outer edges. They moved towards me and enveloped me in their light, completely taking me in. Instantly, I felt the most intense joy I'd ever experienced. Joy without limit, without fear, unending and all-consuming. Pure, intense joy.

***

I woke up crying, the only thought I had was, *Why am I back? Why did I have to come back?* I tasted the outer corners of the joy that was so real, so intense just a moment ago. It was replaced with sadness that filled every space in my body. I felt disoriented. Nothing was familiar, not even my own body. Understanding crept into my consciousness and brought me back to the present. I was in the hospital bed…the fall and the injuries. Just as I became aware of my current state, the ache in my ribs became acute, and I let out a cry and doubled over clutching my torso. In all the emotion and the confusion that followed the dream, I must have launched myself up to sitting, and my broken ribs were not happy with the sudden movement. I painfully lowered myself back down and tried to calm my breathing. My head throbbed and the room spun.

What just happened to me? It did not feel like a dream…it was too real. Even now as I tried to fully recall the experience, the edges felt fuzzy. What I could mostly remember was the feeling of complete bliss when the beings moved into me. It felt like I was being embraced by them but, in fact, it was more like I diffused into them as they enveloped me. Could that have been God? I was embarrassed to even entertain the idea. My knowledge of God was limited as my parents were not religious in the least. My mom would say she was agnostic. She believed in some higher power but questioned all the sureties that individual religions espoused. My dad claimed he was an atheist, but I heard him tell my mom one night that the fact that “he’d found her out of all the people in the world might make him believe.” My mom called him a romantic at that.

Maybe I just experienced being with God. I had always liked the idea of a loving, kind God versus a wrathful God, and joy could be like love, right? The purest kind of love? I closed my eyes and tried to ignore the throbbing in my ribs and head. Maybe if I try to sleep again, it will happen again. The beings of light will come back. I suddenly felt brilliant, and I was sure I would find the answer if I just went back to sleep. I laid there in the hard, lumpy hospital bed willing myself to sleep, but sleep wouldn’t come. I changed position, pulled the blanket up over my eyes to shut out the machinery lights in the room, and tried the anxiety breathing my aunt taught me. Breathe in—hold—breathe out. Breathe in—hold—breathe out. My pulse stabilized as I continued focusing on my breath.

***

All around me were soft white swirls. They danced and turned and intertwined. They were beautiful and peaceful, and I simply watched them as they moved. They seemed alive, like they knew where they were going. I reached out and they didn’t move away, but rather whirled around my fingers. I felt just a shimmer of touch as they flowed around me, almost like a shift of air. As I moved my arm, they followed. It was like we were communicating. Suddenly, I understood what they were trying to tell me. I reached out and closed my fingers around one of the light strands. Even though it didn’t feel like I was actually holding anything, the strand yielded to my touch. I took the strand and brought it to my side. Gently and knowingly I placed my fingers holding the light to my broken ribs. The light seemed to flow into my body and disperse. I did it twice more, and then pulled three more strands into my head. Once done, I placed one hand on my side and one on my head and whispered, “Thank you.”

***

The light of full morning sun hit my eyelids and I fluttered them open. The border between reality and dreaming was muddled. As my senses finished waking, I heard voices in the hall outside my door. There was a knock and the door opened a smidge. A face peeked around, spied me looking back, and came fully through the door.

"Good morning, sunshine!" said the nurse from yesterday. "How did your night go? Did you sleep?" he asked while busying himself with the machines.

"I think so," I replied. "What time is it?"

"It's about a quarter to eight," he said. "I've been peeking in every half hour or so, but you were out like a light. Your body needed it after what it went through yesterday, huh?" He came over and stood by the side of the hospital bed. "I need to check on your ribs and your head, okay?" I remembered the test from the day before where he flashed the light at my eyes while I looked in different directions.

"Here, I'll get up so it's easier," I said, quickly shifting to a seated position.

"Whoa! Hang on, Leah!" he yelled as he grabbed at my arms. Seeing no reaction in me, he said, "Didn't that hurt? Moving like that—didn't that hurt your ribs?" He looked at me puzzled.

Somewhat perplexed, I replied, "No, actually…is that weird? I didn't think about it and just moved but it doesn't feel bad…" I furrowed my brow and looked down at my side. Yesterday, moving from lying down to sitting literally knocked the wind out of me. But now it didn't seem to be a problem. I gingerly felt along my side. It was a little tender, I guess, but not much. I looked up at the nurse. "Do broken ribs heal that quickly?" I asked him.

"No—never…let's take a look." He lifted my shirt to where I was bandaged and had been starting to turn several shades of purple from the bruising just last night. "What in the world?" he whispered as he saw that the deep purples had diminished to light pinks and yellows. "I'm going to touch the ribs very gently, okay, Leah? You tell me what you feel." Gingerly, he placed two fingers along the bandage covering the top rib and pressed ever so slightly. "Does that hurt? Any pain?" he raised his eyebrows at me as he asked.

"Honestly…no. Yesterday that hurt like crazy…but right now I barely feel it," I answered. The nurse continued to assess the area, but only found one or two little spots where I felt much discomfort at all.

"This is wild—did anyone come in and give you medication this morning?"

"I don't think so," I replied. "You know my head doesn't hurt either, is that strange, too?"

He shined the flashlight in my eyes and checked my head wound. "Your head feels okay? No headache?" I shook my head. "Leah, I don't know what to say, your eyes are behaving normally, and the cut on your head is just a faint scar. I don't know what's going on. I'll get the doc in soon as I can—he's going to want to see this for himself." He slowly stood up and paused, peering down at me, as though an explanation might occur to him if he stared a little longer. He finally sighed. "I better leave this one for the doc. I'll grab your breakfast. Back in a flash." He gave me a smile and left the room.

I brought my hand up to my broken ribs and felt around. Could I really have healed that quickly? Maybe the doctors were wrong about my ribs. Surely, they couldn't have been broken if now they barely hurt. Suddenly, I gasped and brought my hands to my mouth as I remembered the swirls of light that I had pulled from the air into my ribs and my head. The image and experience of the soft, white dancing light came back to me as clear as if it had just happened. I felt my head where the cut was but felt just slightly raised skin. Then I moved to my ribs and pushed harder to see if they gave pain like the day before. They were tender, but nothing like yesterday.

Just then the doctor came in and repeated the tests the nurse had done. Frowning, he ordered me more x-rays. Minutes after I returned from the x-ray room, Mary Ann arrived. I brought her up to speed on my condition. She remembered to bring the box of pastries from Sloane's, and we were about to dig in, just as the doctor came back to the room.

"Oh good, your aunt is here, too. I have some incredible and somewhat perplexing news." He looked down at his clipboard, gathering his thoughts. "Leah," he started, turning toward me. "I can't explain it and it doesn't make any sense, but your broken ribs seem to have healed dramatically overnight." He looked back down at the report in his hand and shook his head back and forth. "I've literally never seen anything like it. It's the x-ray result I would expect to see after a month or two of rehab. You have new bone growth knitted all around the breaks already…it's astounding." He looked at Mary Ann. "I actually had the tech triple check that she didn't give me another patient's imaging by mistake, but this is definitely Leah's. I'm not sure what to say except that it's almost like a miracle. Did anything happen? Did you take anything—vitamins, herbs—last night? Anything not given by the staff here? Anything at all out of the ordinary you can think of?" He raised his eyebrows and waited for me to respond.

"No—nothing at all," I replied. I couldn't imagine starting a conversation about my dream. No way I wanted to end up in the psych ward.

"Well—in any case, it's great news! And I imagine you're feeling a lot less pain." I nodded. "I'd like my staff to come in and take some blood samples to analyze. See if it tells us anything about how your body healed itself so quickly. Does that sound manageable on your end?" I looked at my aunt, she was frowning and replied for me.

"Doctor, my niece has suffered enough and doesn't need to suffer more just to satisfy your curiosity. Let's just chalk it up to good genes and let her continue to heal. Will you be consenting to an early discharge now that she's doing so much better?" She raised her eyebrows and smiled at him. He looked a little surprised—I don't think he expected her to say no to the blood sample.

"Well—I mean, if she stayed one more night we would be able to monitor her vitals more closely and that might give us clues as to what happened," he replied, gaining enthusiasm as this new idea occurred to him.

"It sounds like that would be very beneficial to you, but not to Leah. And isn't her wellbeing the reason you're here?" She spoke the last words a little softer, and it made him turn back to look at her.

He sat forward eagerly on his stool. "Something unusual happened with Leah. What if we could figure it out and it could help others, too? That's all I'm suggesting."

Mary Ann smiled at him. "I believe you, and I agree her recovery is mind-boggling and implausible, but Leah has been through a lot and it's time she came home. If we think of anything that could be useful to you for solving this mystery, we'll let you know. But for now, let's get this girl fully checked out so she can sleep in her own bed tonight."

The doctor opened his mouth as though he was going to argue but thought better of it. He just nodded, abruptly stood and left the room. A short while later my nurse friend returned, checked me out, and gave me my discharge papers. In just over an hour, Mary Ann and I were in her car heading home. I wasn't sorry to be leaving the hospital. We picked up Mexican food on the way and sat in the kitchen unwrapping giant burritos.

Mary Ann and I hadn't been alone at all during the day at the hospital, so I hadn't had a chance to tell her anything about my nighttime experience. I looked up at her.

"Mary Ann…"

"Mmm?" she replied, having just taken a huge bite. I paused and she raised her eyebrows expectantly.

"I might have an idea how my broken ribs, and my head healed themselves so quickly." I said, not at all sure of myself. "It will sound completely crazy to you, though." I quickly added, then sighed and put my hands over my eyes. I had been thinking about it all day—trying to make sense of, what seemed to me, like magic. She patiently listened as I explained my experiences as best I could, at times getting frustrated with how ridiculous it sounded.

When I finished, she slowly shook her head and said, "I think this is only the beginning, sweet girl. There are great things in store for you."

Laotong:
(Chinese) The precious bond of female friendship.

CHAPTER 5:

"You're dropping your arm, Leah. Don't telegraph your strike." Danny coached me from the side mats. "You let him know what's coming and he has time to react. Don't give him the time."

As usual, my hair, slick with sweat, was getting in my eyes. I swiped at it quickly and José flinched. Using his reaction, I faked a jab again, pulling it back just as he parried, and threw a lead kick to his temple. José tried to bring his hand back to cover but I still got him. He hit the deck. Even with practice sparring at half strength, a head kick was enough to rattle you. Danny called time and checked on José. He was fine.

He smiled at me as he got up and held out his glove saying, "Nice one," which sounded like "nishe un" with the mouthguard in. Just then the timer rang for the round. That was it for training tonight. It was my eighteenth birthday, and we were going out to dinner at Chez Joelle, this amazing French bistro. Danny and José gave me big hugs and wished me a happy birthday, then I rode my bike home to get cleaned up.

I had been training with Danny at Intercept Martial Arts Academy for a few years now. I started because it seemed that my injuries from Eric created two camps of people: Those who left me alone (even more than before) because trouble seemed to follow me, and those who thought I was making the whole story up for attention. I ended up only missing a few days of school. As the rumor mill goes, many kids heard what happened, or some version of it, by Monday morning. When I returned to school Thursday morning seemingly unscathed, no broken ribs and not much bruising, the rumor began that I had made the whole thing up.

After about a week of insults or snubbing, one boy from Eric's group of friends decided to confront me. Apparently, Eric had been grounded by his parents for the entire month, and his friend thought this was unacceptable from someone who was obviously lying. He was short and skinny with acne peppering his cheeks. Though I didn't know his name, I had seen him in Eric's group many times. He was always louder and more obnoxious than everyone else.

It was after Mrs. Holland's English class eighth period that I left to find him waiting for me, blocking my path with his hands folded across his chest. I moved to slip around him, and he repositioned himself to block me again. I steeled myself for whatever was about to happen. The halls weren't empty, but most kids had grabbed their backpacks and started home for the day. I looked up at this fool in my way and felt equally angry and anxious. Understanding that he wasn't going to let me pass, I hugged my books to my chest and stood waiting.

"Well?" I asked. "Are we just going to stand here or are you going to tell me what you want?" I tried to sound as calm and unbothered as possible.

"You're a lying witch," he spat at me. "Look at you! There's not a damn thing wrong with you. But you tell everyone how Eric attacked you—it's pathetic!" He was getting red in his pimpled cheeks.

"I haven't told anyone anything," I replied. "Why don't you ask Eric what happened, hmmm? What do you care anyway?" I could feel my own head heating up with frustration and embarrassment as other kids around stopped to see what was happening.

"He's not allowed to do anything all month because of your stupid lies. He suffers while you walk around like something important…as if you were anything but a pathetic freak!" He leaned in a little closer and said in a low voice, looking right in my eyes. "You know what they used to do to lying witches, right? If I were you, I'd watch your back."

Then he straightened up, knocked the books out of my hand, and sneered as he walked away. I followed him with my eyes for a minute, trying to control my breath. Then I knelt down to gather my things.

A notebook had opened and some papers had fallen a few feet away. A girl I never saw before picked them up and held them out for me. As I took them and thanked her, she smiled.

"You're Leah, right?" she asked. "I've only been at this school a couple weeks and have heard nothing but Leah, Leah, Leah." Her hands gestured in the air as she spoke. I was confused how to respond. It didn't seem like she was making fun of me, but I couldn't really tell. I took the papers she offered and waited to see if she would continue.

"I'll tell you what. I have language arts with Eric fourth period, and I believe your side of the story one hundred percent. Though I haven't seen him in a while. I guess he's taking the week off to 'recover' from the emotional toll attacking you took." She rolled her eyes and made air quotes with her fingers. Her hair was fair and bouncy with curls that flew around when she gestured. I still didn't know if I was supposed to respond to that or what, so I kept still.

"I'm Alex." She smiled at me again. "We just moved here from Virginia. It is not fun moving in the middle of a school year, let me tell you." She started walking toward the bay of lockers…I hadn't yet moved. She turned around to face me again,

"You know, you should learn to protect yourself. Like, from jerks like Eric and that idiot who was just here. My uncle owns a martial arts gym—you might want to look into it. It's actually a lot of fun, sparring and hitting the mitts and stuff. I could take you sometime if you wanted to give it a try." She raised her eyebrows at me and waited for a response.

What on earth was I supposed to say to that? Martial arts? What even was that? Wasn't that the stuff the samurai warriors did? With swords and sticks? "Maybe," was all I could think to say.

"Cool—well I gotta go for now. But I'll see you tomorrow, Leah!" She gave me a little wave as she walked away toward the stairs.

I didn't see her the next day or the entire next week. But the following Monday, we ran into each other outside the library after eighth period.

"Leah! There you are! I haven't seen you all week!" Alex exclaimed as she ran over to me. I almost jumped with the attention and glanced around nervously to see if anyone was looking at us. "I talked to my uncle and he says you can come do a trial beginner's class if I take it with you. They have them at seven o'clock every weeknight. Is there a day that works for you?" She was talking so fast I had a difficult time processing what she was telling me. Was she asking me to do something…with her?

"Umm, I don't really have too much going on during the week," I replied shyly, feeling completely flustered.

"How about Thursday night, then? It's called Intercept Martial Arts, you can Google it to get the address. Wear sweats or exercise clothes, okay? I'll meet you there!" She seemed so excited it was hard not to feel upbeat, too.

"Okay, I'll check with my aunt, but I think I can make it." I gave her a half smile as she beamed at me. It was hard to understand that someone at the school was directing all that happiness towards me.

"Oh—and here's my cell in case something changes. Obviously, we have completely opposite schedules!" she added. On a scrap of paper, she wrote with sweeping, curly handwriting; *Alex Newill*, and the nine digits of her cell underneath. "Can you even read that? God, my handwriting has gone to shit!" she exclaimed. Everything she said seemed laced with enthusiasm. Like a little puppy that just wanted to play. She had pep, I decided. Alex Newill was peppy. "I've got to run now, Leah…but I'll see you

Thursday, okay?" She gave me one more big smile and wave and walked down the hall.

That night I told Mary Ann what had happened. I don't know what excited her more, the fact that someone was nice to me, or that I had a plan to do something physical. She was ecstatic.

"Oh Leah—this is just what you need! Get some of that energy out. Hitting things is absolutely wonderful…frankly, I think everyone should do it!"

On Thursday evening, Mary Ann drove me to the address listed on the website. We were greeted by a concrete building in various stages of disrepair. The sidewalk and grassy curb had bits of trash strewn here and there. An empty Coke can shifted back and forth in the breeze. I turned back and looked doubtfully at my aunt.

"Are you sure this is the right address?" I asked, the apprehension growing in my stomach. Mary Ann got out and walked around to where I had stopped outside the passenger side door.

"Not exactly ritzy, huh?" she said, putting her hands on her hips and looking up and down the street. The street was busy, but in an industrial way. Large, boxy, nondescript buildings lined up one after another. A couple had tall metal fences surrounding the property. No one would call it welcoming. "This is the right address—let's go to the door and see what we find." She paused and turned back to make sure the car was locked.

The double glass doors that served as the unassuming main entrance were unlocked, so we passed through them into a dingy entryway. There was a set of stairs off to the left and a small-ish sign on the wall that read "Intercept Martial Arts" with an arrow pointing the way up the stairs.

"This is definitely the place." Mary Ann declared after seeing the sign. "I wouldn't call them advertising pros." She winked at me. "Let's check it out."

We headed up a concrete staircase. The paint was peeling on the walls and there were stains on the stairs that looked like they'd been there as long as the building itself. When we got to the top of the landing, though, we began hearing sounds of life: grunts and thuds and a bass beat of music. A second arrowed sign pointed us down a short hallway to the right toward a door with Intercept Martial Arts stenciled in the small window. We cautiously turned the handle and stepped through.

The scene inside was vastly different than the entrance. About two dozen people were spread throughout the well-lit room. The floor was covered with blue and black wrestling mats, and there seemed to be a cage of some kind in the corner. It looked like a class was in session as a group of people stood in front of a man demonstrating something. Half a dozen heavy bags hung along the wall to our right, and each was being punched or kicked by a very sweaty, red-faced person. In the cage, a man and a woman were doing some kind of wrestling that looked rather painful.

"This is more encouraging!" chirped my aunt. A small office sat to the left of the entrance, and the door was ajar. Mary Ann walked over and gently knocked.

"Come on in!" said a voice, and we moved into the room.

"Welcome! Welcome!" the man sitting at the desk stood. "You must be Leah, right?" I nodded. "Alex has told me about a thousand times that you'd be coming tonight. I think she's just a tad bit excited about you being here." He playfully rolled his eyes. "I'm Alex's uncle, Danny. It's nice to meet you." He held out his hand and I shook it, then he turned to smile at Mary Ann. "You must be Leah's aunt," he said as he took her hand. "So nice to have you both here!"

"Leah, you're going to do a beginner's foundations class tonight. Pierre is the instructor and you'll really like him. It's just the basics—fighting stance, jabs, crosses, and, of course, conditioning." He grinned. "Have you ever taken any martial arts before?" I shook my head. In fact, all I was thinking when he said "conditioning" was a funny old YouTube video my aunt shared with me of an aerobics class in the eighties where these women with terrible cotton candy hair wore pastel leotards and shiny tights and bounced around to the Bee Gees. Mary Ann laughed pretty hard at that video because she said it made her remember her mom's "Jane Fonda phase."

Just then Alex pushed open the door and greeted me with an excited "Yay! I was worried you might not come!" and a hug. I snuck a sideways glance at Mary Ann and when she saw Alex hug me, I thought she might faint from joy. "And now you've met my awesome Uncle Danny," she added, walking around the desk to give him a hug as well. She turned to face Mary Ann and extended her hand, "Hi! I'm Alex!"

"Nice to meet you, Alex. I'm Leah's Aunt Mary Ann. I'm so glad you suggested this!" she gushed.

At that moment, Danny looked out the office window into the studio. "Looks like your class is about to start, girls. Alex, why don't you go introduce Leah to Pierre? Mary Ann, if you're staying you can watch the class from the group of chairs to the right of those heavy bags. I've got some calls to make, but I'll peek in on the class. Have a great time, Leah!"

With that, Alex grabbed my arm and led me to an area to leave my coat and shoes. Pierre was tall and bald and so muscular that I felt I was looking at a superhero. Needless to say, I started to worry about what I'd gotten myself into. But he turned out to be really friendly in a calm, self-assured way, much like Danny was. There were about ten people in the class with Alex and me, all of us in varying degrees of fitness and coordination, so I quickly stopped worrying about how I looked and whether I was doing it right. Alex was my training partner and she didn't seem to mind at all when I made a mistake. In fact, she really seemed to enjoy helping me out, and we ended up laughing through a lot of it.

That didn't mean it wasn't work, though. I was already sweatier than I'd been since elementary school by the start of conditioning—which I soon found out had a lot less pastel bouncing and much more torture like burpees and military-style pushups. Though I had to stop once or twice for a couple seconds, I managed not to die through the series. While Alex did much better than me, she was also a sweaty mess, which made me feel slightly less like an out-of-shape slob. Even more surprising than the fact that I didn't die was that I really liked it. The entire time I was trying to learn the moves or complete the pushups, I was completely absorbed in it. I wasn't thinking about school or what people thought about me, or my parents. I was only focused on the position of my hand or the effort to finish a round. I felt free.

After that first night, I began going to Intercept every Thursday, then added Tuesday nights a month later. Alex could only join me on Thursdays. To my surprise, I developed such an intense desire to learn and train, that being around strangers in the class didn't even deter me. In fact, by the end of a month some familiar faces started greeting me by name, and I found that I knew their names, too. At school I talked about it so often to Isaac that I managed to convince him to join me, and pretty soon he was coming to train as often as I was. Alex and I got to be pretty good friends, and once Isaac started training too, the three of us were together all the time. Isaac fell hard for Alex about sixth months in, but it took a year for them to officially start dating. Now, almost four years later, we were still inseparable.

I had tested for my purple belt just a month prior and was sparring more and more often. José was a regular training partner of mine even though he'd been at it a lot longer. He was good at testing me, but I rarely got a clean shot in. That head kick tonight was a huge deal for me, and I was elated the entire ride home.

Later at my birthday dinner at Chez Joelle, after incredible steak tips and mousse au chocolat, I opened gifts. Isaac knowingly gave me "glove dogs," or inserts for my boxing gloves to help them not smell so bad between training sessions. I'd been complaining about the odor every time I took them out of my training bag. Isaac, usually standing next to me, readily agreed they were disgusting. I joked that the glove dogs were as much a gift for him as for me.

I opened Mary Ann's gift next. It was a book about Noam Chomsky's Theory of Universal Grammar. Speaking to our shared love of language and my success in French and Spanish classes in high school, it was a gift I was excited to receive. I half stood and reached across the table to give her a big hug. The moment I got my arms around her, my vision flashed and the image in my mind's eye shifted to black with crisscrossing electric light blue lines. They were alive and numerous. I couldn't see where they began, but they all seemed to converge in a high spot just right of center. I suddenly noticed the lines were making sound: like humming. And though I hadn't heard anything like it before, I felt an understanding of their meaning.

Just as quickly as it arrived, the vision was gone and I was back in my position above the dinner table, my aunt in my embrace. I startled and pulled away to look at Mary Ann.

Mary Ann noticed the shift in my state. She placed her hands on my arms and looked at me, her face serious.

"What is it, Leah? What's going on?" she demanded. I opened my mouth to speak but couldn't. Tears welled up in my eyes and I looked back and forth between Isaac, Alex, and Mary Ann. I just wanted one of them to make it go away, to tell me that it wasn't real. But by now, I knew it was. I looked back at Mary Ann. She softened her gaze, "It's okay, Leah. Whatever it is, we'll get through it together." I took a deep breath and considered the person standing in front of me. My mother and father and best friend over the last several years. Why did it have to be Mary Ann? My head screamed in protest to the unfairness of it all and I cried even harder. Slumping back into my seat I covered my face with my hands.

"It's you, Mary Ann. It's you."

The vision showed me Mary Ann had a problem in her right breast. When I told her this, she made an appointment for a mammogram the very next day. I insisted on skipping school and going with her. Not surprisingly, the mammogram found something suspicious, and she was sent for ultrasound and thin needle biopsy—which, as we knew it would, confirmed cancer cells. She was scheduled for a lumpectomy a week later. They removed the tumor and three lymph nodes to check if the cancer was contained or spreading.

I moved in and out of places the following week in a dense haze of distraction and depression. I had only had the vision three times in my life now, and the first two had ended in death. The idea of losing Mary Ann was on my mind constantly, which made me think even more than usual of my parents. It had been six years since their deaths, and at times I would panic trying to recall specific memories or experiences with them that seemed beyond my grasp. Other memories would arrive like lightning, fast and intense, and leave me feeling hollow with loss. Isaac and his parents, having known my mom and dad so well, were always willing to help me fill in any gaps, and Mary Ann kept me close to them through stories of when I was little, or when they were first dating. Who would give me that if Mary Ann died? I would be lost at sea without an anchor.

I had just gotten home from school, and Mary Ann had just sat down with tea and a mystery novel "for distraction," when she got the call. Standing and walking over to the small pad of paper we keep in the kitchen, she began jotting notes. I read over her shoulder. Stage 2A. Lymph nodes ok. Radiation. Possibly chemotherapy. Immunotherapy? Proton therapy? All of these sounded terrible and confusing to me. I never knew anyone with cancer before, so words like "stage 2" and "proton therapy" could be good or bad news as far as I was concerned. Then Mary Ann wrote in bigger letters, "Good prognosis" and caught my eye with a small smile. After a minute more she hung up the phone and touched her fingers to her forehead, let out a huge breath and said, "Thank God! Oh, Thank God!" Then she turned to me and placed her left hand on my arm, smiling through tears.

"It's going to be okay, Leah. The doctor says I have stage 2, or rather stage 2A breast cancer. The tumor itself was a little over three centimeters big." She shook her head in wonder, "I never even felt a lump or anything. I guess the A after the 2 means that it hasn't gone into my lymph nodes at all, and that's a very good sign. They want me to undergo radiation, or this other, newer thing called proton therapy, starting next week. They don't believe I'll need chemotherapy as the cells were still contained, but they want to keep it as an option." She moved a shaky hand up to her hair, betraying the stress she'd been feeling waiting for an answer. "She says there's no reason to believe I won't live another 40 years when all is said and done." She grabbed a tissue and blew her nose, then offered the box to me. "Your vision saved me by finding the cancer early. Thank you, sweet girl."

Rswt QD:
(Ancient Egyptian) (Pronounced Rasut Qwed) The state of being awake while dreaming.

CHAPTER 6

The following weeks, Mary Ann started her treatment, and I went on with my senior year of high school. It was suggested that my aunt start a meditation practice to handle the stress that the diagnosis and treatment might bring. Being a yoga instructor, Mary Ann had used meditation many times throughout her life, but had taken a break in the years since moving back to be with me. Much of her "before" life had been put on the back burner to care for me, and Mary Ann decided it was the perfect time to rediscover her previous passions. As soon as her surgeon gave the okay, she committed to twenty minutes of yoga followed by twenty minutes of meditation every morning upon waking. She was a bit surprised when, after a couple weeks, I asked if I could join her. She gladly welcomed the company.

"Every habit needs a little accountability to help it stick!" she exclaimed and said we'd keep each other on track. Mary Ann decided she wanted us to try a meditation to align the chakras or energy "wheels" of the body, whatever that meant. It was supposed to facilitate her body's own healing abilities. She bought a small poster showing the outline of a seated human with legs crossed and hands resting on their knees with palms turned toward the sky. Overlapping the image of the human were balls of color, each to represent one of the seven main chakras: Magenta or purple for crown, indigo for third eye, blue for throat, green for heart, yellow for solar plexus, orange for sacral, and red for root. I was mesmerized by the image.

That first morning, after Mary Ann showed me some basic yoga poses, we sat to listen to a guided chakra meditation she found on YouTube. We got into a position much like the person on the poster and breathed slowly and calmly. A deep, British man's voice slowly and softly instructed us to imagine all our body's processes working together and interwoven to bring us health and vitality: heart pumping, lungs inflating and deflating, and neurons firing to keep everything moving smoothly. Next, we were to imagine our bodies surrounded by soft diffuse yellowish-white light. This was energy surrounding our body and flowing in and out, connecting us to the energy of the universe.

While focused on the energy, there arose a small, familiar vibration in my head. The man then told us to picture a red sphere of light at the base of our tailbone—our root chakra. We were to visualize this red sphere spinning in a clockwise direction while keeping our minds on the intention to release the chakra. I didn't know if I was imagining it, but I started to feel warmth spread around my tailbone as I pictured the red sphere. The voice then guided us up to our sacral area and told us to visualize an orange sphere and set our intention for release. We spent a few minutes at each color and chakra before moving on to the next. The warmth I felt at my tailbone moved up my body with each corresponding chakra: Yellow solar plexus and green heart were next. The vibration in my head had grown and I was starting to feel it traveling down to the rest of my body. Then we reached the third eye chakra, between the brows. As I pictured a spinning deep blue sphere, I could feel space between my eyes and the vibration turning to a pulse. The visual area in my mind's eye felt infinite and deep. As though I could see how, even between atoms, there was distance…possibility. And even though separate, it was all part of a whole. A universal whole. The deep voice guided us to the last chakra, the crown. A purple spinning orb with energy flowing out from the top of our head into the universe above was our visual. I focused on the color and the movement of the orb, though it was getting harder with the increased strength of the vibrations and pulsing.

***

I was sitting in the grand room, again perched on my marble throne, wearing the heavy crown of horns surrounding a solar disc. The layers of my linen sheath were torn, and a deep red stain feathered out from where the spear had penetrated my abdomen. The cavernous room was empty of the usual throngs of sick and maimed poor who had come to seek the healer. I was alone. In my shaking hands was the pink stone, cool and heavy, but smooth like silk. I traced the soft white lines crossing through it with my finger, whispering words of thanks and admiration for its strength and magic. Turning the stone over, my finger located the one soft blue vein. I now praised the stone for its wisdom and understanding. Closing my eyes, I whispered the dedication; "May this body be the vessel of the power of the Healing Stone." I could soon see the dancing soft white lines gracefully swirling around me in the black of my consciousness.

Reaching out my shaking hand, a band of light wrapped itself gently around my fingers. I pulled it down and placed it to my abdomen, just below my navel, where the spear had penetrated deep through my flesh. The light entered my body and I reached out for another strand. With each strand I brought into my wound, the more I felt my energy and life force returning. Finally, sensing I was almost fully restored, I brought the pink stone to my lips, close enough that my whispers left condensation on the smooth surface, and asked it to accept my body as its protector. I then moved the stone down to my abdomen, and slowly, excruciatingly, pushed it fully into the wound. The pain was like ripping open from the inside out and an incredible wail escaped me. But once it was inside the wound, the pain subsided, and my flesh knitted itself closed in healing.

The exertion had exhausted me so much that I could do nothing but slump in the throne for several minutes, drifting in and out of consciousness. Finally, placing my hands over the site, I opened my eyes. I was weak and soaked with sweat. Looking around me for the first time, I noticed the long shadows of an approaching dusk. It would soon be time to move. My breath calmed and I held my hands up in front of my face. Whispering "May this body be the vessel of the power of the Healing Stone", I began to see a faint pink mist arise from my palms. It was the same pink hue of the stone and its energy coursed around my body, testing out its new home. I exhaled, lowered my arms and said, "It is done."

***

I found myself back in the living room, still seated on the fuchsia and orange floor cushion Mary Ann had given me for our meditation. I looked over at her. Her eyes were closed, and she had a look of concentration on her face as her lips moved gently with soundless words. Feeling my abdomen, I was again surprised to find it unharmed. No longer paying attention to the meditation, I tried to focus on the waking dream I just experienced. Could I have really drifted off to sleep for a few seconds? I've never fallen asleep while sitting up. Like before, the experience felt so real to me. So what was it? Was I reliving a past life? I had the stone and used the white strands to heal myself, like I did in the hospital with my ribs. And once the stone was inside my body, the pink mist that I experienced with Eric in eighth grade appeared around my hands. Nothing was clear and I sighed audibly in frustration. Mary Ann peeked out at me. Seeing that I was no longer interested in the meditation, she leaned over.

"What's the matter? Are you finding it too hard to sit still?" she asked. "I know it took forever for me before I could get my mental to-do list out of my head and focus on what he was saying."

"No—it's not that. I liked the experience—it felt good to try to quiet my thoughts. It's that something happened when we got to the crown chakra," I answered. "Do you remember the morning after I—er—got my period…I told you about the dream I'd had? About sitting on a throne and using this pink stone to heal people? And that I woke up when I was impaled by my brother's spear?" Mary Ann nodded. "I always just assumed it was a crazy dream and the real-life pains from my period made me imagine being injured, you know? But it just happened again, while I wasn't asleep. During the meditation," I tried to explain. Mary Ann shifted from sitting cross-legged to her knees and gave me her full attention.

"Once we were visualizing the crown chakra, I was in that room again. I was the woman again. And I used the healing stone on myself to help heal the spear wound. But before the wound was completely healed, I pushed the stone inside my body." I could remember the feeling, sharp and painful. "Then I held my hands up and the same pink mist swirled around them, like I told you about in eighth grade. It looked exactly the same." Holding my hands out in front of me, I looked up at Mary Ann. "What could it mean? Could I be the person in my dream? Like…a past life or something?" I asked. I had never given reincarnation more than a fleeting thought. Could I be envisioning a former life—*very* former—where I was this woman? I shook my head as though trying to clear the fog or cobwebs. *Come on, Leah*, I thought to myself. What I dreamt was hardly realistic. Even if I could see a past life, what I experienced seemed magical, not humanly possible. I sighed. Mary Ann hadn't said anything yet. She was still looking at me but in a far-off way, like she wasn't really seeing me, but seeing her thoughts instead. I shifted on my pillow, suddenly aware of an ache in my midback. My movement shook Mary Ann from her reverie and her focus returned to me.

"It's incredible, isn't it? What's happening to you." She paused, bringing a hand up to pull at her bottom lip in concentration. "I haven't a clue what your vision could mean, Leah, but I strongly believe it's important. It means *something*." She raised herself off her floor pillow gracefully, as only someone who's practiced yoga her whole adult life could do, and walked over to her laptop. I stood up, regrettably with much less grace than my aunt. I think I may have even grunted. Looking over her shoulder, I saw her type the words "past lives and dreams" in the search box. We landed on a site called pastlifepresentlife.net. It read "Dreams often reveal our past lives to us. When we're in them, they seem as real as our waking life, and may feel as though we've dropped into the middle of an ongoing movie. You will understand and know people and places that are not familiar in your waking life, and once awake, it will be hard to separate the dream from reality." Mary Ann read the section aloud and turned to look at me.

"I think your gut feeling that you somehow lived as this woman could be right. Why not? Maybe you should write as many details down as you can to keep track of what they reveal to you."

The next day at school was difficult. I was preoccupied with my waking dream, but also had a big history assignment with a looming due date. Pretty certain I wouldn't be able to finish in time, I popped into the teacher's office to beg for an extension. He was less than thrilled with my request, but reluctantly gave me an extra half day to submit the assignment. Getting up to leave, with my ego down a few notches, my eyes swept the wall to the left of the door. I froze midway through putting on my sweater. There on the wall was a poster of a woman, sitting on a throne with a crown of a disc and horns. It was really a picture of a sculpture of the woman, but it was definitely the one from my dreams. I ran up to it looking for information, but the picture had no descriptor.

"Mr. Carrillo?" I started. "Can you tell me who this is a statue of?"

He barely raised his eyes from the papers strewn around him to give a cursory glance at where my attention laid.

"Isis—Egyptian Goddess." His voice was clipped, and I got the impression there would be no further discussion welcome at that moment. I thanked him and left hurriedly. It was Friday afternoon and I had just gained until Saturday evening to upload my completed assignment. Once I had that off my plate, I would focus on finding out all I could about my goddess: Isis.

Thaumaturge:
A worker of wonders or miracles; a magician.

CHAPTER 7

Sunday turned out to be one of those miraculous late spring days where the air was clear, the sun was bright, and the breeze carried with it the scent of flowers and new grass. I woke up early and decided to walk to the nearby local library branch. A converted brick cottage, it had a fireplace on one end that was always lit during the colder months, and the staff were warm and friendly. In spring and summer, the entryway was framed by gigantic hydrangea bushes and small, flowering trees. I spent a lot of time there over the years. It was the first place my parents let me travel to and from on my own when I was ten years old. I would roam the shelves imagining all the potential stories to lose myself in.

On this gorgeous morning, I had a mission, though. I needed to research Isis. I settled down into a comfy, worn armchair by a large picture window and propped my laptop on my knees. Scrolling through the information online was a bit overwhelming. Turns out there were some conflicting myths surrounding the goddess and her role among the deities. A common variation was that Isis was the daughter of Geb, the Earth god, and Nut, the sky goddess. She had three siblings, Osiris, Set (Seth), and Nephthys. Apparently, she was also the wife of Osiris, which I'm sure made for some crazy family dynamics. "She was a revered goddess," one source wrote, "known as a role model for women, protector of the dead, and magical healer."

The sun filtering through the window illuminated the paper on which I was taking notes, making the black type feel as though it was swimming above the page. I ran my fingers over "magical healer" on the screen and felt an excitement start to grow in my belly. I kept researching.

"Osiris was king of Egypt and ruled justly, bringing culture, agriculture, and religion to the barbaric men and women born from the tears of the God Ra. The land was fruitful and peaceful, and men and women lived equally without want. Osiris' brother Set was married to his sister Nephthys. Osiris had the title 'the beautiful one.' Nephthys had transformed herself to look like Isis in order to seduce Osiris. When Set found out, instead of taking out his anger on Nephthys, he deduced that she was overcome with the temptation of Osiris' beauty and could not resist him. Thus, Set sought revenge on Osiris, tricking him, trapping him in a leaden box, and dumping him in the Nile. Set then took over Egypt but abandoned the favors Osiris and Isis had bestowed on the people. It resulted in drought and famine throughout the land.

"Distraught by what Set had done, Isis sought out Osiris' box, finding it finally at Byblos. She was sure she could bring Osiris back to life, so she brought his box home and went to find healing herbs while leaving Nephthys guard. Set heard about this and tricked Nephthys into telling him where the body was. He then cut Osiris' body into many pieces and scattered them across the land and in the Nile. Isis and Nephthys transformed themselves into birds and scoured the land for all Osiris' pieces. They found all but his penis, which had been eaten by fish. Isis brought Osiris back from the dead, but because he was not whole, he could no longer be ruler among the living. He was forced to retreat to the underworld and become king of the dead. Before this, however, Isis turned herself into a falcon and circled Osiris' body. This allowed her to pull his seed from his body and impregnate herself."

Scrolling down, there was a picture of a bronze figurine of the Goddess, much like the one I'd seen in Mr. Carrillo's office. It was a small image, and somewhat grainy, but my breath quickened, and I felt the vibration in my head nonetheless. She was sculpted sitting in her throne with her baby Horus in her lap and the crown disc with two horns balanced upon her head. I ran my fingers over the image. Isis had her eyes closed and looked peaceful as she cradled her child in her arms. This was the woman of my visions, and she was considered one of the most powerful healers among the gods.

I searched for information on Isis' son Horus next.

"Horus was a god of the sky and often depicted as a falcon. Being the son of Isis and Osiris, Horus is thought to protect all through life and death. He has four sons to help in this sacred duty: Duamutef, a jackal god; Hapy, a baboon god; Imsety, a human-form god; and Qebehsenuef, a hawk god. Each of these sons represented different vital organs of the body, and helped men and women pass from the world of living to the world of the dead."

Another grainy black and white picture of a bronze sculpture sat below the text. The description read "Horus, son of Osiris and Isis, ruler of Egypt." The image was a falcon standing erect with a fierce gaze and a crown of metal upon his feathered head.

I turned away from the laptop and let my gaze settle on the greenery out the window. A soft breeze gently moved the leaves, and one small branch lightly scratched back and forth along the glass. Having the strange vibration sensation, I knew I had stumbled upon the right connection with my dreams/visions. Isis was the woman in my head, and she had a son Horus. None of my visions had included him, but her attacker in the first vision must have been her brother Set. The event was so real to me even now, years later. And reading that Isis was considered a magical healer only solidified my belief that she was the goddess I dreamt of. So I was closer to understanding the visions, but I was still far from knowing *why* I was having them.

As I moved my head slightly, the shaft of sunlight through the window hit my eyelids. I lingered there for a moment with my eyes closed, letting the warmth comfort my thoughts. Suddenly, I was very sleepy. Yawning and stretching my back and arms out, I got packed up to walk home. The cheery weather coupled with my newfound knowledge gave me a buoyant feeling. I turned my gaze up to "Look through the trees," as my mom always said. She felt most people got so caught up in the narrowness of their own lives and problems, that they spent most of their time looking down at the ground.

"We must remember that life is bigger than ourselves, Leah, and look up through the trees at the beauty of the world above," she would tell me, often on a day like this when the trees were in full leaf and the sun was at its brightest.

The memory comforted me and made me sad at the same time. I dropped my gaze back down to the sidewalk. Just then I noticed a baby bird near the trunk of a large maple tree. Walking over, I knelt down next to it. It was just a fledgling, with downy grey feathers and little, unfinished wings. To my dismay, the bird appeared to be dead or dying, as I couldn't detect any up or down movement in its little body. It must have fallen from the nest, the poor creature. I placed my index finger gently on the back feathers of the bird. A sparrow maybe? Suddenly I could see the electric blue lines in my vision leading to a spot I understood was the bird's heart. I gasped, opening my eyes and withdrawing my hand. I stared at the small body, now understanding that the bird was not dead, but would be soon. I suddenly, desperately wanted—needed—to do something.

Remembering how in my dream I had used a dedication before the ribbons or mist appeared, I closed my eyes and clasped my hands in what I imagined was a state of prayer and spoke the words Isis had during the dream.

"May this body be the vessel of the power of the Healing Stone." I stayed this way for a few slow breaths. My head began gently buzzing and the black behind my eyelids was abruptly filled with the soft, white, gliding ribbons. The ribbons of Isis and my dream in the hospital. I reached my hands out in front of my body and the ribbons responded by swirling around, revealing the outline of where my hands must have been. While I couldn't really *feel* the ribbons in the natural way, I could sense their movement around my fingertips. Seeing what would happen, I wiggled my fingers slowly. The ribbons moved with them.

"Please let me help this baby bird," I whispered into my hands, pinching a ribbon between my index finger and thumb. It stayed with me, though I couldn't feel any weight or substance to it. Keeping my eyes closed for fear of making it go away, I felt my other hand down to the bird's small body. Some of the ribbons moved, too, and were encircling the bird, so that I could see its outline. Slowly, I brought the ribbon I was holding down to where the bird was, and it seemed to absorb into its body. I repeated the process a second time. Then a third. It was after the third that I felt warmth and a small movement under my left hand, the one touching the bird's body. It startled me so that I drew back my hands and opened my eyes. I leaned down so that my face was just a couple inches from the baby bird and stared intently. The ribcage moved! Up and down, up and down… and the little eye facing me was now blinking. I let out a yell and a laugh and clapped my hands together in front of my face.

"Oh my God, it worked!" I exclaimed to myself. "I did it! I fucking did it!"

The happiness felt boundless in my chest, like it couldn't stand being trapped by my ribcage and might bust out at any moment. I watched as the little bird, all fluffy and gray, stood up and started clumsily hopping around the base of the tree.

"Yes!" I said. "Hop around, little bird! Hop and hop and hop!" I felt delirious with excitement and started hopping around, too. Something was releasing in me. Unleashing. I had controlled some part of this experience that had previously been random and uncontrollable. I reached my hands out far to either side of my torso and looked to the sky.

"Thank you!" I shouted, not caring who heard. I ran home to tell Mary Ann everything.

The elated feeling stayed with me the next morning at school and throughout the first few days of the week. Mary Ann had listened to my tale and asked all sorts of questions that I couldn't answer, like, what did I think the ribbons were made of? And was I really sure the bird had been dying? Once I convinced her it was real, she insisted we go to dinner to celebrate. I was giddy about the future and what I was now considering a gift instead of a curse. Sharing an appetizer of mouthwatering garlicky greens, olives, and hummus, it occurred to me that I should try to heal Mary Ann's cancer. I almost knocked her out of her chair with my enthusiasm. She agreed we could try, but not for a few days. She just wanted me to enjoy this moment without putting too much pressure on myself. I think she was a little scared that I wouldn't be able to draw upon it again and I would end up deflated. Not me though. My worry was gone. Now that I'd done it once, I was absolutely positive that I could do it again.

It was really hard to quit the buzzing in my brain, so sleep was fitful and incomplete that night, yet I still jumped out of bed in cheerfulness at first light. Nothing was going to shatter this newfound joy. Isaac and Alex didn't know what to make of my changed persona. I was laughing in class, looking teachers in the eye and smiling for no obvious reason. This was not the Leah they had come to know—at least not the school Leah. After school, when I explained to them what had happened, they were flabbergasted, if not a tiny bit skeptical, like Mary Ann had been. I had shared every step of the journey of my vision and power with them, but it always made me anxious. It was just that with each new experience, I was veering farther and farther from being "normal," and I still worried there might come a point where

I crossed a line. But they had accepted all the other things that had happened to me over the years. They were willing to believe.

It was Wednesday after school when life got a little more interesting. The house phone rang. I only used my cell, so I usually let it go to voicemail when Mary Ann wasn't home, but something made me pick it up this time.

"Hello?" I answered with an upbeat, and still unfamiliar, lilt to my voice.

"Is this the home of Leah Brown?" a woman's chipper voice demanded on the other end of the line.

"Yes, this is Leah. Who's calling?" I answered, a bit more uncertainly.

"Leah!" the voice gasped. "I'm so happy I caught you at home! I'm Angela Rossman of Channel 5 News!" She said this with such vigor it was clear it was supposed to mean something to me. And it probably did to any other normal human who engaged in society and did things liked watched the evening news with their families after dinner. Did people still do that? The pause became slightly awkward and the woman cleared her throat.

"Anyway, like I said…I'm from Channel 5 and we've decided to run your YouTube video during the evening news tonight! Congratulations! I would love to interview you live during the segment. Really just get you there to talk about how you did it and what was going through your mind, et cetera. How *did* you do it by the way? The video isn't always the best angle, and the sound was off so we were, so far, only able to guess." The voice rambled on and I was having a really hard time keeping up with what she was saying.

YouTube video? They must have called the wrong person because this made no sense at all to me.

"I'm sorry," I stammered. "But I'm not sure what you're talking about. I don't know anything about a YouTube video. I think you must have the wrong Leah."

There was a slight pause on the other end, and I could hear the movement of papers. “Aren’t you Leah Brown? Senior at Cranston High School? Parents were Marisa and Joshua Brown?”

At the mention of my mom and dad my body stiffened. How the hell did this Angela…whatever…Channel something-or-other know anything about me?

“Yes…” I answered warily.

“Wonderful—then you’re my gal! Haven’t you seen the video? It went viral maybe twenty-four hours ago or something. You have…” Her voice pulled away from the phone slightly as though she was reaching to read a paper just out of view. “…close to a million views on YouTube already!” This obviously delighted Angela because her voice reached yet another octave. “You’re an internet sensation!”

“I’m sorry,” I repeated, knitting my brow trying to understand. “What is this video I’m supposedly in?”

“The baby bird, Leah! You bringing the baby bird back to life! It’s incredible what you did! How did you do it? Clearly the bird is dead…then you go in and do something with your hands and *poof*!”

She nearly shouted, and I startled, jerking my head away from the receiver. I held the phone slightly away from my ear and stared hard at it. There’s a video of me saving the bird? How can that be? I started taking shallow, quick breaths as panic threaded its way through my chest. Did she say a million people had seen this video? Oh my God.

Angela’s voice was distant and tinny as I held the receiver away from my ear. “Leah? Are you still there, Leah?” Suddenly I realized I needed to see the video. I barked into the phone, not wanting to bring it closer to me. “I’m sorry but I have to go now!” and hung up. Racing upstairs to my laptop, I could hear the ring of her calling back. Ignoring it, I went directly to YouTube and typed in “baby bird.” Oh my God, I was the second video launched. The title read, “Girl brings baby bird back to life.” I clicked the link as my heart raced. The view was from above, as if from in the tree, and focused directly down on the baby bird. I stared in horror as I witnessed myself enter the scene. Just like the reporter had said, the video showed me doing the movements with my hands. There was no audio, but you can see me move my lips, so it's obvious I'm saying something. Most of the video is of the top of my head, so you only see part of my face a handful of times. Only when the bird begins moving and I shout for joy do I lift my head to the sky. And there I am in full view of the video. Not a particularly clear image, but I certainly recognized myself. How could I have known I was being recorded? Why *was* I recorded? I frantically looked at the authors of the video—Javier P. was the name listed. Did I know anyone by that name? The picture was small but showed a young boy, maybe ten years old, smiling and holding a fishing line with a fish attached. The posting date showed two days prior: Monday. Below the name was a short description.

It read: "My friend and I found this baby bird near the library. We totally thought it was dead but wanted to try to help it in case it wasn't. I put my phone in the tree with the video on to keep watch if the mom or dad bird came to help, then ran home to get my parents. When we got back to the tree the bird was gone! So, I looked at the video and was TOTALLY AMAZED to see this girl bringing the bird back to life!!!!! Anyone know who this is? How did she do this?????"

Scrolling down through the various comments of "so cool!" and "totally fake video!", I saw one that read. "Hey! This girl goes to my school—she's a senior, I think. People used to call her a witch—maybe they were right!" The thread of comments below stretched on and on. About the 50th comment down, posted late this morning, I was named. Someone responded simply: 'This is our neighborhood witch, Leah Brown."

The commenter's picture was of a dog, not an identifiable human, and there was no other distinguishing way for me to figure out who it was. Posts continued after that, but I couldn't read any longer. I had started hyperventilating and had to sit with my head in my hands curled into my thighs. Close to a million people had seen this. And now they knew it was me. I'd never be able to go outside again.

Wait a minute, I thought. *I didn't do anything wrong or shameful or dangerous. All the video shows is me helping a bird. I did something good. I have a power, and I used it for good.* The only thing scary about this was that people other than my family and two close friends now knew about it.

The doorbell rang. I whipped my head toward the sound but didn't move a muscle. I held my breath, steeling myself. When it rang a second time, I walked over to the bedroom window and discreetly peered around the curtain down to the front door. Isaac and Alex stood there waiting. I exhaled in relief and ran downstairs to let them in.

After pushing past me quickly into the house, Alex pounced on me with an enormous hug. "Leah! We ran here as fast as we could. Are you okay? Do you have any idea what's going on?" she said breathlessly.

Isaac picked up where she left off. "Do you know about the video? Did you see it?"

"Only just now! This tv reporter, Angela something, called me to ask if I could be on the segment live when she aired the video tonight. I'm trying to avoid her, but she keeps calling!" As if I'd conjured it, the phone began ringing. "That's probably her again." I groaned, ignoring the phone. "How did you guys find out about it?"

"You know that asshole Marcus?" Isaac said. "We were leaving school and he nearly ran us down he came at us so fast. He was his charming self, asking if we'd seen you and mouthing off about this video. When he left, I pulled it up on my phone. Then we ran straight over here." He paused. "Do you mean Angela Rossman of Channel 5? She actually called you?" He raised his eyebrows. Isaac's family was more traditional than mine in every sense of the word…of course he knows who Angela Rossman is. "What did you tell her? Are you going to do it?" he asked.

"She totally blindsided me!" I responded. "I didn't know the video existed until she called. I'm sure I sounded like a complete idiot on the phone." My stomach twisted at the memory. "I didn't actually answer her…which I'm assuming is why she keeps calling. I panicked, told her I had to go, and literally hung up on her. I just had to go see the video for myself. You guys showed up right after I watched it." The ringing stopped and I turned my head to look at the phone in relief. "I suppose now I need to figure out what to do." It came out like a whine and I squeezed my eyes tightly and grabbed at my hair.

"Where's Mary Ann?" Alex chimed in. "She'll know how to handle this, because I have absolutely no clue what you should do."

Before I had a chance to answer, we heard the sounds of Mary Ann coming in through the back door.

"Well hello, crew!" Mary Ann sang as she saw us all gathered in the kitchen. Then looking at us closer, she piled her bags on the kitchen counter. "This looks serious," she said, coming over to join us. I brought her up to speed and then Isaac pulled the video up on his phone again so she could watch it. "And you say this reporter called you here at the house?"

"Yes—she keeps calling. She wants me to go on the news with her to 'explain' how I did it, I guess," I replied. "How the hell could I possibly do that without sounding like a crazy person?"

This was the first time I'd been able to make the ribbons appear at will. Just by asking. I wasn't sure if I could do it every single time, but even if it happened some of the time, think about the people I could help. We were all standing around in silent contemplation, when the phone's shrill ring broke our trance. Isaac and Alex looked first at me, then we all turned and looked at Mary Ann.

"What do you think I should do, Mary Ann?" I knew I was putting her on the spot, because she was in uncharted waters like me, but I needed advice desperately.

"Certainly not go on the nightly news! Every wacko for fifty miles around would be at our door!" Mary Ann exclaimed and tugged at her lower lip. "I'm so glad you're learning to use your gifts, Leah, truly…I just don't feel it's time to let the outside world in yet. You don't need this process muddied by people asking questions you don't yet know how to answer. Or by making yourself vulnerable to people like that doctor, who would want to 'study' your gift."

After a long pause, she threw her arms up in the air in a triumphant gesture. "I've got it! Summer break is in a little over a week—you really only have finals left, right?" she asked, turning to each of us for confirmation. "And then graduation the following Sunday…Leah, sweet girl, it's time for a road trip. Let's get outta Dodge for a couple weeks and let this video blow over. The Monday after graduation we'll go to Arizona—Sedona! I've always heard it was a beautiful, mystical place filled with artists and nature!" she exclaimed. "Just what we need to figure this all out. What do you say? It can be your graduation present!"

It sounded perfect to me and such a relief to have a plan, even a short-term one. "That sounds so amazing," I said.

"We can rent a house for a little while, do some hiking and figuring out," she said with a touch of finality in her voice, signaling the decision had been made. Turning to Isaac and Alex, she said, "Well—what about you two? Care to tag along on our little adventure?"

Their eyes lit up. Alex said, "You mean it? We can join you? For the whole time?"

"I think it would be wonderful, don't you?" she asked me. I nodded vigorously. "Do you think you'll be allowed to?" she said to Alex and Isaac.

"Only one way to find out!" Isaac said. Then they both retreated to different corners of the kitchen to call their parents. Our house phone started ringing again. This time Mary Ann strode over and picked up the receiver.

"Hello, Ms. Rossman? This is Leah's aunt and guardian, how are you? Good. I'm afraid Leah is unavailable to join your show this evening. That's right. No, I understand perfectly what it could mean for her. Also, the video may be out of our hands, but I kindly request you avoid naming her during the segment." She looked over at me and rolled her eyes playfully. "Ms. Rossman, I understand it would help your job tremendously, but it will not help my niece— Of course, you are within the law to name her, she is technically no longer a minor, but you'd be putting her at risk for all sorts of attention that she is not prepared for at this age— You have children as well, if I'm not mistaken? I would ask that you think of what this kind of exposure would do to their lives. Thank you… Yes, I appreciate your consideration. Have a wonderful evening." With that, she hung up the phone and sighed. "I'm not sure what she'll decide to do, but hopefully I gave her at least a little pause."

Isaac and Alex joined us. They both stated talking at once in excited bursts. "My parents said yes, so long as it's after my graduation party!" said Isaac. "Can we wait an extra few days to leave?"

"I can do it, too!" Alex continued, "I already promised my uncle Danny I'd work in his gym this summer helping out with the kids' summer camps. But it doesn't have to start right away, so I get to come with you first!"

"So, then what about exams next week? If Leah goes to school, it will be madness around her," Isaac said.

Mary Ann knitted her brow. "You might be right, Isaac. Let me call the principal and see if we can't work something out, given the circumstances." She retreated back over to the now-silent phone. While Mary Ann was talking, Alex and Isaac and I ran upstairs to my laptop to look at pictures of Sedona. None of us had ever been to Arizona, and the desert landscape seemed exotic. The majority of the images we found were of red rocks in crazy formations. They reminded me of a trip to the 31st Street beach in Chicago one summer when I was little. My parents had brought a few buckets to make sandcastles, and if the sand was not quite wet enough when you packed it in, it would retain some of the bucket shape when overturned, but the rest of the sand would ripple out at the bottom. One picture we found of Sedona at night showed a billion stars in an inky black backdrop. Living near a big city, we could usually only make out a few stars here and there due to all the light pollution. I couldn't wait to see billions.

Mary Ann called to us and we headed back to the kitchen. "We've worked it out that you only have to show up for your exams, and I can drop you at the classroom and pick you up again—act as a kind of buffer for unwanted attention. You know how scary I can be, no one will mess with you while I'm there," she said with a twinkle in her eye. "You don't have to go to the end-of-year assembly or homeroom on either day. Your principal was more than gracious and didn't hesitate to provide us with some options." Then she muttered more to herself as she turned to finally empty her abandoned shopping bags, "Bloody well should be helpful with the amount we're paying in tuition."

She looked up from her bags at us. "Well then! Looks like you three have some studying and some packing to do. When exams and graduation are done, we're hitting the road!"

When Mary Ann called me down for dinner a while later, I asked if she was ready for me to try to use my gift with her. Her doctors thought she was doing very well, and she had finished radiation treatments a week ago. In fact, she was now considered in remission and would just be monitored routinely for the next year. She raised her eyes and looked up at me.

"The doctors say it's gone, sweet girl. But I'll tell you what, you can be my 'second opinion.'" She smiled. "I think practice is a good idea. But like I said, if you can't see anything, it's probably because there's nothing left to see, and not because you can't."

We finished dinner and moved into the living room. I sat across from Mary Ann, placed my hands on her shoulders, closed my eyes, and whispered the dedication. Nothing happened. No vibration in my head, no electric blue lines, and no white ribbons of light or warmth. Nada. I tried again with the same result. Opening my eyes, I met Mary Ann's, and shrugged my shoulders. I couldn't hide my disappointment, but at the same time I was reminded that maybe it wasn't working because there was nothing of consequence there anymore.

Mary Ann beamed at me. "Thank you, Leah!" she exclaimed. "Now I truly *do* believe I'm in remission." I laughed and decided that was the best possible result after all.

Eudaimonia:
(Greek) A state of flourishing, prospering or living well. Being happy and healthy.

CHAPTER 8

It took us three leisurely days of driving to get down to Sedona, through Illinois, Missouri, Oklahoma, and a bit of Texas and New Mexico. My aunt's car looked like a trash bag by the end of it, strewn with snack bags and drink containers. The mood was joyful the whole time, if slightly more subdued by exhaustion on the third day. We chose to make the drive part of the trip and see what we could see along the way. In Oklahoma, we stopped at the "Blue Whale of Catoosa," a funny whale sculpture built half in the water and half out. You can walk through its mouth to a dock made from its tail. We took a photo in the mouth and splashed around for about an hour until the mosquitos made us retreat back to the car. In Amarillo, Texas, we found the Cadillac Ranch. It's a crazy place where wildly painted cars are sticking halfway out of the sand in a line, like they'd taken a nosedive and become permanently stuck. It looked like visitors were encouraged to add to the cars' designs. I guess they could have just been vandals, but we grabbed a Sharpie from the car and documented our visit anyway.

In New Mexico, we stocked up at a grocery store and had a picnic lunch at the base of an insane tower of rock called El Morro National Monument. It was a little out of our way, but the day was beautiful, and the hours of hiking were good for our car-weary bodies. Standing at the base and looking up, it seemed as though the rock was reaching its hand to meet the sky. The landscape was already so different than anything I'd experienced before. White, ochre, and tan sandstone beneath our feet made wavy patterns almost like the undulation of the sea. It was dotted with spots of green—little scrawny trees and bushes that somehow, through sheer force of will, pushed their way up toward the sun. There was so much more to this world than I could even hope to glimpse. A yearning took seed in my heart that afternoon. I wanted to see everything. To learn everything. Mary Ann correctly labeled it "wanderlust," and the word would now enter the conversation of who I was and how I defined myself.

When we finally rolled into Sedona on the third evening, the sun had just gone down. The main street glowed with soft yellow lights from restaurants and bars. People walked in pairs or groups, laughing and chatting, relaxing into each other's company for the evening. Aside from our immediate area, an immense darkness extended out in every direction, as though the little town was all that existed in the universe. Though it was exciting, all of our energy was dwindling from three days in the car. Mary Ann suggested we could explore the town tomorrow, and that we should get set up in our house rental before we all collapsed.

We'd called ahead to let the property manager know that we'd be arriving in the evening, and the house was lit up and inviting when we pulled into the driveway. It was cozy and, though in a neighborhood with many other houses, had enough space to still feel somewhat private. It was a ranch-style home with off-white stucco and red ochre tiled floors that were cool on my feet. We threw our suitcases in our respective rooms — me and Alex sharing a room with two twin beds and Isaac and Mary Ann with their own rooms — and met at the back patio where we found a little table with four chairs. Perfect. The day had been hot, a different kind of heat than sticky Midwest summer days, but the night air felt cool and fresh. I breathed in deeply and looked up. The sky was alive with lights. Most soft white, some pink-rimmed, some tinged blue or yellow, and there were billions of them as far as the eye could see. Without the lights of the town, the stars seemed unending. Even the Milky Way was visible across the expanse. There were depths to them as well—layers upon layers that challenged my eyes to focus.

We sat in astonished silence by the magnificence of it. Finally, Mary Ann announced she needed sleep. Giving us all a hug and a kiss good night, she headed to her room. Isaac, Alex and I stayed rooted to our chairs.

Isaac whispered, "The pictures we saw don't begin to measure up to the real thing. I wouldn't even know how to put this into words."

"It's like the world has just opened up," Alex agreed.

I felt the same way. And like the world around me, I felt the world inside me open up just the same. It was incredibly peaceful and bigger than words all at once.

We woke the next morning to brilliant sunshine. Daylight revealed that our little home for the next couple weeks was surrounded by the large red rocks we'd seen in advertisements of Sedona. Only, much like the night sky, the images only captured a fragment of their majesty. Being able to see it in person was a profoundly different experience.

Our rental house was too far to walk to the downtown area, so we hopped back in the car, which did not smell very nice, drove to town, and went in search of breakfast. We had read online that June would be hot, but that maybe it wouldn't seem too bad for us because as a desert heat it was dryer and not humid. By 9:30 a.m., the temperature had already reached 84 degrees, so it seemed the day promised to test that theory. We walked till we came upon a little restaurant called Annie's, painted in shades of pink and green. It was mildly busy on this Saturday morning, but we were seated after only a few minutes' wait. Mary Ann swooned when the waiter brought her a mug of steaming hot coffee, and we all ordered items with names like "Southwest Breakfast Panini" and "Cowboy Hash."

Halfway through my huevos rancheros, I had the feeling I was being watched. Turning around, my eyes locked on those of a woman seated alone a few tables over. She was older, with lined skin the same red shade as the rocks all around Sedona. Her gray hair was piled high on her head messily, with strands escaping here and there. A pair of turquoise glasses on a beaded string hung around her neck. She smiled at me in a familiar way, and I was unsure what to do in response. *Maybe because Sedona is such a small town, people are friendlier in a way I'm not used to?* I gave her a small smile in return and swiveled back to face my friends. The sensation of being watched stayed with me throughout breakfast, but I didn't dare turn around.

"You kids up for a hike this morning?" Mary Ann asked. "There are so many to choose from, but I'm thinking we start with something somewhat small and unquestionably doable—even for me!" Mary Ann laughed at her own expense, though we all knew she was still in wonderful shape from her regular yoga practice. We were definitely on board. Mary Ann paid the bill and we got up to go. Leaving the café, I allowed myself the slightest sideways glance back. The woman still had her eyes fixed on me. It was kind of creepy, but I decided to let it go.

Mary Ann found us a two-and-a-half-mile hike called the Coffee Pot Trail to Coffee Pot Rock. She was absolutely tickled with this option, declaring her body still needed to "wake up" after our journey. Off we went. The trailhead began in town, and the trail itself was well marked. Warm, red dust coated my sneakers as we walked, and my dark hair was hot from absorbing the sunlight above. The first layer of hair along my neck was slick with sweat after only a few minutes, and I wished I had thought to bring a hair tie. The sun was so bright we were all squinting, even with our sunglasses.

"Okay crew, before our next hike we are definitely buying hats!" Mary Ann exclaimed.

Coffee Pot Rock was the end rock of a group of massive rocks in the classic red sandstone. We all agreed it *somewhat* resembled an actual coffee pot, and Mary Ann posed for a picture with her mouth open underneath the spout as if she were drinking. We didn't linger too long at the base, though, because naively we hadn't drawn the conclusion that a hike in the middle of the hot day might be a little intense for our first outing. So, after a few more perfunctory pictures to document our first hike, we headed back to the car. Though the ride back to the house from town was only about ten minutes, every one of us felt completely drained by the time we arrived. A nap was in order, and we stumbled to our rooms.

The house was quiet when I woke up, and I turned over to check on Alex. She was lying with her back to me, her chest gently rising and falling under a thin cotton blanket. I quietly slid out of my own little twin bed and tiptoed out the door. Through the glass patio doors, I spied Isaac sitting and reading. Feeling desperately thirsty, I stopped at the kitchen. A note on the kitchen counter read, "Headed out for groceries—back soon! XOXO – Mary Ann."

Sliding the glass doors to the patio aside, I smiled hi to Isaac. My heart swelled for him as I sat down. My best friend for most of my life, my only friend for parts of it; in fact, Isaac knew me better than anyone. There was incredible comfort in someone like him existing in the world, and I had vowed never to take it for granted.

"Whatcha reading?" I asked, settling into the metal patio chair, delighted to discover it rocked. The book jacket had an image of skyscrapers below a clouded sky.

"Just a mystery I brought from home. Tried to start it on the way here but just couldn't do it." He gave me a slight grimace, alluding to the carsickness that plagued him whenever he tried to read in the car

He closed the book and relaxed back in his chair. "I feel like a different person here," he said, letting his gaze go to the horizon. "You know? I mean, we've been here less than twenty-four hours, but I *feel* so different already. Calmer, maybe. I would say powerful, but I don't mean, like, Power, you know?" He looked at me. "Like the power of being in control of yourself. Does that make any sense?" It made perfect sense to me, and I told him. I'd been trying to place it, too. It was like finding the inner peace people were always talking about. Even if it was fleeting, it was an astonishing feeling. "I think there's a different energy here, too," he continued. "Almost like a low current of electricity. It feels like anticipation for something, but I don't know what. Makes me believe this trip will be eventful." He raised his eyebrows at me.

"Me too." I replied. "Actually," I continued, pausing to collect a thought, "it's like leaving home has freed me to feel more like the me I want to be, you know? I mean, at home, I have all this history that follows me around. Either the history of being the kid whose parents died, or the kid who got her fourth grade gym teacher fired…or the kid who might be a witch," I said, making air quotes. The sense of what was different here was taking shape in my head. "And leaving, having this adventure, feels like it frees me from all that. I can decide who I feel like being today, not how the world feels like seeing me. I know it won't last, but I don't care, it feels so good now."

The sliding door opened and Mary Ann stuck her face through. "Hello, sleepy heads! Anyone hungry?" At the mention of food, I was suddenly ravenous. We headed inside for sandwiches, a bleary-eyed Alex emerging just in time to join us.

It was decided we'd spend the evening looking around the little downtown, buying hats and finding a fun place for dinner. Everyone was still a little out of it from the journey, the naps, and the heat. The mood was light and happy as we walked in and out of shops. Being a Saturday, there were lots of people all around, many we recognized as tourists like ourselves. Once evening hit, the air cooled to comfortable, and we found a restaurant with outdoor seating. I didn't have a care in the world.

The next morning, we headed out early to catch a trolley that would take us to a church built into the red rocks themselves: The Chapel of the Holy Cross. Donning our new hats, we boarded an already packed green and yellow trolley. The morning was warm, and a not-so-pleasant odor, like sweat and sunscreen, joined us for the ride. The tourists that morning included an older Russian couple who seemed to be in the middle of an argument, the wife gesticulating wildly with her hands and seeming to scoff at everything her husband said. Many others seemed to be friends or relatives traveling together from nearby Texas. This was apparent after a burly man dressed in a loud Hawaiian shirt that didn't conceal his beer gut complained, "If this was in Texas, you *know* they'd find a bigger dang trolley!" The four of us just sat and looked out the window.

We eventually disembarked at the strangest building I have ever seen. It was tall and rectangular and seemed to ascend toward the sky directly out of the rocks. With massive, two-hundred-fifty-foot-tall solid side walls, the front and back of the chapel were top to bottom windows. As we walked in the back door, the light streaked through brilliantly and the view made me catch my breath. Basic wooden pews lined toward the pulpit directly in front of the window, separated by about a dozen rows of red votive candles.

As we shuffled slowly along with the rest of the trolley throng, a low vibration took root in the base of my skull. Not unlike I'd felt many times before, but I didn't know why it was starting now. Mary Ann came up and put her arm around me.

"Your mom and dad would absolutely love this, wouldn't they?" She gave me a slight squeeze. She was right. They could spend hours wandering through incense-scented cathedrals, pausing to take in each stained glass. It wasn't religion that instilled a sense of awe in my parents. It was the regular humans who had the vision and the ingenuity to create such incredible structures, often knowing they would not be alive to see their dream finished.

The vibration had expanded from my skull up to the top of my head and behind my eyes, to the back of my calves and soles of my feet. It was stronger than I'd felt in a while. Though there were many people in the church, the din was low and respectful. Except every few minutes one or two of the Texans would bellow some inane comment about this tapestry or that crucifix—often receiving admonishing glances from other visitors, which they either missed or decided to ignore. Alex shot me a look and mouthed, "Loud Americans," while shaking her head. We moved to the front of the chapel and paused to take in the incredible view through the tower of windows. The crucifix behind the altar was unlike any I'd seen before. Jesus' body was set not on bare wooden beams, but rather in the boughs of a beautiful, winding tree. His body was sculpted strong, and his face was not in despair or agony, but peaceful. He seemed to be looking right at me. It was a face that spoke to the strength and love inside me, and I didn't want to look away.

I felt the boorish movement of people behind me, and a voice much louder than necessary exclaimed, "Well, this ain't the way Jesus is supposed to look! This guy is nailed to a freakin' tree, his God has just forsaken him, and he looks as simple and calm as if he's here for afternoon tea." His voice was grating and angered me immediately. I willed him to go away, but he just kept talking, "Jesus was *suffering* for us, and *dying*!" His voice gained volume and emotion and other tourists were turned toward the commotion. My ears burned as I felt like their eyes were on me, too. "And look at his dang muscles! Looks like he's just come from a workout or something. That ain't *my* Jesus!" He threw his hands on his ample hips and shook his head. I was disgusted. The sculpture was beautiful and tragic and felt electric with love, and whoever made it was a genius.

This man was just the kind I couldn't stand. They spent their lives tearing down the beauty in the world because they were too cowardly or stupid to create any themselves. I felt Alex's hand on my arm, gently pulling.

"C'mon let's move away from them," she whispered. As we pushed through people making our way back to the exit, I noticed that the vibration so strong a moment ago, had left me. Out in the sunshine and stifling heat, I let my anger flare. Not only did that jerk ruin my experience of the chapel, but he'd chased away whatever magic was happening in my body, too.

"God, I can't stand people like that!" I shouted as we moved off to the side of the parking lot. "They don't care about anyone or anything except their own pompous selves! The more ignorant they are, the louder they yell!" I yelled, ignoring the irony in my own statement. The others looked at me curiously.

"Leah," Isaac said, "they were really annoying, but why are you letting them get to you like this? Just forget them—be happy you aren't like them." But I couldn't seem to let it go. The vibrations always meant something special was happening, and they ruined it for me. I felt like I'd missed something important. "But they ruined it! It was the most beautiful crucifix I'd ever seen, and his big, stupid mouth just wouldn't shut up!"

In a calm voice I understood was meant to try to settle me, Mary Ann said, "I agree he was the worst…but, Leah, you seem so upset. Is there something else going on?" she asked.

I threw up my hands and exclaimed, "Yes!" I was pacing now, barely noticing the heat from the pavement licking at my toes. "I had the vibrations, Mary Ann! They were strong and felt linked to the chapel. You know they always mean something important is happening. And I was close to understanding, I think. Or something was close to happening…I don't know. Then that ass started running off his mouth, and they disappeared! I lost them! Now I feel nothing at all, it was wasted!" I kicked a small rock and pale red dust swirled around the air by my foot. "What if I missed something? What if they don't come back again?" I could hear the whine in my voice, but I couldn't help it. I felt loss.

"Ah. Now I understand," Mary Ann began. "You are right to be upset. But if it can happen once, it can happen again. I don't think you've missed anything. Maybe for the moment, but not forever." She came over and put her hand on my shoulder. "Don't let this man wreck the whole experience for you. The fact that the vibrations came means that change is afoot! You'll understand them soon enough."

That night we made a feast together of spaghetti and meatballs, roasted asparagus salad, and garlic bread. Afterwards, sitting around the patio table, we laughed till our sides hurt listening to Mary Ann's tales of her own young adulthood. Apparently, she spent an entire summer as a traveling mime in upstate New York, sleeping in tents with her friends and "performing" at music festivals. We cajoled her into giving us a demonstration, and I don't think I ever laughed so hard in my life. In college, after a few drinks and a dare, she let her friend shave off all her hair, forgetting she was to be a bridesmaid for her cousin's wedding one month later. Her parents were completely mortified and found her a wig like a southern debutante, big and full. It was heavy and horribly itchy, but she wore it like a good daughter. She drew a picture of it for us so we could fully appreciate its awesomeness. Halfway through the ceremony, she sneezed so hard that the wig fell down to her nose. All she could do was slide it back into place and hope everyone was too busy looking at the bride and groom to notice, but it was all anyone wanted to talk about at the reception. Her cousin, the bride, thought it was hilarious and ripped it from her head on the dance floor. Mary Ann was thrilled to be rid of it and, though it then passed from person to person throughout the reception, the wig didn't touch her head again.

Finally, the darkness was full, and the stars came back into view. What could primitive humans have thought about them? No wonder the "heavens" were part of so many religions—it was impossible to see something like that night sky and not believe it was pure magic. As if on cue, a streak of white shot quickly among the clusters. I bolted upright in my chair. "Did you guys see that? It was a real shooting star!" I exclaimed. Isaac had, but Alex and Mary Ann were looking in different directions.

"Shoot! I totally missed it!" cried Alex. "I've never seen a shooting star before! Quick! You guys make wishes!" she demanded. I immediately closed my eyes and wished to find a way to use my newfound powers to help people.

Even though it was only technically our third full day in Sedona, Monday was scheduled to be the coolest day, so we figured we should take advantage of it and head north to visit the Grand Canyon. Like everything else we'd seen so far on our journey, it was almost beyond description. We did a little hiking down into the canyon on our own, paying close attention to every step as the path was not what anyone would call roomy. At one point, two runners passed us heading back up the trail, and I couldn't believe they could go that fast on such a difficult, dangerous pass.

"Some people are just nuts," Mary Ann exclaimed.

"Actually, I would love to do something like that!" Alex responded. Alex was never one for sitting still very long. She was constantly moving her body and trying new physical activities. She still trained at her uncle's gym and was often running or biking or anything that interested her.

Isaac drew her in and kissed her forehead. They didn't usually show affection publicly, and I was happy to see them more relaxed as a couple.

When we got back, no one felt like cooking, so we headed to a restaurant nestled in the hills that got great reviews. It had a huge covered patio and panoramic views to take your breath away, almost like being one with the environment. The sun was beginning to set as we settled into our table. Our meals were fabulous, and we were all peaceful and sleepy from our excursion and hike. Just as we ordered dessert and Mary Ann got a chamomile tea, I had that same sensation of being watched as I'd had two days prior at breakfast. It hit me so suddenly that I whipped my head around to look for the old woman. There she was, sitting at a table closer to the main restaurant. She gave me a little wave and smile, then tilted her head to her companion to say something. Her companion, an older, white-haired man, also turned to smile at me.

Isaac noticed my sudden agitation and checked in. "Hey, Leah. What's going on? You okay?"

"That woman over there. I've seen her before. At breakfast on Saturday, I had the strong sensation someone was watching me, and every time I turned around this woman was staring me down," I said. "I just felt the sensation again, and turned to find her there, smiling and waving like we were long lost friends." Everyone at the table turned to look.

"That's weird. They seem totally normal," Alex added. "You don't think they could be recognizing you from the bird video, do you?"

That hadn't even occurred to me, but now I was nervous. "Oh man, you don't think that could be it, do you?" I directed my worry towards Mary Ann. She stood up with her hands on her hips.

"Mysteries only usually stay mysterious because we're too afraid to investigate. I'm going to invite them to join us." She walked over.

Before I knew it, the old couple were scraping extra chairs along the decking to squeeze in around our table. Alex was right. They looked like nice, normal people. So what was her deal? Once at the table, they introduced themselves.

"I'm Frida and this is Carlos. We live here in Sedona." Mary Ann introduced us, and then Frida turned to me. "I'm sorry if my attentions made you uncertain. I just noticed your aura immediately at Annie's on Saturday morning and wanted to acknowledge you." She said this simply as though she had said she'd noticed my brown hair or sandals and wanted to compliment me on them.

"I have an aura?" I asked her.

"What's an aura?" Isaac added.

Frida turned to him first to answer. "Auras are like light around a living thing. It's essence or energy. We all have them, but we can't all see them. I was lucky to learn how to tune in to that ability. They show different colors depending on the energy of the person or animal. And your friend here has an incredibly strong one." She smiled at me again. "She has the rose-colored aura of a healer—like me!" This seemed to bring her delight, and her face erupted in a wide smile that went all the way into her eyes.

Suddenly recognition came to me. "Rose-colored! Yes!" I almost yelled. Then turning to Mary Ann and Isaac, "Like that time in middle school with Eric, remember? I saw it then! And then in my visions, Isis had the rose mist around her hands!" I couldn't believe I was face to face with someone who not only understood what I was talking about, but who claimed to have the same ability. I stared agape at Frida. "You know what it means? You can see it now?" I asked her. She chuckled at my earnestness.

"Yes, my dear. Even now. You are practically effulgent in pink. Of course, I have to be in tune to see it, and I can choose not to see auras when I want, too. Sometimes they can be distracting, but I definitely see yours now." She nodded at me. Isaac, Alex and Mary Ann squinted at me intensely.

"Can any of you see it, too?" I asked them, but they all shook their heads. "Why can't I see it? I did once before, a few years ago, but I don't know how and I couldn't make it happen again."

"Not everyone has the ability, I'm afraid. But you obviously do. It just takes learning how to tune in and concentrate. And lots of practice, of course, to be able to do it at will. But you can learn easy-peasy, my dear."

Mary Ann chimed in. "And you say the rose color of Leah's aura means she's a healer?"

"Yes," Frida replied. "A fairly powerful one based on the strength of her aura. Much more powerful than me, even." Then she paused as a thought occurred to her. "Do you not know this about yourself yet? Oh dear—that would be dreadful if you haven't even started knowing your powers!" Her face looked stricken, as though she'd just realized I was eighteen years old and never learned to tie my shoes.

I looked to Mary Ann for encouragement. She gave me a little nod and I answered. "I've had different things happen since I was little, but it's gotten more intense over the last few years."

Frida nodded her head at that. "Yes—usually when a person reaches puberty the abilities start to reveal themselves. It's the hormone shift, I think, though no one really knows why that should make a difference."

"That's when I had the first dream! The dream about the goddess, Isis. Remember, Mary Ann?" Suddenly, I realized we were talking about the first time I bled with my period, and my cheeks burned with embarrassment. Alex, who knew this story, raised her eyebrows. Frida was looking at me with surprise.

"Dreaming that you are the goddess Isis shows just how powerful a healer you must be! I'll even bet you're a direct descendant, Leah!"

"Wait," Alex chimed in. "You're saying that Leah is a descendant of the goddess Isis? The Egyptian mythical goddess?" The doubt this new revelation brought clearly displayed in her tone of voice. "How can that be possible? Isis wasn't real. Gods and goddesses are just myths, stories people believe to help them make sense of the things in the world that make no sense."

It was Carlos' turn to speak. "You are so right, Alex. Myths, and whole religions for that matter, are often the product of reasonable people trying to make sense of unreasonable occurrences. We don't know how or why the sky rumbles during thunder, so we believe there is a powerful being up there making it happen. Most of us can only wrap our heads around ideas that are in line with our experience in the world. So many of our gods and goddesses look like humans or animals, talk like humans, so we can relate to them. But they are assigned powers as a way to explain away the terrifying unknown."

"Yes," Frida added. "Imagine you met a woman. And she made your pain go away just by touching you. She was flesh and blood but could do something that no one else seemed to be able to do. She was special in an inexplicable way. This is always scary, so people create a story. If she is no longer a human like everyone else, but a goddess on high, then it's not so difficult to accept that she has gifts you don't." Frida let this sink in and took a drink from her wine glass. My mind was reeling.

"So you're saying that Isis was a real person? A person born with the gift of healing? But I saw her on a throne…with a crown of horns and a disc." I furrowed my brow in concentration.

Frida answered, "Isis was a queen, alright. She ruled with her husband Osiris, and she had gifts of healing to be sure." Then she added as she relaxed back in her chair, "We believe Isis was real flesh and blood, but with special abilities. And her descendants received varying degrees of that power down the line. Me? I have a moderate amount. I have intuitive healing and can read and sometimes manipulate the energy fields of a person. Oh, and I can see strong auras. But that's about it. I'll take it, though. There is nothing quite like connecting with a person and helping them heal." She sighed contentedly.

I really didn't know what to say. This sounded so silly to me. I was a descendant of a goddess from Egypt? How could I possibly buy into that? At the same time, this woman seemed to know about my gifts and have at least the outline of an explanation for how I have them, however implausible. A thought occurred to me. "Wait. If you and I are descendants of Isis, there must be thousands and thousands of us. There must be so many people with these powers throughout the world!" I said.

Frida smiled and nodded. "Yes, we think there are many descendants, all with varying degrees of power. Not only healing, though. Osiris had different gifts than Isis. He could communicate with spirits and travel between the realms of the living and the dead. Some believe he also had the gift of foresight, or precognition. Their abilities melded with their first descendant, their son Horus, and then way on down the line to you and me.

"I have met quite a few other descendants in my life," she continued. "Many with a moderate amount of ability end up in healing professions—whether medical or mystical. I, myself, am a reiki practitioner, because it is in tune with my abilities…and my affinities." Her smile turned sad as she continued. "Unfortunately, many of us never understand why we have different gifts and are treated poorly when we try to show them. So, we bury them deep, believing there must be something wrong with us, instead of something wonderful. This usually ends in a difficult life. Drugs, alcohol…when a person ignores or denies who they truly are there is pain, physical or emotional, and many choose to numb that pain." Turning to Carlos, she added, "It's Carlos' theory that our prisons are probably filled with healers. Isn't that a terrible thought?" Carlos nodded.

Mary Ann turned to me. "This part makes a certain amount of sense, doesn't it? I mean, think about how often you hated your gifts for the negative attention they brought. And you had a loving, supportive environment."

She was right. Up until recently, my abilities had mostly made me hide away or feel like an outcast, friendless and lonely.

Frida continued. "There's a theory that there was a small group of early Egyptians, direct descendants, who migrated further West into Africa. For a long time, they lived in peace and seclusion, until word of their abilities spread beyond their borders. Outsiders began visiting to seek help, which they were happy to oblige. Can you imagine how a tribe of peaceful healers might draw the attention of other tribes hoping to extend their might? These Egyptians became the prize between warring tribes, and they were attacked repeatedly. Many died in the attacks, and those rumored to be the more powerful healers taken as slaves. There are some who escaped, however, and the lineage continued."

Carlos added, "Of course, most of this tale is pure conjecture, but we figure it's as likely as any other scenario."

Mary Ann was tugging at her bottom lip again, "My grandmother, Luisa, Grammy-Lou, had the visions, so we already assumed Leah inherited them from her. I guess she probably inherited them from someone further up the chain." She turned to face me again. Setting her jaw and sitting up straighter, she said, "Right. Like Carlos said, it's as good an explanation as any, and before it we had absolutely nothing at all. So, I vote we follow along for now with this narrative." She then turned to Frida. "Do you think you can help Leah understand her gifts? Or figure out how to control them? We are here for another week and a half." We all turned hopefully toward Frida.

"Oh my! Of course I'll help! In any way I can. And I'm sure if you spend a little time in the vortexes, the more in tune you'll feel," she said. We looked quizzically at her.

"What are the 'vortexes'?" Isaac asked.

"Vortexes are powerful, swirling energy centers that flow up from the earth or down into the earth from the sky above," Frida explained. "The energy is alive and healing and helps with meditation and inspiration. Actually, Sedona itself is considered a vortex, but there are pockets around the city where the energy activity spikes. I'm so surprised you never heard of them. People come from all over to visit the vortexes. There are other places in the country—and world, for that matter—that have concentrated energy activity centers like this, but Sedona is one of the absolute best. If you align your energy with a vortex, I bet we can get you tuned up." She beamed. "I'm off tomorrow if you'd like to try. Bell Rock is the strongest, so we may as well just start there. I can meet you at the trailhead around 10 a.m. Will that work?"

"Yes!" I practically yelled, then looking to the others, "We can do that, right?" Everyone approved heartily and we exchanged cell numbers. With a plan in place, Frida and Carlos said good night. Once they left, the four of us stared at each other. I started giggling, throwing my hand over my mouth. The others joined in and we all ended up laughing at our luck. Then we headed home to get ready for the morning of enlightenment.

Oneirataxia:
(Greek) Inability to differentiate between dreams and reality.

CHAPTER 9

The early morning sun woke me a little before 6 a.m. My mind was full and spinning. When we'd returned to the house after dinner, I Googled "Vortexes in Sedona." One site I found described them as "Energetic centers of the earth known for healing and spiritual power that correspond with electromagnetic earth energy. They are not electric or magnetic themselves. Vortexes seem to have been mapped all over the world, not just here in Sedona. Though the combination of these energy centers and the natural beauty of Sedona make it a destination for vortex hunters everywhere." Apparently, the energy flow of a vortex was to bring a person to a higher place of spiritual awakening or peace.

I wasn't sure what I was hoping I would feel at the vortex, but my expectations for *something* to happen were already high.

Grabbing my phone from the nightstand, I checked the weather for the day. By the time we met Frida and Carlos at the trailhead, the temperature would already be mid-eighties. I tiptoed out of the bedroom and into the kitchen. It looked like I was the first one up, and I went to sit outside and read to distract myself. Instead, I found myself staring into nothing in particular.

A shuffling sound to my left broke the spell, and I spied a small, brown lizard scuttling along the mulch and patio stones. He moved fast, then stopped abruptly to stare at something for about ten seconds before darting off again. Fast and stop, fast and stop. I stood up and took a closer look around the garden. The outer edges of the patio had about two feet of garden space where dangerous-looking plants with incredibly vibrantly colored blooms were scattered. I leaned in toward a low cactus with paddle shaped arms and bright yellow flowers. Its spikes were about an inch long and the tips of the round arms seemed to be turning purple. It was so pretty and alien to any of the nature I'd grown up around. Grabbing my phone off the table, I leaned closer to the cactus plant to get a picture, then jumped back in surprise as another little lizard darted out and ran over my toes. This place was very cool.

We met Frida by an old-fashioned signpost stuck in the red dirt. Wooden destination signs were bolted to the top half with the names of the trails and little arrows etched in pointing the way. It was like the ones you see in movies, where a car pulls up to a four-way stop in the middle of nowhere. Usually one direction leading to a decision of the heart and the other of the mind. Clearly, I'd seen too many Lifetime movies.

Frida had a floppy straw hat and massive black, round sunglasses, and waved to us theatrically from aside the sign.

"Good morning, everyone!" she greeted us. "Ready for an adventure?" She explained how Bell Rock Trail wasn't very difficult, but a lot of people—mostly young people—climb up the rock face itself, which can be a bit more challenging. After checking that we all brought hats and water and were wearing sunscreen, Frida led the way.

The path was packed red earth and we were not the only hikers that morning. Frida explained that June was still a busy time in Sedona as kids were just off school, and the temperatures weren't too unbearable yet. My northern blood wasn't used to the heat, and only ten minutes in I could feel a little bead of sweat drip between my breasts and my shirt sticking to my low back. Frida seemed relaxed, cool and comfortable.

"I'm sorry Carlos had to back out on us last minute, but he had an employee call in sick at the art gallery he owns, and had to cover the shift himself. Anyway, he'd love to take us all out to dinner tonight if you don't have other plans. No rush deciding, it's your vacation, after all. You may not be interested in hanging out with a couple old people," she chuckled.

Just then a bell chimed, and I jumped as a group of mountain bikers came up the trail behind us. We moved over to let them pass, and the last of the group raised a hand in thanks as he pedaled away.

"I'd love to try mountain biking!" exclaimed Alex.

"Ah, an adventurer, huh?" asked Frida. "The world is your playground, kids. Never be afraid to live fully and deeply…and that goes for love, too." She winked at Isaac. It would seem that nothing much got past Frida.

Before long, we arrived at the base of Bell Rock. There were several other hikers milling about and dotting the sides of the rock itself. It was a long way up to the top, but something in me was desperate to get there. The vibrations I'd felt in the chapel had begun again in earnest as we approached. Frida noticed a shift, too.

"Oooh! Leah, your aura is showing!" I gave her a shy grin. "Let's climb a little higher. These old bones can handle at least a level or two of elevation," she laughed.

"I was thinking that the top of that rock would make a pretty awesome panorama," Isaac added.

The first section of the climb wasn't too strenuous, and in many sections, the rock was naturally striated, almost like there were steps built into the side. My whole body was on high alert, and my vision seemed more focused than usual. We reached a flat section after climbing for a while, and Frida declared we'd made it to the upper Bell Rock Trail. After that would be the ascent, and it would be more strenuous of a climb. Frida declared that was as high as she planned on climbing.

"Frida? What do we do once we get to the top?" I asked.

"You find a safe place to sit, close your eyes, and ask for the vortex to guide you." She smiled. "After that, I can't tell you. The vortexes affect people in many different ways." She offered suggestions on a way to begin the meditation once we were situated.

I nodded my head, making up my mind. With no more discussion, and a few directions from Frida, Isaac, Alex and I began the ascent. Mary Ann chose to stick with Frida. Most of the climb was as simple as before, and we were moving quickly. When we got to the first switchback section of climbing, our conversation lulled, and our full attention was on the section of rock under our fingers and toes and in our faces. I was trying hard to pay close attention, but a low humming had joined the vibrations in my body, and it was a little distracting. At one point, my left foot slipped on loose pebbles and I let out a yell. Frantically grasping at the straggly plants around me, I was able to quickly stop sliding and regain my footing.

"Holy shit, Leah. I swear you just gave me a heart attack!" Alex cried. "Don't you do that again!" Even though I couldn't have fallen too far at that point, the lack of control was unsettling.

We made it around the tightest section to scramble up to the flat head of a narrow spire. It was oval-shaped and the three of us just had enough room to sit without worrying about sneezing and falling over the edge. We were panting but exhilarated by our accomplishment. The view was spectacular. Towers of red earth rose up around us, some skinny, some wide, in varying shades of reds and burnt orange. On our little perch, I felt small but not insignificant. For me, being up there gave me the sense of connectedness to all things. A peaceful feeling of belonging, but not needing to do anything to prove it. *It's funny how we can create all this noise in our heads about what's most important in life,* I thought. *I have to have excellent grades, I can't risk looking foolish...* We tread the water of thoughts like these our whole lives. But here, getting outside the normal and experiencing a different view of the world, the noise seemed to quiet down. In the new quiet spaces, other thoughts had room to stretch. *This life is a journey and an adventure*, or even the most surprising thought: *I am the luckiest girl in the world.*

The three of us settled down and took deep breaths of the clear air. The sun was strong, but there was a breeze that made it bearable. After a couple minutes, Alex suggested we start our meditation. To be honest, I already felt some strong sensations during the climb, and I had a moment of doubt whether I could keep it together with focused meditation. I moved a few more inches away from the edge and toward my friends, just in case.

I closed my eyes. My whole body was buzzing, but I tried calming my breath. In the distance, I heard a bird call and that helped to ground me. I pictured white light flowing in and out with each breath, filling my fingertips and toes and ears and lungs. After a few minutes of this, I found I could focus on the image without my mind racing through a hundred other thoughts. I exhaled audibly and felt a release through my whole body.

***

The evening light was beginning to fade. I sat and waited. The sand beneath my sheath had been trod recently, and I recognized the small curves of antelope hooves. It was lucky that they have already passed through here. I didn't want any distractions. Leaning my back against the hard bark, I looked up through the canopy of leaves. This tree had seen the mysteries of this world: life, death, and the spaces in between. The leaves were like many fingers reaching out from the branches—extending offerings of nourishment and shelter. How many generations of our people have been saved by this gift of life? I took deep breaths and let my hand gently pass over the bark. My fingers landed on a hard lump of amber gum—a healer's find. I pulled it from the bark to inspect it. Clear and smooth, with hardly any imperfections—I slipped it into the satchel at my waist. All amber gum is sacred to a healer as it absorbs negative energy and diminishes pain, and the find was a positive omen for the meeting I awaited. It helped calm my nerves. In only a handful of minutes, the light of day was replaced with the indigo of night, and a few points of light lost their shyness to come out to greet the moon. The air shifted.

"I feel you there," I said to the night. A dark form emerged from the dark background.

"I can arrive unannounced to rulers and warriors, but I can never sneak up on you," he responded with an amused tone, entering the circle of sand around the acacia tree.

"My son, you have the cunning and stealth of the falcon you are so aptly named for. But your blood is my blood, and we are connected in ways that go deeper than that which can be seen or heard."

Reaching me, he bent down to kiss my forehead. "Mother. How are you?"

"As well as can be expected knowing what I know," I said. "Do you know what I am tasking you with tonight? Were you given the whole message?"

He paused and took a deep breath. "I was. And it has filled me with dread ever since." His voice took a harder edge. "What you ask of me no mother should ask of her son." I could only barely make out the whites of his eyes, but the pain he felt I sensed clearly.

"It will not kill me—that will come at another's hand than yours. It is too important, Horus. If I am taken to Osiris in the underworld before it is done, the living world will suffer." I paused. "I am sorry to ask it of you, but there is no one else I would trust." I sighed. Ever since I knew the threats to my life were imminent, I had fought to find a way to ensure the stone's power is not lost to our people. Horus shares my blood but does not have the same strength of healing that I do, his power is different. It must be this way. With resolve, I continued, "You understand what is to be done? The stone must be removed and coupled with your

blood and mine to create new life. The new life will be stronger and will pass the powers on to its offspring in a way that I was not able to for you. The power of the stone will become the power of the healer. It is in this way our people will be able to help themselves forevermore, and the healer will live on in too many than can be struck down."

The more I spoke the more confidence I felt that this was the only way forward. Horus did not have my healing gifts, but he possessed the powers of resurrection, fertility and vision from Osiris. Our blood mixed with the stone could give us the power to create life, I was sure of it. Horus just needed to cut it out of my body first. He was right, it was a heavy burden I was laying on his shoulders.

It took us until the stars regained their shyness of the sun and sky showed hints of green to finish. Though I felt weak from the exertion of the stone's removal, it had not killed me, as I promised Horus. I was still able to draw forth the healing light before I was too far gone. Horus had screamed along with me as he did what was required, begging me for forgiveness, though it was I that had forced him to this act. Cutting his own leg deeply, he let his blood mix with the sand already slick with mine. Together we placed our hands on the stone and held it over the mixture. It became warm to the touch as we spoke our wish, white light ribbons swirling around us. We asked for four sons. Four beings born from our ritual who could possess the stone's powers and pass them on through their lineage.

The stone got even hotter and became painful to hold. As though melting, the stone morphed into four smaller ovals of pliable mass, almost like clay. My hands burned with the heat, and I couldn't help but cry out. Just as I thought I could bear the pain no longer, the four pieces of the stone turned to liquid that bled through our fingers to the blood and sand below. There was a brilliant flash of light that threw me down onto my back. When I stood again, four babes lay at our feet. Four boys, looking as perfect as if they had just been birthed from the womb. Horus looked at me wide-eyed and panting.

"It worked! You were right, Mother!" he exclaimed.

I nodded at him and brought my hand to my mouth to stifle a cry. They were a miracle, flesh from stone and blood, and I was awestruck looking at their smooth skin and tufts of dark black hair. Just then, two of the babes began wailing the angry cries of newborn hunger and confusion. I picked up two and cradled them in my elbows, laughing as they rooted for milk.

"Not for a long time, precious ones. Not this body," I answered them. Horus carefully picked up the other two and cradled them the same.

"They look like brothers, but not identical. They shall be brothers in every way," he declared.

"We must feed them," I answered, looking earnestly at Horus. "You are now a father. You have a sacred duty to these boys. They and their descendants will bring help and healing to the people forevermore." Then more quietly, I added, "You must not let on they are gifted until we know they have passed on their seed. They will have important roles in this world, but do not tell them they are healers until they have given the power forward. They are not safe once their secret is known. Trust me."

We walked into the grasses, leaving the wise and wondrous acacia tree to greet the dawn alone.

***

I opened my eyes and found myself back on the top of the red rock spire. Bringing my hands in front of my face, I could see a soft pink mist swirling around my fingertips. I felt strength and power pulse through my body and a peace of understanding enter my chest. I now was certain that I was a descendant of the four sons of Horus, and of Horus and Isis and the stone as well. The visions had always come to me like memories, and this last one the most vivid and intense. Every pain felt like my own. Every emotion was raw and real. How could I not believe it to be true?

Alex and Isaac had opened their eyes, too, and were now looking at me wide-eyed. "Can you see it?" I asked them, holding out my hands where the pink mist delicately swirled. They both nodded, and I felt such relief. Even though I believed in what was happening to me, it helped that my friends could validate this one aspect of it for me, so I didn't need to feel like a crazy person.

It turns out they each had different visions with their meditations, too. Isaac had seen himself as a sculptor, feverishly and joyfully creating beings out of clay. When he finished a piece, it would come to life and thank him. Alex had become a bird soaring above the earth. She said she could see us down below but that her thoughts didn't stay there. Instead, it was as though she was disconnected with the humans on the rock, and her focus was the sky, the breeze under her wings, and the promise of exploration. Each of our experiences were short and fleeting, but so vibrant and real, we couldn't not be changed by them.

We descended back down Bell Rock and met with Frida and Mary Ann. Over lunch, we told them all that had happened to us. Frida was amazed, as usually the vortex responses were more subtle, but we three had had profound truths revealed to us. And the idea that Isis and Horus had created life with the stone left Frida questioning her theory that gods and goddesses were just stories of normal people with gifts that were explained away with fanciful tales. She said we gave her much to think about.

Back at the house that night, our fourth, the four of us spent a lot of time on the back patio just staring at the stars. Each of our heads was filled to busting with all that we'd experienced, that everything in the physical world around us took on a different quality. Colors and light seemed more intense and vibrant. Natural sound like the wind or a bird call became more acute. It was as though a separate part of our spirits had been awakened that had just been lying sleeping, waiting to be freed.

The next week and a half week were busy. Seeing as we were in an artists' mecca, Isaac set forth finding a place to learn sculpture. One of the sculptors whose work Carlos sold in his shop was open to having an apprentice for a short while, and Isaac began spending each morning in the studio. He came back to the little ranch house at lunchtime, coated in clay dust and happier and more enthusiastic than I'd ever seen him. Even though he was starting with simple shaped bowls and vases, he could glimpse future creations and had even bought a sketchbook to draw project ideas. Isaac researched a studio back at home and was already signed up for lessons before our Sedona time was done.

As for Alex, the freedom and exhilaration she'd felt as the bird during her meditation made her realize that she wanted to live a life that wasn't tethered to any one place—that she was someone who could be happy as long as she made time for adventure and exploration. Fueled by her enthusiasm, we spent more time hiking and visiting sites of early inhabitants. It was impossible not to be moved by dwellings literally built into the side of rock as far back as 1150 BC. Inside many of the caves were pictographs of animals or people. It was truly mind-blowing.

As for me, I dedicated most of my remaining time to Frida. We met for a couple hours every morning and practiced sensing auras and energy. Though I had seen the mist of my aura on top of Bell Rock, it hadn't appeared to me since, nor could I see anyone else's aura. Frida assured me it was a talent I had, but I just needed to practice to make it a skill. So we practiced. At first, I tried softening my gaze and sensing the borders around a shape, while not looking directly at it. Apparently, our eyes and our brains are very good at filtering out information we don't necessarily need, so training is essential for this kind of sight. Once I got the hang of it practicing with Frida, Carlos, Mary Ann, Isaac, and Alex, we went down to the town to try with people walking by. It made me extremely uncomfortable because I was not good at it yet, which basically meant I was staring at people. More than once, while focused on a person, they turned in my direction, and shot me a nasty look when I couldn't turn away in time. I got embarrassed and whined to Frida that I didn't really need to read auras to help heal people anyway. She assured me that to read the energy of another would make me an even more effective healer because I'd be able to communicate on a deeper, energetic level. She did a couple reiki sessions on me in the week after Bell Rock, and it felt like my body was floating on top of a lake, bobbing gently with the waves. I definitely felt more balanced and clear-headed after the sessions, and my aura reading seemed to improve as well.

Ever since Bell Rock, I'd been even more anxious to try healing again. Much to my dismay, Mary Ann was cool to the idea. She was still reluctant to expose me to anyone who might talk about it to others. But the following week, I got lucky. Carlos was unpacking inventory for the shop and his hand slipped while using a box knife. The knife slid too fast through the tape as he dragged it toward his body and ended up giving him a nice little gash on his thigh. Nothing too deep, but probably needing a handful of stitches. Carlos came home instead of going to the hospital, though. He knew I'd be there and said he wanted me to have the first crack at it. Frida clucked, but Carlos held firm. With a pair of scissors, he cut his ripped and bloody pant leg off so I could clearly see the wound.

"Does it hurt? It looks like it hurts," I said, trying not to convey how excited I was.

"Not too bad. Happened so fast I barely felt it. Sayonara to these pants, though. I'm just happy I didn't bleed all over the artwork in the box!" He pulled a chair into the middle of the room with a hand towel under his thigh to catch the drops of blood still slowly making their escape. I pulled another chair and positioned myself right in front of him.

"Ready?" I asked. He nodded and smiled.

I placed my hands over the wound and breathed deeply. Then I closed my eyes and spoke the words from Isis in my vision. "May this body be the vessel of the power of the Healing Stone."

The ribbons appeared to me, alive and active. I carefully took one and placed it to Carlos' leg. Though I couldn't "see" the cut, the ribbon seemed to dissolve down into space. I grabbed one more and repeated the process. After the third ribbon was absorbed, I felt heat emanating from the leg beneath my hands, and it startled my eyes open. To my amazement, the cut was gently glowing with soft white light as scar tissue formed over the gash. Carlos and Frida stared too, all of us a little afraid to move or make a sound lest we break the spell. My hands still above the leg felt the heat lessen and I sensed the cut was almost done healing. Smooth pink skin tissue now covered where the cut had been. It was lumpy and looked like a misshapen scar, but the wound was definitely closed. My eyes wide, I looked up at Carlos.

"Does it hurt?" I asked.

"I'm still aware of it, but…no…it doesn't hurt." Then turning to Frida, he said, "Do you believe what just happened?" She shook her head in wonder in response, then looked at me and started giggling. I jumped up and laughed too, and the three of us carried on like we'd just won the lottery.

"Can I see it again, closer?" I asked Carlos. "It's really all closed up, isn't it?" I wondered aloud. Then it occurred to me that the scar was quite big and ropey and not smooth at all. "I guess stitches might have been a good idea first…then at least the skin would have healed close together and you wouldn't have this big scar."

Carlos just laughed. "You think I would trade an itty-bitty scar for what I just saw? Not a chance. I could care less about that scar. What I just witnessed—experienced! —was nothing short of dumbfounding." He beamed at me. "I'm going to have to wear a bandage on my leg if I wear shorts in case my employees see it healed."

The days flew by and suddenly it was time to head back home. I felt so melancholy on our last night. Frida tried to cheer me up, but it was a sad attempt as she was just as upset about our leaving as I was. Mary Ann had gotten into a groove with her painting, and Isaac was finally feeling comfortable with the wheel and using clay tools.

The thing that was eating at me the most was that here in Sedona I had this incredible support system and could focus on just understanding more about myself. At home, we all had responsibilities and other family, friends, to take us away from each other. I wasn't ready to give up the daily rhythm we'd created. And I was scared. Scared that I wouldn't be the same Leah I'd discovered through this trip. Scared that the people who'd known me all my life and had caused me trouble all my life, would still be there waiting for me when I returned. That this last three weeks would turn out to feel more like the fantasy than the reality.

The five of us went out to dinner on our last night in Sedona. To the same restaurant with the outdoor patio where we met the first time. We laughed and tried to make light, but there was a strong undercurrent of heavy at the table. Carlos was seated to my left, and at one point when Frida was telling Mary Ann a story that he and I had heard before, he pulled me close to talk.

"You know, it's up to you now. You need to dig deep and find the strength you uncovered on this trip, and let it continue to carry you forward. You are not alone—remember that. We are all here for you whenever you need us. Let that settle your heart so you can have the courage to continue on your journey. Nothing important ever came from succumbing to fear. You can be afraid, but you have to decide to move forward anyway. That is what will set you apart from other healers that never realize their potential. Feel the fear—and keep striving anyway."

He finished his speech with a squeeze of my hand, and I felt like a weight had lifted. He was right, I had people who loved and supported me. I decided then not to let my fear get in the way of realizing my full potential. Just as quickly, the thought of Amanda Rossman of Channel 5 wormed its way into my mind. I took a deep breath and told her she'd just have to wait until I was ready.

PART II

Kopfkino:
(German) 'Head cinema,' playing out a scenario like a movie in your head.

CHAPTER 10

Returning home was less eventful than I had worked myself up to believe it would be. In truth, the only people who would've really missed me were on the trip with me, so no one marked our homecoming. Alex began her routine of helping with the summer camps at her uncle's gym, and Isaac immediately filled his schedule with wheel throwing and sculpting classes in the mornings, and a part-time job bussing tables in the evenings. His parents were a little baffled by this sudden, unforeseen passion for working with clay, but they supported it as they did all his endeavors.

I was really worried that the hoopla surrounding the bird video would still be waiting for me. After the weeks away, however, it seems I had been mostly forgotten. While YouTube views of the video had increased, the comments seemed to have dropped off. I was equally relieved and alarmed at people's ability to simply move on. Our voicemail box was filled at the house with media looking for interviews. Mary Ann just deleted them all.

A couple days after we got back, there was a brochure in the mail from a small liberal arts college one town adjacent to ours. Scrolling the summer course list just out of curiosity, my eyes landed on a class titled "Ancient Healing Traditions," and I caught my breath. It felt as though the course was calling to me, and a week later I was registered and sitting in a small classroom with twenty or thirty other students of all ages. The professor, Dr. Vihaan Anand, was a slight man of Indian descent, his accent melodious and pleasing. The ends of words turned up as the corners of the mouth in a smile, and it made everything he said feel happy. In fact, as he told us on the first day, his surname Anand, was a derivative of "Ananda," which meant "bliss" in Sanskrit. The class was to be three weeks long, three hours per day, and I quickly immersed myself in it.

Dr. Anand began with the Indian traditional healing practices of Ayurveda and Siddha-Veda the first week, which are based on the principles called doshas; Pita, Vata and Kapha. Health and vitality come from balancing these doshas, stemming from the elements of air, water, fire, space and earth, within our bodies. Illness, instability and pain indicate that a person is out of balance. Changes in diet and lifestyle and special herbs are usually "prescribed" to someone suffering. Dr. Anand spoke passionately and personally about how his mother helped cure her rheumatoid arthritis after seeing a Siddha-Veda healer and following the principles. It changed the way he thought about modern medical approaches.

The second week was focused on shamanism around the world, and how important a role the natural environment played in maintaining health. Aided by natural spirits with whom they could communicate, shamans believed that our survival depended on the harmony and survival of other species, as well as nature, and that they could not be separated. Aided by plants, some psychedelics depending on their native regions, shamans could reach an altered mind state to help them with healing and spiritual growth. Shamans were born with certain gifts of seeing or understanding of the human spirit and nature, and were taught healing practices developed and passed down through generations.

Dr. Anand taught that shamans or "healers" exist in all cultures and traditions. There are people who are born with gifts that extend beyond what we expect a normal human to possess. These are the people who would often end up becoming shamans or healers. But when a person is born with gifts and chooses to deny them for any reason, it is believed their own health will suffer greatly—that shamans who deny their gifts will be afflicted throughout their lives.

I couldn't help but think he was speaking directly to me, as he echoed the sentiments of Carlos and Frida weeks earlier.

The final week was focused on ancient healing societies of Africa, including Egypt. Using names such as High Priests and Priestesses, diviners, or herbalists, many traditions believed that human beings were made of the physical, the spiritual, the moral, and the social. Illness could stem from any of these attributes, just as healing could. It was during the time of colonialism that many African healing traditions were lost or buried. Western medicine was considered more advanced and ancient healing considered inferior, superstitious, and backward—sometimes even labeled as witchcraft. This left many healers unable to practice freely for fear of persecution, and Western medicine took the place of healing traditions. On our last day of class, Dr. Anand, usually very focused on topic, allowed us the gift of his opinion on modern medicine.

"The medical communities are always looking deeper and deeper into whichever aspect of health is their specialty. This, of course, can result in amazing discovery and understanding, and reveal new ways to approach health issues!" He swept his arms open wide. "The problem with this focused approach, is we end up with fractured and narrow views of health. Your endocrinologist looks at your organ function, your orthopedist looks at your bones and muscles, your cardiologist looks at how your heart and blood vessels are functioning. And they are very good at their jobs! But they miss what the ancient traditions follow. That our ailments are not narrow and fractured, because our bodies are wide and holistic. They function with many systems working synergistically as a whole. This includes our spirit or energetic portions, our mind and thought patterns. Ancient healers throughout the world understood this in a way that seems lost to many of today's medical leaders. You cannot look at a torn meniscus in the knee and only look at the meniscus. Because a torn meniscus hurts. This changes how we move our bodies throughout the day. We become more sedentary and alter our gait to accommodate the pain, which creates changes in how the rest of our joints function. In addition, changes occur in our breathing patterns, our nerve conduction, our mood and our thought processes. Even our spirit! Each of these plays an important role in healing and overall wellbeing. You cannot truly separate the body into parts and only address one or two." His emotion betrayed deep feeling.

I stayed after class that last day, waiting for my turn to speak one on one with Dr. Anand. It had been a great course, and many of the students took a moment to personally thank him and express their happiness with what they'd learned. I waited back, vying for the last slot, where I might be able to speak with him alone. When, finally, it was my turn, Dr. Anand spoke first.

"I'm thinking this coursework spoke to you on a deeper level than perhaps the rest of your classmates?" He raised his eyebrows. I must have looked surprised, and he let out a little chuckle. "You think someone who made a life's work of studying healing traditions didn't learn a little bit about how to recognize when he's in the presence of a healer? I'm glad you stayed because I want to speak to you about something. What are your plans for the fall?"

Most of my friends would be headed to college in a month's time. Alex was going to the Northeast. Cashing in on her dual citizenship granted by her Canadian father, she'd be attending McGill University in Montreal. Isaac, reluctant to admit that Alex's decision colored his, would also be in the Northeast, going to Skidmore College in Saratoga Springs, New York. Not only was it a quick and easy three-hour train ride to Montreal, but they had a solid English Lit program. He'd also recently discovered, happily, they offered a minor in studio art with an excellent sculpture studio.

My grades were good, and I had dutifully applied to and been accepted by a few schools. Nothing felt quite right, though, and I had dragged my feet on making a decision, much to Mary Ann's growing consternation. Truth was, I was scared to death. A big part of me was desperate to get out and be independent. But with me still understanding so little about my abilities, I was too afraid to be on my own. And I wasn't sure what I wanted to study. After a few heated discussions with Mary Ann about the importance of higher education and my parents' expectations, I made the decision to delay my decision.

I—or we—decided I should take a gap year to do some traveling and "self-exploration" and then see how I felt the following year. I was still self-conscious when anyone asked me about my plans for the fall, as they inevitably assumed I would be going to college *somewhere*. The reactions to my time off were often awkward, including some form of "Good for you!" as though I needed cheering up about it. It led me to qualify my answers with, "Well, I'm hoping to get lots of volunteering done," or "I'm just not ready to begin real life without seeing more of the world first." These extras felt and were contrived to cover the fact that I was unsteady about the decision and really had no clue how I would occupy the time. But they made me seem much more put together in the face of all those well-meaning teachers and acquaintances. I worried now that Dr. Anand might judge my lack of plans, and I hesitated to answer. Luckily, he didn't wait for me to fill the silence.

"Here's why I'm asking. I will be taking on a lighter course load this fall because a grant just came through for a research project of mine. Do you remember I mentioned that when a person is born with special healing talents, and they deny or suppress those talents, they often suffer themselves? Whether physically or mentally?" I nodded. "It is my theory that many of these people end up in our prison system. People with exceptional insight or intuition, skills they might have felt as children, but the environment they were born to was not supportive." He paused to let that thought sink in. "Now, I'm not saying there aren't simply awful people in the world—but in my mind, it makes more sense that the people who commit small, petty crimes, especially those who also have substance addictions, are the gifted ones. Because when you're born with healing gifts, it is not in your nature, no matter how awful your life, to cause suffering to others. It goes against your very being. Of course, this is just my theory, but I have learned to trust my own intuition in life, and this is where it's leading me."

"I've heard this before," I said. "This summer when I met a healer, she echoed the same idea, that physical and mental pain is suffered by those who deny their gifts." Dr. Anand nodded along with me.

"Yes, yes, good. I'm planning on testing this theory in the fall. There is a minimum-security adult prison—mostly white-collar crime, drugs, thefts—located about ten miles from here. Truthfully, I wanted to work with the juvenile centers, but the legal hurdles of working with minors proved to be an absolute nightmare, so I gave that up for now. It is my theory that if we can work with these prisoners, test their intuition and teach them skills such as meditation in a supportive environment, it may help them change the trajectory of their lives moving forward. The hope is then that they will not end up as repeat offenders—though I'm working to temper my expectations for sweeping change." He sighed. "Adults have built up lifetimes of beliefs about the world they live in and their role in it. I do not have the illusion that this study will result in a massive shift in criminal behaviors. But maybe we can reach just one…or maybe two." He grinned at me.

"It sounds like an interesting plan, Dr. Anand." I hesitated. "How are you going to find out which criminals have abilities?"

"That's where you come in. I would like your assistance. I have known several healers of different abilities in my years, and I sense a strength in you. Often, healers are drawn to other healers. I'm thinking you may be able to help me figure out who we can help." He looked right at me then.

He wants me to go into a prison? I thought. *With criminals?*

"Of course, I'd be with you the entire time," he added as though reading my mind. "You would act as my research assistant, which would, of course, mean you'd need to be enrolled in the college for at least the semester. We will begin with a simple questionnaire that the inmates can fill out. Based on their answers, we will choose with whom to conduct follow-up meetings. We'll have less than an hour with each inmate—perhaps only a half-hour, accompanied by guards, of course, to go through a more advanced series of tests, and to speak with them in more depth."

I didn't respond right away. He had just dumped a load on me, and I was still processing.

"Here's my contact information," he said, holding out a business card. "I want to get this sorted by the end of next week, so let me know before then. And if you have any questions, just shoot me a note. I believe your assistance would be very helpful to me, Leah, but I understand that enrolling at the college and jumping right into research may not have been your vision of the summer." He gave me a warm smile and started to leave me in the classroom.

"Dr. Anand?" I asked. "Isn't it too late to apply for entry in the college? Won't that have been decided already? Would I have to go through the entire application process?"

Dr. Anand thought for a minute. "If you decide you'd like to help me, I will speak to the dean and we'll go from there. You won't have to do a full application to attend. Any other questions right now? I'm afraid I'm late for a tennis lesson." He smiled apologetically. "Let me know! Then we'll figure out the details." He spoke over his shoulder as he left the room, waving one arm overhead in goodbye.

I headed home to talk it over with Mary Ann. I knew that the cost of college was figured out in the trust left by my parents, but this wasn't exactly the route we had planned on me taking. I needed a sounding board, even though my heart was already growing warm to the idea.

A week later, I found myself in his office on campus. It was surprisingly neat for how much was crammed into it. He had a large walnut desk with the kind of green-glass desk lamp you'd find in stately libraries. His chair was leather and high-backed but swiveled and rolled. I sat across from him in a smaller chair made from the same leather. Mine neither swiveled nor rolled, however, and I was finding it too far from the desk. When I tried to shimmy up, it was really hard to move. I tried lifting my weight ever so slightly off the chair and squatting, then slowly shifted the chair forward a few inches and let my weight rest back down. I didn't think Dr. Anand saw me, but without lifting his eyes from the papers in front of him, he said, "Everyone tells me to replace that chair…that it's so cumbersome, but I rarely have anyone sitting there for very long. Now that you're here, however, I will look into something more suitable for sharing a desk."

The east wall held the only window and faced the quad area. It was flanked by two framed prints of medicinal herbs. Almost every other wall surface was covered by shelves filled with books, figurines, and pots with ivy spilling down the sides. I wondered if Dr. Anand even knew half of what he had arranged on those shelves. But while the clutter framed the room, his desk was surprisingly tidy.

"I want you to look over the questions I have so far. Tell me if there's anything you feel we should add or take away or change the wording of." He reached across the desk and handed me a stapled packet of about three pages worth of questions we would be using to weed out potential healers from the nearly 2,500 inmates at the correctional facility. Even if only a third or a quarter of the people responded, we had our work cut out for us. I sat back in the notorious chair and began reading over the questions. A handful touched on the person's relationship with plants, animals, and health problems. An entire page was dedicated to "Intuitive Abilities" and included questions like, "Do you often sense who is calling before you pick up the phone?" or "Did you ever have a dream that came true the next day?"

"Dr. Anand, will some of these questions not be as relevant for someone who has been incarcerated? Like this one about the phone calls?" I asked him. He nodded. "Good. The questions can relate back to time throughout their lives, not just current. Why not add a clause in there or something that helps explain it?" He rolled a red pen across the desk in my direction and I snatched it up before it fell to the floor.

For the next few hours, we traded ideas and suggestions, rewording, removing or adding questions as they occurred to us. Unlike Dr. Anand, my knowledge on the subject of ancient healers and questions that might reveal their truths was limited. But as a healer, myself, I had an inside view into some experiences that another healer might go through. So, we added a group of questions dealing with things I experienced on my own journey thus far: waking dreams, auras and sensing another's energy, flashes of insight. Dr. Anand teasingly called this the Woo-Woo section and winked at me. By the end of the day, we had almost seventy questions on the list. Deciding that the inmates would probably take one look at that and toss it in the trash, we spent the next two days culling. For finances' sake, we needed to keep it to one page, front and back, so we weren't making five thousand copies. In the end we managed to fill that space requirement with forty small-type questions, most of which required only yes or no answers. Dr. Anand seemed satisfied and pleased with my first week's contribution to the study. He would be delivering the questionnaires the following day, a day off for me, and would go back to collect them a week later.

I spent most of my day off arranging photos from our Sedona trip into an online photobook to order. Mary Ann kept bringing me food and sat down periodically to talk about our adventures. Shortly after we'd returned, she received a large oil painting commission, and it was taking up a lot of her time but was making her so happy. I was struck by Mary Ann's talent every time I caught a glimpse of her canvas. She was truly gifted.

The following week, Dr. Anand walked me through the interview process he expected us to complete with each inmate whose answers to the questionnaire hinted at suppressed healing abilities. I would mostly be assisting and trying to read energy while Dr. Anand would complete the interviews. There were some physical tests and follow-up questions, but it would mainly be a conversation that flowed depending on an individual's answers. My duties would include taking detailed notes of the conversations and chiming in if anything occurred to me to add or ask.

At the end of the week, Dr. Anand headed back to the correctional facility to collect whatever questionnaires had been filled out. I anxiously awaited a text from him letting me know, and it came at about 5:30 p.m. on the Friday evening. Bright and early Monday morning we would begin the process of analyzing around 700 responses. He told me to dress comfortably because chances were, we weren't leaving the office except to eat for the next couple weeks.

When I arrived Monday, a sleek, wheeled, curved-back desk chair sat in place of the leather behemoth. It even swiveled. Dr. Anand nodded at me, handed me a piping hot mug of tea, and chased it with a one-inch stack of completed questionnaires.

"Here we go!" he exclaimed. "I didn't expect these many responses, but it just reinforces the idea that maybe many of our petty criminals are healers in denial!" His mood seemed jovial and I smiled.

We worked out ahead of time which "Yes" answers, as well as the total number of "Yes" answers, would indicate strong candidates. Now, we began the arduous process of going through them. After each ten, we stopped to record the data in a simple application the computer engineering department had designed for Dr. Anand. It would compare the data and allow us to pull up, match, and cross-reference the individuals' information easily once entered. The first day, we managed to complete thirty forms. I was totally exhausted. Dr. Anand said, with the intent of cheering us, that we would get faster and more efficient as the days went on. And we did. After two nonstop weeks, we were done. Dr. Anand took Mary Ann and me out to dinner to celebrate. Even though he said it might seem cliché, he introduced us to his most beloved Indian restaurant in the city.

In the end, we had one hundred twenty-one inmates who tested high enough on the questionnaires to warrant follow-up interviews. This number seemed daunting, but Dr. Anand assured me some of them would be quick. We would be allowed at the correctional facility three days each week, Monday through Wednesday. Thursday and Friday would be spent evaluating and uploading the data from the interviews. We needed to get as much done as possible before the end of summer, because then my classes began, and I would be more limited with time to help.

The first Monday we arrived was hot and humid, with a heat index close to one hundred degrees. Dr. Anand had leather seats in his car and the backs of my thighs were sticking to them. I was nervous. I had never spent any time around criminals, at least not that I was aware of. Would they be rude and profane? Would they be disrespectful to Dr. Anand? We had five interviews lined up that first day—to get our feet wet, Dr. Anand said. The next two days had double that amount scheduled.

We arrived in a large concrete parking lot framed on one side with a chain link fence coated on the inside with barbed wire. The building face was red brick and inviting, like a public library, while the remainder of the building was cream-colored concrete: massive, blocky and not inviting at all. As we walked toward the main entrance, I was taken aback by the neat flower beds and bright blooms in planters framing the walkway. They were directly in front of the barbed wire and chain link fence, and it was a jarring juxtaposition of images. We checked in, went through a series of doors, and then another series of doors. Through hallway windows, I saw a row of chairs and cubbies separated by what I assumed was bulletproof glass and a large room with round tables and chairs. This was the main visiting area. Dr. Anand had arranged a private consultation room for our interviews, and we would have a guard with us at all times.

Today our guard was named Tommy, and he walked on his toes with a bounce as though he couldn't wait to get to wherever it was we were going. He smiled and cracked jokes, and we liked him right away. After showing us where to find the bathroom, Tommy brought us to the room where our first inmate interviewee would join us ten minutes later. There was a gray table with four chairs surrounding it, and the room was framed with windows so nothing was hidden from view. Otherwise there was nothing at all in the room. It was colorless and gloomy.

A few moments before the interviewee arrived, Dr. Anand turned to me. "Remember, you don't need to do anything but take notes and help me if I've forgotten anything. If you happen to get a sense of their energy, put it in the notes. Don't bring it up during the interview. We will have a few minutes between sessions to chat about it. But don't feel bad if you don't feel anything, either. This is a research study—we don't know if our theory is correct or not, so try not to place too much expectation on the outcomes, okay?" He smiled at me. I got the impression the pep talk was as much for himself as it was for me, as I knew how much he wanted his theory to be right.

A few seconds later, our first interviewee was led in. He wore the standard issue gray top and bottom and was, much to my surprise, unshackled. I guess I'd watched too many movies. Even more surprising was that he was kind and gentle and deferential to Dr. Anand, and even to me. He answered all the questions the best he could, pausing to knit his brow and correctly remember experiences when asked to recount them. After about forty minutes we were finished, and he thanked us for the time and was escorted out. Once he was gone, Dr. Anand turned to me and smiled.

"That went very well, don't you think?" he asked me with raised eyebrows. I guess he was as nervous as I was about the reception we'd get. We met with two more inmates, then had a short break for lunch. None of them gave off any remarkable energy, and I was too nervous to try to read their auras, since I figured it wasn't a good idea to stare at someone who'd been locked up. The first interviewee was so far the most promising of the three, and we both agreed we'd nix the two others as possibilities.

"Did the morning go as you'd expected, Leah?" Dr. Anand asked me.

"In truth, I wasn't sure what to expect. I guess I imagined all offenders as 'hardened', you know? Different from other people simply because of where they'd ended up. But the people we met today all seem so normal," I answered.

"It takes some personal experience, I think, to be able to separate a person from their circumstance. Many of these people in here have lived lives quite different from what you or I know," Dr. Anand replied. "Don't get me wrong, I believe committing a crime is still a choice someone makes. But I wonder if I, too, would choose to steal from a convenience store if I knew it would feed my family for a couple weeks?" Then he shook his head as if to get the cobwebs out and sighed. "Of course, I'm romanticizing it, too. Not everyone needed the money to survive, or the car for anything but a joyride with their boys—a stupid decision on an otherwise boring Saturday night. Life is a series of decisions that bring us toward one destiny or another."

The last two interviews went as smoothly as the first three, and we left for the day feeling optimistic for the rest of the study. The correctional facility with its immaculate entryway and cold, unfeeling furniture became a second home over the following few weeks. I got over my fear of trying to read their auras and decided it was excellent practice instead. So that by the second week, I was actually pretty adept. There had also been a few men from whom, upon them walking into the room, I felt waves of energy. I made notes of everything.

Now we had to slow our operations down because college was in session, and my coursework was beginning. I managed to cluster all my classes on Mondays and Wednesdays, leaving Tuesdays and Thursdays to spend with Dr. Anand at the facility. Friday was for compiling notes and data entry. Weekends were saved for actual coursework. I had never been this busy in my life, moving from one task to the next, like a hummingbird flitting from one flower to another. My classes were interesting, though, as I was registered as an anthropology student. The college was small and there were few majors to choose from. Anthropology wasn't really where I saw my future, but for now it was interesting, and it allowed me to work with Dr. Anand.

It was mid-October when things shifted for me in a big way with the study. We only had a couple weeks of interviews left. Dr. Anand and I had a total of seventy-eight men who were some level of natural healers based on the information we gathered, a lower number than expected. Still, it was a positive result. The next step of the study would be small group sessions where we revealed our findings and showed them some techniques to practice that supported their gifts or career options that would be suited to them. Then we'd say goodbye, and if they agreed, we would track them over the next two years with check-ins and supportive therapy to see how their lives progressed.

I woke Tuesday morning on our last week of interviews, and the air had a bite to it. Something was gnawing at me in a way I couldn't explain. Like the feeling that I was forgetting something or that something was about to happen. It was a nervous energy and it was driving me crazy. First, I dropped a mug and it broke into a million pieces, spraying my clothes with hot tea. After cleaning up and changing, I walked into the coffee table so hard that I toppled over, ripping my sleeve and bashing my knee. After changing again and putting a Band-aid on my knee, I had to run back into the house twice: the first time because I forgot my purse and the second because I forgot my phone.

"What is wrong with me this morning?" I shouted to my steering wheel. Once on the road, though, it was as if the universe changed its mind and was rushing me forward instead of holding me back. Already stressed because I was running late, I managed to get every single green light on my way to the college, so that in the end I arrived five minutes early. Dr. Anand was ready to go as well, something I had come to disbelieve was possible. If he seemed like a polished lecturer in the classroom, he was the absent-minded professor when getting ready to go somewhere. But not today. We only caught one red light on the way to the correctional facility, which was actually yellow, and I say we could have made it, but Dr. Anand was a cautious driver, so we stopped. In the end, we arrived fifteen minutes early for our first interview, which meant we could prepare a little in advance, instead of catching up afterwards.

I was still not myself, however, and when we entered the interview room, I tripped on what I can only imagine was air, dropping my notebook and a file folder of papers all over the floor. Frustration threatened to come screaming out of me as I knelt down to pick up the mess. I was still off to the side trying to arrange the fallen papers into their correct order when our first interviewee arrived. To say that I felt him before I saw him was not an exaggeration. I was focused on the papers but was suddenly hit with an energy stronger than anything else I'd experienced. I whipped my head around to meet the eyes of a beautiful man. He was taller than Dr. Anand, but not quite as tall as Isaac, maybe around six feet, and he was muscular in a subtle way. At first glance he looked to be young, maybe twenty-one or twenty-two. His dark, wide eyes were fixed on mine, and he wore a perplexed expression.

"Welcome, Rafi. I'm Dr. Anand, and this is Leah, my research assistant. We appreciate you coming to talk with us a bit today." Rafi's eyes only flickered briefly to acknowledge Dr. Anand before returning to me. "Please have a seat and we'll get started."

I almost couldn't breathe under the weight of that gaze and the power of the energy it conveyed. Once Rafi's eyes moved off me to Dr. Anand, some of the pressure released.

Dr. Anand and I took our usual places at the table, he in front of the inmate and me in front of the laptop. Every time Rafi looked at me, I felt a wave. The tension in the room was palpable, and I could tell Dr. Anand was trying to figure it out as well. I kept my gaze down and tried to seem as uninteresting as possible, but Rafi kept looking at me. In order to bring him back to the task on hand, Dr. Anand switched tactics and suggested Rafi describe his childhood while looking at a picture of the seven chakra colors over a drawn, seated figure. This was supposed to help the person focus and tune into their body while thinking about their answers. It seemed to work slightly in Rafi's case, as to my relief, his attention shifted away from me, and he launched into a long tale.

His history didn't not seem to contain much happiness, but he didn't speak with resentment or anger. He matter-of-factly relayed how he was born to a single mother with a drug addiction and was raised in his early years by his grandmother and great aunt. All he knew of his father was that he gave him his name before disappearing from his life. Though they were loving to him, his grandma had diabetes and could hardly walk from the bedroom to the kitchen six feet away. He couldn't remember her ever leaving the apartment, and he was frequently sent to the corner store to get her cigarettes or food. His aunt, his grandma's younger sister, worked afternoons and evenings as a home health nurse, and was gone most of the time. He started school at age five, and getting out of the apartment felt like freedom to him. He loved school.

A couple months into first grade, when he was six years old, his mother stole him away in the middle of the night. The event was vividly scorched into his memory, as it had terrified him. Though his aunt wrestled for him and his grandma screamed, his mother, whom he barely knew, was stronger and managed to get him out of the apartment and into a waiting car, driven by a man he'd never seen before. He tried to fight and yell, but his mom hit him hard enough that he stopped. He spent the next year with his mom and her boyfriend, a man who turned out to be a drinker and a cheat. The three of them were on the road almost constantly, chasing this hustle or that, and fighting endlessly about money and other women. Rafi learned to keep his mouth shut and stay as invisible as possible, lest they decide to turn their anger in his direction. It was around that time he said he developed what he called his "sense about people." He could read their moods or their intentions without so much as a word. This became his saving grace because it helped him understand when to speak and when not to. Which stranger might help him if he needed it, and which would not. It became like a game to him wherever they were. Though it was a small comfort, it wasn't enough to make up for the fact that during the entire year his mother never once brought him to school.

He asked her a couple times in the first few weeks where his new school would be, but by the second or third ask, she smacked him and called him a selfish little shit, asking what made him think he deserved to sit around all day while they busted their butts just to feed his greedy ass. He needed to start pulling his weight, she said. So instead of a classroom, Rafi spent his days on the side of the road or in the subway station begging for money. People were horrified to see a young boy alone, and their guilt brought in lots of money. He couldn't stay in any place too long, though, because people would often call the cops when they saw a small kid by himself. His job was to run like hell when he saw anyone reaching for their cellphone.

When begging was slow and no one was around, Rafi would spend his time reading the signs along the road or picking up dropped pamphlets or receipts from the ground. He had learned to read during kindergarten, greatly impressing his teacher. She lent him books throughout the year, encouraging him and calling him smart. As a present for the summer, she sent him home with a used copy of the Harry Potter series. His mom had stolen him when he was only halfway through the series, and he remembered being angrier at her for that more than anything else she'd done.

It was during one of his shifts in the subway when he was finally caught. His mom had left him there only ten minutes before to go get a drink and some air, which he knew meant she was seeing her dealer. The first cop came around from the left so he bolted, but ran headfirst into another cop coming from the right. Rafi confessed that when he finally realized he wasn't going to be able to get out of the cop's grip, he just started bawling. He stopped fighting and cried his eyes out because he was so relieved. They took him to a station where he told them the whole saga. He spent two days in a child services home while they looked into his story. Turned out his grandma and aunt had tried to find him, even putting his picture in one of those "Have you seen me?" ads in the saver papers. Six months after his abduction, though, his grandmother had died from a stroke. They tried to find his aunt, but she wasn't living in the apartment anymore, and the phone number from the ad was no longer in service.

Rafi spent the next eleven years of his life in several different foster homes, some better than others. Since turning eighteen, he'd been on his own. He'd graduated with all As from high school, despite everything he'd had to deal with, and was working as a manager at a convenience store when he got arrested. Some friends from school had the brilliant idea to steal a suburban mom's car while she was picking her kid up from daycare. They showed up at the end of his shift and took him riding around the city. Rafi didn't know the driver and didn't realize the car was stolen. Though, he admitted, he could've guessed, but it had been a shitty day, so he decided not to ask. They got beer and drove around the city. The car was nice, expensive with leather interior and power everything.

The police arrested them when they stopped for snacks at a gas station two towns over. Two of his friends who were in the store saw the cops, ran, and got away, but Rafi and the driver were still in the car and couldn't get out in time. The public defender got his sentence reduced to a misdemeanor and he had been in the facility for nine months. He was getting out in two weeks' time.

I had sat riveted, listening to his tale. It was hard to believe he wasn't describing a movie or a fictional story. Once Rafi was finished talking, Dr. Anand began asking questions.

"Will you still have your job at the convenience store when you get out in two weeks?" he asked.

Rafi chuckled. "Uh, no. They don't hold a job for someone doing jail time."

"What do you plan to do? Have you considered college? You said your grades were outstanding…have you applied anywhere?" Dr. Anand continued, taking on a surprisingly fatherly tone.

Rafi looked at him, sighed and leaned back into his chair, folding his arms across his chest. "Sir, I have no job, almost no money, and I now have a criminal record. I can't imagine how higher education is in my immediate future, no. I have also been evicted from my apartment for failure to pay rent while incarcerated, so I can't even tell you what I will do two weeks from now. I suppose a friend's couch is my first option but, as I've mentioned, I don't have the most reliable friends," he said with a sardonic smile.

The exhaustion of his situation showed through in his face and his voice, and Dr. Anand fell silent. I couldn't imagine what Rafi was dealing with. No one to support him, no job, no one he could rely on, and soon to be homeless, too. My gaze shifted to his eyes. They were a shade darker brown than his skin but with an outer rim that was almost golden, and framed by long, dark lashes. His dark brown hair looked recently clipped, but his face had the stubble of a week or more. I was struck again by how attractive he was. *Oh my God, Leah! This man just bared his soul and all you can think about are his eyes?* I thought, embarrassed by my lack of shame. In exasperation, I mirrored him, crossing my arms and slouching to the back of my chair. Rafi noticed and turned his attention to me again. I started to feel the crazy pull of his energy return. Then Dr. Anand saved me.

"I'm not sure how, but if we can be of service, please let me know." He handed Rafi a card with his contact information on it. "Also, the reason we are conducting this study is that we believe there are gifted people in the world who, for one reason or another, have denied their gifts. My theory is that this denial leads to disruption in health or behavioral decisions, sometimes leading people towards a lifestyle of crime. That's why we came to this correctional facility, because we assume a fair number of those in here, or in prisons everywhere, are here because they are denying their power." He had never explained this to the others, and I wondered where he was going. "Do you think you could have power that you have never explored?" he asked Rafi directly.

Rafi looked back and forth between us, furrowing his brow. "What do you mean by power?" he asked cautiously.

"Much like your ability to read people. Some call it intuition or a sixth sense. You most likely have other parts of this that have gone under-expressed because of your situation. Can you think of anything else you've just always felt you could do?" Dr. Anand asked.

Rafi turned to face me, deflecting the question. "Is that your deal? Do you have 'abilities'?" I felt heat and redness rising in my cheeks with his focused attention. "I started to read you, and there's something different in your energy, not in a bad way."

"I'm a healer," I declared and waited to gauge his reaction. He nodded slowly as if working through something in his head.

"A healer makes sense. Your energy feels positive. But you must be crazy strong. Are you like those people in revivals who place their hands on foreheads and push people to the ground, and when they get back up they can see even though they've been blind all their lives?"

I wrinkled my brow. Was he mocking me?

"Um…no. I'm pretty sure those people are scam artists," I answered, then guardedly continued. "I can sense what is wrong with a person, like when they're sick or hurt…and, well, it's kind of complicated." I stammered, aware that Dr. Anand was looking sideways at me. I hadn't told him everything about my gifts, I just figured it was better that way so I didn't feel weird while we worked together. Now it occurred to me that Dr. Anand might feel hurt that I didn't share with him what I was willing to blurt to a complete stranger in a correctional facility. The room was suddenly very hot, and I wanted the attention off of me. "Are we finished with the questions?" I asked Dr. Anand, rather aggressively.

Dr. Anand squinted at me, nodded and turned back to Rafi. "How do you read someone, Rafi? What do you have to do? Is it as easy as just looking at them?"

Rafi considered the question, and shook his head. "It's not quite that easy, but I've gotten really good at it by now that I can do it pretty quickly. It's not so easy to explain, to be honest. I have to be focused on the person, and I need to want to read them…does that make sense? It's the intention, I guess." Now, it was Rafi who was getting uneasy.

"And there's nothing else you've experienced that you can think to share with us?" Dr. Anand asked again.

Rafi shifted his gaze to his hands resting on the table. "I have had premonitions. Situations that I see in my mind that then happen in real life." He quickly added, "But it only happened a few times and not in years." He seemed suddenly agitated.

Dr. Anand sensed it, too, and smiled kindly. "We certainly appreciate you taking the time to meet with us today. I would say you are exactly the kind of person we were hoping to find with this study. I meant what I said about giving me a call if you think of a way I could be of service. And we wish you luck when you leave in two weeks."

We all stood and shook hands, and then Rafi was gone. I thought I'd be relieved, but I was suddenly, inexplicably sad. Like I'd just lost something vitally important. It was as confusing to feel this way as the wave of energy had been when Rafi first walked into the room. Worrying I might actually cry, I turned away and busied myself with unnecessary paper shuffling. *What the hell was wrong with me today?* I thought. Thankfully, I was distracted by the next interview beginning. Nothing else remarkable happened, and soon Dr. Anand and I were back in his car heading home. I had been pretty silent since Rafi's session, and it hadn't escaped Dr. Anand's attention.

"Do you want to talk about what happened during Rafi's interview?" he asked gently.

"What do you mean?" I tried to feign ignorance, but my heart started beating harder.

"I mean you had a reaction to him, and he had a reaction to you. You sensed each other's abilities. The tension in the air was thick enough to cut with a knife."

I had forgotten that Dr. Anand was sensitive to these things, too. Of course, he would have noticed the shifting between us.

"He was reading me, when he first walked into the room. I almost couldn't breathe for the power in his attention. It was really unsettling, actually." I frowned. If it was so unsettling, why have I felt like my best friend just died ever since he left? It didn't make any sense. I shook my head in an effort to clear it.

"How about your gifts?" he asked. "Have you ever tried to heal someone?" His question was innocent enough, and made sense considering I called myself a healer, but Mary Ann cautioned me about talking to people about what I've been able to do. I wasn't thinking straight enough to decide whether I could trust Dr. Anand yet.

"I'm really tired, I'm sorry. Can we talk about this another time?" I asked. He paused, still looking at the road, then nodded his head. We rode in uncomfortable silence back to the campus. "I'll get all the notes from today entered in tomorrow," I offered as he waved goodbye and drove off.

Solivagant:
A lonely wanderer.

CHAPTER 11

I couldn't get Rafi out of my head. Like an earworm song that drives you bonkers. To make matters worse, I had secretly copied his personal information from the study and obsessively read it. His full name was Rafi Wilson, and prior to being arrested, he lived in an apartment in a not-so-great part of town, about three blocks from the convenience store where he worked as a manager. I wasn't sure what good any of it would do me, since he mentioned he no longer had that apartment or that job. But I took it, nonetheless. I wanted him out of my head, but I wanted him in my presence again equally as much.

The worst part about it was that I couldn't stop imagining the bow of his lips and the way his eyes had flicked to mine. My body ached in a way that it never had before. It was truly awful. Especially because there was no way he was even thinking of me. I was being a first-rate fool, but that didn't stop him from occupying my thoughts day in and day out. A day after he was released, the date of which I knew because I'd copied his file, I was in a terrible state. At least in the correctional facility, I knew where to find him. Now, he was out in the world and it was very likely I'd never see him again.

I got on my bike just to ride around and clear my head, but I rode in a cloud. A car horn scared me out of my daze, and I stopped fast. With alarm, I realized I had ridden toward Rafi's old apartment address. Where I came to a stop was the last street before the neighborhood shifted from questionable to outright dangerous. I stood frozen on that corner, a war waging in my mind over what to do next.

What if I just rode around one time to see if I spied him on the street or something? It's probably not nearly as dangerous as people say it is; after all, Rafi had lived here, right? It's not like I'm walking, I have my bike to get away quickly. I'll just ride a few blocks and then return, no lingering. It will be fine, I convinced myself. I got back on my bike and shaken, crossed into Rafi's territory. It was still dusk, so darkness was at least a half-hour away, and I'd definitely be out by then. I rode past a liquor store and a boarded up house. Most of the small houses were in some state of disrepair, and the apartment buildings were cold brick and boxy. I didn't see many people, except a mom with her two kids walking down the sidewalk on the opposite side of the street. They didn't seem dangerous or in danger, just completely normal. I started to relax a little bit. *See? It was all just hyped up nonsense.*

I turned a corner and there was the convenience store where Rafi had worked. Peering quickly through the windows, I tried to see if by some chance he'd gotten his job back, but I didn't see him. I rode further along the sidewalk until I noticed a group of men ahead on the front stoop of a small brick house. There were about six of them smoking and drinking. I stopped abruptly and turned back the way I came, but not before one of them spied me.

He hopped down onto the sidewalk and yelled after my retreating form, "Hey baby! Why don't you ride on over here? We won't bite." Hearing them laugh, I pedaled even harder.

Now all I wanted was to get back to a familiar street. I had to stop for a red light, breathing hard from the effort of riding. I focused on the streetlight, willing it to turn so I could go. Just when I thought it would change, I was yanked backwards off my bike. Two arms snaked around me, one under my left arm and across my chest, the other across my neck and face, in front of my eyes so I couldn't see. Jerkily I was dragged back, my feet scraping the sidewalk, my bike left clattering to the ground.

I was whipped around and shoved to the ground. A man straddled my hips and tried grabbing my arms. It wasn't fully dark out yet, but I couldn't see well. We seemed to be under a tree or hedges. I began shouting, and he put his hand down over my mouth, hissing at me to shut up. His other hand kept trying to control my arms. I bit him, and he reared back and howled. Then he hit me hard in the face. I was jolted and immediately tasted the acid of blood. I was really in trouble. My mind froze in alarm, but my body realized it was time to fight. I pumped my hips up and drove my knee into his back to propel him forward. He lurched with the sudden hit from behind and ended up hovering over me with his hands out on the ground to catch himself. I grabbed him in a hug and held tightly so he couldn't hit me, threw my hips up again with all my effort and rolled us over so that I was now on top. I hit him once in the face before scrambling to my feet and kicking him hard in the groin. He doubled over with the pain from my kicks and I turned to get away.

I pushed through branches that scratched my arms and face. It was a group of tall bushes about ten feet back from the sidewalk. The guy must have just been waiting there. As I cleared the hedge, I stumbled and fell, tripping on a root or something. He grabbed at my ankle and tried pulling me back again. I kicked him off and got to my feet just as he did. Now we were face to face, and I didn't hesitate. I used the heel of my palm to hit his nose, then threw a rear elbow across his temple. Grabbing the back of his head, I shoved him down into my knee twice, pushed him off me, and kicked him hard in the head. He hit the ground moaning.

A split second later, I saw a second figure closing in on my right and I swerved around to strike. The figure stopped and jumped back.

"Whoa! Leah? Are you okay?" he said, narrowly avoiding my side kick. I stopped—did he just call me by my name? I shook myself and looked at him. I couldn't believe it, but Rafi was standing next to me.

"Rafi?" I said somewhat stunned. "Rafi?" I repeated.

"Yes, it's me—are you okay? Oh man, your face!" He moved in closer, reaching his hand toward my jaw, and I flinched. He quickly pulled his hand back. "I'm not going to hurt you." Just then, my attacker moved to get up and Rafi switched his attention to him.

"You like to hurt women, you piece of shit?" He was shouting as he dragged the man back into the bushes. I heard the sounds of Rafi beating him and I panicked and desperately needed to get away. I ran back to where my bike still lay on the pavement. Rafi came out as I was trying to pick it up.

"Come on, we need to get you out of here. You ride, I'll run alongside you, okay?" I tried to get on, but my body was shaking uncontrollably, and I couldn't seem to make it work. "You're in shock, Leah," Rafi said. "Is it okay if I help you? I'll need to pick you up, though, is that okay? I promise I won't hurt you, and if you need to get down, you just say so, okay? But I just want to get us out of here." He looked directly into my eyes to show me how serious he was, and I just nodded. He returned my nod. "Okay then. You sit on the bike and just hold on here, I'll steer the bike where you tell me to go, okay? Steady…"

I wrapped my shaky arms around his shoulders. He lifted me onto the bike like he might have a child and told me to hold on tightly. With a fair amount of wobbling, he started pushing us away from that horrible place. I pointed this way and that to tell him which directions to go. Twenty minutes later, after one almost terrible fall, we pulled the bike into my driveway. Rafi let me down and draped his arm around my shoulder while his other hand held my arm closest to him, as though he felt I might not make the walk up to my front door.

"Is anyone home?" he asked. There were lights on inside, and it had become dark while we were making our way back. I nodded, and Rafi rang the doorbell. I could hear

Mary Ann's footsteps as she approached, opened the door and gasped.

"Leah! Oh my God—what the hell happened?" she shrieked. "Come inside, let me look at you!" I had regained a little of my control and the shaking had subsided a bit, but the knocks and bruises from the ordeal were starting to make themselves known to me. My lip was swollen and split, and my cheek ached from where the attacker had hit me. Rafi sat me down at the kitchen island and Mary Ann frantically looked back and forth between us.

"If someone doesn't start talking, I might actually scream!" she pleaded. "Who are you? Who did this to her?" Rafi looked stunned, "She was attacked on the corner of Randolph Street. She was yanked off her bike. I didn't see everything."

Mary Ann turned to me, eyes wide. "What were you doing over there? My God, Leah. And on your bike?" Her eyes were wide with disbelief at my stupidity.

I nodded, and there was an ache in my head. "I was heading back home, just stopped for a second waiting for the light to change so I could cross." I winced as my lip moved while speaking. I would need to keep my lips more still. "I didn't even see the guy coming. He grabbed me off my bike from behind and dragged me backwards. It happened so fast." My breath caught. Mary Ann had a protective hand on my back, and I tried to focus on the solidity of it. I took a deep breath and tried to continue.

"I was yelling, I think. No, I know I was yelling. I was telling him to get off me, because in the bushes he was sitting on top of me trying to grab at my hands. I think he hit me in the mouth to shut me up." I was starting to shake again, and my face was wet with tears. I hadn't realized I'd started crying. Mary Ann moved to stroke the hair out of my face, then reached the tissue box across the island and handed me a tissue. It hurt to wipe my face.

"When he hit me, it stunned me enough to make me realize what was happening. That's when I started fighting harder. I almost got away once, but the bushes were in my way and I tripped, and he got my ankle." I put my hands over my eyes. "It's not all clear."

Rafi, who had been silent up until this moment, spoke up. "You have no idea how amazing she was. When I got there, she was basically beating the shit out of the guy." He shook his head back and forth. "How did you learn to do that?" he asked me.

Mary Ann turned to Rafi as though just remembering he was there. Before I could answer, Mary Ann interjected. "I'm sorry, but I still don't know who you are. You obviously helped Leah home, and for that I'm grateful, but how were you there?"

I answered for him. "This is Rafi, Mary Ann."

She turned to look sharply at me, "The man from the correctional facility?"

"He was the reason I went there," I said meekly. "I was looking for him. I didn't expect I'd actually find him, but I couldn't stop myself. Like I was compelled. My brain knew how reckless I was being, but my body didn't seem connected. I just found myself pedaling there." I looked up at Rafi, embarrassed by my admission. He was studying me intensely, but I didn't feel him trying to read me. Then it occurred to me that *he* found *me*.

"Wait. Rafi, what were you doing there? I had looked for you and didn't find you, then you appeared out of nowhere." The coincidence of it was startling. He shook his head in disbelief.

"I had to go. I only got out a couple days ago, did you know that?" I nodded. "I didn't want to go back there at all. I called about my job yesterday and my boss basically called me an imbecile, in not so nice words, and hung up on me. I had just been wandering around, trying to figure out what to do. Feeling helpless. Feeling sorry for myself, embarrassed and angry. Then I put my hand in my pocket and found Dr. Anand's card. I hadn't even remembered putting it there." He ran his hand through his hair and looked at the ground. "I called him. I begged him for a job. Anything, cleaning toilets, sweeping sidewalks, anything he thought he could help me with. I felt so desperate that I had no pride left." Rafi's voice broke with emotion. "He said he'd been waiting for my call. That he had already arranged with the university for me to be part of his staff. An administrative/research assistant, and if I wanted the job, it was mine. I won't lie that I sat down on the ground and cried. I couldn't believe anyone could do something like that for someone like me. Let alone a stranger." He blinked hard and cleared his throat, trying not to cry again.

"He told me I'd be helping you with the study," Rafi told me cautiously. "I wasn't sure how you'd feel about that. The session we had…I… I didn't handle it well. Like I made a bad impression and creeped you out. That was in my head while walking around. Next time I looked up, I was back at the convenience store. I didn't try to go there, but my body brought me unconsciously. It was a very strange experience. One of the guys I used to work with saw me and waved me in to say hi." He looked up at me. "Not five minutes later I saw you, Leah. Through the window, you went screaming by on your bike. I thought my eyes must be playing tricks on me, that it couldn't possibly have been you. But I ran after you anyway. I saw your bike just lying there on the corner and I freaked out. Then I saw you stumble from the bushes and beat that guy."

Rafi was going to work for Dr. Anand, too? I would see him every week? Could I handle that? I ran my hand through my hair and caught on a scab.

"Ow!" I exclaimed, pulling a thorn out of my hair.

"Let me see," said Mary Ann, moving me slightly into the light. "Christ, Leah, your head is all cut up!"

"It must have been when he was on top of me, there was gravel, roots and stuff." I winced as I brought my hand up to feel what she saw.

"I'm calling the police, and we're going to the hospital."

"No!" I was surprised by my reaction. "We don't need the police or the hospital—I don't want to explain this again. And I know I'm not seriously hurt anywhere—it's just surface wounds. They wouldn't be able to do anything for me at the hospital."

"Leah, you were attacked! We can't just let him go!" she replied.

"Yes, we can. Rafi beat him again, then we took off. I don't know what kind of shape we left him in, and I don't want Rafi to get in trouble if we really hurt him. Trust me, he got what he deserved! If I feel something is really wrong tomorrow, we can go to the hospital then, okay?"

Mary Ann frowned and tugged on her lip, weighing the choices. She looked uncertainly at me, then gave the slightest of nods.

"We need to get you cleaned up. Maybe a bath will be gentler than a shower." She stood and started to help me up. Rafi stood, too, and Mary Ann jumped again, clearly nervous. Rafi noticed her reaction.

"I should probably go, then. If you think you're okay, Leah." He hesitated and then looked to Mary Ann. "Unless there's anything I can help you with."

"No. Thank you, but I think I can handle it now. Thank you so much for bringing Leah home." He nodded, looking so sad about leaving that Mary Ann added, "Maybe you could come back in a couple days and check on her?"

At that, he brightened a little and nodded. "Okay then. I'll see you in a couple days, Leah. Get some rest." He turned to walk toward the door, then paused and looked back at me. "You are tough as hell." Then he walked out the door.

Everything hurt. The bath water was a mixture of dirt and blood so that we had to change it three times to get it clear. A shower would have made more sense, but I couldn't handle the pressure of the water on my head. Mary Ann confirmed that none of the cuts seemed big enough to need stitches, but she wanted to make really sure everything was clean and didn't get infected. I had bruises all over my body, most I didn't remember getting. I imagined a lot were just from the drag from the bike and the fight on the ground. Halfway through the second filling of the tub, Mary Ann started asking about Rafi.

"Why were you looking for him? He just got out of prison," she said quietly, with emphasis on the word "prison."

I groaned. "I don't know. I lost my mind or something. I know how stupid it was. I don't know what the hell I was thinking! It's my fault this happened." I was sobbing now and shaking all over.

"No, Leah. Look at me," she demanded. "It is *not* your fault this happened. This man—this complete asshole—chose to hurt someone. He decided to attack you. It had nothing to do with you. That man is one hundred percent to blame. And I have never truly desired to murder someone before this moment." Her eyes were steel. She pushed me back and held me at arm's length to look in my eyes. "You saved yourself, Leah. You fought, and you got away. I'm so damn proud of you, my sweet girl. You are *fierce*, and you saved yourself." She paused. "Just don't ever do something so foolish again!"

I started slowly. "I know you're worried about Rafi. But there's something different about him, some connection between us. And he did help me tonight."

"He was in prison, Leah. What do you really know about him?" I looked at her, exhausted, and she sighed. "Let's talk about this another time. You need to try to sleep. Let me get you some Advil, okay?"

I nodded, grateful not to have to argue. I was so tired, emotionally and physically, that it was hard to even walk to my room. Mary Ann returned with a glass of water, and sat at the edge of my bed. Most of my wounds were bruises and small little cuts and didn't require visiting a doctor. My face was the worst, but even that was just a bad bruise on my cheek and a fat lip.

"Do you think you could try to heal yourself?" she asked.

I nodded and lay in the bed. Closing my eyes, I called up the ribbons and recited the dedication. I hadn't tried to heal anyone in months, and it felt a little awkward and still somewhat shocking to bring the ribbons out. I took one around my finger and brought it to my lip. Immediately, I could feel tingling in my cut. I grabbed another ribbon and placed it on my cheek, then repeated the process everywhere I felt pain. Once finished, I said thank you, moving my mouth without pain and sighing with relief. Mary Ann came closer to inspect me more carefully.

"How do you feel now? Any pain?" she asked.

Only a small scar of healing flesh remained just below my bottom lip, and my cheek was a faint yellow. "Just a little achy," I murmured.

"It's remarkable," she exclaimed, gently running her hand over the back of my head where there were so many little cuts just minutes ago. Then she hugged me hard. "You are amazing, Leah. But just take it easy on yourself, okay? Just because the visible scars are gone, it may take a while for the emotional strain of what happened to go away."

She wasn't wrong. Despite my fatigue, sleep did not come easily. I kept remembering bits from the evening and living the terror and anger all over again. When I finally did drift off, I woke in a panic, feeling as though someone was on top of me. I yelled out. Mary Ann heard and decided that she was setting up camp in my room for the night. She brought a bunch of blankets and set up a nest on the floor next to my bed. With her there, I could actually sleep. The next day I didn't leave the house and took up residence in front of the television instead.

Mary Ann and I had gotten into a little tiff that night about Rafi. She brought up her concerns—namely, what would make me lose good judgment and go into a dangerous area by myself on the off chance that this man I met in prison might be wandering around too? When she put it that way, it sounded awful. I tried to explain how I had thought of almost nothing but him in the weeks since our short thirty minutes together. And that our connection made me act without really understanding what I was doing. Of course, that just made me sound like a lovesick teenager. Frankly, that's how I was feeling. More so than with any other boy before. Trying to sound more reasonable, I brought up the point that even Dr. Anand trusted Rafi enough to hire him to work with us after only a thirty-minute session, and didn't she trust Dr. Anand's judgment?

To that, she'd declared she was starting not to. In the end, she was willing to trust my intuition to a point with this relationship, but I should be understanding that she may not be happy about it all. I went to bed feeling somewhat relieved, but also saddened. Mary Ann and I almost never fought or even disagreed, really, and being in discord with her didn't sit easily with me.

It was late the next morning when the doorbell rang, and I felt a jolt of electricity run up my spine. Rafi. My heart leaped out of my chest at the thought of seeing him again. I was moving much more quickly today and got to the door before Mary Ann. I pulled it open and he was standing there. *My God, you are a total lovesick teenager*, I thought in dismay as the sight of him made my stomach flutter.

He took one look at my healed face and said, "What the hell? Two days ago you looked swollen, cut and bruised, and now I hardly see a scratch. Am I remembering it wrong?" He looked at me completely confused.

"No. I was pretty beat up," I said slowly. "Remember in the interview session when I told you I'm a healer?" I raised my eyebrows at him, waiting to gauge his response to that.

He nodded. "I do. I spent a lot of time thinking about what that meant for you, actually. You did this to yourself? Your powers are that strong?" His voice rose with the thought of it, and he looked at me wide-eyed. I nodded and he just shook his head. "That's unbelievable. No wonder when I read you it was like nothing I'd ever felt before."

"Do you want to come in?" I asked him, stepping a little aside and opening the door more fully. Rafi walked in and greeted Mary Ann, who had entered the kitchen.

"She looks quite a bit better, don't you think?" Mary Ann asked. Then she turned to me and whispered, "Does Rafi know?"

"Only a little. I think this…" I pointed to my healed face, "…might have been a bit of a shock."

Mary Ann nodded at Rafi. "Why don't I put on some tea and Leah can tell you about it?"

For the next couple hours, the three of us sat around the kitchen island. Mary Ann wasn't about to leave us alone, though I could sense her softening a bit toward Rafi as we talked. A lot was just filling him in on everything about my gifts. I was usually cautious sharing details of my experiences. Even Dr. Anand only knew the bare minimum of what had occurred. But with Rafi, I found myself spilling it all. It was like once the floodgates were open, I couldn't stop the flow of words from gushing forth. And he was absorbing it all like a sponge, asking smart questions and making comments about what I might have been feeling that were spot on. By the time we'd had way too much tea and eaten all the banana bread Mary Ann had made the day before, it felt like we'd gotten everything out. Rafi sat back in his stool and sighed.

"This was an enlightening morning, no doubt," he said. "I feel like I know almost nothing about pretty much everything in this world."

Mary Ann and I shared a look of understanding. Then she turned her attention to Rafi. "Please don't tell anyone what we talked about. I don't want Leah to be hounded about it, as I'm sure you understand."

I sighed in exasperation. "I want to be able to heal people, Mary Ann."

"You're not ready, Leah." It was an argument we'd had a couple times since Sedona. "You have no idea how people will react."

Changing the subject, she turned back to Rafi, "So are you starting with Dr. Anand tomorrow?" That was when I was due back to my research work, too.

"Yes. I'm a little nervous about what he wants me to do. I mean, working on a college research project is a far cry from managing a convenience store. I can't exactly afford to mess it up." His face clouded over with worry.

"Don't worry," I told him. "Dr. Anand walked me through everything he wanted me to do and was super patient if he needed to explain or if I did something wrong. If he didn't think you'd be good enough, he wouldn't have offered."

"But I think he was just trying to help me out, you know? Feeling sorry for me or something."

I looked at this man, so used to getting the shit end of things that he couldn't see he might actually have something to offer. "Rafi, do you know how many inmates we met with? Over a hundred. The majority of them seemed like decent people who fell on hard times and could use some help. Dr. Anand did not offer any of them jobs. You are not a charity case. Dr. Anand would only make this happen if he thought it was best for his project. If you got helped along the way then all the better." I finished, looking right into his eyes. He held my gaze for a long while and gave a small nod. Suddenly, I felt that whoosh of energy coming from him that nearly knocked me over the first time in the correctional facility. I felt a little dizzy and out of control. "Are you reading me again?" I asked him, putting my hands to my temples. "God it's so strong, I can hardly breathe when you do that!"

Rafi's eyes widened. "You feel it that much? Most people either don't feel anything or it's just a bit. I'm sorry…I couldn't help it. I was just trying to see if you were being real with me. It's that strong?" He furrowed his brow as I squeezed my eyes together, trying to concentrate. I felt the energy dissipate and opened my eyes to look at him.

"Did you get your reading?" I asked. He smiled and his eyes crinkled up in the corners so beautifully.

"Yes, I did," he replied. I was suddenly feeling anxious as a thought occurred to me.

"Um, you can't tell what a person is thinking while 'reading' them, can you?" I asked timidly.

He laughed. "If I could do that, then I'd be a billionaire and not a homeless ex-con! No, I can tell moods though. And real versus fake emotion." I let out a breath.

Mary Ann, always paying attention, didn't let Rafi's off-hand comment pass. "You're homeless, Rafi?"

Rafi's expression became guarded as he realized he'd let that slip. "Oh, no big thing. Just temporary," he said brusquely, showing that he didn't want to talk about it. But Mary Ann didn't let it drop.

"So where have you been sleeping this last week?" She kept her voice completely neutral, so she neither conveyed pity nor disdain.

"Umm, some nights I find a friend's couch. There's a shelter not far from where I used to live." He mumbled into the table, not meeting our eyes. He slid his stool back and stood. "I should probably be going, I've taken up enough of your time. But I'll see you tomorrow, Leah? Thank you very much for having me over—" he said to Mary Ann, finally meeting her gaze.

She smiled. "I know you don't know me very well, but I'm an artist by profession." Rafi nodded, unsure where she was going with this. "I recently rented a studio for painting a few blocks away. It's a small room with a couch, kitchenette, and bathroom. I only paint in natural light and so once the day is done, I'm done, and the studio sits empty. I would like to offer you to stay there for the time being until you are able to get things sorted out. You could pay half the water and electricity once Dr. Anand starts paying you. What do you think?" I stared at her agape. Mary Ann is and has always been a generous and loving soul, but this was such a turnabout from our discussion the night before and the "but you barely know him and met him in a prison!" argument.

Rafi looked back and forth between us, unsure how to respond. "That's very kind of you, Mary Ann, but I can look after myself. I would never dream of imposing on you like that," he stuttered.

Mary Ann held up a hand to stop him. "Rafi. Much like Dr. Anand, I'm no fool, and, like you, I have an ability to read people, albeit in a much more subtle, intuitive way." She dropped her hand. "I'm not offering this out of pity or guilt that I have a house and you do not. It is simply a way to help a friend. It will cost me nothing and might make it easier for you to focus on work instead of worrying where you will sleep in the evenings." She moved over to the junk drawer and rooted around, then held up a spare key with a keychain of a blue heron on it. "I even have a spare key and can walk you over there now if you're free." She raised her eyebrows expectantly at him.

Rafi seemed so moved by the gesture he could only nod and say a quiet "Thank you."

Mary Ann nodded back and said to just let her grab her coat. While she was gone, Rafi stood staring at the floor in front of him. Then he nearly whispered, "I'm not sure what to do with all this kindness." I had an impulse and walked over to take his hand. He started and looked up at me.

"I've learned this last year that kindness is actually the most important thing and accepting it from someone is a gift for you both. Thank you for coming after me, Rafi." I reached up and kissed his cheek, heat immediately rising to my face. I pulled away again, just as Mary Ann came back in the room.

"Shall we go? Leah, I'll be back in a minute." She winked at me, and out the door they went.

Turtledove:
Expression of endearment for a sweetheart.

CHAPTER 12

Since Dr. Anand and I had finished all the interviews at the correctional facility by the time Rafi came on board, the three of us were mostly confined to his office and the big walnut desk. All the information we'd compiled over months needed to be cross-referenced for similarities and documented in a way that would present well in a research paper. In the end, out of one hundred twenty-one inmates that showed promise from the initial questionnaire, we found forty-eight who tested positive for some level of gifted or intuitive ability. This made Dr. Anand very happy as it was a high enough number to make his experiment a viable one. Rafi quickly got into the groove of the project, and to my surprise, he had a wicked dry sense of humor that kept us in stitches all day.

We were nearing the November 15 deadline for submission of the project and paper, and we were right on target. The weather turned, and a late fall rainstorm stripped the leaves from the campus trees overnight. The last week before the deadline, Rafi seemed preoccupied and heavier in spirit. It was impossible for us not to notice, but he was enough in his own world not to be aware of the change it made in the office atmosphere. When I asked if everything was okay, he just brushed me off, saying nothing was wrong.

He and I had gotten closer over the last month or so, but I didn't try to hold his hand or kiss him again, and he didn't bring it up. There was a tension between us…or at least I felt it. I just had no idea how to address it. Like I said, I had zero dating experience. I confided in Mary Ann about it though. Or rather, she noticed and asked me point blank if I had feelings for him. It would be dishonest to say that Rafi wasn't on my mind most hours of most days. I couldn't seem to get him out of there. At the end of the week, Dr. Anand took us out to dinner to celebrate a job well done. Rafi sat mute, pushing his food around his plate. He was being a total drag when we should have been congratulating ourselves. I caught Dr. Anand's eye and he gave me a half smile and winked.

"Leah, I know you have your studies to finish up, and the semester ends in a month. Have you decided to stay on for the remainder of the year?" he asked. In truth, I hadn't decided anything. I knew I had to register for next semester's classes—and pay tuition—before the Thanksgiving break next week, but I was procrastinating. While I enjoyed my anthropology classes, I wasn't passionate about them.

"I'm actually not sure yet, Dr. Anand," I replied. "I think the best thing about me being in this college was the research project and working with you and Rafi. I'm not sure I'll enjoy my time here without those components, you know?"

Dr. Anand nodded. "I thought that might be the case. So I have a proposal to make to you—and Rafi." He inclined his head in Rafi's direction, and Rafi looked up in response to his name. "I have been thinking about your gifts in particular, Leah. And forgive me if this is forward, but it's time to start using them. You've healed yourself twice now. Don't you want to see if you can help others?"

"You mean, like, heal other people? Yes! I have wanted to do that for a long time. But what will happen if people find out what I can do? Mary Ann is reluctant for me to expose myself like that," I answered.

He nodded in understanding. "I would want to converse with your aunt, of course. But I wish to gauge your interest first. I have a sabbatical coming up after this semester. I want to use it to study your gifts in action and write about them. As scientifically as possible, of course. My former colleague works at a small liberal arts college in New York State. He has a studio he rents out not far from the campus, and it is currently available. I'm proposing that we go there for a few weeks or month next semester. We can spread the word that there is a healer in town for a short time and get you practice using your gifts. What do you think?"

The idea equally excited me and filled me with dread. "I would need to talk with Mary Ann about it."

"Of course, of course." Dr. Anand replied. "But does the idea interest you at all? That's what I want you and Rafi to consider." At this, Rafi came back to attention.

"Me?" Rafi asked.

"Yes, Rafi. You have proved to be invaluable as an assistant this past month. If it interests you, I would like you to continue as my assistant for this next—shall we call it an adventure?" His eyes twinkled. "Of course, you'd both need to be willing to live in upstate New York during the winter months, but frankly, it's not much different than living here as far as cold and snow are concerned. And, as you know by now, the pay for a research assistant is dismal." He grinned. "But I could provide the housing and it should be enough to get us along just fine. Assuming it interests you, Leah. Do talk it over with Mary Ann, but I would need to firm up the details before the semester's end." He finished just as the food arrived. I felt energy flow over me and turned to find Rafi studying me. I smiled knowingly at his attempt to subtly read my energy, and he shyly grinned back and looked down at his food, knowing he was caught.

Not long after, Dr. Anand excused himself to use the washroom, and Rafi and I found ourselves alone at the table. It occurred to me that we had almost never been alone since we first met. "You know, you can just ask me what I think. You don't have to try to read me," I said in a teasing tone. Rafi's mouth turned up in an embarrassed grin.

"Sorry. I didn't want to ask you right then, but I didn't want to wait either. It's tough with you being so sensitive to it. I was just trying to feel if you were excited or not. So…what do you think?"

"To be honest, I'm as much excited as I am terrified by the idea. It feels like a big responsibility, but I'm desperate to start helping people. I feel pulled to it in a big way, and that is overriding the fear of being seen and judged. I do want to get Mary Ann's opinion, though. Before I make any final decisions. What about you? Do you like the idea?"

"Hell, yes," Rafi said. "I like working with Dr. Anand a lot. And, to be honest, I've been freaking out about this project ending."

"That was kinda obvious," I joked. "You haven't been yourself all week."

"That's fair, I haven't been sleeping much. I don't exactly have a lot of options other than Dr. Anand at this point. But above that, I love the work. The idea of going back to a mindless job has been making me sick to my stomach, now that I know what it means to use your brain for work." He quickly added, "But don't factor that into your decision! I have a fire in me now that will keep me on the right track, even if this isn't the right opportunity." I felt like he finished the last statement in a more formal tone. I didn't like it.

"Rafi, can we agree we're friends now? I mean, you don't have to watch your words with me. And I don't want to watch my words with you. Can we agree to that?"

He nodded and gave me a thoughtful look. "Okay, you're right, Leah. I didn't want to read into our friendship because we were kind of thrown together. Glad we're straight now—no watching words."

He held out his hand and I shook it, sealing our agreement. The touch of his skin on my hand sent goosebumps up my back, and I let go. Thankfully, Dr. Anand returned at that moment, and we finished our dinner much more relaxed.

The following Thursday was Thanksgiving. Mary Ann had invited Dr. Anand and Rafi to join us, as they didn't have any family to celebrate with. Isaac and Alex were home for break, but busy with their own families' dinners. I planned to meet them at Isaac's house the next day. Dr. Anand and I decided we'd bring up the proposed project, now playfully dubbed the "White Ribbon" project, while everyone was seated around the table with full bellies, and Mary Ann had had a couple glasses of wine. She had a fair amount of questions, and trepidation, but in the end reluctantly agreed it was time for me to at least try. And if I could do it with all this support in a different place where no one knew me, maybe it was the best way to get my feet wet. She thought it best that she come along as well, and I didn't argue. Frankly, knowing she'd be there made me feel less nervous about taking such a big step. Her other idea that I should try and stay as anonymous as possible by hiding my face when I healed people was less appealing. I wondered aloud how I would pull that off, but she just said we'd figure something out. I decided to let that one go for the time being.

"Where exactly is this town?" Mary Ann asked Dr. Anand.

"It's about two hours north of New York City, called Saratoga Springs. My colleague is a professor at a college there called Skidmore."

I sat upright in my chair. "That's where Isaac goes to college!" I practically shouted. "You didn't tell me we would be in Isaac's town!"

"My dear," Dr. Anand replied. "Who is Isaac?"

"Isaac is only my best friend and my favorite person in the whole world! I can't believe we're going to be near him!" I gushed. Rafi made a face and looked down at his plate.

"Wonderful!" exclaimed Dr. Anand. "We must recruit him for our team, then." Now Rafi looked a little ill and slumped back in his chair. When Dr. Anand looked his way, he gave a half-hearted smile. By the end of the evening, we had settled it. I was finally going to be a healer, and I wasn't alone, just like Carlos had said.

The next afternoon, I met Alex and Isaac at Isaac's house. Though we kept in touch with calls and texts, it was not the same thing as being together, and I had missed my friends desperately. I told them about Rafi's behavior at Thanksgiving dinner, and how we'd agreed just last week that we were friends. Isaac rolled his eyes at me and moaned.

"Friends? Really? Jesus Christ, Leah, be real. You are so freaking in love with him you've become boring!"

Alex agreed, "It's been all 'Rafi this' and 'Rafi that.' Get over yourself—you are in deep."

I covered my face with my hands and whined. "I know! But what the hell do I do about it? I'm even sick of myself, but I can't think of anything else! I don't know if he even likes me back!"

Alex and Isaac laughed at me. "Are you serious?" Isaac said. "Open your eyes! You mention your favorite person in the world—thanks for that by the way—is a guy and you're super excited to have him join you on this new project that was supposed to be just you and Rafi? He was jealous as hell!"

The next couple weeks felt like torture. Since our current project was finished, I had no good reason to go to Dr. Anand's office. Rafi kept on to help with some administrative tasks, so I still got to see him when I popped in on my class days, but we were never alone. Once I stopped in to find Rafi wasn't in the office at all, and I thought I might actually cry. This was getting ridiculous. I just had to make it until the second Saturday in December when exams would be finished, and Dr. Anand's department was having its holiday party. The time dragged on painfully slowly.

The evening of the party, I had Alex, newly returned home for winter break, over to help me get ready. I agonized over what to wear, so she brought some options from her closet too. Finally, I settled on a wine red, spaghetti-strap, knee-length dress that Alex had brought. With a pair of black boots and my hair done, I stood in front of the mirror to assess our efforts.

"You look so beautiful!" Alex cooed. I always figured I was pretty enough, but not anything exceptional. Looking at myself all dressed up like this, though, I really did feel beautiful. I smiled. It was a good feeling and gave me a boost of confidence for what I had planned.

The party was held in the department chair's offices, a group of four rooms joined with a small hallway and foyer that held a seating area and a reception desk. Most of the rooms were personal offices of professors in the department, as well as one conference room for meetings. This was where the food and drink, and by default, most of the attendees, had gathered. I was meeting Dr. Anand and Rafi there, and by the time Alex and I finished getting me ready and I had driven over, I was almost an hour late. The foyer was filled with faces I had never seen before and a few I had passed in the halls. People nodded hello and made room for me to pass through. Christmas carols played on a speaker somewhere. I passed the first two rooms on the left, craning my neck to see around bodies if my friends were there, but they weren't. Not in the conference room either. The department chair's office was the last one down the hall, and I took a deep breath as I approached. I stood in the doorway and looked around. It wasn't a big room, but there was a fair amount of people in it. Finally, my eyes landed on the figures of Rafi and Dr. Anand speaking with another man off to the right. Rafi dressed up for the evening and was wearing a suit jacket over a button down and dark jeans. My heart did flip-flops looking at him. Just then, he turned in my direction and caught my eye. I could tell he was affected by how I looked too, as he opened his mouth in surprise when he saw me. I smiled and held his gaze as I walked over to join them, feeling dizzy with his attention.

Dr. Anand turned to welcome me in a warm embrace, "Leah! You are a vision!" he exclaimed, then introduced me to their companion and invited me to join the discussion. Rafi kept stealing sideways glances at me and nervously shifting his stance. I had never seen him this uncomfortable. A little while later in the evening, I told Rafi I needed some air and asked him to join me. I believe I saw Dr. Anand give a knowing grin just before we turned to walk out, but I didn't turn around to confirm it. The offices were so hot due to the number of bodies crammed into the small, unaired space, and the cold December air felt good for a moment on my skin. Then I shivered and Rafi took off his coat to place over my shoulders.

"Won't you be cold?"

"Yes," he laughed in response.

I turned to him, my heart feeling like it might explode for how fast it was beating. "Rafi. I like you." I looked him in the eye so he wouldn't doubt I was serious, but he didn't respond right away. "I like you more than a friend. I have from the beginning. I think you like me too, and I'm tired of guessing. Do you want to be with me?"

Rafi exhaled. "Hell yes, Leah. Desperately." He leaned down and threaded his hands through my hair and brought his lips to mine with a hunger that sent shockwaves through my body.

Alpas:
(Tagalog) To get out and be free, to break loose as from confinement.

CHAPTER 13

The snow was coming down in big, puffy white flakes when we pulled into the driveway of the cute stucco carriage house that served as our temporary home. Stepping out of Dr. Anand's car, I took a good look around. Even in the dead of winter, Saratoga Springs was a beautiful and charming place. The carriage house was positioned behind a grandiose mansion on a lane about a quarter-mile from the campus of Skidmore College, where Isaac attended. Trees lined the opposite side of the lane, and the bare, sleeping, winter branches were heavy with white. We'd arrived only three days ago, and I already loved it here. The carriage house had three bedrooms, and Mary Ann, Rafi and I each claimed one. Dr. Anand chose to stay in the spare bedroom of his friend and colleague. I think the idea of running the project, being with us twenty-four/seven, and never having a space to be alone was overwhelming. Our rental had a small kitchen with all the amenities, two full bathrooms, and so many windows it felt the house was an extension of the outside. There was even a spacious yard, though it was currently a thick carpet of white.

There was some discussion over where Rafi should sleep, considering the new status of our relationship. The truth was, Mary Ann had come to love Rafi over the last several months, but he was my first boyfriend, and she was on unsure footing with how to handle it. Though I was an adult, she was still my guardian and worried I'd fallen too hard, too fast. We agreed that everyone should have their own space in the house for sanity's sake, but she would also try to give us time to be alone together.

The studio we were to use as our "treatment" space was a few miles away, near a horse polo field, and set apart from other homes. Privacy was important, and there was a long driveway shaded by trees on either side leading up to the house. It was a small open living space with a bathroom and kitchenette, almost like a fishing cabin you'd find on a lake, though there were only fields and groves of trees surrounding it. We checked it out yesterday, brainstorming how to create a separate waiting area and treatment space. We wanted to provide people with some privacy from others waiting their turn. In the end, we engineered a series of sliding curtains we could jerry rig from the ceiling. They'd be positioned to create a 'walkway' from front door to back door, so those who wanted to remain private had the best chance and didn't have to pass back through the waiting area to return to their cars.

There was no rest for us, as Dr. Anand already set an opening date for the following Monday, eight days away. To say I was anxious was an understatement. Mary Ann reiterated her suggestion that I should try to keep my identity hidden so I could walk in the town without being recognized. Reluctantly, I agreed but threw a little fit when Dr. Anand presented me with my "costume." It was basically a tent of white polyester fabric and putting it on felt immediately claustrophobic. I made it clear in no uncertain terms that there was no way I was spending day in and day out in that getup. He was taken aback by my outburst, but Rafi had to put the back of his fist against his mouth to hide his laughter. He later told me it was "cute" to see me freak out like that, and I stormed into my room and slammed the door, indignant. I apologized to Dr. Anand later that evening, but stuck to my guns about the outfit. Mary Ann and I went shopping to find something I could live with. In the meantime, Dr. Anand, through his colleague, had placed some anonymous advertisements in the local papers, and pinned up photocopied announcements in coffee shops and the community center bulletin boards. The announcement read:

The Healer

No matter what ails you, the healer uses ancient wisdom and descended gifts to make you well again. No gimmicks or false promises, just the healing power of the ancestors.

To schedule a visit with the Healer, please leave a message at the following number and you will be contacted with a time and location. Your session will last no more than 15–20 minutes and you will meet with the Healer directly. You may bring a friend or family member if you prefer.

A number to a temporary cellphone Dr. Anand purchased for the purpose of the project was listed underneath. So far no one had called the listed number. Frankly, I didn't think I would trust an advert like that to be safe, either. Rafi suggested we put the notice up in retirement homes, because, of course, there is enough suffering to be found among the residents there. I worried they'd have *too* many ailments for me to heal in one session. The rest of the week, our days were spent getting the little studio set up. We added plants and some lighting to make it a more inviting experience. Our plan was to be there for the few weeks, and I hoped we'd have enough interest not to be bored to death. Mary Ann and I found a multi-hued blue headscarf to wrap around my hair and face for privacy. It felt so much more like me and was super comfortable. Mary Ann didn't want me to speak at all during sessions. She wanted nothing that would help people identify me outside the studio, but I doubted that would be an issue, and it would keep me from fully connecting with people. The closer we got to opening our doors, the more apprchensive Mary Ann was becoming, and her nervousness was creeping under my skin. I realized that if I was out and about in town, then one of them would most likely be with me. Couldn't I be recognized through them? We agreed to all wear scarves over our faces and hoped it wouldn't scare everyone off the moment we opened the door. This was an experiment, after all, and we had no idea what to expect from our participants.

I started calling them participants as I didn't feel I had earned the right to call them patients. Dr. Anand had a difficult time with this and kept messing it up, then getting frustrated with me about it. Like the costume, however, I stuck to my guns. They were participating in their own healing after all, and I wanted to separate myself from the doctors and specialists they had visited over weeks and months and years of their disease. The people with actual educations trying hard to work within the normal order of nature, not cheaters like me born with gifts that I often didn't feel like I had earned.

Two days before our start day, two people left voicemails for Dr. Anand: One was a gentleman living in a retirement home who had late stage emphysema, and the other was a woman in her mid-forties who had been living a couple years with ovarian cancer, but the treatments were starting to fail. Dr. Anand played the voicemails on speaker so we could all hear. There was skepticism mixed with desperation in their voices, and my heart ached to help them. Rafi called them back to schedule, and we had our first two participants. One more call on Sunday gave us three people for day one, and at 9 a.m. Monday morning we were dressed and ready to receive. When no one pulled into the drive at 9 a.m. sharp, my mind started betraying me with doubts. Why did I think anyone would trust me? What if Sedona was a fluke, and healing myself was a fluke, and someone comes in with too many ailments and I don't help them and I'm labeled a charlatan? I voiced a few of these worries to Rafi, who listened calmly and then came over to the table where I sat waiting for my first participant.

He took my hands in his own and looked me in the eyes, smiling softly, and said, "Get over yourself, Leah."

"Wait. What?" I asked, surprised by his unsympathetic words.

"Look. You have gifts. You've used these gifts, and you know they help people. You have friends and family supporting you. You're not chained to a post or imprisoned with no choices. You're a free person with a gift to share. It's up to you whether you approach this one life you have with fear and small-mindedness, or if you decide to embrace it fully and make it incredible. People with far less than you have made the decision not to waste their time on useless self-doubt and anguish, and they are living a life that is *worth* living. You have no excuse not to do the same. But it is entirely up to you. You can feel scared and you can feel unprepared. But how you respond in your life to those feelings will be what sets you apart from those who live a half-assed life and whine about it, and those who fall, dust themselves off, and believe the amazing and unseen possibilities for positive change that they still can't see." He paused and kissed both my hands. "If people come or not, if you heal them or not, if you are labeled a fraud or not—you have a choice in how to handle it and keep living your life. What do you choose?" His words were direct and impactful—and oddly inspiring. I took a deep breath and nodded just as the front door opened.

Our first appointment was the elderly man with emphysema and his son. The son was clearly leading the charge from the moment they got in the door. He stood with his hands across his chest, eyeballing our covered faces with suspicion and his brawny arms looked ready to sock anyone he deemed deserved socking. It was not a very comfortable feeling.

"What the hell is this?" he demanded. "You can't show your faces? I knew this was a scam. Dad, we can't trust these people. I told you. Let's go." His father had just painstakingly managed to sit in one of the waiting room chairs when his son grabbed his arm to try to lift him up again, his portable oxygen tank nearly falling over in the process. Dr. Anand rushed over and placed a hand on the son's arm. The son flinched and I worried he might strike out. But he simply stood to his full height, about five inches above Dr. Anand.

"Don't touch me!" he scowled. Dr. Anand took a step back as Rafi came to stand beside him. Then Dr. Anand unwrapped his head scarf, putting it aside.

"Here. You may see my face. I understand that it's disconcerting to have us covered up. But please try to understand why we chose to do it. It is of utmost importance to keep our healer anonymous, for her own safety, so we thought we, those who would be with her out and about, should also remain anonymous for her protection. I can see now that it made for an awkward start to this meeting, and I apologize. My name is Dr. Anand, and I am a helper for the healer." He held out his hand to the son. After a few moments of pause, the son shook his hand and introduced himself, the scowl remaining on his face.

"I'm Ike and this is my father Benjamin." Dr. Anand leaned down to shake the seated man's hand. "Dad here saw your flyer on the community board in his retirement home. I don't believe in hokey voodoo crap healing, but he demanded we come." It was hard to imagine anyone demanding anything of this imposing man. "I mean, he's got end-stage emphysema and has had the best medical care money can buy. What the hell do you propose to do for him? Sell him some herbs? Coat him with healing oils and give him false hope? I think it's despicable," he snarled.

Dr. Anand kept his composure. "I understand your feelings, I do. First of all, let me say there is no cost for you or your father for being here. The healer is new to her craft, and we are testing the waters, so to speak. This is our first time offering help to the public. We are selling nothing and ask nothing of you, except perhaps an open mind." He opened his hands out to his sides and smiled humbly while he spoke. "The healer has been given a gift, one that a simple man like me doesn't fully understand. She only wishes to offer this to others who suffer and wasn't sure how to go about it. This setup is our first attempt at trying it out. And we absolutely appreciate your willingness to at least give us a chance." This last bit he directed at the father, who had thus far not uttered a word. But now he nodded and responded, directing his words to his son.

"I have nothing to lose, Ike, nothing but thirty minutes of a day I would otherwise spend sitting uncomfortably watching stupid TV, in an uninspiring room with other people living uninspiring lives. I'm living my life like I'm waiting to die. Why wouldn't I try something that doesn't seem to have any downside except maybe it doesn't work, and I'm in exactly the same place I was before." His words were halting and raspy as he labored for breath. Then turning to Dr. Anand, "Let's meet this healer of yours, Doc."

When they entered my section of the studio, I stood, smiled as broadly with my eyes as I could. Holding out my hand, I walked forward with an overeager voice and said, "Welcome." Rafi led the men to the seats across from me and came over to stand behind me. Dr. Anand, who had followed the men in, stood behind them. The dad smiled and nodded in my direction.

"The healer just has to place her hands on you, is that all right?" Dr. Anand asked the father. "It's how she reads what's wrong."

"I already told you he has end-stage emphysema, didn't I?" said Ike, looking at Dr. Anand like he was an idiot.

"Yes, of course, but she needs to connect with your father, and placing her hands is how she does it. Does she have your permission to continue with the healing?" Dr. Anand asked the father, who quickly nodded.

I reached out my hands and placed them on Benjamin's shoulders. The blue lines appeared to me, and I could hear the humming. Yes, his lungs were suffering. Keeping my eyes closed, trying not to imagine how silly I might look to anyone else, I whispered the dedication and the white ribbons of light appeared to my relief. I coaxed a ribbon around my fingers and placed it near the man's chest. Once it was absorbed, I calmly found another willing ribbon and repeated the process. After four ribbons, I felt slight heat emanating from his chest, and the humming diminished. I knew it was enough. I withdrew my hands and opened my eyes to look at Benjamin. His mouth was agape, and he stared at me wide-eyed as he took breath after breath of deep, satisfying air. His chest expanded and deflated to its full capacity and he placed his hands over his body to feel it further. Jumping to standing, he removed the oxygen tubes attaching him to the tank and life-giving air.

His son Ike jumped up, too. "Dad, what the hell are you doing? You need that!" Concern fought with the gruffness in his voice. His father just shook his head no and smiled hugely.

"Look at my chest, Ike!" he exclaimed, grabbing his son firmly by the shoulders. "I'm breathing! I'm breathing for real!" He nearly shouted, the rasp and wheezing greatly diminished. "Ha ha!" he shouted in excitement, "How the hell did you do that!? I feel amazing! I could feel it while you were moving your hands back and forth to my chest. It was like each time you did it I could get more air and feel strength return! Then it was all warm! Holy shit, I can't believe how good I feel!" He smiled at everyone in the room in turn.

Ike was not as convinced. He had moved around his father to retrieve the abandoned oxygen tank, uncoiled the tube and held it out to his father, "Dad, please. You need this. Put it back on. Your mind is playing tricks on you, like, what do they call that, the placebo effect. You can't be better just like that. It's not possible. Put the tubes back in, now." The last bit was said more forcefully. I could tell he was scared. My mom always told me when I was little that the strength of her yelling correlated with how scared she was in any given situation. And I could hear the fear for his Dad coming out in the way his voice had changed.

But his dad brushed off his hand and said, "I don't need that blasted thing anymore, Ike! Look at me. Listen to my voice! Don't I sound better? Can't you see me breathing better? I don't understand it any more than you do, but I sure as hell *feel* it." He practically giggled and turned to me again. "Girly, you are something else. I don't know what you did, or how you did it, but I can't possibly say thank you enough. Can I give you a hug?" he asked while walking over to me. "I would love a hug," I said. His embrace was full, and I thought he might lift me off my feet, but he didn't. When he let go he looked me in the eyes. "Keep doing what you're doing, girly. You just gave me my life back." His eyes watered slightly.

Ike, still fumbling with the oxygen tank, came over and yelled at his father. "Will you stop this nonsense and put your tubes back in, you stupid, gullible, old man! They tricked your mind into thinking you're healed, but you're not! You can't be! But if you don't have your oxygen, you'll be dead before I can even get you to the hospital. Put it on!" He shoved it toward Benjamin's face. None of us knew what to do, and Rafi had moved from me to the old man protectively. Ike's eyes were wild with fright now, and his father finally looked at him, recognizing his fear.

Reaching out, he took the tubes from his son's outstretched hand and gently said, "I will make a deal with you, son. I will wear these tubes all the way to the hospital. There we will get me checked out as much as will satisfy you to believe I'm better. Then—" he paused to hook the tubes back around his face and head, "—I'm throwing this shit away and we're going to your house so I can play with my grandchildren. Do we have a deal?" With his father's oxygen flowing again, Ike calmed a bit.

"Fine." He acquiesced. "Let's go." Then turning to the rest of us, "I hope for your sakes you aren't pulling some scam. It's a cruel thing to do to people. How the hell do we get out of here?" Mary Ann led them out the back and watched until the car completely disappeared from view.

I was elated. "Did you see him?" I asked everyone. "He was so happy, completely changed! And I got to give that to him!" My exhilaration was overflowing.

Rafi engulfed me in a huge bear hug that lifted me off my feet. "You did so great," he whispered.

"I should have better anticipated what happened with the son," allowed Dr. Anand. "I know we agreed to keep ourselves covered up and anonymous, but I guess I didn't fully appreciate how disconcerting it would be to walk into an unknown place and find us all that way. I will be the point person, and Leah, you and I will just have to try not to be out in public much together."

We didn't have too long to wait till another car made its way up the drive. Dr. Anand spaced sessions apart enough so that participants wouldn't encounter each other in the driveway or waiting room, in case they were wary of having anyone know they were there. Once parked, a teenage girl got out of the driver's side and walked over to the passenger side to help out a woman who appeared very frail. Her gaunt face and slight body seemed swallowed up by the big winter coat she wore. Dr. Anand went out to help when it seemed the recent snow was proving difficult for the mom to navigate. We had shoveled, but there was still a thin layer of icy slush that coated the walk. Once they entered the room and were seated in the waiting area, introductions began.

The girl, Adeleine, was the eldest daughter of the fragile woman in the big coat, Helen. Helen had been diagnosed with stage 3 ovarian cancer two years ago and had recently run out of options as the disease kept proving stronger than the treatments. Helen looked lovingly at her daughter as she explained her mom's situation.

Then Helen herself chimed in, "The morning I saw your advertisement in the *Saratogian*, I had just been told I had a month or two at best, weeks at worst. My husband and family were advised to get me in hospice care. Shortly after, I was sitting in bed looking at the paper, not really able to focus on any of the words, my mind not settling. Facing death is an incredibly disorienting experience. But your advertisement almost jumped off the page at me. I certainly have nothing to lose at this point, and my children—you see, I have two younger as well—and my husband have suffered a lot with this illness. I asked Ady if she would be willing to bring me, and she said yes. I didn't bother my husband with it, just in case it didn't pan out. No offense, but we've had so many false moments of hope over the last couple years, I couldn't bear putting him through it again. So, my wonderful Ady promised to help me out, and keep my secret." She smiled at her daughter, who was struggling to keep her composure.

Ady turned to Dr. Anand. "Can you help her?"

Dr. Anand kindly replied, "Alas, I'm not the healer, so I can't answer that question for you. I'm so sorry for the struggle your journey with this disease has been. Shall we go in and see what the healer has to say about it?" A moment later, after Dr. Anand explained why our faces would be covered, they joined me in the healing room. I was moved by the emotion they had shared in telling their story, and the obvious love they had for each other. Once I gained permission to place my hands on Helen, I started the process. The blue lines confirmed what she had said, but the humming told me the cancer was elsewhere in her body as well. She was certainly at the end of her life, and her energy was weak. But, like the baby bird, she was not dead yet. I placed six light ribbons to her lower abdomen before I felt the warming. Then I placed two by her heart in hopes they would reach her blood and travel where needed. When the humming died down, I removed my hands and opened my eyes. Unlike Benjamin, who immediately felt the return of his lung function, Helen's experience was slightly more subtle. Her body had been weak with damage for years. Though I helped heal the cancer, her body processes still needed time to adjust and return to health.

"I feel different," Helen offered, cautiously, once I was done. "I don't have pain," she whispered, turning to Adeleine. "I don't feel any pain right now." She raised her eyebrows at this revelation. Then turning back to me. "I've had pain nonstop for the last six weeks at least. I forgot what it felt like to *not* be in pain. How did you do that? Is my cancer gone?" Her eyes pleaded with me to say yes.

Reluctantly, I answered, "I felt healing in your ovaries—but I believe the cancer has spread to other areas. I focused healing on your heart and blood, that it might travel where it is most needed, and bring you back to health. But—it's just that I've never tried healing someone with multiple diseases, and I don't know what to expect. I don't really know what else I can do at this point." My answer felt wholly inadequate.

Helen looked me in the eyes, nodded, and stood up with more energy than before. Her daughter smiled.

"You look better already!" she exclaimed.

Helen nodded. "I do feel a little better, for sure." She walked around and offered me a hug without asking, and I took it without hesitation. As they left, Dr. Anand asked that she follow up with the number on the phone to let us know how she was doing a week from then. While much less dramatic of a healing than the first participant, I felt confident Helen was going to start recovering, much to the surprise of her doctors and family.

The third participant was a man in his thirties, who'd recently been diagnosed with Lyme disease and was having some neurological symptoms that were interfering with his work and life. This one felt like a piece of cake after the last two, and he was in and out in less than fifteen minutes. I was happy and relieved with how the day had gone, as was everyone else. But I was also emotionally spent.

We ordered takeout and shared an evening feast to congratulate ourselves on the success of the day. My mind was still racing when it came time for sleep, and I found myself tossing and turning. Finally, I got up and went out to the living space. I came upon Mary Ann there, battling her own sleep difficulties. She agreed it was hard to process all the emotions from the day, and it was still overwhelming to imagine what this gift I had allowed me to bring to the world. Above it all, she worried a lot about the consequences of exposing me. It frustrated me that every conversation seemed to circle back to this. I was too tired to argue, though, and headed back to bed, not wanting her anxiousness to dampen the joy I'd experienced healing people.

Hinky:
Dishonest, suspect.

CHAPTER 14

The next day, Dr. Anand received three more voicemails from the retirement home where Benjamin resided. By Tuesday evening, two others had responded to the flyers hung in the community center. I saw five participants on Wednesday. By Thursday evening, when Dr. Anand checked the mailbox for the cellphone, it was full. Most messages were from people calling because they either saw or heard about our success with those who had already come. I was now officially healing people and, though many sessions were as fraught as that first one with Ike and Benjamin, I felt more and more confident in my role. Soon the three weeks of sessions were booked solid, and Dr. Anand was turning away so many people, we agreed to add one more week. To handle the surprising emotions that flooded me after each day of healing, Mary Ann bought me a journal. She suggested that once I got my thoughts onto paper, they wouldn't burden me so heavily. As usual, she was right.

But by week three, I was starting to fatigue. We kept a grueling pace of eight to ten hours of treatment each day, as the demand was so high. Mary Ann tried to talk me out of attempting to see everyone, but I felt a new sense of obligation to all these suffering people. Who was I, with this gift, to selfishly guard my time when a person's entire life could be changed for the better? But my mood was souring with my fatigue, and by the end of the third week I caught myself snapping at Dr. Anand or Rafi for nothing in particular. Maybe they took too long escorting one participant out and letting the next in. Maybe they laughed too loudly with the waiting room participant while I was in the middle of healing someone. Even with all my friends around me to help, no one but me could do the actual healing. Resentment was creeping in. It helped knowing I could soon stop for a while. Knowing there was an end in sight helped me push through. But that Friday evening when I yelled at Rafi for being clumsy when he accidentally bumped into my session table, upsetting a cup of tea I had just poured, it was clear I needed a break.

Though there was a lot of work to do even in the off hours, we decided to all go out to dinner. Isaac came along as well. For the sake of anonymity, we chose a restaurant thirty miles from the studio. Dr. Anand wore his reading glasses as an extra layer of "disguise," and off we went. Scanning the restaurant for any face that looked familiar, I just couldn't settle down. Mary Ann finally put her hands on mine and Rafi's—because he was apparently doing the same thing—and told us to relax. Halfway through dinner, when I was feeling human again, a group of older adults, two couples, were seated at a table within earshot of ours. My head shot up and my eyes found Rafi's when I heard one of the men start talking about us.

"I'm telling you, he's been on death's door for a year. Last night I saw him at the tennis club playing singles with his wife. I was completely blown away, so I had to ask what happened."

"This is Alfred we're talking about?" asked the woman from the other couple.

"Yes, Alfred," he confirmed. Then turning to who I assumed to be his wife, he said, "Remember how frail and sickly he was over Thanksgiving? You even mentioned you were afraid he wouldn't make it to the spring." His wife nodded along.

"What did he tell you?" asked the other man.

"He said he visited a spiritual healer." He paused, looking them each in the eye for dramatic effect. "What do you think about that?"

"Like one of those traveling pastors in revival tents?" asked the woman.

"No, I asked him the same thing. This is a young woman. She and a small group of employees, who all cover their faces, by the way. All except one, and Alfred called him the doctor. Though he couldn't tell me what he was a doctor of! Only that he had an accent like a foreigner. The rest of them keep everything but their eyes completely covered. It's all very secretive. They are here for only a month, put flyers in the community center—that's where his wife found out about it. You have to leave a voicemail at this cell number and wait for someone to call you back with an appointment time and location. Alfred said they set up camp in a small house in Saratoga. The woman puts her hands on you and then gives you 'healing energy.' No talk of God or Jesus or Spirit at all, and he has no idea how she does it. But he left there and felt almost immediately better," he said with an incredulous tone.

"I bet she hypnotized him," added the wife. "Made him think he was better and that she performed some miracle—while the cancer still grows inside him." She shook her head in disgust.

I narrowed my eyes toward Mary Ann and mouthed, "Hypnotized?" How could someone believe that? I remembered this Alfred. He came in with his sweet wife. He had been diagnosed with brain cancer the year prior and was failing rapidly. When he came in the room, his face was ashen, and he was, like the man said, very weak. His wife cried when he stood up straight after the session. She held his face in her hands and, with tear-streaked cheeks, asked him how he felt. He laughed back that he felt like dancing, and he took her hand and slowly waltzed her around the room. It was an incredibly sweet exchange, and one of my favorites from the week.

"If there was nothing shady about what they were doing, why would they need to cover their faces? I'm telling you, something isn't right about it," the wife continued. The friends nodded their heads in agreement.

"Do you think someone should call the police to investigate?" asked the female friend.

The husband joined in. "I plan to talk to our pastor on Sunday. Get his advice. I mean, if someone is claiming to be a spiritual healer, I'm sure he'll have an opinion on the validity of it. If he thinks calling the police is prudent, then that's what I'll do."

Their conversation rattled me and stole my sense of calm. It was shocking that these people saw their friend, healed of a terrible illness, out enjoying life, and their first inclination is that it must be a hoax—that we must be taking advantage of people. And what would happen if they actually went to the police? Was anything we were doing technically illegal? I waited until we were in the car to bring these questions up to everyone else, who were thinking along the same lines. Dr. Anand asked us to all just take a deep breath.

"It's not a surprise that people doubt your healing abilities are real, Leah. Think how long *you* spent doubting them. People are always wary of things that can't easily be explained, and for good reason! Things that scare them because they seem too good to be true, or impossible. It will take time to earn their trust. And the only way to do it is to heal people. Your work must speak for itself. Of course, this will require we thicken our skin a bit and expect it won't always be simple and rosy. What all of you have to decide is—is it worth it?" He paused to let his question sit with us. "Leah, now that you've spent three weeks healing people, do you think you could go back to keeping it to yourself?" he asked me. The answer was so simple.

"No. No, I couldn't."

"So then are you willing to suffer the ups and downs of what that may bring?" He didn't wait for my response. "You are still so young and, like Mary Ann, I have no interest in you losing your freedom or control over your life, so we wouldn't blame you for wanting to stop, even just temporarily. Only you know in your heart what you're willing to put up with to bring this gift to the people." He was thoughtful for a moment. "How about we make a pact among us that whenever you need a break, or you change your mind, you just have to say the word and we will make that happen? We are here to support you, Leah. Let's have a code word!" He smiled. "If you need to stop, your code word can be falafel!" Dr. Anand had recently discovered the falafel at a Middle Eastern restaurant here in Saratoga, and he'd been besotted with it ever since. I laughed. "Okay, falafel it is." The mood in the car lightened substantially. How lucky I was to have these incredible people on my side.

Monday morning of our last week was frigid, and the threat of a snow squall was all over the news. Rafi went out to three hardware stores searching for rock salt for the front walk and bought an extra shovel, just in case. We arrived about twenty minutes before 9 a.m. and got the coffee brewing. After week one, we invested in a percolator for the studio, for us as well as our participants. Never a coffee drinker before, I became one on this adventure. The aroma wafted through the studio and it helped create a feeling coziness and warmth.

Our first participant was on time and we got right to it. Shortly after she entered my room, another car came up the drive. We scheduled participants on the half-hour, so this person was quite early. As Dr. Anand watched them approach from the window, he saw there were about five people in the car. They got out, but instead of coming immediately to the front door, they gathered around the trunk, retrieving what looked to be placards with black writing. Four of them stayed in the driveway while the driver came to the front door. I was just finishing with the participant when I heard Dr. Anand exchanging gruff words with the man. The participant heard, too, and Rafi went to investigate. The door closed heavily, and Dr. Anand huffed into the session space. Mary Ann was just about to walk the participant to her car.

"Please wait one moment. I would prefer if Rafi went with you. It appears we have some protesters from the local evangelical church. They have just taken up residence in our driveway to protest what they believe to be witchcraft or Satanism or some ridiculous idea about what is happening in here." Dr. Anand sounded very flustered, and I moved to the window to see for myself. Indeed, five people had formed a circle in the driveway. Each held signs with various messages: Jesus is the only true healer! Playing God will anger God! Put your faith in Jesus, not witchcraft!

"This is absolutely absurd," I said. "They know nothing about us and our relationship with God or Jesus—they didn't even ask or speak to us before deciding they knew the truth. And jumping to the conclusion that we must be doing witchcraft is just insulting."

The participant who was waiting to leave spoke up. "I can tell them it's not Satanism or witchcraft if you like? I feel so good, I can tell them it's okay."

It was such a generous offer, and I told her so. But there was no way we were going to throw her to those wolves who were obviously not interested in the truth, considering they didn't even try to talk to us. Mary Ann walked her to her car while Rafi stood guard.

"You are consorting with evil!" one of them yelled at the participant.

When they came back in, Rafi said, "These people have got to go. Should we call the police? It's not going to be good for our participants to arrive and be yelled at and shamed, and it certainly doesn't make us look trustworthy." The next participant was due in thirty minutes, and I anxiously looked out the window at the group.

"Maybe I should go talk to them?" I asked. Could it be as simple as that?

"No way, Leah," Rafi said. "I know you think there can be a reasonable solution here, but these people aren't reasonable. They are frightened because we threaten their belief system. You can't win."

"So, then what?" I asked.

In that moment, out of nowhere, snow started to fall. Big, wet flakes. A minute later, the wind shifted and picked up speed, and the snow fell even harder. This was the squall the news kept predicting, and it was a doozy! I could barely make out the people in the driveway anymore, they were so camouflaged by the snowstorm. After about twenty minutes of struggling, we watched as the group, leaning forward against the wind, carefully picked their way back over to their car, packed the signs back in the trunk, got in, and drove away.

Not five minutes later, our next participant made a slow and cautious trek up the driveway. Rafi and Dr. Anand, braced against the wind, met their car to help them to the house. A man got out the front and, with difficulty, pulled a girl out of the back seat. Holding her in his arms, he carried the girl through the storm to the studio, with Rafi and Dr. Anand flanking him for support on either side. Once inside, the father sat the girl in a chair, and introductions were made. I was not in the room, but I felt an energy shift as they entered. Instead of waiting for them to come to me, I joined them.

The minute I saw her, I knew the girl must have gifts. She was probably twelve or thirteen years old, and her legs were shriveled from lack of use. One look in her eyes and I could see she was in pain, but she smiled fully nonetheless. I pulled Rafi aside while Dr. Anand was explaining the head coverings.

"Rafi, this girl is different. Can you read her?" He nodded and moved off to the side so as to be less conspicuous. Dr. Anand was surprised to see me standing behind him, but smiled and introduced me.

"Ah! Here is our healer now. This is Magda and her father, Patrick. Magda is thirteen, and over the last six months has slowly lost the use of her legs, and has pains that move around her body in random fashion."

"The doctors don't know what's happened to her," her father said, "And she just keeps getting worse." His voice was strained.

"Magda, can you tell me anything unique about when this began? Even if it seems silly to you." Magda looked sideways at her dad, then began slowly. "Yes. Though I'm sure it has nothing to do with anything, but I had a dream the night before the pain started." She hesitated, judging my reaction to the fact that she was equating a dream with her physical symptoms. No doubt she'd had not-so-great responses from medical professionals when she dared bring this up in the past. Her dad seemed to slump a little further into his chair and didn't look at her. Maybe he was tired of hearing about this, too.

"Dreams can be very powerful communication tools," I assured her, "though also confounding because they almost never tell us anything directly." Frida had schooled me on dream patterns during my time in Sedona, and I was so grateful now. "Would you be willing to share your dream with me now?" I asked, pulling a chair over so I could sit directly in front of her while she spoke.

"I was in a classroom, like in school. I was the only student in the class, and I sat at a desk up front. The teacher was pacing the room as she talked to me. She seemed frustrated and—it was like she was scolding me. She said, 'Magda, if you keep denying this, you will suffer greatly. Do you want to suffer?' and I replied 'No,' but I didn't know what it was she thought I was denying. Then she said, 'You are the only one who can save you, so don't even bother looking elsewhere. And you're being bullheaded.' Then the teacher went over to the blackboard and wrote, in big chalk letters: 'Denying = suffering,' underlining it and asking, 'Do you get it?' I was afraid to say no, but I didn't understand any of it!

"Then the teacher in the dream sighed like she was so disappointed in me, and told me to gather my things and go home. That morning I woke and couldn't put my left leg down without pain." She paused. "The dream was so scary and confusing. I understood that if I couldn't figure it out, I was somehow going to fail. But I don't know what I would fail at! No one thinks the dream has any connection to my actual pain, but I can't stop feeling like it's super important. I just have no idea how!" Exasperation came through in her voice.

I paused to look briefly out the window; the snow squall was just as strong as before. "Dr. Anand? Will you cancel the rest of the participant sessions for today? I don't want anyone getting hurt trying to get to a healing session." Then I turned to Patrick. "Is your car good in this weather? I don't want you to be unsafe, either, but I think I would like to take a little bit longer than normal with you and Magda. Would that be okay? Maybe an hour?" The father agreed. Turning to Magda, "Your dream is vitally important to your story, Magda. And I want to share something with you, and you tell me if it resonates as true." I went on to tell her my own gradual growth into becoming a healer and the wisdom Frida shared about how those that deny their gifts often suffer physically or emotionally.

While I was talking, Magda suddenly whipped her head around to look at Rafi. "What are you doing?" she demanded.

Rafi held up his hands in surrender. "Whoa, Magda— it's okay. I was just trying to read you. It's kind of like looking at your soul, but gently." He shrugged his shoulders, knowing full well hearing someone was "looking at your soul" sounded somewhat alarming. "What did you feel?"

Magda shuddered. "It was like losing control of my mind. Powerful— like a wave flowing over me. I couldn't think straight while you were doing it. I felt all muddled. I didn't like it."

"I won't do it again without your permission. Can I share with the healer what I read in you?" Magda nodded, looking back and forth between us.

Rafi looked at me. "She's a healer like you. Not sure if she's quite as strong, but she definitely has gifts."

At this, her father spoke up. "Wait. You're telling me that you can *read* someone's —what? —energy or something? And it tells you about them?" His voice was incredulous and somewhat mocking. "What about me, then? What's my favorite meal? What do I do for a living?"

Rafi, with the patience of a saint, replied, "No sir, it's not exactly like that. I sense things like emotions and intentions. So, for example, in your daughter I sensed a very strong desire to help people. A desire to be good and understood. And the strength of her energy is almost that of the healer here, which means she is very gifted indeed. It's not an exact science, it's just an ability I've always had. I can tell her intentions are good in every part of her. And I equate her energy to the healer's because I've only ever felt that kind of energy from one other person, and that's the healer. Does that help? I know it's a lot to take in." He had such a knack for explaining something that didn't make the listener feel patronized, without a trace of defensiveness.

We could tell that Magda's dad wasn't entirely convinced that we all weren't loonies and he shouldn't take his daughter and run this very instant.

"Patrick," I interjected, "I've told you and Magda already how I was born with certain gifts. Gifts that are very difficult to understand, but I have them nonetheless. I asked Rafi to read Magda, because I felt something very special in her as we met. Rafi, using his born gift, felt the same thing." Then I turned to Magda. "Have you ever felt things happen that you couldn't explain, or that made you think that maybe you were different? Before the pain, that is."

Magda hesitated, and glanced at her dad. Her dad nodded his head just the slightest bit, and Magda seemed to exhale in relief. "I can tell when someone is going to die." It came out as almost a whisper. "I mean, it's happened a few times anyway. It's not the most popular gift—people don't usually like to hear those things. The first time, I was—what, Dad—eight years old? And we went to visit my grandma for spring break. The air got all buzzy around her, which was new, and when I touched her, I had a feeling that she was dying." She paused. "I told my mom and dad, and they asked my grandma about her health. She said she did have a little nausea and felt out of breath a bit. It was bothersome but nothing to visit with the doctor about. She had a heart attack that night.

"That really scared me, actually. I thought somehow I'd caused her heart attack—that I was making it happen with my thoughts." Her dad wrapped his arm tighter around her shoulders. "The second time was maybe a year later, when my mom and dad and I took part in a walk for breast cancer. Not long after we started walking, I heard that same buzz again, concentrated near this woman walking about ten feet away from us. I told my dad, and he, pretty stealthily, struck up a friendly conversation. She revealed she was newly diagnosed with breast cancer and due to start chemotherapy the following week."

Her dad joined in here. "She said she was stage 4, but hopeful that she could fight it and win." He shook his head sadly. "We don't know if she made it or not."

"The last time was the worst." Magda picked up the story again. "I was on the school playground about eight months ago, at the end of sixth grade. Our assistant principal blew the whistle for us to come in and dropped a sweatshirt she was carrying. I picked it up to give back to her and touched her arm." She grimaced at the memory. "Not only did I immediately get buzzy, but I sensed that she was going to die. Not that she was sick—but that she would soon be dead. She was hit by a car and killed on her way home from work. After that, I started listening to music all the time, or having white noise or some sound always around me to drown out the buzzing. It's a terrible feeling knowing someone is going to die, but it's worse when there's nothing I can do about it!" she cried. "My pain started a couple months later."

This wasn't what I expected when Rafi said she had a healer's energy. I could sense a lifeforce or illness, but I didn't know exactly when someone was going to die. "Did you ever see blue electric lines when you touched anyone?" I asked her.

She shook her head no. "I never see anything—I just hear a buzzing sound. And there's a pulling sensation in my head. It's hard to describe. It doesn't hurt, but it's as though I'm wearing a stocking around my head and someone is pulling it forward. That's the only way I really know how to explain it. And it doesn't last long."

"I don't exactly know what it means that you have this ability, Magda. But I believe there is more to discover with it." I turned toward Mary Ann. "Do you think Frida would be willing to get involved here? Our friend Frida is also a healer, and she helped me understand how to better use my gifts. Would it be okay if I talked to her about you? Maybe I could take your contact information to let you know what she says?" I aimed this last question at Patrick, who nodded his assent. "Okay. For now, though, we need to get you home before the snow gets any deeper out there. Can I place my hands on you?" She agreed and I put my hands on her shoulders. The blue lines were erratic, and the humming wasn't clear. Hmmm, that had never happened to me before. "I'm actually having trouble reading you. Maybe it's because you're a healer, too? I will focus the ribbons on your head and heart, and we'll go from there."

After placing three ribbons into her third eye, and another two near her heart, I said, "My sense is that this will heal you temporarily. But the pain will come back if you continue to ignore your gifts. Do you feel that's true?" She nodded. "I will call our friend and connect you with her. And here is my cellphone number." Seeing Mary Ann begin to protest out of the corner of my eye, I quickly added, "Please don't share this with anyone. I'm trying to keep a low profile as I navigate this healing business."

Once they were gone, and we had managed to slide the car to our rental house, we had to figure out how to deal with the protesters that had shown up. The snow, though it had yet to subside, wouldn't keep them away for long. We knew they'd probably be back tomorrow. Dr. Anand decided to start by calling the pastor of the church, and he retreated to Rafi's bedroom to make the call. He returned only minutes later, looking dejected. "The Pastor said he is only a shepherd of his flock, not their master, and if they want to peacefully protest acts they deem profane, then he is not one to stop them. He didn't wish to listen to how un-profane what we're doing is." Dr. Anand's voice betrayed fatigue.

"Then we just move," I said. "No one coming has any expectations, so we can really do the healing anywhere. Let them arrive to protest tomorrow and the next day to an empty studio. We only have four days of sessions left. Let's figure it out."

After brainstorming, we arrived at a few different options. Logistically, it would be a bit of a nightmare, but, like I said, no one really had expectations, so we could just send them wherever. 'Wherever' for the next day seemed to include a few sessions at a covered pagoda in the state park, and a shopping mall food court. By the end of the day, we were spent. But we'd managed to see everyone and that's what mattered. We asked Isaac to drive by the studio between classes to see if any cars or people were in the drive. Tuesday, he reported seeing the protesters in the morning, but not when he went again after lunch. Wednesday was the same report. Thursday, when we had all had enough of the moving around, he didn't see them at all. So we returned for our last day on Friday to see participants at the studio. It went fine, and we all felt satisfied by the time the last participant left for the afternoon.

This first step of our project was finished, and by all accounts, was a success. We had helped over sixty people in the four weeks of residence—so many leaving voicemails of thanks and messages of renewed hope for life. After we'd packed up the studio and rental house, and hit the car for the ride home, I let the reality of that sink in.

Vaticination:
Prediction, The act of prophesying.

CHAPTER 15

"Leah, did you remember to get more sunscreen?" Mary Ann called from the other room.

"Shoot, no! We can buy some when we're out later." I called back. Southern Florida in summer was no joke for heat, but we still tried to make it to the beach every couple days. This third project location was my favorite so far for temperature (it had rained almost the entire three weeks we were in Asheville, North Carolina!), but was proving to be the most challenging for healing. So many people here were older and had multiple health problems.

Using my gifts consistently for the past six months seemed to hone my abilities and I was more confident as a healer every day. This time around, we'd had many requests to go directly into hospitals to serve those who were bedridden. The barriers to that were numerous, including simply getting permission to be in the hospital performing any kind of unknown treatment. Also, I was still covering my face, so it was harder in an outside environment. We broke the rules last night, though, and I wasn't sure what the repercussions would be.

I couldn't say no to helping a little baby, so I took risks. They told the hospital I was a cousin, and I wore a head scarf and a surgical mask. The sweet little baby boy, born six months earlier, was hooked up to tubes and monitors, quiet and sleeping. It was heartbreaking. Mary Ann came with me and kept a tissue in her left hand to wipe the tears she couldn't stop. It was the first time I'd ever heard of a neuroblastoma. I focused the white ribbons on the small lump visible in the baby's neck and thanked Isis for passing this gift on to me. The hardest part was seeing all the other suffering families at the children's hospital and not being able to help them right then and there. Mary Ann and I cried freely in the car on the way home.

Today was a day off, and we were meeting Dr. Anand for lunch to go over some business details and decide the next location for the project. After the initial clinic in Saratoga Springs, it was clear we couldn't continue to offer the clinics for free because he would run out of money. In order to be available to keep doing them, Rafi, Mary Ann, and I would all need to start making money too. For the three weeks we were in Asheville, we tried asking for donations after the service. Some gave nothing or a small amount because that's all they could afford. But many, especially those who'd suffered (and paid for) years of treatments that didn't help them, were extremely generous. Dr. Anand set up a bank account, as well as an email address and P.O. box under the business name "The Healer." Many participants asked how to know when and where the next clinics would be, so they could tell friends and family around the country, and we wanted a way for them to connect with us after the sessions.

Several weeks after the contact info was set up, communication began pouring in. It turned out that many of our participants were sharing their stories on social media and sharing the contact info for The Healer along with it. Most initial emails were letters of thanks or pleas for us to set up a clinic in this town or that. I stopped reading them all because the sheer numbers of people desperate for healing was starting to give me panic attacks. How could I possibly help all of them?

Then something curious happened. We received a few emails from people stating they, too, believed they had gifts of healing.

My initial reaction was to connect these people to Frida as we had done with Magda in Saratoga Springs. But Frida gently declined. She and Carlos loved their peaceful life in Sedona, and while she'd be happy to talk on the phone with one or two people, she didn't want her calm upset by a large commitment. I admit I was disappointed, but had to face the fact that I didn't want to be solely responsible for helping them either. We ended up creating an online forum where they could connect with each other, share experiences, and ask advice—and not feel so alone in the world anymore. Currently, the forum had five members, including me, all with usernames that kept us anonymous in real life.

We had been in Tampa for two weeks now, and only had one week left. I realized three weeks was my max for any place before I would completely burn out. Rafi joined us for lunch, having spent the morning returning correspondence. He didn't have as much free time as Mary Ann and I did during the project weeks, as he was helping Dr. Anand with the business and the research. We still had separate rooms at rental houses, though Mary Ann was giving us way more time alone this last trip. I was now nineteen and Rafi twenty-three, and she decided she didn't feel like playing the role of chaperone anymore.

During lunch, we settled on a small town outside Richmond, Virginia, as our next location, spurred by a particularly gut-wrenching request. I brought Rafi and Dr. Anand up to speed on our evening visit to the children's ward at the hospital. The sky had darkened while we were inside the restaurant and a storm was imminent, so the four of us went back to our rental to watch a movie. Over the past six months, we had become as close as any family, even bickering from time to time. I swelled with love for them all as we huddled in the living room with a huge bucket of popcorn.

The next day was Sunday, and that was my day to recharge and do calming things like read and take long, solo walks to get geared up for the emotional days ahead. I felt anxious as the evening drew near, though, more so than usual. I watched another movie as a distraction, tried journaling and finally took a long bath. At 9:30 p.m., I decided just to try to sleep. It took me a while, but I finally drifted off.

***

The air in the hut smelled damp and stale, and in the hot humid early morning it was already oppressive. Surprise rains overnight left the vegetation bursting with health this morning, and insects came out in swarms to investigate. I was no longer on a marble throne in a stately room, but rather in a mud-walled hut where no air circulated with all the bodies that had forced themselves in. I tried to keep my head straight and stay focused on my duties, but I had not eaten in two days, and I had barely taken time to sleep. A bead of sweat made its way from my temple down my cheek, pausing just a moment to rest before slipping over my jaw and down my neck. The neck of my robe was already soaked and heavy from the sweat that never ceased falling. I supposed I could stop drinking, but then my own health would suffer. Besides, the poor often only had a drink of water as an offering for the healer's gifts. We were not far from the sea here, but you would not know it for the way the air hung in the hut. If only we could stem the waves of bodies that kept arriving. But I knew we could not. And now that I no longer had the stone's power coursing through me, my own powers of healing were weakened, and took longer to call upon.

The boy in front of me couldn't have been more than eleven or twelve, but he was already missing one leg and had scars of battle on his torso. "What is happening to our people?" I silently despaired. The least I could do was continue to help as many as I could. This had become harder since going into hiding, but so be it. I knew it would come to this, and I would help as long as I had healing gifts and a living body with which to use them. I did not fear bodily death as many do. I knew Osiris would protect and comfort my spirit when it came time to separate. Still, most were not lucky like me, and so I helped.

When the stone first left my body, I didn't know if I would still be able to heal. But the power had been a part of me so long that it fused with my spirit. This was a joyous thing, as the boys would not be able to use their gifts knowingly until they became men. That left many years where our people would suffer without a healer. But, thanks to the gods, I was still able to help. Not like before, when barely a breath of life lingered in a person and I could still call them back. No, now there were many who were too far gone to the edge of this realm to do anything but jump the chasm into the next. I took comfort knowing Osiris would help them navigate the journey. Until then, however, I would do my part to help with the suffering. If only my gifts could create food as well. So many were now dying from starvation. There was nothing I could do about that.

Horus' four sons were only fourteen years old. Too young for battle, though Horus himself was already challenging Set at the same age, and they were certainly trained in the art of war. No. We needed just another year or two.

I could continue like I was for at least that long, and Horus needed to do what he could for the people in the south. Set was hoping to lay siege on the lands, again. Killing the one (known) healer would give him an advantage in that he could rely on the suffering ones to not live to fight him another day. But I did not believe that was Set's plan for me. Instead, I would be enslaved to keep him, and him alone, in health to do battle again and again. That was the fate I ran from. For I knew that if I was captured, Horus would forget his charge and focus his energy on my release. This was what Set wanted, Horus weak and distracted. I would not allow it.

I turned my focus back to the boy in front of me. Placing my hands on him, I saw that his blood was poisoned, and it was too far gone for my weakened magic to change. I had a difficult choice to make. Do I do what I could, pretending that I could cure him, so he would believe he was cured and leave with hope in his heart? The danger was that he would die soon anyway, and his people would begin to question my gifts. Or tell him now that there is nothing I can do, let him leave with death in his heart. His people would still question my gifts, or scorn me for not even trying. I chose the path of hope for this boy and called forth the ribbons of light. They were weaker than they once were, and each ribbon only did so much. Still, I fed three into the boy's chest, hoping his heart would pump it through his blood. When done, I placed a hand on the boy's head.

"Go and help your family, my child. My blessings are with you." He knelt and kissed the tops of my dust-covered bare feet, then he was gone. I allowed myself a small wish that his family would blame a snake bite when the poisoned blood finally took him, and not me.

I swayed a bit as the next person stepped forward, and my helper Anis placed her hand on my elbow to steady me. She announced to the throngs that I needed a few minutes' break. If I were stronger I would scold her for speaking for me without permission, but I was too weak to even do that. Anis brought me the jug of water, warm and mixed with herbs. I took only as much as I thought would get me by, though my body longed to drain the entire jug. I knew this was the water to be shared all the day among myself, Anis and my other helper Cheres. In fact, where was Cheres? I looked around the hut, but there were so many people I couldn't see him. I asked Anis.

"He went to get more herbs, my queen, but that was long ago. I do not know what could be keeping him." Anis was nothing if not proper, but her eyes held fear and doubt.

Though we took pains to hide the locations of our healing visits, there were always ways for the news to get out. Set had begun placing spies in villages. Cheres rarely left my side for long, and I worried his absence was not of his own accord. Something was wrong.

"If Cheres is not back after the next healing, we must abandon this place and send these people away for safety."

Anis nodded at me, though we both understood how easy a task this seemed in theory, and how difficult a task in execution. Plus, it was Cheres who determined our escape plan whenever we arrived at a new healing place. We needed him to lead us, but it seemed that was not to be. I turned my attention to a woman at my right. She held a baby in one arm while the other contorted painfully into her chest. A toddler clung to the fabric at her shins. I motioned her forward, and laid my hand on her. This woman had a problem with her power to move. Her brain was not connecting with her arm properly. The humming told me her blood had failed to nourish her brain for a few minutes, and it meant parts of the brain needed to shut down to protect the whole body. Though this woman wanted me to treat her arm, it was her head that required the healing ribbons. I explained this briefly and as plainly as I could to her, as she just nodded, wide-eyed and accepting. I placed four weak ribbons to the woman's temples. When finished, she was able to move her hand, but her arm still remained frozen at her chest. I asked for her patience, as the magic of the brain took slightly longer to respond, but was more powerful in the end. Satisfied, she and her children pushed through the crowd to leave.

Cheres was still not back. It was time to go. Anis first packed up our meager belongings discreetly as I pretended to need another drink from the jug.

She then leaned in to whisper, "You will stand and pretend to fall. I will enlist help to carry you outside the hut for air. Once outside, tell the people you sense mortal danger lurking near. They will believe you, Queen. They will run, and you and I will move. I saw a papyrus boat covered with fabric maybe fifty paces from the hut. We will set our sights there, as a hiding place. I will lead you." I nodded my approval and stood, only to pitch forward into the crowd at my feet, my eyelids fluttering to show loss of focus. Anis immediately enlisted the strongest man in our first circle to help carry me out for air. Once outside the hut, I was lain on the hard, dusty earth, surrounded by dozens of the faithful, Anis fighting to remain the closest at my side. I roused myself and made my eyes wide.

"There is danger here! I sense danger coming!" I weakly shouted. "Please, everyone, find safety quickly!"

The panic spread immediately, and people ran this way and that. Suddenly, the man who helped carry me outside the hut, grabbed my arms and pulled me toward him. "Queen! You must come with me to safety!" he cried. I was weak and it was difficult to resist, but Anis came forth to block his way. "You must not touch the queen when she is not healing you! It diminishes her powers!" she screamed in mock anguish.

The man quickly removed his hands and looked at me horrified. "But I helped carry her from the hut!" he protested.

Anis, thinking ever quickly, responded, "Yes—she was not in her mind—otherwise, I would never have allowed it. If the queen is awake and present, her power can be stolen!" she improvised.

This man seemed to consider the validity of such a claim, so I added, "You must protect your children! I have the protection of Osiris, do not worry for me!"

After one more moment's hesitation, he bowed and took off running. Anis quickly threw a scarf over my head as disguise and led me around to the abandoned papyrus boat.

Not a moment after we had pulled the cover down over our cramped bodies, we heard the shouts of fighting. Carefully peeking under our covering, I saw a group of five armed men, beating the people around them back to get toward the hut. My heart screamed for those caught in their way. Anis watched the scene next to me, both of us trying not to breathe.

After a moment I heard a man shout, "The hut is abandoned! Scan the area, kill anyone in your path!"

My heart stopped as I heard the voice of my beloved servant Cheres answer his call. "They are weak. They will not have gotten far!" A tortured, guttural noise came out of Anis. She and Cheres were lovers, so his betrayal was not only to me. She turned her anguished eyes to look into mine, and without words, I asked her to will her body to ignore the treachery until we were free. Then she could suffer the physical blow of it. I also placed my hands on her to calm her breath. We must not move. We must not let them see us, or all hope would be lost. Cheres. The one who was named for the Lion, strong and in command. Perhaps his name was never the right one for someone placed into service. I should have known.

***

I awoke in a panic. The room was still dark, but I could see the green light of early morning through my window. A tapping on my door startled my racing heart again, and I jumped up to answer. Rafi came in, looking agitated.

"Good, you're awake. We need to talk about something." He was clearly upset and spoke quickly, leading me to sit but pacing the floor in front of my bed himself. "You can't go to the clinic today. We need to cancel."

"Why? What's going on?" I answered. I had rarely seen Rafi this upset.

"Something is going to happen. To you. I had a …a premonition," he stuttered, getting more and more frustrated. "It was so unclear, though! Why was it so unclear? That's not what usually happens." He had switched to talking to himself, and I decided in my own confusion to just listen. "No clear face except yours, no clear location, only the damn red stripe of paint. How is that supposed to be helpful? I mean, I could see you so clearly, but it's like seeing you through a camera lens this time, limited—so limited!" He kept pacing. "But your face is terrified, Leah. I can tell that so clearly. You are absolutely scared out of your wits." He turned to look at me, his eyes wide with fear, too.

"Rafi, I don't know what you're talking about. You had a premonition?"

"Remember the first time we met I told you and Dr. Anand I have visions, too? Well, it just happened. It's been years since the last time. They have always come true—every single one. I had a vision just now when I woke up. A vision of you with that terrified look on your face in front of a white background with a red stripe. It flashed so quickly, so different than before. I don't understand it. What were you so afraid of?" He started pacing again, pinching the bridge of his nose with his eyes closed trying to bring the vision back. "I can't see anything else, damnit!"

"Back up a bit. You say you've never had a vision that didn't come true? Could you just have been dreaming, since this one seems different?"

He shook his head. "No. No, the quality is the same, and it's different than a dream. More vibrant, like I'm there. Like I imagine your Isis dreams feel. The only time I experience that is with visions, and this was definitely the same. I just usually get more information. A broader frame, you know? More context."

In truth, I had forgotten his mention of visions until this moment. Now it seemed strange it hadn't come up in all the time we'd been together. "Why haven't we ever talked about them?" I asked, hurt that after almost a year together, dealing with all sorts of gifted people, he didn't want to share this with me.

"I'm sorry, okay? It's just that they always show me something awful. I've never had a vision that was good or wonderful, only bad—and occasionally terrible." He sighed, dropping his defenses a little. "I worried that if I spent time thinking about them, or talking about them, maybe it would bring them on more frequently or something. I don't know." He seemed very fragile.

"Maybe I just saw something scary—or *will see* something scary, like a car accident. You don't know that I'm scared for myself, do you?" I asked him.

"I do. I get emotions from my visions, too. And I could clearly tell you were being threatened somehow. Enough to be scared shitless. But I can't see anything else." Despair lined his words and I went to him and pulled him to me.

"You only see me scared—not hurt, not dead. Let's not assume the worst. Besides, it's not like I haven't been terrified by something before and everything turned out fine—my fear for nothing." I was looking into his eyes, trying to get through and calm him. "And I'm very tough, you know." I gave him a half-smile.

He sighed and pulled me in again. "Yes, you're tough. But you are also my entire world, Leah." I caught my breath. "Something is going to happen today, and I'm terrified I won't be able to stop it. Can we please cancel the clinic?" he pleaded.

I didn't want to cancel. The idea of telling all those hurting people that I couldn't make it on the odd chance that I was going to be scared of something at some point during the day—it wasn't enough. Then a thought occurred to me.

"There's no place like that at the clinic—white with a red stripe. So it can't be there where it occurs. It won't make any difference if we cancel, it will just leave people in pain longer."

Rafi thought this over. "I guess you're right." I thought he was coming around to my view when something new occurred to him. "But I know that there's no place like that in this house, so if you don't leave the house then you can stay safe!"

"But all those people. We don't have time to reschedule them. I don't want to sit here doing nothing when I could go straight to the clinic and straight home, too. And didn't you just say that these visions *always* come true? So how can I avoid it anyway?" This logic caused him even more discomfort.

"I know—but I'm scared, Leah. I'm not leaving your side today, okay? Have Mary Ann walk the participants out. I'm not letting you out of my sight."

The day went fine up until the last appointment. A young woman came in stating she had just been diagnosed with liver cancer. Her energy was off, and she kept nervously darting her eyes between us and giggling at inappropriate times. I told myself she was just having a hard time processing her diagnosis, but I had an uneasy feeling. When I put my hands on her nothing happened. No blue lines, no humming. I asked her again about her diagnosis, and she assured me that the doctors found a tumor and would be operating in a couple weeks. She was hoping to avoid the operation altogether, and had heard how "ahmaaaazing" my healing abilities were. Her tone was mocking, her exuberance over the top. I put my hands on her again—still nothing.

I excused myself for a moment and gave Rafi a meaningful look, letting him know I wanted him to read her. When I came back to the room a moment later with water for her and me, Rafi pulled me aside.

"She's up to something. Her energy is angry, almost hatred—and sad. Let's get her out of here."

I told her I was sorry, but I couldn't feel anything wrong with her liver. I suggested perhaps she should get a second opinion before she let anyone cut into her. She angrily called me a "fucking fraud" before storming out. I was so shaken up even after we watched her get into her car and drive away. Where had she come from, and why was she pretending to be sick?

We packed up and, as promised, headed straight home in the car. Not far from the rental, we stopped at a red light. Almost immediately a car screeched to a stop behind us, hitting our back bumper. We couldn't see the person behind the windshield. The light turned green, and Mary Ann slowly pulled over to the side of the road to assess the damage. The car that hit us pulled up behind. We all got out first and stepped to the sidewalk. Dr. Anand was already calling the insurance company and Mary Ann was walking over to the other car when I got a bad feeling.

"Mary Ann! "I yelled. "Don't go over there! Something's wrong!" But she was already too close. The front door opened and an arm with a gun pointed right at Mary Ann emerged. Behind it was the woman from the clinic—the liver cancer participant without liver cancer.

I moved forward and shouted, "What the hell are you doing? Mary Ann!"

The woman grabbed her roughly and pinned the gun to her back to hide it. She guided Mary Ann over to the sidewalk with us.

"I'm so sorry I hit your stupid-ass car—actually, I'm just sorry I didn't hit it harder. Let's take a little walk, shall we?" She motioned for us to move ahead of her while she and Mary Ann took up the rear. "Just up ahead a bit. There, turn right onto that sidewalk." The sidewalk turned out to be some sort of entryway. It was flanked by tall shrubs and trees, and once we passed through, we were invisible to the rest of the street.

We stopped walking and faced the girl with Mary Ann still in her grip. "What are you doing? What do you want?" I asked her, my mind desperately trying to think of a way to get Mary Ann away from her.

"You. Who the hell do you think you are asking me anything! You think you're God? You just touch people and make them better—but you don't know anything about the people you help. Maybe they are *supposed* to suffer and die! Did you ever think of *that*? That maybe it was part of God's plan for *their* life? Do you ask them if they are worthy of your help? You are playing God and you need to be stopped!"

What is she talking about? Is she just a crazy person? Was this about the session today? About me saying she wasn't sick?

"I'm so sorry my gifts didn't work today, and I couldn't sense your cancer. Maybe we can try again?" I offered.

"I don't have fucking liver cancer, you egotistical phony!" She sneered at me with disgust. "This isn't about me! It's about you—how you think you can just change the way the world is supposed to work. Some people are supposed to die. Some people are too awful to be saved—the scum of the earth. Yet you take away their pain like they didn't earn every shred. What gives you the right? You are not God! It's not up to you if someone lives or dies!" She was yelling now. "I fucking hate you!"

At this, she shoved Mary Ann hard to the ground and pointed the gun at my head, not three feet away from me. Dr. Anand rushed to Mary Ann's side while Rafi started toward the woman, but she hit me hard in the head with the butt of the gun and then resumed pointing it. "Move again, lover boy, and I'll use the right end of this gun!" He stopped about six feet away from us both. "Go lie down next to your friends over there." She pointed to Dr. Anand and Mary Ann, who was still on the ground where she fell, tears falling down her face.

"Please, please don't hurt her!" pleaded Mary Ann. "She only wants to help people."

"Shut up! Do you know how reckless that is? When you know nothing about any of them?"

My head hurt and I was terrified, but wanted her attention back on me and off Mary Ann.

"What happened, Anne?" I asked, remembering her name from the session. "Tell me what happened to make you this angry with me."

She turned on me with such venom, I recoiled. "My fucking name is not Anne! It's Alice. Alice Parker. My father Winston Parker came to see you in Asheville—ring any bells? Dying of liver cancer, on his last breath! You fucking cured him. Cured him! Did you even use your voodoo shit to see that he was a vile human being and *deserved* to die? *Deserved* the pain he was in? No! You just waved your fucking wand and gave him his life back. You want to know what kind of life that was? What kind of man he is? What he did with his new health?" Her eyes were wild and her crying intensified.

"He came back to his house. We'd been free of him for four weeks while he was at the hospital. Four weeks without terror, without beatings. Four weeks where my little sister and I didn't find him on top of us at the end of the night, reeking of liquor and sweat. Four weeks where my mother could speak more than two words without being called a stupid slut and getting backhanded across the face for opening her mouth. It took two solid weeks of that for any of us to trust he was really gone! To actually sleep!

"He deserved his disease! I prayed for him to die every damn night of my life, and God answered my prayers with that disease. He was finally suffering, too weak to hurt us. The pain was horrible, and I relished every tormented scream, because he deserved every bit of it and more. We thought we were free!

"Then he came back. Tore into the house while we were making dinner, the three of us. Happy! We had been singing and dancing along to the radio and he roared in—took one look at us enjoying life with him gone and lost his mind. He grabbed the iron poker from the fireplace and beat my mother with it till she wasn't moving! Her chest and head shredded! My sister and I tried desperately to pull him off her, but he was too strong, too crazed! I got the poker away from him, but he hit me hard and I fell back into the stone around the hearth. When I woke up, they were dead. Do you hear me? He *beat them to death*!" She was shoving me now, back and away from the others. I was crying, too. "You let him live! What gave you the right? We were finally free, and you made him come back. I hate you! I fucking hate you!" She moved in and shoved the gun right to my head. I had never been so scared in my life.

"I'm so sorry! I'm so sorry!" I meant it. Misery flowed through me.

"Alice, please!" I heard Mary Ann from behind her, she had gotten to her feet. "Please don't do this! You're not a murderer. I'm so sorry for what he did to you, for what he did to your sister and your mother! But she didn't know. *You are not like him*!"

Her misery wracked her entire body now, and she didn't realize that the gun had moved slightly away from my head. I stepped back a little and the movement made her look at me again.

"Please," I whispered. "I'm so sorry."

She seemed to awaken to her surroundings for the first time. She looked at the gun in her hand and then at me and the rest of them, her eyes widening.

"Oh God!" she exclaimed, her voice full of pain. "Oh, God!" She took a couple paces back from me, not lowering the gun. Her facial expression turned from sadness to horror as she looked at all of us. Then in one flash of movement, she pulled the gun from my head to her own and pulled the trigger. I recoiled in terror at the sound, then screamed when I saw her lying there, dark red blood coloring the grass and absorbing into the dirt around her body. I turned away from the awful sight, and there behind me was a brick wall, painted all white, except for one deep red stripe.

Tristesse:
(French) A state of melancholy sadness.

CHAPTER 16

"Leah, it's time for your appointment. You've got to get out of bed." Mary Ann poked her head through the sliver of lit open doorway. "I'll make you some coffee. We leave in thirty minutes, sweet girl."

I didn't respond, so she opened the door fully, shining the hall light in my eyes.

"I'm up, I'm up!" I said, shielding my eyes.

She chirped, "Love you!" before closing it again and heading downstairs.

I swung my legs over the side of the bed and sat there for a moment, trying to clear the fogginess. A byproduct of the sleeping pills I'd been taking the past couple weeks—doctor's orders. I slowly got dressed, brushed my teeth, put a brush through my hair. That's how my therapist knew I hadn't gone off the deep end completely (my words, not his), because I still brushed my hair. He found that incredibly hopeful. My legs felt heavy on the stairs, and I slumped in a kitchen stool while Mary Ann slid a glass of water and a hot mug of coffee in front of me.

"Here. This will hold you over until the appointment is done and we can get some actual food in you. Water first!"

I obliged, and the smell of coffee felt comforting and precious. "I'm always a little sad when my coffee is done in the mornings," I said. "Is that strange?"

Mary Ann laughed. "My dear, I go to bed excited because when I wake up it means I'll get to have coffee again! I'm right there with you."

The small kitchen television was playing the news as I cradled my steaming mug. Mary Ann sat next to me as the headlines changed to a story that had been everywhere for the last week. Seems a small, illegal container ship had been found in the Caribbean when a mechanical fire sent plumes of smoke hundreds of feet in the air. When the patrol boarded after a deadly standoff with the crew, they encountered a living hell. In addition to twenty million dollars' worth of cocaine and heroin, seven of the containers were filled with humans: women and girls as young as ten packed into crates with nothing but a case of water bottles that wouldn't last more than a day and a half and a few holes for air. They had been on the ship for three days like that, covered in urine and feces. Mary Ann and I gasped at the video footage of the women emerging from a crate. The newscaster had choked up telling us about the three women who had died, including one who was pregnant, and the living who had been trapped with the dead. The ship was presumed linked to a drug kingpin originally from the Juarez cartel in Mexico who went by the name of "El Padrino," whose whereabouts were unknown. The latest information tied the trafficking ring to several prominent U.S. businessmen and the shockwaves were being felt throughout the country.

"How does someone become so evil?" Mary Ann shook her head and turned off the television. "Sorry, but I can't stomach more of this today."

Thirty minutes later, we were in the car to the therapist's office. Dr. Marshall was recommended by my emergency social worker in Tampa. They had gone to undergrad together, and she knew he would have the right experience and temperament for me, and would not be frightened off by the *unusual* abilities Rafi and I possessed. Also, he worked only about twenty minutes from our house. I was surprised to find I liked going. I never thought therapy would be a positive thing, rehashing upsetting situations or bringing up every little thing that ever went wrong and blaming it on other people. But I liked the sessions I had in Florida and now home with Dr. Marshall. It felt good to get some feelings or fears out and be given a different perspective on them. Mary Ann wouldn't let me out of it anyway, so twice a week she woke me at 8 a.m. to make our 9 a.m. appointments.

The building was plain on the outside, but inside it was a sensory dream. Soft leather chairs and sofas, plush area rugs, gentle sounds of a water fountain, and soft stained-glass lighting. It was such a comforting space, I was surprised when Dr. Marshall said it was he himself who decorated it. I know it is sexist of me, but the room seemed to have had a feminine touch, and Dr. Marshall did not have a feminine personality. I didn't share that opinion with him, though, just Mary Ann and Rafi. In the waiting room I settled into a bucket seat that enveloped me in a hug. We managed to arrive a little early to the session this time, and Dr. Marshall was still with another patient. I closed my eyes as we waited. Last session, he asked me to talk about Alice, and I tried. We'd dabbled with it, for sure, since that's the main reason I was seeing him in the first place, but I had talked more about what actually happened, not Alice herself. It was not so easy.

Alice had been in my dreams for weeks now. She was the reason I was on sleeping pills, because in the end, I was hardly sleeping at all. The minute I closed my eyes, her face would appear to me. Tortured and accusing, or confused and sad—or mangled and torn apart by the bullet. In the dreams, she would tell me she hated me or ask me why—no matter what I did, I couldn't stop seeing her face. Everyone told me it was normal after a trauma, but when you can't sleep, you can't function. And in the weeks after the incident I was in a very bad place. Obviously, all of us were upset, and suffered in different ways. Rafi wouldn't leave me alone except to go to the bathroom for an entire two weeks afterwards. We even began sleeping in the same bed, to no objections. I think Mary Ann felt more at ease knowing I wasn't alone overnight. But while Rafi gently snored, I got up and tried anything and everything to distract myself. Online solitaire, movies, headphones with soft music, headphones with hip-hop or heavy metal—these would help for a little bit, but then the minute I felt I couldn't keep my eyes open any longer, Alice would come back.

Dr. Marshall thought it was time we figured out why I was holding on to her so tightly. This week the plan was to focus on Alice and see what came up for me. I was deeply dreading it.

"Leah, Mary Ann, good morning." His deep baritone voice woke me from my thoughts. He held open the door to his session room and motioned for us to join him. "Ready?"

Dr. Marshall's office was designed with a back door where people could leave a session when finished and not have to face whoever was in the waiting room. Considering I broke into heavy tears pretty much every session, I thought this was absolutely brilliant. We settled in.

Mary Ann didn't join every session, but he, and I, wanted her there for this one. I sank into the couch. "Like we talked about last time, I want to bring Alice to our conversation today. If at any point you need a break, you just let me know, okay?" I nodded. "Good. So tell me about your first meeting with Alice, at the clinic." I took a deep breath—this was the easier part. I told him how I felt uneasy with her behavior, and could tell something was off. How at first, when I didn't get a reaction from touching her, I thought I must have it wrong, but by the second time, I knew she wasn't sick. And how when Rafi read her, he saw anger bordering hatred. That scared me, and I was glad to be rid of her once the session was over. I felt a pang of guilt over this, but also felt stupid not to have seen her as dangerous at that point. I conveyed all this to Dr. Marshall, with my eyes closed, which he suggested would help my visual memory.

"Was that all you felt in her presence?" he asked me.

"No. I felt sadness and pity, though I wasn't sure why. At the time, I thought maybe she was pretending to be sick for attention, or was given a terrible diagnosis in error, and each option made me sad for her."

"Good, so your heart was already open to her."

"I guess so," I reluctantly agreed. He prompted me to continue, asking me to try to see the emotions on her face as the situation unfolded. "I was feeling good in the car, not too tired from the day, and happy that nothing bad happened like Rafi feared. Then she hit us, and that was an awful, jolting feeling. But it wasn't until she had the gun on Mary Ann that I knew something terrible was happening."

"Try to see her face when she first exits the car and grabs Mary Ann," Dr. Marshall prodded me. My breath quickened, remembering how scared I was for Mary Ann. But I tried to do what he asked.

"She is so angry. She looks in control and like she knows exactly what she's doing. Evil." I shuddered. Dr. Marshall asked me to continue. "It was when she was telling us about what her father did to her…" I couldn't think about this part without crying. "…what she was finally free from, and what I brought back into her life…"

Dr. Marshall interrupted me. "Leah, we've been through that. What I want you to focus on this time is Alice herself. What did her face, her voice, her mannerisms tell you?"

I was sobbing now. "That she was in so much pain! So much pain that she blamed me for. She had hatred in her eyes, yes, but the pain was more. She was tortured." I focused hard on Alice and my senses during the event, and something occurred to me. "She had guilt, too. So much guilt because she couldn't save them. She tried and failed to save them."

"Do you think her guilt was stronger than her hatred for you?" Dr. Marshall asked. "Try to keep your own guilt out of it for now. What do you remember from her energy?"

"I don't know." I tried to concentrate. "I think she really hated her father, and since she couldn't physically direct it at him, she focused on me." I could see her eyes, like those from my dreams at night. I squeezed my own eyes tightly to try to block out the image.

"Leah, I know it's painful, but I need you to feel these feelings—not try to block them out."

"Why? What's the point of that!? It's like being there all over again. Why are you making me relive it? It was horrible!" I shouted at him.

"I know, but it will continue to torture you until we can get through it. I know how brave you are, so let that come out here. The more you deny it the longer it will haunt you." He spoke calmly in response to my shouting, and I tried to breathe.

"When the gun was to my head, her eyes were wild, like she wasn't in control anymore. Like she wasn't really with me." A thought occurred to me. "It was as though she was seeing her father, and not me." This resonated with me as truth. "She wanted so badly to kill her father, but it was me she had instead. I think she realized this when Mary Ann told her she wasn't like him. She changed completely in that moment." I pictured her eyes, wild just seconds before, get confused. Almost like she woke up and didn't know where she was. "It was as though what she was doing actually dawned on her. She saw that I wasn't him. She saw she was terrorizing us like she'd been terrorized by him. Mary Ann told her she wasn't like him, but in that moment, she realized she was. And it horrified her." I curled into a ball.

"What are you feeling for Alice now?" Dr. Marshall asked.

"So much sadness. I feel terribly sad that she didn't wait. I feel like we could have helped her if she'd only talked to us instead of threatened us."

"Do you think her life could have ever been happy— or even normal?" he asked in his calm voice.

I considered this. "No. I don't know. Right now, I don't think so. She was too broken by everything. And consumed by guilt and hate. I think seeing her father in herself was so terrifying she couldn't live with it. I think that's why she killed herself." This idea about Alice now gave me more peace, about what happened in the end. But then the guilt came back. "But it's my fault he killed her mom and sister! I brought him back to life when he was on death's door! I unleashed a monster!"

"Leah, do you believe in God? In 'God's Plan' for us all?" There was no judgment behind his question.

"I think there's something bigger than us out there," I gestured to the sky above, "But I don't really buy that's it's some guy in a robe and beard who controls what happens in our lives. I think we control our lives with our decisions."

"How about fate? Do you believe in fate?" he continued.

"I don't really know. I can't deny I feel like things happen for a reason sometimes. But Alice believed in God—she said God gave him the cancer and made him suffer in answer to her prayers."

"Yes, she did. She believed that God had a plan, a just plan, and a plan that you unwittingly ruined. But let's explore that a little bit. If it's true there's a master plan for each of us, and all of us collectively, then your involvement would be part of that plan, wouldn't it? Not separate from it. Who are we to know what God's wishes are? Maybe this was the way it was supposed to unfold all along. Because do you believe that you, a mere mortal, could truly change any plan that God designed?" He waited for a reply, but I couldn't think of anything to say. "If we believe, like Alice did, that God is in charge, then you were just fulfilling the plan he has for you, too, right?"

He didn't wait for an answer this time. "Let's forget God for a moment and consider fate. The universe this time is our master planner, and fate rules our lives. If his fate was to die of liver cancer, would her father ever have come across your healing clinic? One might argue that his fate was to live and to murder. In either case, God or fate, this destiny was preordained, and you couldn't have 'ruined it' or changed it if you wanted to, right?"

He continued. "Let's just talk about this gift you've inherited. How many people do you think you've helped since you started the project?"

I knew the number by heart. "Two hundred seventy-eight."

"That's two hundred seventy-eight people whose lives have been considerably better since they saw you. How do you feel when you think of them?"

"I'm happy. Fulfilled—" I hesitated. "—proud, I guess."

"Does helping Winston Parker negate every other person you helped?"

I had certainly been feeling that way. "I don't know. Sometimes I think it does."

"Really?" He raised his eyebrows at me. "Out of the two hundred seventy-eight, how many of them would be dead now if not for you?"

Mary Ann, who had been quiet this entire time, answered for me. "One hundred fifty-three. I've kept track."

"So you have given one hundred fifty-three people more life. One of them ruined three lives with the time he had left. By the way, I heard he was living out the rest of those healthy days in jail for double homicide." I heard it just a few days ago, myself. It took them a few weeks to track him down. But now he was serving a life sentence—our testimonies helped put him there. "Would you trade all those one hundred fifty-three people, have them not have been healed, in order for Winston Parker to also not have been healed? Or let me present another idea to you. If you knew Winston Parker was a terrible person, and he came to you for help, pitiful and in pain, would you refuse to help him? Couldn't that also be considered 'playing God'? Deciding that someone deserves to die?" I had been grappling with this question a lot lately.

Dr. Marshall continued. "I'm not really looking for answers here, Leah. I don't think it's as simple as one right and one wrong choice. I'm just trying to get you to understand that there are multiple ways to look at this scenario, and you have to delve deep within yourself to see what your truth is. If you can see another possibility for moving forward. Winston Parker was being treated by multiple medical doctors to heal his cancer and ease his suffering. Do you think they shouldn't have given him medical care because of the kind of person he was? Should they have refused? He certainly would have died a lot quicker."

I hadn't thought about that, to be honest. While I did help him recover, I wasn't the only person working toward making him better. "I guess not," I agreed. If the doctors had cured him, would Alice have gone after them, too? She might have, her sorrow was so deep.

"Do you believe doctors should be made aware of each patient's character before deciding to treat them? Should it be up to the doctors if someone is allowed to die or if we try to save them? Could they bear a burden like that day in and day out?" Dr. Marshall asked.

"No. It would be too much for any person, you're right. I can see that. Doctors just help whoever shows up to receive help—so long as they have health insurance."

Dr. Marshall smiled. "No doubt. I want to give you one more scenario to consider before we end for the day. What if Mr. Parker, after being given a second chance at life, decided to change his ways. What if he left your clinic, feeling the best he's felt in months, and decided he was lucky? Decided to become a better man? It happens all the time—people who live through near-death experiences decide to change their lives for the better. Couldn't it have been just as possible for Mr. Parker to have had that reaction following your help?"

"I suppose so, yes."

"You are not responsible for what Winston Parker did during his life. That much I can tell you for damn sure. We are all responsible for our own actions, not those of anyone else. This includes you. Only *you* can decide how you want to move forward from this. I hope you'll spend some time writing and thinking it over. And, like I said before, there is room for gray areas and changing your mind. Life has a way of testing our beliefs and giving us many perspectives that disprove them."

"It's really super annoying," I replied, and Mary Ann and Dr. Marshall laughed. Our session time was up, and we left through the back entrance.

Mary Ann and I had a quiet ride home. I was lost in my thoughts, and I think she was, too. About a mile from the house, my phone rang. It was Rafi and he was frantic. "Leah! Where are you? Are you home yet?"

"Almost, why?"

"Don't go home! We've been outed. Our names have been leaked to the media—they know you're the healer. I drove by your house a minute ago and there are about ten media companies parked out front waiting for you!"

"What? Oh My God. Mary Ann! Don't pull onto Adams!" We were just arriving at our street when she stopped, and I could see the vans lining the road even that far from the house. "What the hell?"

Rafi continued. "Dr. Anand said they're all around his office on campus, too. Come to the studio for now, no one is here."

Dr. Anand arrived just as we did, and the four of us fought for floor space as we paced like caged animals.

"Those bastards!" I shouted. "They promised us!" The deal we struck for our testimonies against Winston Parker was that our identities would be kept secret. The suicide and the details around it were all over the news immediately. At first locally, then within a few days it was national news. Not only was it an attempted homicide turned suicide, but it included a person who heals with her hands and an escaped murderer. It was way too juicy a story. They didn't have our pictures, though, and so far we'd believed we could remain unknown. All of us except Rafi, that is.

"I tried to tell you it was only a matter of time. You think these people have your best interests at heart?" It's true that Rafi warned us over and over again we couldn't trust the police, the media, the doctors and nurses at the hospitals even—eventually someone would betray us for money or fame, simply because they could. I just assumed he was jaded by his past experiences and didn't believe the people who helped us so earnestly would sell us out. I was wrong, yet again. "They have the email, too. I woke up to hundreds more messages than yesterday."

I felt myself beginning to spiral. Could we ever go home again?

Dr. Anand took a big breath in and exhaled audibly, "Okay, we all need to calm down. What are the facts? They know who we are and where we live and work. Fine, what do they want from us? Right now, we're in reactive mode. We need to gain some control over the situation. Leah, when the YouTube video of the baby bird went viral, what worked for you and Mary Ann?"

"We ran away," I said. "We left town until interest died down. People mostly left me alone after we got back, but I didn't give an interview." The voicemail box had been full of requests for interviews when we got back from Sedona, but Mary Ann just deleted them all. "I don't think we'll be able to run away from this one. It's too big." Everyone agreed.

"So if we can't run away, how can we gain back some control? What do they want from us?" Dr. Anand asked.

"Me," I answered. It was obvious now that I would have to face them; there was no other way. "I can't hide anymore. I understand that. It scares the hell out of me, but there's nothing I can do about it."

Mary Ann came over and held me by the shoulders. "I don't want this for you. Why should you have to face them? I think we should go away again. Let it blow over like the YouTube video."

"I don't know, Mary Ann—won't this follow me wherever I go now? Who knew it would be so crazy?"

"I did," Rafi said. "Leah, you know I love you, so understand that I'm saying this from a place of love. It's time you stopped being afraid of who you are. You have been playing it safe for the last year. But you are so much stronger than that. You're an adult, and you have adult choices. Think of all that you've been through and survived in your life. A weak person would have been crushed by now. But you don't own your strength. You live half out of fear. It's time to get over it." He turned to Mary Ann. "I know you want what's best for Leah, but I don't think running away is the answer this time." Then facing me again, he said, "If you don't step up now, you will be forever running from this, and what kind of life will that be? It's time to own who you are and decide how you want to share it with the world."

He wasn't coddling or telling me, "There, there, it will all be okay." He was being straight with me. At first I bristled, but only because deep down I knew he was right.

Mary Ann started to defend me. "Rafi, I think Leah has a right to want some privacy! To be cautious and—" I interrupted her.

"He's right, Mary Ann. Thank you and I love you. But he's right. I have spent my entire life afraid. Easing into everything with baby steps in case the floor dropped out from underneath me, because it did, over and over. And, like Rafi said, I've made it through each of those experiences. I have been strong but still believed myself to be weak. I'm tired of living like that. In truth, it has been exhausting to live in fear." I looked at all of them in turn. "I will continue to need your help, as old habits die hard, but I'm ready for change. I'm a fucking descendent of gods—it's time I acted like it. Let's make a game plan."

Abience:
Strong tendency or desire to avoid a stimulation or situation.

CHAPTER 17

Mary Ann reluctantly called Amanda Rossman of Channel 5 that afternoon, and we offered her our exclusive interview with "Leah Brown: The Healer" for the evening news. We decided ahead of time that I wouldn't mention the whole "My great, great, great, great, grandmother was the Egyptian Goddess Isis" thing. Instead, I did my best to answer Amanda's questions as simply as possible.

Amanda: "Do you have to touch the person to know what's wrong?"

Me: "Yes, though I can sometimes get a read on a person just by looking at them. Well—staring, I guess." I chuckled. "When a person is hurt or diseased, I can tell where or how by touching them. My vision sort of blacks out, like if you had your eyes closed, and light blue lines that look like electricity, crisscross to a meeting point. Usually the meeting point is somewhere related to the body part that's suffering. For example, if you have a brain tumor, I might see the blue mass where your head would be."

Amanda: "And the blue mass tells you what the problem is?"

Leah: "Partly. It shows me more where the problem is focused. I also hear a humming noise. I have no idea where it comes from, but it could almost be likened to the electric buzz you hear when walking near power lines. It's the humming that really tells me what's happening. Don't ask me how I understand it, but somehow I can."

Amanda: "Is the humming coming from within you?"

Leah: "It feels like it is, yes. I don't really know. It's like another language that my brain just remembers, deep down in my subconscious or something. And it's fast, maybe a second or two before it goes away."

Amanda: "What happens if the person isn't sick or injured? And can you turn it off?"

Leah: "Then I see nothing when I touch them, it's just a touch. And no, I don't seem to be able to turn it off. It happens without me trying."

Amanda: "Have you ever wanted to turn it off?"

Leah: "Oh yes. The first few times it happened, I was young. It was really scary because I didn't fully understand it then, and after I'd seen the lines the person or animal died. Part of me worried I caused the deaths, instead of just reading the illnesses." Amanda tilted her head to the side and furrowed her brow in a concerned look. "And I read my aunt's breast cancer, which was really scary. But in the end, that was what helped me begin to recognize it as a gift, because the knowledge meant she found and treated the cancer in the early stages, and it is now in remission."

Amanda: "That must have been a shock. Did you heal your aunt?"

Leah: "No, I didn't know how to heal yet. But she got wonderful medical care."

Amanda: "How *do* you heal? And how did you learn?"

Leah: "To be honest, I learned through my dreams. I dreamt of a person who healed by pulling ribbons of light out of the air. Then when I was in the hospital with broken injuries, I dreamed that I pulled the ribbons of light to heal myself. When I woke up my injuries were almost completely healed. It was through dreaming I learned how to call forth the ribbons—and use them."

Amanda: "Like the baby bird?" She turned to the camera. "Let's look at the YouTube video from last summer where we first heard of Leah Brown." The video played in its entirety. "Was that your first time healing something? You look very happy."

Leah: "I was ecstatic. Yes, other than my own injuries, I hadn't ever used the ribbons to heal someone. I still doubted myself very much. Seeing that bird hopping around was life-changing and wonderful."

Amanda: "Have you ever *not* been able to help someone?"

Leah: "I don't think so. If they are too close to death, I might not be able to save them, but those people weren't the ones visiting in the clinics, because they would have had to leave the hospital to get there. There were a few participants who had multiple ailments, and I think I was able to heal at least one of them."

Amanda: "So you see these ribbons of light and—what?"

Leah: "I ask them to help me, and I pull them one by one into the person suffering. I think of them as life force, but I don't know how they work, really. People's bodies just heal."

Amanda: "That's remarkable! Let's shift gears a little bit here, and talk about Alice Parker. You healed her father, who then killed her mother and sister, and nearly killed her. She blamed you for their deaths, didn't she?"

Leah: "Yes." I winced. "Alice's father was a terrible person, and he was dying. He came to me to ask for help, and, without knowing what kind of person he was, I helped him."

Amanda: "Do you think Alice was right to blame you?"

Leah: "I think Alice was treated horribly her whole life by a horrible man. She blamed me because I healed him, and she had prayed for his death. At first, I did feel responsible. Once I found out what he did to Alice and her family, I was overtaken with grief and self-doubt about my role in it. But then a wise person reminded me that I'm a healer. Like doctors and nurses are healers. Winston Parker was helped by a number of doctors and nurses prior to seeing me, and they all tried to save his life. They knew it was their job to heal, and people don't have to pass a 'good human' test to receive their care. I had to have that perspective, too. I'm not going to do a background check on every person I heal. I have a gift that is meant to help people, not just the people I deem worthy enough. I'm not sure how I'd even test that. If Winston Parker had walked in the clinic saying I'm a bastard and I beat and molest my family, I might have chosen not to help him—I honestly don't know. But he didn't. He was gracious and pleading."

Amanda: "One last question—how can the needy people of this world find their way to you for help?"

Leah: "Right. We've set up an email address for people to contact us, and we have another clinic coming up in a couple months in the east and will be taking appointments. We will try to make the clinics in different parts of the country so we are more accessible to the whole country."

The interview ended with us exchanging a few more pleasantries, and Amanda wishing me the best of luck. The story ran nationally, then internationally. The police set up watch at our house and at the college for Dr. Anand. Though it was still summer, he found that all his fall courses were filled overnight, with extensive waiting lists. The dean suggested that maybe he could add a class or two, whatever topic Dr. Anand felt like teaching. With Rafi's help, he submitted both research papers for publication a week before the semester began. He had also been invited to speak as an expert on many podcasts and shows about healing, ancient medicine, and life in general.

Rafi moved into the house with us, and we kept the studio as a secret hideaway for when we needed some relief. The night after my interview, I was able to sleep without Alice taking over, and I ditched the pills after that. The first week we felt completely confined to the house. A trip to the grocery store had us followed by two reporters. Trying to be civil, we told them we'd give them a statement if they left us alone to shop. It didn't matter. In the store, with milk in one hand and yogurt in the other, a woman approached us to pepper me with questions—and a list of ailments she was hoping I could get rid of right there in the dairy section. We gave her the email address and suggested she try to get an appointment at the next clinic. She thought this was ridiculous since I was just there in the store—couldn't I just put my hands on her quickly and be done with it? When I said no, she called me a selfish bitch and actually grabbed one of my hands and placed it on her head.

"Here! Just do the thing!"

I snatched my hand away and told her, somewhat forcefully, she could make an appointment like everyone else.

She yelled at me her whole way out of the store. "Greedy bitch!" The reporters, of course, got her statement before ours, and suddenly, my behavior toward the woman was debated by every talk show and evening newscaster nationwide.

After that, I didn't want the hassle, so I stayed at home. By the fifth day of confinement, though, I'd had enough, so Mary Ann and I made a plan to get out of town for a short while. Dr. Anand said he had a friend with a lake house in northern Michigan that we could use. Rafi engaged the reporters out front while Mary Ann and I snuck through the back alley to his car, parked one street over. We drove one more block to pick him up, then the three of us, blissfully anonymous, drove six hours north.

The lake house was on a smaller lake about an hour outside Traverse City and Lake Michigan. We had the house for a full week. Rafi drove back after the weekend in order to keep working with Dr. Anand, who was busier than ever. He told us that whenever Dr. Anand was approached outside the house to get to me, he just switched to Hindi, and usually the person left him, confused that they had the wrong man. I thought that was brilliant.

The air was cool near the lake and the water was refreshing, and there were kayaks for us to use. Mary Ann and I went on dusk cruises each evening to see the sunset from the lake. When we went to the store or walking around, we both wore hats and sunglasses, and no one bothered us a bit.

The Virginia clinic would take place over the fall break at the college, and Rafi had been making appointments from all the voicemail requests. We could only be there two weeks because Dr. Anand didn't have a long break, so the clinic days would be longer. Already there was a waiting list for appointments over a hundred people long, and more email requests were coming in every day. As usual, the location was kept secret until we were there and the appointments were set.

Rafi returned Friday evening after spending the week back home, with a little bit of news. It turns out that there were close to two hundred more messages from people around the world who believe they, too were healers like me. Who wanted to talk to me to find out how I learned to use my gifts. One even had the electric blue lines, but didn't know what to do with the information. The most interesting was a woman out of Australia who claimed to have had a series of dreams about the goddess Isis, and wanted to know if that was important or not. We helped Rafi connect those people with the information for the forum. It felt very satisfying to learn how many people across the world were opening up about their experiences.

We couldn't hide away forever, though, and at the end of our week, we headed back. Rafi had been staying at the art studio while we were in Michigan, periodically driving by our house to see if the media vans were still hanging around, and by the last check, they had gone. We still had several weeks before the next clinic, and though I planned to spend a fair bit of time on the correspondence now that Rafi was busy with Dr. Anand's classes, I was feeling restless.

We were back exactly twenty-four hours when our doorbell rang. It was 8:30 a.m. on a Monday. Rafi had already left for the college, and I was still in bed. The muffled noises coming from downstairs sounded like Mary Ann might be in some distress, so I threw on my robe and rushed down. At the door was a woman and her son. The woman was crying and pleading with Mary Ann.

"He's dying! Can't you see that!? Don't you have a heart? We drove an hour to get here, can't you just let us in for fifteen minutes?" She caught sight of me coming up behind Mary Ann. "Leah! You're her, right? Look! Look at my poor boy! Won't you help him? You can't look at him and not help him—you're not a monster, right?"

I could see and sense the truth behind the mother's anguish, and I looked at her son. He was probably about three years old and lying in a stroller. He was awake, but listless and pale. Of course, I was going to help him. But we couldn't have people just showing up at our door at odd hours demanding to be seen.

I looked at Mary Ann and nodded slightly. Turning to the mother, I asked, "Where are you staying?"

Her eyes widened. "At the Quality Inn right off 55."

I ran and grabbed a scrap piece of paper from the kitchen. "Write your name, number and room number here. We will be there in one hour. I will try to help your son then."

She grabbed me and pulled me in to a forceful hug. "Thank you! Thank you! We'll wait for you, one hour." They piled back into her car and left.

"Leah, I know you want to help. I do too, but she just showed up at the door demanding service. We can't live like that," Mary Ann cautioned.

"I know, but she's just one and she's from out of town. We can do this, right?"

"My worry is it will never be just one. I guess we'll just have to play it by ear." She sighed, clearly bothered. I was elated to be helping someone again, and the boy was in trouble. When we left the hotel room, with promises of confidentiality from the mother, I felt light.

That afternoon, however, the bell rang again. Another family was at the door, and right behind them was a man in his sixties or seventies, all asking for help. These were neighborhood people who had been watching the house and saw we were back home. Everyone was in desperate need, and when they saw one person who came to the house, it emboldened them to come too. I looked at the people at the door, my frustration mounting as yet another man ran over to join them. All of them pleading for me to take a few minutes to help. My stomach twisted in knots.

Mary Ann addressed them. “Look. This is our home! How would you feel if strangers showed up at your door at all hours and demanded help?” she nearly yelled. “Of course, we want to help you, but we have lives, too!”

The man from the back of the group yelled back, “What are we supposed to do? I emailed a week ago and got a response that you’ll be in Virginia, in a secret place, in November. My wife could be dead by November! And you’re only two streets over from me. Why should we go to Virginia when you’re right here and could save her right now?” The others murmured their agreement.

I wished we hadn’t canceled the police presence when we left for Michigan. The tension in the group was mounting and I was nervous they might decide to try to force their way in. I squeezed Mary Ann’s hand and stepped forward.

I summoned my most authoritative voice. “Please understand I want to help you. But I will not do it out of my house. There is a picnic shelter at the forest preserve on the corner of Thatcher and Chicago Avenues. I will be there in two hours, and I will help you then.”

They seemed mollified and grateful—all but the family of four who first arrived, who left grumbling, “I don’t see why we have to be inconvenienced like this, we’re here now.” But at least they said it to each other as they were leaving and didn’t challenge me while still at the door. Once the door was closed and double bolted, Mary Ann and I collapsed at the kitchen island.

"I will not have our home become a doctor's office," Mary Ann said. "You know this will only continue, right? Once word gets out that you helped these people, and they *will* talk about it, it will be a madhouse here."

I knew she was right, and there was no way we could handle that. "I think we need to ask for the police guard to come back. But any hope of privacy for me—for us—is gone. I see that now." I sighed, feeling heavy. "They're right, though. There's no reason for me to wait until Virginia. I want to help people now. We need to find a place and think of a scheduling system."

That night, Dr. Anand, Rafi, Mary Ann and I went to the studio to brainstorm. We found an empty storefront for rent online we could use as a pop-up clinic. The money in the Healer account would cover upfront rent, but it wouldn't last long. It was decided we would start charging people forty dollars to see me. Rafi suggested more, but I didn't want only wealthy people to get help. Forty dollars was a typical insurance co-pay, so we settled on that. An online scheduling site was set up, and we left instructions for users on the voicemail. It took two more days to get set up and start at the clinic, and people were continuing to show up at our front door. It got so bad that the police added another officer to the two we asked back, and they set up a barricade around our driveway with a sign that read: PRIVATE RESIDENCE: TRESPASSERS WILL BE PROSECUTED.

It didn't deter people from coming though. Each day we had groups perched at the barricades yelling at us to help, to open the door. I added a sign about the clinic, and how to schedule, and this got rid of some of them. It was insane. The morning of the pop-up clinic, there was a group waiting outside. Once they saw who we were, they moved aside so we could get to the door and waited a few minutes for me to set up.

It was a steady stream of people all day, and there were many disagreements outside between those with appointments and those who just showed up. Once we finished all the scheduled appointments, it was 5:30 p.m., and I had taken only a few fifteen-minute breaks to eat and go to the bathroom. I was exhausted. We locked up to leave and saw there were still about twenty people or so waiting outside. They yelled protests at our leaving,

"We've been waiting all day!" an angry man shouted.

"So make an appointment!" Rafi shouted back.

Obviously, we would need help at the clinic, too. Dr. Anand hired security guards for outside, and that seemed to ease the tension a little bit. But each day we arrived, the group of people waiting outside had grown. By the fourth day, Sunday, the police came to shut us down. The crowds were a public nuisance, blocking the sidewalks and causing traffic hazards.

When the people saw us closing down and leaving early, I thought there might be a riot. "But we have an appointment!" This time the police escorted us out and dispersed the crowds.

As I was walking to the car, people reached out to touch me, as though just contact would heal them. One woman grabbed my shirt and I pitched backward. Mary Ann caught me and the officer on my side pushed the woman away so forcefully that she fell back onto the concrete, taking two other people with her. Everything was out of hand. Crowds were still gathered at the barricade at the house, too, now joined by a group of religious protestors holding signs like the ones in Saratoga. Everyone seemed to be shouting at each other, and a fourth police vehicle was parked with its lights on, telling everyone to leave or be arrested.

Inside the house, I screamed in frustration. "I'm trying to *help* people and they're acting like animals! Can't they see they are ruining everything? Where can we go? Will it be like this everywhere? What can we possibly do?" I went into our basement where there was a heavy bag, and punched, kicked, and screamed until I was spent and could think again.

"We need to leave again, Leah," Mary Ann said as I came back upstairs. "I'm afraid you're going to get hurt, and you can't help people at the rate you've been going. You'll collapse." She was right about that, but I didn't want to leave again.

"Mary Ann, I don't want to run anymore, remember? Besides—where could we even go? I'm internationally known now! Is there anywhere that won't be the same as here?"

Dr. Anand, who had friends all over the world, answered. "Yes. I know where you could go. I have a colleague in Boston who has a second home in Costa Rica. The hardest part will be getting you there without anyone finding out. You'll have to take a roundabout flight to throw them off. I'll call him now. How soon can you be packed?"

"I don't want to run away!" I retorted, but Mary Ann yelled back.

"Leah—you need to protect yourself, too! If you are harmed, the world loses the only person we know of who can make people better just by touching them. What good is that?"

Rafi nodded, taking Mary Ann's side, and that made me even more frustrated. "What about your speech?" I yelled at him. "I'm an adult with adult choices, right? I'm living half out of fear, right?"

"Mary Ann is right, Leah, you need to survive —and we need time to figure this out," Dr. Anand added. I was overruled.

Once Dr. Anand arranged for us to visit his colleague's vacation home, Mary Ann booked us a flight to Miami, then from Miami to Mexico, and Mexico to Costa Rica. One person seemed to recognize me in Miami, but I played dumb and she decided she must have the wrong person. After that,

I bought a pair of weak reading glasses at an airport boutique, just to change my look a little. They gave me a headache, but seemed to work. I passed the time on the Healer Forum, reading the hundreds of posts. There were so many gifts shared by so many people. While the language of the forum was English, I counted members from thirty-two different countries. I longed to talk to them all, these men and women who were building a community together. I felt lonely and apart, even though it was me who brought them together. When I mentioned it to Mary Ann, she furrowed her brow and rubbed her bottom lip.

"We have our focus, sweet girl. Let's find a way to make it happen."

The vacation condo in Costa Rica was cute and secluded, and the first few days, we managed to get some quiet. But then news came in from Rafi and Dr. Anand: A crowd of people continued to show up at our house each day, along with the group of protestors. The police called Rafi four days after our escape to say that someone had thrown rocks and eggs at the house, breaking several windows. They arrested three members of the Evangelical Free Church found on or near the premises, but Rafi didn't think they had enough evidence to keep them. He boarded up the windows, people shouting at him all the while.

Dr. Anand also suffered more now that we were gone. Thinking they could get to me through him, people started showing up at the college and waiting for him after class. Campus security found they were overwhelmed with this turn of events at their little, sleepy college, and police were called. After the third day of this, the school had to cancel Dr. Anand's lectures for the remainder of the week, and police were placed at every entrance to the campus. The protestors were the fastest growing group, but it seemed a Healer Fan Club also formed. People started showing up holding blown-up pictures of my face on sticks.

The media couldn't get enough, and Rafi sent me a video from a national news program that contained candid interviews with various members of the mob outside the college. The reporter stood a few feet in front of what looked like makeshift gates, with people, five rows thick, jumping and hollering behind him.

"As the world wonders what happened to the woman who calls herself, 'The Healer,' many have come to look for help, show support, or protest what they believe to be black magic. It is hard to imagine that a person exists with the power to cure the sick just through touch, but the dozens of stories of those she's cured are undeniable. This has led many to go so far as to compare her to Jesus of Nazareth, claiming her presence is a gift from God." The screen shifted to a twenty-something woman with excited eyes and a t-shirt printed with my face superimposed on the image of what I could only guess used to be the Virgin Mary in flowing robes of linen.

"She has been sent to save us! A gift from God come to show us that we aren't alone! That the good shall be saved!" The good?

The camera shifted to a man yelling behind the woman. "Only God can heal the faithful! This is *not God's work*! She is a false idol! She let that murderer loose on his family in North Carolina! A horrible man that she purposefully helped so he could continue her devil work! She is evil incarnate, and she is playing all of you for fools!"

The next frame showed a group of a half-dozen people, sitting in a circle on the pavement, eyes closed and holding hands in what looked like prayer. The reporter's narration continued.

"It's no secret that the public is strongly divided by the idea of a woman walking among us with the ability to heal the sick and dying. While some see her arrival as a signal for hope, others feel her very existence is heresy and signals danger." The screen switched to an image of the religious protestors mutely shouting and carrying their placards. "No matter where you fall on the spectrum of belief, there is no question that The Healer has stirred people's emotions and imaginations. The world is waiting to hear again from the woman, or Goddess as some have begun calling her, herself." The reporter now looked directly into the camera. "Healer. Leah Brown. However you wish to be called." He gestured to the throngs behind him. "The world needs to hear from you."

The recording ended. Mary Ann and I sat in silence for a moment, too stunned to speak. The video was from last night's evening news broadcast, meaning it was already eleven hours old. A weight had settled in the pit of my stomach. I looked down at my hands.

"I've been going about this all wrong. You were right, Mary Ann. I wasn't ready for the world to know me yet. I just wanted to help people, and the clinics were a good way to ease me in. But what happened with Alice threw us into the spotlight. I wasn't ready. I didn't know people would react like this. Irrationally and without care for each other. I can't bear the thought of me being the reason for division and anger. It's not what I wanted being the Healer to be like. I have been so naïve."

"No—you have been brave and wonderful," she responded. "But the world has no rights to your life."

"They do now, I gave them the rights. Not fully, I mean—but I can't turn back now. Now that I'm out in the world, I need to accept the responsibilities that come with that. I need to go back." I looked up at her. "You know that, right? I need to be there to face this. I'm so sorry for what it's done to our lives, Mary Ann. I know you only ever wanted to protect me, and I've thrown us to the lions."

"Leah, I love you. From day one when we were bound together, I have always thought about what your mom and dad would have wanted for you. In every situation. Marisa and I would talk sometimes about her dreams for you—that you would find love, something to be passionate about, self-reliance. And she talked about her worries for you, too—that you would let your differences cause you to lead a fearful life. That you'd shy away from being seen or really known, because you were different, and you'd never fully embrace life. Through every stage of this crazy journey, I have worried that you might crumble under the weight of it all. It terrified me. But you didn't. Everything you've gone through in your short life, and you still greet the day smiling and hopeful, ready to keep going." Her voice was full of emotion. "After your parents died, I made a vow to them that I would love you and keep you safe. I've tried to hold onto that vow like sand running through my fingers, and I've taken my fear about not being able to protect you and projected it on you. It was never really yours. I realize now that you don't need protecting. You need love and support, but not protection. Because we haven't been thrown to the lions, sweet girl—you are the lion. Pack up, we're going back."

Lambent:
Lit with a soft, radiant, glowing light.

CHAPTER 18

As I was waiting backstage to be announced, one assistant fussed over my microphone while another smoothed out my hair. I just stood there with my eyes closed and focused on the speech. Though I knew it so well, I worried the lights and cameras would make me freeze up, and I needed to seem put together. Trustworthy. With everyone's help, I had written a detailed message to be shared with the world. It took us a couple days and a dozen revisions to arrive at the words filling one college-ruled sheet of paper folded in my pocket right now. It was there for comfort, not that I planned to pull it out during the segment. I needed to convey compassion and caring with confidence and understanding. Set the world straight without being divisive at all. I had to basically pull off a miracle. I guess it's a good thing I come from a goddess, then.

The speech didn't worry me too much. It was the question-and-answer period that was to follow. The host, Isabel Hargraves, only the most recognized name in talk show history, suggested we ask the audience (all 4.2 million of them per episode) to send in questions ahead of time. Then they would scroll through and choose ones that reflected major themes to focus on during the live show. I would have to wing it during the Q and A, and as much as they encouraged me with words, Dr. Anand's and Mary Ann's faces betrayed worry that I might just blow it completely. My stomach cramped, and I just wanted to get started. Finally, a man with a headpiece and a clipboard came over to me.

"We're ready for you. Please follow me," he said, already turning to walk away. I followed him to a spot offstage where I saw Isabel finishing her prep work and getting ready for the segment. It was a special airing that

Mary Ann was able to arrange. Every media outlet in the country—or perhaps the world—was vying for an interview, and The Hargraves Studio was based in Chicago, not far from our house. Mary Ann had a friend who worked there, and she was able to connect us with the scheduler. Isabel was dressed in a chic, cream-colored pantsuit, her hair framing her angular face in a perfectly coifed bob. She sat with perfect posture as her legs crossed to reveal cream peep-toed heels. She was the picture of sophistication. I, too, had been coifed and dressed for the segment, and for the first time the statements "clothes make the man" or "dress for success" finally made sense to me. Being put together like I was gave me a slight edge up in the confidence department.

The cameras were rolling, and Isabel began setting the stage for our show. "My guest for this special airing has become a household name in the last couple weeks. Not only here in the United States, but around the world. Her abilities and even her purpose in the world have been debated by the religious communities, the medical communities, and around the breakfast tables of every American. She has been compared to witches, demons, shamans, and even Jesus himself. She chose to speak with me today to put a hopeful end to the divisiveness that has occurred in the wake of her abilities becoming known. I, like all of you, am incredibly excited to hear what she has to tell us. Without further delay, please let me welcome Leah Brown, The Healer."

She turned and smiled in my direction and the man with the clipboard gave me a gentle push forward. "That's your cue! Good luck! Don't forget to smile!" he said as I made my way across the stage to sit on a tan couch angled so I faced both Isabel and the cameras. I quickly threw a smile on my face and focused on not tripping.

"Welcome, Leah! May I call you Leah? Or should I say 'Healer'?" she asked.

I chuckled. "Oh no—Leah is perfect. I called myself The Healer when I was still trying to be anonymous. But I think it's safe to say that ship has sailed, don't you?" I wondered if I was smiling my normal smile.

Thankfully, Isabel laughed and nodded. "Yes, your story is pretty much all anyone is talking about this summer—and I include myself in that mix. It's truly extraordinary to think that you have the ability to simply heal someone with your touch. But you mentioned in our phone call while planning for this segment that you are saddened with the response many people are having to someone like you walking amongst us."

"Yes, many people are wrongly speculating about me and my abilities, and they're causing division and anger. It is my hope today to answer some of the assumptions that are flying around with truth." Here was my moment to begin.

Isabel made a sweeping gesture with her hand to tell me to go ahead. I took a deep breath and looked into the camera.

"I was born with certain abilities. They are as much a part of my genetic code, my DNA, as my hair color or my gender. They are not religious in nature, but they do connect me to a different level of awareness. It all started when I was a child in fourth grade. It was then that I placed my hands on my friend in gym class and first experienced the crisscrossing blue lines like electricity. My body was able to understand what this meant, albeit on a fourth grader's level. What I couldn't figure out, though, was why or how it was happening to me. It was not something I could choose to see, it just happened. The understanding I had that afternoon was that my friend's heart was sick. There was a problem. I felt it as real as the ground beneath my feet. When I learned the next day that my friend had died, my experience was even more upsetting. But it lent a bit of validity to what I felt so strongly. The vision of those blue lines happened twice more in the following years, but with no more clarity. Then, when I was thirteen, I had the first dream. I will not reveal exactly what I saw, but it showed me that my gifts are a genetic link to ancestors in ancient Egypt.

"I experienced a few more sporadic dreams after that, each uncovering more pieces of the puzzle. Such as how to use my abilities—to learn how to go beyond just reading a person's illness or ailment, to knowing how to help them heal. All of it was revealed through dreams, and then through trying to replicate what I learned. I had guidance along the way from a teacher who recognized my experience and understood more than I, though their abilities were different. Through this teacher, and through the dreams, I learned that I'm not the only one born with the gift of healing, or other gifts for that matter. In fact, there are probably thousands and thousands of us living now who share some level of the gene. It might show up differently for them than it does for me, but they are gifted, nonetheless. We have had communication from many of these individuals over the last several months, as my story became known. So many who feel they, too, have experienced some of the things that I spoke about. But they don't know how to use what they've been given."

Isabel interrupted me here, "Wait. I'm sorry, but you're saying this is a genetic predisposition? And others around the world share it? There are others who can do what you do?"

"Yes! Maybe not exactly like I do, but yes! So many have already reached out to me via email." I turned now to face Isabel who was the picture of raptured attention. "I'm not a disciple or a prophet. I'm just as human as you. I don't practice any particular religion or belief system. I'm not a signal of the apocalypse or the world's change. I was simply lucky enough, through generations and generations of humans, that my particular genetic soup is strong with the ability to heal. I'm not the only one, I'm just a particularly strong example. If my gifts—or rather my understanding how to use them—is anything more, maybe it's a beginning for the world to notice others with similar gifts. To support them, and learn that the human race is far more powerful than we once believed ourselves to be.

"Yes, I can heal someone by touching them. It is an incredible honor and responsibility to realize this, and to put it into action. But I'm not ever going to replace the medical community, and I don't want that. I have incredible respect for doctors like those who treated my aunt's cancer, researchers who are discovering why disease happens in the first place and the millions around the world whose sole purpose in life is to quell the suffering of others. My hope is that we can work together. I don't know how my gifts spark healing in someone's body—I just trust that they will. Doctors learn everything they can about how to heal and work tirelessly to help people. In my mind, they are heroes and should be treated with the utmost respect.

"As for the religious groups who have decided I must be conferring with the devil or am performing acts of sacrilege, I offer another way to look at it. Why couldn't it be God who gave me the gifts in the first place? If we live by the doctrine of 'God's will be done,' couldn't I just be fulfilling his higher purpose for me? I have only ever eased suffering—I'm not able to cause it. If healing the sick can't be considered in line with God's work, then I'm not sure what can. I wish to work in peace with religious groups around the world, as I can only really heal the body. The spirit is beyond my paygrade." I turned a wry smile to Isabel.

"How do you see yourself moving forward, Leah?" she asked me in response.

"Someday soon, I hope it will be revealed that the world has many more healers just as powerful, or maybe even more so, than myself. If we can bring them together to explore their gifts in a supported space, with guidance, just imagine how healing could change! This is my goal moving forward. And I say to all those watching who believe deep down they, too, have gifts—don't give up! You are not alone. A wise woman taught me that when we deny our gifts, or hide them away, they will cause us to suffer either physically or psychically. Find even one person you can trust and talk to, and allow yourself the dream of becoming more fully who you were meant to become.

"Obviously, I cannot, as one person, help the staggering masses of people in need. I tried and was exhausted and physically run over by those not willing to wait. If I'm to be able to continue helping people, which I desperately want to do, it must be in a controlled way. So I'm asking you," I turned to look directly into the camera. "Please respect the times and places we hold our clinics. Especially those of you who are not suffering life-threatening ailments. I know you're desperate. I feel it. I want to help you, but I can't if I'm forced to continuously close clinics and run away because of protesting or angry demanding mobs. For now, I will continue the practice of keeping the locations of clinics secretive except to the scheduled participants. Please help me by not revealing the location to others, so that we can keep peace and I can continue to work.

"If you see me on the street, of course, say hello! But please do not demand me to heal you right there, or physically maul me because you believe just touching me is enough. It's not, and I will not choose to help anyone who does this. Instead, I ask that we rejoice in the discovery of this genetic gift, and come together to explore where it can take us."

I had gotten through it. Now it was the question and answer period, and Isabel spoke to the cameras as an image of hundreds and hundreds of tweeted questions displayed on the screen backdrop. "I asked you, the public, to submit questions for Leah. As you can see, the response was overwhelming. We have chosen a few to finish the segment with. Let's start with this question from Robert in Tallahassee, Florida. 'Healer, what if someone has multiple illnesses? Can you heal them of everything? I was in a car accident eight years ago that left me paralyzed from the waist down. In the last two years, I have also developed multiple sclerosis and melanoma. If I came to see you, could you heal all of it?'"

"Thank you for your question, Robert," Isabel said. "There were many who had similar questions. Can you heal multiple things at once, Leah?"

"First, I want to say thank you to Robert, and that I'm sorry he's suffering. The short answer is, 'I'm not sure.' The blue lines usually show me the most important issue, but the humming will hint at what else is happening in the body, too. In the past, I've sent healing energy to the heart when I felt it needed to travel throughout the body, but I don't have any feedback from participants on whether everything else was healed, too. I have suggested they stay under their doctor's care to make sure nothing gets neglected. The research is still out on the answer for this question, I'm afraid. It is something my team and I will focus on as we continue to work with people." Isabel nodded at me, so I felt satisfied enough with my answer to move on.

"Next is Delphine from Paris. Delphine writes, 'My cousin in the states visited your clinic in Saratoga Springs with diabetes. Now six months later, she's starting to have symptoms again. Can you explain that?'"

"What do you say to Delphine, Leah? And to anyone who might have a recurrence of a problem." Isabel asked me.

"Right. Delphine, thank you for letting me know, and I'm sorry for your cousin. The reality is that we are continuously aging and how we treat our bodies matters for our health. If someone comes to me with type 2 diabetes and I get their body functioning properly again, but they continue with the lifestyle choices that brought on the disease in the first place, the disease will probably return. The way you live your life matters to your physical health. It's the same way for the strung-out executive with heart disease. If I make your heart healthy, but the stress doesn't go away, then the heart will most likely suffer disease again. Maybe not immediately, but down the road. I cannot heal someone indefinitely, just in that moment. And I cannot stop the aging process, we all get older and our bodies begin to shut down. I can help ailments as they arise, but others will most likely take their place. It's normal and natural to age. We all have limited time with these bodies—respect them and treat them well."

"Here's a quick question from ten-year old Mason in Atlanta, Georgia," Isabel said. "'Does it hurt you when you heal others?' Good question, Mason! What *does* it feel like for your own body when you are healing?" Isabel said.

I shook my head no, "Mason, I appreciate you asking about my wellbeing while I'm trying to help people. You are a very empathetic person, I can tell. Maybe you even have abilities yourself! No—it doesn't hurt me at all. The only thing that happens is that each person I see drains my energy a little bit. So downtime is very important to me. You know, recharge the batteries. Other than that, I might feel some vibrations in my body while I'm healing someone. Sometimes there's a little pulse around my eyes, but it's not painful at all."

"This one is from Wei Ming in Hong Kong. Wei writes, 'Can you bring the dead back to life?' Wow. That is a doozy of a question, thank you Wei. Do you even know the answer to that, Leah? I'm assuming you haven't tried to bring back the dead—have you?" Her eyebrows rose expectantly.

"No, I haven't tried. But I do know the answer because my dreams have touched on it. A person must have enough life energy left in their body for my gifts to work. If they are too close to death, then I can't do anything for them at all. That is also true if they are already dead. I can sense this when I feel their energy flow through touch," I answered.

"Okay, Leah, last question, from Charlie in Minnesota. Charlie writes, 'I lost my left leg during my last tour in Afghanistan several years ago. Can you help limbs regrow?' Charlie, that is a great question. There are so many of our brave men and women who have suffered similar loss of limb while on duty. Is that something you can heal, Leah? Can your powers regenerate limbs?"

"Charlie, I so appreciate everything you, and your fellow troops, sacrificed for the good of us all. I wish I could tell you that regeneration of limbs is within my power, but it isn't. I have tried without success. I do know that I can stimulate regeneration of nerve tissue, muscle tissue and bone, just not when the bone is missing. It's the body's own process of healing regrowth. What I've found is that I can quell the pain and neuropathies associated with the lost limb, giving the person back some quality of life. But, sadly no, I cannot make your leg return. If I could, I would."

That was the last question and I felt a sense of relief that we were finished and I hadn't done anything stupid. I exhaled and smiled at Isabel, expecting her to wrap things up. "Leah, that's all the time we allotted for questions, and I think the world learned a lot from you today. I know I did. I thank you deeply for allowing me to be a part of bringing your message to the people." She smiled back at me and then hesitated. "I do have one more small request before we finish. In response to the hundreds of messages we received asking you to do a live healing, I have asked a dear friend of mine to join us here today. It is my hope, though not my demand, that you could heal my friend. I'm sure the world will appreciate seeing a healing session just as much as she would." She said the last phrase excitedly and looked back and forth between the camera and me.

I stared at her frozen. Was she really sandbagging me like this? I couldn't refuse in front of millions of people. After a few seconds of silence while I processed what she was doing to me, the realization that I had no choice but to play along hit me. This was the most beloved and famous talk show host in the country, if not most of the world. She was just 'giving her public what they needed.' I gave her a tight-lipped smile. "It's not what we'd planned, but I will be happy to help your friend."

"Wonderful! I just knew you wouldn't say no!" She motioned off the stage to the man with the clipboard, and moments later, he brought a woman in a wheelchair over to us. "Leah, this is Abigail Wright, my oldest friend in the whole world," she said as she got up and walked over to hug her friend. Then with tears in her eyes, she continued. "Abigail was diagnosed with ALS almost two years ago, and it has quickly ravaged her body. Last week, she lost the ability to walk. Would you do me the tremendous honor, and gift her three young children with their mom again? Would you heal Abigail for me?" She brought a tissue from some mysterious place behind the chair and wiped her eyes.

It's just another clinic participant, I told myself. *Don't think about the people watching, just focus on the one in front of you.* I took a deep breath and stood up.

"It's nice to meet you, Abigail," I started. "I'm so sorry for what you've been going through. It's hardest when you see your pain reflected in the eyes of those you love, isn't it?" I had been told as much by countless participants who asked for my help: "So my children don't suffer…So my husband doesn't have to be alone in the world..."

Abigail nodded, tears welling up. In a thick, slurred voice she responded, "It's been the hardest on my children. They want to help me and can't." She paused before continuing with difficulty. "I'm not the mom they knew anymore."

I nodded and wiped my own eyes with my sleeve. "May I put my hands on you?" I asked her. She nodded and I closed my eyes, placing each of my hands on each of hers.

The blue lines came immediately, and the mass was centered near where her head would be. Her nervous system was failing. Opening my eyes briefly, I moved my left hand to rest my finger on her forehead while I turned my right palm up to the sky. Closing my eyes again, I whispered the dedication and asked to help. The ribbons appeared like they always did, and I began drawing them from the air and placing them through the forehead where my finger was. After four ribbons diffused into Abigail, I felt the heat under my finger. I heard a small gasp from Isabel, but I didn't stop or open my eyes. After two more strands, the heat dissipated, and I knew it was all I could do. Slowly, I opened my eyes and removed my finger from Abigail's forehead. She was smiling at me wide-eyed.

"Do you feel any different?" I asked her. She held my gaze and quickly nodded her head up and down. "Can you describe it?"

In a much clearer voice, she responded, "I will show you." Abigail stood. A collective gasp went through the studio. Isabel ran over to her friend and embraced her.

"Do you really feel that much better that quickly?" she asked incredulously.

Abigail laughed through tears. "Yes—I mean, I'm weak, but I couldn't stand up five minutes ago, and look at me, Isabel! Listen to me! I can speak again!" She wasn't talking quickly, but the slurring was completely gone.

Isabel turned to embrace me. "Thank you, Leah! Oh my God. Thank you!"

Isabel and I sat back down then looked expectantly at Abigail. "I'll stand if it's all the same to you!" she answered, and we all laughed.

Isabel turned to me again. "Leah, that was incredible to witness. I saw the light! When you had your finger on her forehead, I saw it surrounded in soft white light! That wasn't my imagination, was it?"

I shook my head. "I had my eyes closed, but I have seen the light before. When I feel warmth under my hand, it usually means the body is accepting the healing, and a light surrounds the area." Then I looked up at Abigail. "I'm so glad you're feeling better. Please go slowly into recovery. Your body will continue to heal, and it may take some time to feel like your old self again. But I hope you have the best hugs from your kids tonight."

We were all crying again as Isabel turned back to offer the camera a final address. "The world has witnessed an incredible event this evening. One that I don't think we'll soon forget. I can't thank you enough, Leah, for sharing your gifts with us. And, as Leah implored you earlier, do not let the existence of her, or others like her, lead to divisiveness. Instead, remember she heals out of love. Leah, I cannot wait to see where you go from here, and if you want to share with me again, I'll be here. That's it, all. I'm signing off with a renewed wonder and hope for humanity, and I send my love to you all."

Fernweh:
(German) A longing for travel to distant places.

CHAPTER 19

After the broadcast, life moved at a harrowing pace. Dr. Anand received a letter at his office at the college from a woman only revealed as Pam. He called a meeting at the art studio, still our secret hideaway, to show us.

Dear Leah and Company,

I can't tell you how much your speaking out meant to me and my family. My son Max was born with gifts like you. He talked about living blue lines and feeling sickness. We tried to laugh it off as an overactive imagination when he was young, but by the time he was fourteen, it was happening with too much frequency and accuracy to deny it. He also had visions, seeing things that would later come true. Some of his visions scared him, and he often didn't want to talk about them. Needless to say, he suffered greatly. In the second grade, he told a teacher, within earshot of the class, that she was going to die. She did, a few days later. Kids started teasing him, and the rumor that he caused her death spread almost immediately. Over the next several years, he was physically attacked repeatedly. But it was the psychological abuse that he couldn't escape from. We tried changing schools, then home schooling. But he couldn't leave the house without having a terrible encounter, and we couldn't afford to move. The stress led my husband and me to divorce, and Max took it very hard.

One night some people put an effigy of him in our front yard and set it on fire. I was out at the store and returned to find it blazing in front of the house with a sign that read, "Burn in Hell." I ran into the house looking for Max, and found him lying down in his bed, an empty pill bottle next to his hand and a note telling me how sorry he was on his chest. If he had known that there were others like him in the world—if he'd just held on a little longer. But his pain was too great.

I tell you this not to upset you, but to let you know how important you are to others in the world who are suffering because they think they are alone. It's too late to help my Max. But maybe I can try to do something positive with his death. He was supposed to receive an inheritance from his grandparents in a trust fund on his eighteenth birthday. I'm giving that money to you so you can continue to help people. Thank you for all you do, and God bless you.

Pam

Inside was a certified check for $125,000, made out to The Healer, LLC.

We were stunned. It was so much money and such a horrible story.

"That poor boy," Mary Ann said, tears streaming down her face like the rest of us.

"We have to reach people," I stated.

"What about the forum, Leah? That's definitely letting them know they're not alone," Rafi chimed in. He was right. The forum was several hundred members strong and growing.

"Yes, like the forum, but in person," I responded. "Like a center or something! Where they can be together but also practice using their abilities!" I nearly shouted as the idea opened up to me.

Mary Ann tugged at her lower lip. "I wonder if a center would work—it would cost a lot of money to build, but the donation from that family could definitely get us started, right?" She looked around the room. I was nodding enthusiastically, but Rafi and Dr. Anand were more subdued.

"It might work if we just found a building to rent, but we'd have to charge tuition or something to keep paying the bills," Rafi said. "Do you want the attendees to pay?"

"Not really," I replied, "But I know you can't run a business for free."

"You would have to recruit suitable staff, too," Dr. Anand added. "And pay a livable salary." Their reality was cramping my excitement.

"You guys—can we at least agree to start looking into it? In the meantime, I know how I want to spend the next several months. It's time I met other healers."

A couple weeks hadn't allayed the tides of people who gathered outside our house or the college, and the police department started fining us for the headache it was causing. I hardly thought that was fair, even though I knew our presence was the reason for the crowds. Once I decided to visit other healers, I didn't want to wait. Rafi and Dr. Anand worked to move the Virginia clinic up to the next week, calling all the scheduled participants and working through the chaos of the change.

Dr. Anand was not going to be able to help us with this one, as he was inundated with his teaching schedule. Since Alex wasn't starting school until the following week, we enlisted her to come with us and help in his place. Her parents were not thrilled with the idea. They feared for her safety after everything that had been happening. But they supported it in the end. It didn't hurt that she would be able to add an internship with The Healer, LLC, to her resume. We made it through the two weeks without too many hiccups and only one sighting that might have closed us down if it hadn't been on our last day. Alex helped me order a couple different wigs and sunglasses to use as disguises while there, and they seemed to do the job beautifully. We returned to the Midwest without incident, having helped another forty-five people.

In the meantime, Mary Ann and I narrowed our list down to three people, from either the forum or those who had emailed, who seemed to have the most similar experiences to mine. We planned to visit them all. The first was the Australian woman who wrote that she was having dreams of the goddess Isis. We decided to spend about three to five days with each healer. More and we'd risk exposure, less and we might not learn everything we needed to. Then we would take a few days or a week to play tourist before coming home to have short clinics in different towns. It took days and days of arranging, but we were ready to leave a week after finishing the Virginia clinic. Rafi was coming with us, of course.

Dr. Anand planned to meet us over Thanksgiving break when we'd be in Germany, right outside Berlin. It just so happened that Berlin was also home to the largest shamanism school in Europe, the Centre for Shamanic Studies. He arranged for us to tour the facility and see how they managed the school. Alex and Isaac would meet us in Spain right after Christmas for their winter breaks. Then we'd visit the last forum member on our list, and that's where our trip would end. After careful consideration, I contacted the three participants before leaving and asked them to quietly arrange places for us to hold short one- or two-day clinics near their homes. They could sit in and see what it was like, or maybe even practice.

The air was colder when we stepped out of the airport in Sydney, and I was reminded that winter was just finishing in this end of the world. I dug my hoodie out of my bag, and we loaded into our rental car to head north. We almost didn't make it out of the rental car parking lot, though. Mary Ann instinctually moved to the right side of the street, the same moment a truck was entering the lot—on the same side of the street. Rafi yelled, "Wrong side!" and she swerved just in time as the truck driver flipped her off.

"At least we can count on Australians being as charming as us Americans!" she chirped. Then playfully slapping her cheeks to wake up, she started again—this time on the correct side of the street, meaning the left.

The healer's name was Charlotte and she lived in the city of Newcastle, about two hours' drive from Sydney. We sped along the M1 Pacific Motorway, and the turquoise ocean that framed much of the drive was incredible. The city center seemed to be made of a few fingers of land mass that swirled around each other. It was absolutely beautiful. GPS led us to Charlotte's address, and we pulled into the driveway of a neat row of townhouses. Charlotte's was a light blue color and it felt calm and cheery at the same time. As we were stepping out of the car, the door to the townhouse flew open and a woman with a toddler clinging to her hip dashed out.

"Oh my God! Is it really you?! Leah? Mary Ann? And Rafi, right?" The baby on her hip was flung wildly about as she ran over to swallow us in massive hugs. Her hair was light blonde and piled in a messy bun on her head. She wore an apron over her clothes and the child had a spatula in his hand with some brown goo dripping off. "I'm Charlotte!" she exclaimed as though we hadn't already guessed. "And this little guy is Alphie—can you say hello, Alphie? These are the magic people I was telling you about! They are gonna help mommy figure out what all her crazies mean! Yes, they are!" She sang more than spoke, and her energy was like a sparkler on the Fourth of July. I liked her right away.

"Come in! Come in! Alphie and I were just baking you a little welcome cake, weren't we?" She snuggled his neck. "Of course, we meant to start hours ago so you could actually *eat* the cake when you arrived, but life happened!"

We followed her into a narrow foyer that led straight back to the kitchen. The house was more tall than wide, and a staircase and half bath sat to the right of the foyer. The kitchen was spacious, though, and made up the entire first floor. The foyer was painted a light lavender that bled into a deep plum in the kitchen. It looked really chic with the white cabinets and countertops. There was a large table to the right of the kitchen with six chairs, each a different color and shape. A huge vase of flowers took center stage on the table, and the rest was strewn with coloring pages, oversized Lego blocks and a mermaid doll. The kitchen counters were covered with flour and baking paraphernalia and the smell of chocolate wafted through the air.

"I absolutely adore your kitchen!" exclaimed Mary Ann. "Are you an artist? The color is so uplifting and fun—but not overwhelming at all."

Charlotte did a little happy jump. "Oh, thanks for saying so! I'm an interior decorator, actually, and 'fun without overwhelm' was exactly what I was going for in here. It's our favorite place in the house, isn't it, Alphie? We spend most of our time here, so I wanted to make sure I absolutely adored it. Now, make yourselves at home and have a seat, there's a hook for coats just behind that door. I'm making tea and we can have ourselves a fabulous tea party later! Are you hungry?" She put Alphie down and, with a sweep of her arm, scooped everything on the table into a basket stored underneath. Then she disappeared to the bottom half of her fridge. Pulling out a tray, she kicked the fridge door closed with her heel and accidentally got her apron string stuck, jerking her back, and nearly causing her to drop the tray. Rafi ran over to grab the tray so she could free herself. "Wooo! A near disaster! Just land that over on the table—thanks, mate! Some munchies for us to start off with." The tray was laden with sliced cheeses, curls of meats, little pickles, olives and two little pots of jellies. My mouth watered as Charlotte dropped a bowl of crackers and little plates down.

"Please don't hesitate, mates, it's meant to be eaten!" After two more trips, two bottles of white wine and four glasses were added to the finish the scene. Charlotte plopped down across from me and began pouring the wine. "Newcastle is on the edge of the best wine region in the country, Hunter Valley. This is a Semillon I've been chilling. Heaven in a glass, I say!" Just as she was passing one to me, she exclaimed, "Crikey! You're so young, Leah! Are you even old enough for this?"

"I'm not sure, actually—how old do I have to be?" I asked, desperately hoping I was old enough.

"Eighteen," she responded, and I smiled.

"I'm nineteen and a half, so I guess we're good!"

She nodded and passed me the glass. "Thank God, I'd have been so disappointed not to share it with you!" She raised her glass and we all followed suit. Little Alphie threw his sippy cup in the air. "I can't tell you how grateful and excited I am to have you here. Cheers to many discoveries and laughs over the next few days!"

"Cheers!" we responded, and the 'Heaven in a Glass' tingled on my tongue. We spent the next few hours chatting, eating, and drinking. When the cake was cool enough, Charlotte switched our wine glasses for tea mugs.

"Do you all want tea?" she asked. "The cake is choccy so hope that's to your liking." It was over unbelievable chocolate cake with hazelnut frosting and herbal tea that our talk shifted from reality to dreaming.

"Right. So I've had three dreams about the goddess over the last decade or so. The first I was holding a pink stone with white and blue lines through it. I was just turning it over and over in my hands and feeling its energy coursing through my body. I understood that it was very powerful and would help heal the sick and wounded. I didn't want to, but I reluctantly handed it back to a beautiful woman with dark hair and wearing linens, who I knew was my mother. She took it like it was the most precious item in the world, and I could still feel the energy linger on my fingers after it was gone. The loss was palpable." She sighed. "I was about fourteen when I had that dream. It was lovely, but I just decided it was a dream and that was that." Her eyes lit up as she spoke.

"Wait," I interrupted her. "In your dreams *you* aren't Isis?" I had been equally elated and disappointed when I learned Charlotte had dreams about Isis. The former because it meant I wasn't the only one. But the latter because how could the dreaming mean I was Isis in a previous life if someone else was dreaming the same thing? Now, I realized Charlotte had always said she'd dreamt *about* the goddess Isis—not that she *was* the goddess. If she was Horus, it was even more exciting!

"Oh no—definitely not Isis herself. I was her son, Horus! Though I didn't know that until after the second dream nearly three years later. I was actually in a movie theater if you can believe it—one of the Spider-man movies, you know, with what's his name in it? They make so many now it's hard to keep track!"

"Andrew Garfield? Tobey Maguire?" Rafi offered. He was a die-hard Marvel fan and had seen every movie about every character. I smiled at him.

"The first one, I think," she replied. "Anyway, I was seventeen and in the theater with a boy I liked, and suddenly my mother, Isis, and I were running through the desert with a mass of other people. I knew it was my uncle chasing us, and I knew he was trying to get the stone. If he caught us, he would kill us—especially me. My mother shoved me into a narrow, hollowed-out crack in the bark of an acacia tree and kept running. It was the most terrified I'd ever been, and I didn't want her to leave me, not knowing if she would be captured or not. In the rush to escape, her crown of a disc and horns fell off her head, and we paused as she jumped back for it. That's how I figured out it was Isis, or that my mother was Isis, because I recognized the crown. It felt just like a memory, you know?

"When I was alone in the dark tree trunk, shaking with terror, a deep voice that I recognized as my father's came to me. He said, 'Close your eyes and envision the sky, Horus. You are god of the sky, feel the wings in your back. Feel the wind in your face. The moon is calling you.' And I could feel it. When I opened my eyes again, I was a bird, a falcon.

I flew out of that tree and into the night sky just as a man arrived at the entrance to look for me. I'm telling you it was as real to me as sitting here now with you. Then it was over, and I was back in the movie theater. I had a bit of a mini panic attack and rushed out.

"Needless to say, the boy I was with thought I was completely bonkers when I tried describing what happened, and our first date turned into our last." She smiled a mischievous grin then and continued, "Worked out for me, though! When he abandoned me trying to catch my breath on a bench, the cute guy working the popcorn came over and asked if I was okay. Said he heard my story and thought dreams were really powerful messages from our subconscious, and shouldn't be taken lightly. That man became my husband a few years later, sweet love that he is!"

"You're young, too, then!" Mary Ann exclaimed.

"Yeah, I got married at twenty-one and had Alphie here at twenty-three. I'll be twenty-five in a couple months. I feel like I've lived a lifetime already, though, the way this one keeps me on my toes!" She scooped Alphie up into her lap, where he immediately lunged for her cake. She let him sink his chubby little fist into it, spraying crumbs all over the plate, and his fingers, which he then carefully licked off, a look of complete concentration on his face.

"It was after that dream in the theater that other things started happening. Like your electric lines, Leah! I was giving my mate a hug and saw them for the first time. Just like you said on the television: I couldn't describe *how* I understood, but the blue lines and humming just made sense. I freaked out and told my friend that something was happening with her head. Something terrible. She admitted to having a few headaches and some tingling in her face here and there, but nothing too crazy. But a doctor's appointment a few weeks later led to a CT scan, and don't you know, they found a large tumor pressing on her brain stem! Well! After that I was totally freaked out and didn't want to touch anyone. My love reassured me it was a good thing that I could sense what was wrong with her. He calmed me down. That happened once more between then and now, with a stranger. I never told the man what I saw, I was just too intimidated by the idea of telling him I knew he was sick just by handing him back his jacket. I chickened out, and the idea that I might have saved him by letting him know has haunted me ever since."

She took a sip of her tea and shook her head as though to cast away the unpleasant thought. "I can't fix that now, but maybe I can learn to help other people." She looked expectantly at me. "Oh! And that's when I started communicating with spirits." She said it so nonchalantly that I thought maybe I'd misheard her.

"Spirits? What do you mean?" Mary Ann asked, knitting her brow.

"At first it just felt like I had random voices in my ear from time to time calling my name. 'Charlotte!' and I'd turn but there'd be no one there. Every couple months it would happen—always different voices. Almost like they were calling my name from inside my head, you know? Does this never happen to you?" she asked me.

"No—never. I don't hear voices ever!" I was fascinated.

"I guess I just assumed whatever I have is the same as what you have. Anyway, once I had the third dream it became clearer. I was twenty-one, and it was about a week before the wedding. I had just closed my eyes to lie down in the tub with some ambient music, you know, the kind they play in spas? No words—lots of pan flute." She playfully rolled her eyes. "Well, I was just trying to de-stress from all the planning and wedding madness, and the most detailed 'dream' came rushing at me."

"The night was filled with the sounds of the desert. Swishes of snake bodies through sand, chirps of crickets, and the buzzing of flying insects were all around me. I sat very still under a wide-branched acacia tree. It was the oldest tree

I knew of, and I had spent many a night seeking wisdom at the base of its trunk. This night was no different. I had felt the call of my father and knew he needed to speak with me. The acacia tree was the best way, as the roots were a bridge between the world below and the world above. I waited, deeply engaged in disturbing thoughts. I had challenged Set for Egypt's throne and our battles had been fierce and damaging. I was stronger and cleverer, and though I won most of the trials the elders ordered, they were not satisfied. Unsure what more I could do to sway their judgment, I sat in frustration. The moon was a slight sliver in the inky blue sky, and I felt its presence— calming and supportive. The energy shifted and the leaves of the acacia waved as though a breeze passed through, but the night was still. I knew Osiris was with me.

"His deep voice resonated in my head. 'I'm in need of help, Horus. If you are to rule Egypt once again, you must strengthen your connection with the spirit realm that you may help ferry the spirits through their transition. Set has somehow cursed the banks of the Nile, preventing the souls of the dead to be guided peacefully through to the underworld. They are unable to reach the water. Some are using the acacia trees, but many are becoming lost. The longer they linger in the physical realm as spirits, the more confused they become. They latch onto the living. Lost spirits confuse the living and create madness, pain, sickness of the head and rage, as two spirits vie for control. Set is doing this to weaken our people. You must become the channel. You must use the power of mine that courses through your veins to guide the spirits to the next phase of their journey. You must draw them from the physical hosts they've contaminated.'

"I asked how I was supposed to accomplish this task. He told me to bathe in the Nile until I felt the space in my own spirit opening. The Nile would awaken my powers.

"He went on to tell me—er, Horus, to use himself, and, when the time was right, to teach his children to be bridges as well. I asked for his help with Set in return. He told me to have peace and patience. That Isis would be the one to deliver me to the throne of Egypt to rule justly and restore abundance and peace to the people once more.

"After that dream, the voices in my head became more frequent, but still not more than my name being called, like someone wanting my attention. I mean, the dream made me believe I was hearing lost spirits, but I still didn't know what to do about it. Then one night when I was pregnant with Alphie here, a male voice called to me. It was frustrating, actually, that I never heard anything else. Then I got an idea. I sat very quietly, closed my eyes, and, like in the vision, thought, 'I'm listening if you want to talk. I'm here. I'm ready.' I got a buzzy sensation in my body, like little vibrations, and the same male voice started talking. He said he was stuck between here and the underworld and asked if I could help him bridge to the other side. I told him I had no clue how to do that."

She paused and looked meaningfully at us. "I mean—can you imagine? What would I know about any of it? I told him as much, but he calmly replied I was a channel between worlds and could help if I allowed myself to open. He couldn't tell me how to do it, though, so I tried getting creative."

"I pictured myself standing beside a beautiful garden fountain that had a stopper in the bottom so no water could flow through. With my eyes still closed, I envisioned reaching down and pulling the stopper. Water flowed up from the hole high into the air above me and cascaded down as gentle rain, back into the fountain basin. As I envisioned this, I thought, 'I've opened the channel now and will help you.'

"Suddenly, there were lights in my mind's eye. Spheres of soft yellow-ish white light that serenely floated around me. I heard the voice say 'Thank you' to me just as the lights floated into me. When I tell you I felt nothing but joy, pure joy in that moment, it is not exaggeration. I was moved to tears with how beautiful they were. And then once they shifted into me, they were gone! I was so sad—devastatingly sad!

"The sadness lingered the rest of the day, but then I went back to feeling my cheerful self—until the same thing happened a couple days later. First, the voice in my head, and me offering to help. This time I didn't even close my eyes, my vision changed to the light spheres anyway. Again the joy, again the sadness. The third time it happened, it was a terribly inconvenient time as I was in a client meeting. So I excused myself to the bathroom and sat on the loo with my eyes closed. I thought, 'I hear you and I want to help, but I can't right now.' I couldn't really see me explaining the sudden need to weep over paint colors to my client, you know? The voice told me that if I wasn't able to help, I should close the channel I'd opened. It was brilliant! So I envisioned physically putting the plug back in and stopping the flow of water—and that was that! From then on, I could choose when to open myself to help the spirits and when I needed to control it.

"I still hear them call my name from time to time while the channel is closed, but if I think, 'Not now, please, but soon,' they don't bother me. I try not to take too long before I take the stopper out now, as there are many spirits that need help. I still don't exactly know how or why they get stuck, but I've been able to figure out that they channel through me when they're ready to take a different form. I won't say it doesn't take me for an emotional roller coaster, though! I need to be very careful when I decide to open the channel, and not to forget to close it."

I couldn't believe it. "Mary Ann! This is what I experienced in the hospital that night! Remember me telling you about the spheres of light that surrounded me? I thought they might be God—but you're saying I was channeling spirits through to another dimension or something? This is incredible! And I felt the same extreme joy when they diffused into me that you described. And the terrible sadness after."

Having someone to understand that experience was incredibly relieving; I didn't realize how much I needed it. Charlotte seemed over the moon, too, as she jumped up and ran over to my side of the table to lift me in a hug.

"I'm so happy!" she cried.

"I never heard voices, though. And it hasn't happened since that night. Do you think I should try what you did with the fountain and plug?" I asked Charlotte.

"I don't know, but it might be worth a shot. It's such a relief knowing I'm not a complete nut job! Or if I am—you are right there with me!" She winked at me.

"Leah, doesn't this make a certain amount of sense? Horus was the son of Osiris, who supposedly ruled the underworld, right? When he and Isis used the stone to make the four children, doesn't that mean their children had a mixture of everyone's abilities? Osiris and the underworld, Horus and fertility and justice, and Isis with healing?" Rafi asked.

"Ummm—Isis and Horus *made* four children?" Charlotte asked. "But they were mother and son!" We filled her in on my dream as she sat wide-eyed, absorbing every syllable. Alphie, who had fallen asleep on the soft rug under the table, let out a little snore. "Oh! Poor Alphie, mum's forgotten you were even here. What time is it anyway? 11 p.m.! Let me get this little love to his bed."

The time since our arrival had passed so quickly, I couldn't believe it was so late.

"We should get to the house, too," Mary Ann added, more quietly now that we remembered we had a sleeping toddler with us.

With the promise of returning for lunch the next day, we all took our travel-weary bodies to bed. I fell asleep the moment my head hit the pillow, and my dreams were filled with colorful lights and animals and spirits, all dancing happily around me.

The next morning none of us woke early; the Airbnb had blackout curtains in every room, and it was 9 a.m. before even Mary Ann stirred. I woke to the smell of coffee brewing and rolled over to find Rafi gently stirring beside me. I put my hand on his back and he turned to face me.

"How did you sleep?" he asked.

"Crazy dreams. I think the excitement mixed with the time difference was messing with me. You?"

"Like the dead, actually. Felt like I just shut my eyes for a moment and it's already morning." He sighed contentedly. "Yesterday was pretty enlightening—how are you feeling about it?"

"Relieved, actually," I answered. "I didn't realize how much I needed to connect with someone else like me." I stretched my arms overhead lazily.

"Do you think you're a channel like she is? Does that freak you out at all? Communicating with spirits?" he asked.

I thought for a minute. "It's not that it freaks me out. The experience I had in the hospital wasn't scary at all. Being able to hear spirits might be a different story." I gave a little shudder at the idea of speaking with the dead. "I'm just a bit concerned that the emotional ups and downs will be hard. The joy and the sadness really were as extreme as she said. I wonder if I'll be able to do it and still function throughout a day." I moved back in to lay my head on Rafi's chest and intertwined our limbs. "I'm so grateful you're here with me," I told him, and meant it. Having him near was incredibly comforting. Like home.

He kissed the top of my head and pulled me in closer. "With you is where I'm meant to be. I feel that every day."

When we arrived at Charlotte's a little after eleven a.m., a tall, thin man with blue eyes and wavy, sun-kissed hair opened the door.

"Ah! Here you all are. I'm Simon, Charlotte's husband. It's so wonderful to have you here." He gave us each a hug as we entered. If Charlotte's energy was like a waterfall, Simon's was a lazy river. Happy and comfortable, but calm and in no hurry.

Charlotte bounded on us as we entered the house. "I hardly slept a wink! Poor Simon got in around midnight and I didn't stop talking till at least 1:30 in the morning! There was just so much to process, and I wanted him to know all of it before we met again today. He's my center of gravity, this man—keeps me from falling over at any moment."

She laughed at herself and ushered us all into the kitchen. Alphie was happily waving at us from his highchair, spraying the room with Cheerios in the process.

"We've prepared a little luncheon for this afternoon—but it's such a crisp morning I thought we could start with a walk. I always do my best thinking after a bit of fresh air and exercise, don't you? Plus, we'll work up an appetite!"

We all agreed, and once Alphie had his shoes and coat and was strapped in his stroller, we headed out. There was a lovely wooded walking path not far from their townhouse, and the sounds of birds called to us. Simon took one long, languid stride for every two of Charlotte's.

"Rafi, you have some abilities, too, right?" Simon asked him. "Do yours come from the god genes as well?" It was a funny but apropos way to describe it.

"Actually, I'm not sure. I can read people's energy. Kind of like seeing a broad stroke of their intention or mood in the moment. It's not very detailed, but usually lets me know who I can trust, or if someone's being straight with me." We'd had debates about Rafi's abilities many times before. There were others on the forum who could read energy, but we weren't sure if it was because they were descendants or got their abilities from some other source.

"That would sure be handy for a relationship!" he laughed. "Not that Charlotte hides her emotions at all—I pretty much know exactly what she's feeling at all times," he said with a wry grin, and Charlotte turned around to bat him with her hat.

"I can't use it with Leah," Rafi lamented. "She feels it immediately and calls me out."

"Oh, too bad," Simon agreed. "I do understand a little bit about the challenges of having a partner with 'special' talents." He chuckled and Rafi smiled.

We were heading back to their house when a woman's voice called out to us from across the street. "Yoo hoo, Charlotte! Is this your healer?" A stout woman with a bright purple dress and flip flops yelled loudly from her front stoop. She smiled and waved at us, a kitchen towel in her hand. "Shall I still come over tomorrow so you can work on my head?"

Mary Ann, Rafi and I looked around frantically to see if anyone could overhear us. Charlotte seemed unconcerned.

"Yes, Colleen, come on over around 2 p.m., and we'll see if I've learned my magic yet! See you then, love!"

The woman waved her towel at us one last time before closing the door. Charlotte looked at our stricken faces and seemed surprised. "You said to set up a mini clinic for while you're here, so I sent a mass email to all my neighbors. We have about ten people to heal. Colleen there suffers recurrent migraines that are just terrible." I must have looked as horrified as I felt. "My goodness—was that wrong of me to do? What's the matter?" she asked me.

Mary Ann spoke first. "Charlotte, we need our visits to be as secretive as possible. Remember about all the protesting and craziness that Leah mentioned on the phone? It's really important that people don't know where we are when we go to visit a place; otherwise, it will be mayhem!" I nodded along. Charlotte was unbothered, however.

"Oh, no worries about all that, mate. These people all know me, and I've talked about my dreams and the spirits for years. In fact, I saw the blue electric lines on Colleen a month ago when she was in the midst of a migraine—I just didn't know what to do with them!" She patted my shoulder. "No one is going to rat you out while you're here, I'm sure of it. And who better to help than the people I'm closest with, right?"

I was still uneasy about it, but what could we do? We went back to their house and had an absolute feast of roasted Cornish hens with thyme and lemon, wild mushrooms and small potatoes in gravy, and wilted arugula with garlic. It was quite possibly the best meal I'd ever eaten.

"Charlotte, where did you learn to cook like this? You're incredible!" Mary Ann exclaimed.

Charlotte smiled in her delight at the comment. "Like I said yesterday, the kitchen is my favorite place and where I spend all my time pretty much. I love cooking almost as much as I love eating."

That afternoon, I taught Charlotte about the healing ribbons and how I called them to me with intention and the dedication. She meditated on the image of them, and when she asked, they appeared for her. She nearly jumped out of her chair in her excitement, and sent Alphie into a startled crying fit.

"They're beautiful and yellow, almost like they're alive!" she exclaimed.

"Yellow? Do you mean white?" I asked. "The ribbons I see are soft white."

"No, definitely yellow—soft yellow for sure—but yellow." I was confused that Charlotte should see different colored ribbons than I did, but I didn't worry much about it. It was my turn to learn.

I tried envisioning a fountain and pulling the plug to open my channel. No beings arrived, nothing happened at all actually. I will admit I was disappointed.

"Maybe you need to find your own way to open your channel," Charlotte suggested. "Something that makes sense to you."

We ended the night and went back to our rental house, promising to return bright and bushytailed at 9 a.m., because Charlotte's neighbors would start arriving promptly at 10 a.m. That night I asked Mary Ann and Rafi if they had any ideas about why Charlotte should see different colored ribbons of light, and why nothing happened when I tried to open my channel.

"Maybe every healer sees a different color of light," Mary Ann suggested. "Maybe Charlotte was right and you need to find your own image to represent the opening of the channel?" In the end, I went to bed with a lot more "maybes" than I expected. After much tossing and turning, I finally fell asleep.

Psychopomp:
(Greek) A mythological creature whose purpose is to guide deceased souls to the afterlife, the spiritual guide for a person's soul.

CHAPTER 20

***

Horus stood before me, just barely a man, but already heavy with experience. He was out of breath for having run to my hut—my secret place of solitude where only a worn mat and clay walls let me focus my thoughts in private. Horus knew of this hut, of course, but I was surprised to find him here. He usually respected the sanctity of its purpose, even from him. His face was troubled.

"Horus! Peace, son—what has happened?" I asked, fearing our location had been revealed, somehow.

"It is Set. Osiris told me he has cursed the banks of the Nile so spirits cannot cross through to the underworld." I gasped. "How? He could not have managed this on his own." I thought for a moment. "The spirits will grow confused and infect the living!" I cried, realizing what this would mean for our people.

"That is what Osiris said. He believes Set has done this to weaken our people. He says I must bathe in the Nile to open my own spirit to its channeling powers. I need your help, Mother." Set was spreading evil to the living and the dead alike with this move. "We must go at once."

We took off running, and finally arrived at the bank of the great river just as dusk was descending.

"We must hurry, the animals that feast at night will be our company too soon. Wade to the center, Horus. Take a large breath of air and submerge." He waded as I spoke and paused when the water was at his waist, looking left and right for signs of crocodiles. I could see his chest rise and fall rapidly with fear, but he did not give his fear voice.

"What do I do once I submerge? How will I know when I've opened?" he asked.

"This I cannot tell you. But the great river is the gateway for our spirits and the lifeblood of our living world. Have faith that it will give you what is needed."

He waded until he could no longer stand. Facing me, our eyes locking, he filled his lungs and descended into the dark water. I kept a sharp eye on the water's surface for signs of movement, though the light was rapidly fading. Far off to the right—there! —a ripple interrupted the calm. And another! Horus was not yet risen, but I sensed he was now being hunted. Racing forward quickly to the water's edge, I began splashing. I stepped into my ankles and kicked up silt and water. The ripple changed direction in response to my movement, and I watched it race toward me. The ripple grew bigger, revealing a large body below the surface. My heart raced at what I would encounter. I frantically reached through the folds of my linens looking for my dagger. Finally, I pulled it forth as a large snout crested the surface not far from where I stood. I let out a cry and turned to leap out of the water and onto the bank. It was faster than me, though and the moment I heard its feet on dry land I turned and raised my dagger. I struck down hard as the creature lunged at me.

The blade met the flesh of its snout, making it turn its head just in time to miss my arm. Its thrashing teeth met my left foot, however, and I screamed in pain as it took hold. It started to drag me back into the murky water and certain death, and I clawed at the dusty earth for something to hold onto.

Just then its body lurched and began thrashing. My mangled foot was released as I saw the form of Horus take strike after strike with his own dagger to the animal's legs and belly, and finally its throat. Horus, covered in blood, dragged the massive crocodile's now-limp body back into the water and let it float away from us. Then he ran as best he could to my side.

"You're hurt!" he yelled.

"Just my foot, have peace, Horus. You are hurt too, are you not?" I scanned him in the dim light, but every inch seemed covered in dark red.

"Only scratches, Mother." He splashed himself with water to reveal torn up skin, with one massive cut across his chest.

"Come here, Horus. Help me to the top of the bank." He supported me on my left side. The pain was intense, and I fought to control the urge to cry out. Once a safe distance from the river's edge, we sat. "Come closer, I need to heal that gash." I held out my hand to Horus, but he hesitated.

"You first, Mother. That foot will not last long if you don't act quickly." I looked at my ragged flesh, my foot hanging limp on my ankle. I nodded.

I said the dedication and brought the dancing light into my foot. After seven ribbons, I finally felt the warmth of healing and looked down to see new pink scars covering my foot. I wiggled my toes and rotated my ankle. Good. It would not look pretty, but it would function again. Horus moved to my side and I directed the light into his wound. When finished, he had a shiny horizontal stripe of new skin extending from his right armpit to his left ribcage—a mark of honor to remind him always of this day.

"What did you discover in the depths, Horus? Did you get the answers you sought?"

Horus nodded thoughtfully. "I was nearly out of air when suddenly I felt every cell in my body expanding. I needed no air. I was filled with air and space and eternity spread out before my mind's eye. I saw beings of light float along with me. I offered them passage. Then they passed through me and I had full understanding."

"Can you sense spirits now?" I asked him. If what Osiris said was true, there would be many stuck on the other

side of the banks. "Wait, we are still on the bank. We must move further from the water."

Once settled, Horus closed his eyes and opened his arms. "I offer you passage!" he shouted. I watched for several minutes as he did not move except for his eyes flicking back and forth under his eyelids. Finally, he exhaled audibly, dropped his arms and opened his eyes. Tears streamed down his cheeks and he sank to his knees to catch his breath. I rushed to his side.

"Is it painful?" I asked.

"No...no. It's the most joyful feeling you can imagine. It's just that when they have finished passing, the joy passes with them, and in its place sits despair." He got to his feet and I embraced him.

"You must fulfill your father's wishes now, Horus. Help the spirits that have bound themselves to the living. Free them both and channel the spirits to their rightful place."

"How do I know when a living person has been bound by a spirit?" Horus asked.

"They will have changed," I answered. "They might have gone mad, or become angry when once they were happy. And they will usually have pain—bouts of intense pain in their head as the spirit tries to gain footing, but cannot. Seek out those people. Disguise yourself and go through the villages. When you find a lost spirit, place your hands on them. The blue lights should appear and will confirm a lost spirit is present. Ask to help guide the lost spirit to the underworld. I am not sure, but I think a form of healing light energy will appear to you, as it does for me. Use the light and the contact of your hand to pull them out and through to you instead. You will understand when the time comes. Now go, my son, because night is coming, and the living need your help."

***

I woke up soaked in sweat. I grasped at my left foot but found it unchanged. The room was dark and Rafi lay beside me, sleeping soundly. I shook him awake.

"Rafi!" I whispered. "Rafi—wake up!"

He stirred and turned toward me. "What is it? You okay?" He sat up, trying to rouse himself.

"I had another vision. Horus was a channel. Like Charlotte today. Horus had the ability to help spirits move from this world to the next." I explained the whole dream as he patiently listened.

"So you must have this ability, too, right? I mean, you channeled the spirits in the hospital, right?" he asked.

"Yes, but I couldn't do it today. Couldn't open the channel, I guess." A thought occurred to me. "Wait! Charlotte said it finally happened for her when she sat quietly and offered to help them. And then Horus did the same thing in the Nile! He offered to be their guide, and they came forward! Maybe they will only be able to pass if someone announces they're willing to let them pass." This sounded right to me and I sat up and closed my eyes, ready to try.

"Leah, wait!" interrupted Rafi. "It's the middle of the night. Can't we wait until the morning to try? We have a big day tomorrow and we need to be rested."

I sighed. "I guess you're right. Okay—let's try in the morning." I kissed his forehead and we both lay back down to try to sleep again.

It took me a long while to get to sleep after what I'd discovered with the dream, but I finally did because it was light when I next opened my eyes. I looked at my phone on the nightstand. It read 7 a.m. I carefully sat up so as not to rouse Rafi, closed my eyes and placed my hands palm up on my thighs. I breathed carefully and slowly.

When I felt relaxed and ready, I thought, "I'm ready to open my channel. I want to help you get to the next realm. I offer myself as your passage."

I felt a tingling in my head and some vibrations in my body. I then imagined a fountain with a plug at the bottom. I reached down and pulled open the plug allowing a spray of water to flow through. A moment later a female voice whispered, "Thank you" just as spheres of light became visible. There were two and they wafted toward me through the black backdrop of my mind's eye. Soon they passed into me, and I felt the intense joy like I had in the hospital. A moment later they were gone, and the despair took their place. Rafi woke to the sounds of my crying.

"What's happened?" he asked, wrapping one strong arm around my shoulders and pulling me gently in.

"I did it," I said, gathering myself together and stopping the tears. "I am a channel."

I was mostly recovered by the time we pulled into Charlotte's driveway. We stepped into the house and were met with the scent of rich coffee and the table laden with crusty breads, jams, meats, cheeses, and a green salad.

"I'm a savory breakfast girl—none of that sugary stuff first thing—yech!" she exclaimed as we took seats to eat. She then narrowed her eyes at me. "What's going on, Leah?" she asked. "Something's happened, hasn't it?"

I filled her and Simon in on the dream and my experience with the channeling. Charlotte stared wide-eyed, as though not to miss a single word. We didn't have too much time to talk about it, though, because when I finally finished the tale, we only had ten minutes before the first neighbor was due to arrive to start the clinic. We all pitched in to clean up from breakfast, and just finished as the doorbell rang.

"Here we go!" chirped Charlotte, running over to open the door. Simon scooped Alphie up, "Come on, mate. You and I have a date upstairs to play with some cars." Alphie clapped and they disappeared around the landing.

The first arrival was a gentleman named Richard who lived one street over and complained he suffered from gout. I placed my hands on him and saw the blue lines, then instructed Charlotte to do the same.

"I don't see anything," she said sadly, and tried again to no avail.

The next two arrivals were the same. One had a heart condition and the next had MS. Each time I saw the blue electric lines the moment I touched them. But Charlotte saw nothing at all. After the fourth visitor, an older gentleman with prostate cancer, I thought Charlotte might cry.

"Why isn't it working?" she asked as we had our lunch break. "I saw the lines before! Twice! So why can't I see what you see?" She looked at me, her eyes pleading for some explanation, but I had none.

After lunch, it was Colleen's turn. Charlotte was dejected and it showed. "Hey, mate, come on in. How's your head today?" she asked her.

"No migraine today, thankfully, but last night was a doozy! It's a good thing we scheduled after lunch because I didn't even get out of bed until an hour ago." Colleen sat at the table and smiled at us expectantly.

"May I place my hands on you, Colleen?" I asked her.

"Of course!" she replied, and I placed my hands over hers on the table. Nothing happened.

"You say you have chronic migraines?" I asked her.

"Yes—bloody awful. Every other day it seems. Doctors have no idea what's the matter with me." I tried again, but still no electric blue lines.

"I don't feel anything wrong," I said.

Charlotte looked at me confused. "But I saw the lines before with Colleen. And I know how she suffers."

"Charlotte, you try. It worked for you before, but I'm not getting anything," I offered.

"Don't get your hopes up, mate. I haven't had any luck yet today," she told her friend. But the minute Charlotte placed her hands on Colleen, she gasped. "I see the blue lines! Clear as day, running this way and that. Like they're alive!"

I tried again but still I saw nothing. "Where are they centered, Charlotte?" I asked her.

"Nowhere. They just run this way and that. There's no center." I wished I could see inside her head. "Try to call up the ribbons of light," I instructed her.

She whispered a dedication and then raised her eyebrows in surprise. "The yellow light ribbons appeared! Now what?" she asked, keeping her eyes closed.

"Place the fingers of your left hand on Colleen's forehead—good—now try to grab one of the ribbons and feed it to where your fingers are touching Colleen." Charlotte moved her right hand through the air as though grasping something and brought it toward her other fingers. "Okay—I have one end of the ribbon to Colleen's forehead. Oh! And the other end of the ribbon attached itself to my head. Is that normal?"

This is going so strangely, I thought. "I don't know—it might be normal for you. Just go with it and let's see what happens."

"Oh my! There's light traveling along the ribbon. A white sphere of light! Traveling from Colleen to me! Oh!" she cried out and opened her eyes wide. Tears started flowing down her cheeks. "It was a spirit! A spirit traveled through from you to me!" She looked wide-eyed at Colleen.

"Of course!" I yelled, jumping out of my chair. "The migraines! Like my dream last night. Colleen suffers unexplained migraines—she had a lost spirit in her body! And you—" I turned to point at Charlotte. "You could sense the spirit and draw it out with your energy lines!"

"Could that be it?" Charlotte asked.

Rafi added, "It makes so much sense! Leah, you heal illness and injury and could sense what was wrong with everyone before Colleen—but Charlotte could not. Then Colleen comes and you couldn't detect any illness or injury, but Charlotte could! Because the trouble with Colleen wasn't with her body, it was with her spirit! Leah—you're a physical healer. But you, Charlotte, you're a spiritual healer! Just like Horus was!" He finished and we all looked at each other amazed.

Finally, Colleen spoke, looking back and forth between us. "So—I have a ghost haunting me? And who the devil is Horus?"

The rest of the clinic went fine, even though Charlotte wasn't able to do much for anyone. She still placed her hands on them to check if they had an extra traveler. We spent the next couple days eating and talking about how Charlotte could best use her abilities. She had a nurse friend who worked at John Hunter Hospital in the city. Her plan was to reach out to her and see if she had any connections in the psychiatry department. There was also a prominent headache clinic in the city, so we helped her find wording to approach that practice so she wouldn't seem like a complete loony. In the end, she felt at peace with not being a physical healer.

"It's such a bloody relief to understand more about what I can do, I can't even tell you," she said. "And now I have my focus, I can help loads of people get their lives back.

We said goodbye to Charlotte, Simon, and Alphie the next morning, with a few tears and promises to keep each other posted on everything. Then Mary Ann, Rafi, and I drove back to Sydney to spend a few days sightseeing. And while the opera house and the tower were incredible, my favorite excursion was the whale-watching cruise. We were lucky enough to see one Minke whale and three humpback whales during the tour. One even came over to check the boat out, swimming alongside us for ten minutes or so. To see such a large animal that close was really intimidating, but such a thrill. I did worry for a moment when the guide announced the whale and everyone on the boat ran over to the side to see, that we would tip over with the shift in weight, but it was fine, and I got an awesome picture from the upper deck. Eight days after our arrival, we boarded a plane bound for home.

McCarthyism:
The act of discrediting people with baseless accusations.

CHAPTER 21

A couple weeks after getting home, we held a clinic in an event room at the local Hilton. For a ridiculous fee, we could have the room and security on staff. We used the back catering entrance, so as not to be a nuisance to the guests or clog the main parking area with a mob of people. It worked so well that we decided we'd try to rent out hotel event rooms for the next two scheduled clinics. Hotel staff put out water, coffee, and tea, and there was a restroom directly outside our event space. We didn't even need to hang curtains for privacy, as the room had a folding half-wall that could open and close as much or as little as we needed. A few of the participants had driven quite a way to make their appointments, and ended up booking rooms at the hotel to make it more convenient, especially for those who were very sick and not easily transported.

Fall passed quickly with the two additional clinics we held in Denver and Minneapolis. Denver went pretty well aside from the time I tripped on a curb and fell to the ground, dislodging my blonde wig. We were downtown, near Pearl Street, and a group of partying college kids ran over to help. When they saw my face, they freaked out and made a scene, taking photos and shouting they'd "found the Healer!" Luckily, a yellow cab passed at that moment, and we flagged it down. One of the college group ran to a car parked not far away and made to follow us. We promised the driver double the fee if he lost him, which he managed to do, thankfully.

Things could have been much worse in Minneapolis. The hotel security was having some difficulty with the crowd getting rowdy outside the barrier set up to separate participants from the simply curious. One group of about five protestors then began acting strangely and huddled together, their backs to everyone else. A security guard saw what looked to be a bulge in the rear waistband of one, and went over to investigate. They not only found the one gun, but between the five protestors, there were three handguns and two semi-automatic rifles with extra magazines. I was horrified to think what might have come to pass if the guard hadn't seen that bulge. Even though the men and woman were arrested, we cancelled the final couple days of the clinic as a precaution and left early for home.

Finally, in late November, we headed to Berlin. While I wasn't sure what would be waiting for us in Europe, I was glad to not be in the states for a couple months. The experience in Minneapolis had rattled me. Dr. Anand was set to join us in a couple days for his two-week term break, and then Mary Ann, Rafi, and I would tour Europe for a couple weeks before meeting Alex and Isaac in Barcelona just after Christmas.

I was also looking forward to meeting Jeorg, the next healer on our tour. Jeorg was still a teenager and lived with his sisters and parents in a small apartment about a ten-minute train ride out of the city. He had been difficult to communicate with, not readily answering emails.

In stark contrast with our experience with Charlotte, Jeorg's parents were not welcoming, nor did they offer to feed us. When we arrived on their doorstep, the mother scowled at us and only reluctantly let us in the house. Rafi squeezed my hand hard in warning when he realized I was about to tell them where they could shove their attitude. The parents hovered on either side while we spoke with Jeorg. He had experienced the blue crisscrossing lights a couple times in the past and had more recently had them appear when he touched his dad, Claus. Claus didn't say much, but nodded briefly when I asked if I could place my hands on him. Once done, I turned to Jeorg but didn't say anything.

"It's his heart, right?" he asked in perfect, clipped English. I nodded and gave Claus a small smile, which he didn't return. "He's been short of breath lately, and feeling somewhat queasy," Jeorg said.

His mother spoke to him quickly and harshly in German, and he looked chastised. "Sorry, I shouldn't have spoken about private matters with strangers." He looked at us apologetically, but we smiled and told him it was okay. "So, what do I do to fix it?" Jeorg asked.

I took a little time with Jeorg explaining the dedication—the ribbons of energy. His mother kept sighing and rolling her eyes every time I opened my mouth. It was clear she thought we were full of nonsense. Eventually, hesitantly under his parents' judgmental gaze, Jeorg called for and received the lights in his mind's eye. His face lit up with excitement when it happened, and he began waving his hands around to play with the ribbons. To an outsider, I knew very well, it looked somewhat ridiculous.

"Jeorg!" yelled his mother abruptly. "Stop that at once, you look like a fool!" She slapped his hands out of the air. His eyes startled open, the smile erased from his face and was replaced with fear. He quickly placed his hands in his lap and looked at the floor.

Mary Ann turned to the mother. "I understand it can seem very strange to us, who aren't seeing what Jeorg and Leah see. But I assure you they *do* see it, and it is the key to being able to heal someone."

The mother frowned and crossed her arms, "My son will not be made a fool by American charlatans. You show him what you came to show him and then leave. I don't need the neighbors talking about the kind of people we let into our home."

I stood up. "Do you not understand we are here to help your son? And your son will in turn heal your husband! Jeorg, please believe I want to help you, but we won't sit here while she insults us and treats us like intruders. Now you know how to call the ribbons, you can begin to heal people. I have faith in you, and reach out whenever you need a friend, okay? We're leaving." I reached back and grabbed Rafi's hand in mine, then turned to stare down the mother as we walked out. Jeorg looked distraught. Out of the corner of my eye, I saw Mary Ann discreetly hand him a small piece of paper which he quickly hid in his pocket. I couldn't get out of that house fast enough.

"Poor Jeorg! That woman is a nightmare!" Suddenly, I remembered something. "Mary Ann, what did you give Jeorg when we were leaving?"

"Once it was clear what kind of hell he lived in, I knew I needed to give him direct contact to you," Mary Ann said. "It was your personal cell number. When I excused myself to the bathroom, I wrote it on an old receipt with a note that said, 'Please call Leah when you're feeling helpless. You have friends in us.' Then I added the postscript, 'Please never share the number with anyone.' It's obvious he will find no support at home, and I kept thinking of that poor boy Max, who was about Jeorg's age. And Max's mom believed in him! I don't want Jeorg to get to a point like Max did, where it felt too painful to go on. I figured if he knew at least we could be in his back pocket when he needed us, it might make the difference."

I grabbed her in a massive hug. "I love you, Mary Ann. Thank you for doing that!" I felt so much better just knowing he had a way to reach us, and the walk became a little lighter.

Dr. Anand was waiting for us at the hotel when we got back, having just flown in. We brought each other up to speed over dinner. He was in a terrible state, more upset than I'd ever seen him. There had been an altercation at the college. A group calling itself God's Army had marched through the campus just as the evening classes were letting out. Carrying placards, they shouted at students and faculty passing in their midst. They claimed loudly that Dr. Anand was defaming God's name by proclaiming a human to be more powerful than the Almighty, which was utter garbage.

Even less relevant, but more upsetting, they shouted that Dr. Anand was a foreign terrorist—that he'd been arrested back in India, and the university was supporting a criminal. Dr. Anand was not present during these verbal attacks. Some of his students had apparently yelled back in his defense, and the confrontation became physical. Campus security used batons, and when the police arrived, they used tear gas to break up the melee. Three students were sent to the hospital. It was all over the news. The president decided to close the campus a day early for the Thanksgiving holidays, and told Dr. Anand that when he returned from Germany they would "have a discussion." Dr. Anand worried they'd fire him over the incident.

"Were you ever arrested in India?" Mary Ann asked him. "Will they find anything there if they look?"

He nodded. "Yes. It was during The Emergency period in the mid to late seventies. Indira Gandhi was prime minister. She orchestrated a campaign of 'forced sterilization' that swept through states. The law mandated that men who fit a certain criterion, such as advanced age or already having a certain number of children, to have vasectomies, and some women to have tubal ligations or forced IUDs. It disproportionately targeted Muslims and poor areas, and by the time the campaign ended, roughly eleven million people had been sterilized. Can you even imagine?

"They imposed horrible tactics such as withholding pay or denying food rations unless people complied, or they would physically force the procedures. I was arrested during a protest after an incident in the village of Uttawar." He shook his head sadly. "Police surrounded the village and announced over loudspeakers that every male above the age of fifteen needed to assemble, then they searched homes for anyone who might be trying to hide. They separated all the men, like sheep or cattle, into groups based on eligibility for sterilization, and then immediately took the eligible groups to have it done. It was disgusting.

"I can't even imagine how this group would have found record of it." He was beside himself with misery. "It was supposed to be a peaceful protest, but people were poor, and angry, and terrified, so in the end it turned violent. Several government and military vehicles were set afire, and many protestors set upon the police with whatever weapons they could find—bats, rocks, really primitive stuff." He looked at us sincerely. "I had no part in the violence! I was just a young man—and I was not a target of the campaign, but I just couldn't sit idly by. I spent three nights in a holding cell with about fifty others who had also been arrested. If I get let go from the college for this, I will never find a viable position again. And those poor students! One girl, Sasha, had just been telling me in class how she was so homesick and couldn't make the hours until break move fast enough. Now she's stuck in the hospital with a concussion and the doctors don't want her to travel."

"Did you go to the hospital?" Rafi asked Dr. Anand.

"Yes. The moment I heard what happened. I sat with the three of them most of the night. Nothing too serious, thankfully. A broken thumb, Sasha with the concussion I just mentioned, and a busted nose. I just feel so responsible. They were defending my name." He dropped his head into his hands.

"Who even are these people? God's Army?" Mary Ann asked.

"Apparently they're a Christian terrorist group," Dr. Anand said. "They like to blow up abortion clinics and the like. This was supposedly a local contingent, so not too big of an operation. But things are getting out of control."

The next day the four of us set off to tour the Centre for Shamanic Studies. About an hour's drive outside Berlin, we approached a long driveway flanked with forest. Many trees were bare as it was the end of November, but there were evergreens peppered throughout. The driveway opened up to a large resort in the style of a country manor. It had ochre stucco and a red-tiled roof, and branched out in three sections, each four stories tall. Dr. Anand's acquaintance, and our guide, Karl Becker, met us in the driveway to begin our tour.

Karl was tall and broad, with a full beard of jet-black hair except for two white streaks on either side of his mouth. His affable demeanor immediately made us feel welcome. As we walked the building, Karl told us he, along with most of the staff of ten, lived in the building year-round. Two wings were set up more like a hotel, with individual suites and bathrooms for the staff and those wishing to stay during longer seminars. The center of the building down below held a large conference room adjacent to a smaller conference room, both with floor to ceiling windows that looked out over a field and woods. Beyond that were the kitchen and dining room where three "health-conscious" meals were served daily. The third wing had smaller classroom-sized rooms as well as spaces for meditation and a music room filled with musical instruments of all sorts, the majority being drums, some as large as me. The music room ceiling opened up two stories, and it was an octagonal shape covered in windows, with dozens of multicolored cushions in rows leading away from a small, raised stage.

We ran into several people during our tour, as a weeklong seminar called "Advanced Shamanic Healing: Assisting the Dying" was just finishing up. Everyone we passed smiled and said hello, and I was amazed at how much energy there was in the building. One man in particular had an aura of yellow and light blue that I saw without even trying as he stood on the far side of a room, speaking with another man and woman.

Karl leaned in to whisper, "That's Michael During. He's leading the seminar. Perhaps you can feel his energy?" I nodded. Dr. Anand had briefed Karl on my peculiarities before we arrived. "He is a very strong intuitive shaman. I will introduce you while they are in break."

We moved over toward the group. Michael During's back was to us, but he turned when we came within twenty feet and raised his eyebrows. Looking straight into my eyes, he rattled off something excitedly in German while taking my hands in his. I looked pleadingly to Karl for help.

"Michael, they are visitors from America," Karl said. "They don't speak German, I'm afraid. Michael During, may I present Leah, Mary Ann, Rafi, and Dr. Vihaan Anand. They are here touring the facility today."

"Ah! How wonderful! I felt your energy as you came into the room. How exciting to have such a powerful shaman pay us a visit!" His hands were warm on mine and they vibrated slightly. I looked down at them.

"I'm not exactly a shaman, at least I don't think so," I explained. "Are you doing something with my energy with your hands?" I asked him, furrowing my brow.

He let go and colored slightly. "Ah! You are correct, I'm sorry. I'm sensing energy through touch. Perhaps I should have asked first? I'm so used to the people around me being practiced shamans, but you are visitors and I forgot my manners." He freed my hands gently. "I'm about to begin my lecture again, but perhaps we can all dine together this evening?" He looked to Karl for agreement. Karl nodded and said, "You would be most welcome to stay for dinner. The drum session is first, and that is a wonderful experience for all." We agreed to stay, and Michael bid us all goodbye to walk back toward his students.

We spent the next hour or so touring the grounds while waiting for the drum session to begin. Karl told us there were eight different hiking trails on the property and led us on one that circled a large pond. The wind had picked up, and I tucked my chin into my coat to lessen the bite. The pond was silvery and alive in the wind, and it smelled of dried leaf and wet earth. It was easy to feel connected to the land here. Mary Ann commented on the beauty of it all, her voice betraying chattering teeth. Karl insisted on leading us back for tea and warmth in front of the lobby fireplace.

Once cozy and comfortably seated in front of the blaze, I started to doze off, just as Karl returned to let us know it was time to head to the music room. We each took a cushion with a couple dozen other people on the floor as two women and two men, one being Michael, made their way to the stage with their instruments. Three held different-sized circular drums with intricate drawings on the skin in one hand while striking a beat with a mallet, and one woman held what looked like a rattle. The beat began, each drum creating a different tone and weaving their rhythms together. The sound pulsed through my chest and head and I closed my eyes to experience it deeper. Like waves on a shore, the rhythm kept cresting and falling, quickening and slowing, and all musicians expertly feeling the play. When it was done, I still felt the deep beats in my chest.

Rafi took my hand and leaned to my ear to whisper, "Wow."

Over a simple dinner with ingredients sourced from the Centre gardens and farm, Michael talked about the class he was leading.

"The way we look at death and dying is not as a final act, but a transition from one state of being to another. Shamanism is deeply intertwined with the natural and spirit worlds, and leaving the physical form of our bodies just frees our spirit to travel home again. The spirit is eternal. You, Leah, might have the ability to connect with the spirit realm. I sensed it when we met earlier."

"I can, yes. I, well, it seems I can help spirits transition—but I've only had it happen twice, so I don't know how strong I am," I answered, feeling silly claiming it outright. Then a thought occurred to me. "Can you do it, too?"

He nodded. “Yes, I have been a bridge for many years. It’s a unique experience to be sure. There are many who gravitate toward the shamanic arts because they’ve felt they have talents they can’t explain. I meet many through the Centre who are bridges. And we’ve had several healers come through here, too, from all over the world. It’s good you’ve shined an international light on the fact that humans are awakening to their spiritual and shamanistic powers. For so long, we’ve been shunned as frauds. I’m sorry to learn of the difficulties at home. I saw the event at your college on the news just before dinner. So many misguided people…” He shook his head sadly.

We talked to Karl and Michael about what it takes to start a Centre like theirs—what they felt worked and what didn’t. The cost was astronomical, but Karl said they saved some money by reducing pay for staff who got free rooming. While many people were opening up to learning about their gifts, they said it was still sometimes hard to fill a seminar with participants. Finding teachers to help them, Michael added, was not so easy either. It was difficult to verify someone’s shamanic ability, as much of it took place in their own consciousness. You needed to have a bit of faith and find people who love what they do, and were authentic in what they did.

In the end, Karl and Michael seemed excited for our idea of finding and bringing together other healers and offered to help in any way, including hosting meetings and teachings at the Centre. It was a very encouraging dinner.

We got back to the room a little after 10 p.m. and I turned on the television. The news was on, in German, of course.

“Ummm, you know none of us speaks German, right?” Rafi asked.

“I know, but I’m pretty sure I just heard this guy say, ‘the Healer,’” I answered.

We gathered around the TV and tried to figure out what was happening. A picture of Pope Francis speaking flashed on the screen, with my picture following shortly thereafter. Then another image of a robed man appeared.

"Rafi! Google 'healer' and 'Pope Francis,' and see what comes up," I said quickly.

"Holy shit, you're right that it's about you, Leah. Turns out the Pope and other religious leaders—I think that other guy on the TV was an important rabbi—have issued statements about you in response to the college event!"

We all gathered around his laptop screen and watched as Pope Francis declared the Catholic church a friend of the Healer. He stated in his graceful, earnest way that God's will is for me to heal, much like Jesus did, and that is not at odds with the Church. He ended by saying the Vatican would welcome a visit from "Ms. Brown" whenever it was possible, and he felt the exposure of my abilities signaled great hope for mankind. The same sentiment was expressed by a chief Rabbi of Israel. It was an incredibly big deal.

"This could change so much!" Mary Ann exclaimed. "Stop the protests, the talk of devil and evil. The world's religions saying they stand with the Healer—who could've imagined it?" She shook her head in wonder at me, and I felt in awe of the dizzying way life could turn positive or negative on a dime.

Leal:
(Scottish) Faithful and true.

CHAPTER 22

We spent the rest of the week as tourists in Berlin, and even managed to find turkey on a menu in a gastropub on American Thanksgiving Day. We said goodbye to Dr. Anand, planning to meet him again in Spain in three weeks' time, then boarded a train for Aachen, Germany, to see what was rumored to be one of the country's best Christmas markets. The quaint town was all aglow, and the market, framed by giant gingerbread men, sat at the base of the massive Aachen Cathedral.

The cathedral was unlike any I'd ever seen. The minute we walked in, we were surrounded by rich color and light. The ceilings, the floor, the marble, the gold-painted chandelier, and the mosaic of the dome were all elaborate designs that gave the experience of looking through a kaleidoscope. Behind the altar sat an intricately carved golden box from the thirteenth century called the Shrine of the Virgin Mary. We marveled at the craftsmanship and beauty of something made over 800 years ago. An equally beautiful second shrine sat behind the first, containing the mortal remains of Charlemagne, the ruler of Western Europe for most of the late 700s and early 800s. On the second floor sat a simple wooden throne. It was the throne that served to crown thirty Roman-German kings between the years of 936 and 1531. The cathedral blew me away.

The market beside it was a fun mix of lights and little pop-up shops made to look like tiny chalets. Our second day there, it snowed, and the white flakes only intensified the feeling that magic was in the air. We ordered hot chocolate and pastries and let the snowflakes catch on our mittens. For a few hours, the rest of the world, along with all its challenges, drifted away.

That night, we got a call from Dr. Anand. While he was with us in Berlin, correspondence had come through to the college that he'd been awarded a massive grant by the American Psychological Association to continue his work with the prison systems. It seemed he was now bringing a boatload of money and potential esteem to the little college. He received a light slap on the wrist from the president about his failure to disclose his prison stay, and in the next breath, was offered a bigger office and the ability to hire three graduate students to help with his research. Dr. Anand was jubilant at the turn of events, and Rafi, who hadn't said anything out loud, was ridiculously relieved to learn that his job was also secure upon our return. It seemed as though things were taking a turn for the better.

Continuing by train from Aachen through Brussels, we stayed a few days before heading for a week in Paris. Getting off the train in Paris, we discovered the air had a deeper bite and the wind had picked up. It turned out to be the start of an arctic event that brought cold air down from the northeast and sent us frantically searching shops for better hats and gloves. The Eiffel Tower lit up at night under a blanket of white snow was an incredible vision, though, and not even the cold could dampen our experiences in that beautiful city.

Rafi suggested a walk our last night in Paris. "In this cold, are you sure?" I asked him. Mary Ann said she was happy to cozy in our apartment with tea and a book, thank you very much. Bundled with every winter layer we had, we set out into the Parisian night. Our breath came out in thick clouds as we talked. Though it hadn't snowed since our first night there, a sheen of frost covered every surface and sparkled like diamonds under streetlights. We passed cafés and restaurants filled with diners laughing, finding warmth with good food and company. Windows were foggy with condensation. I thought we were just walking aimlessly, but after about twenty minutes of twists and turns, I realized Rafi was leading us somewhere.

"Are we going somewhere in particular?" I asked him, blowing on my fingers through too-thin gloves.

"Just a couple more minutes. There's something I wanted to check out before we left for Spain." We turned another corner and came upon a bridge. Rafi led us to the center, and we stopped to watch the lights dance off the surface of the Seine.

"This bridge is called Le Pont des Arts. You can't see it now, but just five years ago, these panels that are now glass used to be linked fence. At some point several years before that, people started leaving 'locks of love' attached to the links. They would take a simple padlock, declare love and commitment to one another, sometimes writing their names on the lock, then they'd lock it onto the fence and throw the key into the Seine. It became such a popular thing to do, that the bridge walls became filled with locks. Locks were attached to every available space, and even to other locks when fencing was too full." I tried to picture what it must have looked like with all those locks; a bridge filled with love.

"Where are the locks now?" I asked him.

"Turns out the weight of so many locks was starting to break the bridge itself, and they were taken down. In the end, the city estimated there were close to a million locks and over forty-five tons of 'love' attached to the bridge."

I thought about how amazing that must have been to see. "What a shame we missed seeing it! How inspiring it must have been!" I said. Now it was a nice enough bridge, but nothing extraordinary that I could see.

Rafi began looking around and spied a wooden bench. He sighed with relief and took my hand, leading me over to the bench to sit. Bending down, he seemed to be checking the underside.

"What are you doing down there?" I asked.

When he straightened up, he was holding something partially closed in his gloved hand and looking at me seriously.

"Leah, I know we're young. I know we haven't known each other very long. But I can't imagine my life without you in it." He opened his hand to reveal a small, gold, rectangular padlock with a key. "I wanted to bring you here, even though the bridge has changed, because it's a place where people declared their love for each other for years. I know it's not a ring, not yet anyway, but it's a way for me to tell you…that I don't ever want to be apart from you." He looked at me so earnestly.

My heart was beating out of my chest as I stood up and placed my hand on his with the lock. "I don't ever want to be apart from you either, Rafi." His shoulders dropped in relief and he gathered me into his arms. "How are we going to attach it, though? I don't see any surface small enough for the lock to fit around."

Rafi smiled and pointed to the base of the bench. There, around one of the iron legs, was a zip tie.

"Where on Earth did you get that?"

"I brought it with me from home," he said. "Ever since I found out we'd be coming to Paris, I knew we needed to find a way to do a lock—pretty ingenious, right?" From his pocket, he pulled a black Sharpie.

"Also brought from home?" I asked, impressed with his forethought.

He nodded with pride, then wrote "Rafi loves Leah" on one side and passed the lock and the Sharpie to me. I turned it over and wrote "Leah loves Rafi" on the other side and handed it back. We knelt down and Rafi attached the lock to the zip tie, retrieving the key out of the base and holding it out to me.

"Do you want to do the honors?" he asked. I took the little gold key, and we walked over to the railing. Sending a silent thank you to the universe for sending Rafi to me, I wound my arm back as far as I could and sent the key soaring out into the night over the river.

Quadrumvirate:
(Latin) A group or association of four men.

CHAPTER 23

Once our week in Paris was done, we embarked on the last leg of our journey south to Spain, relieved to be heading toward warmer weather. We spent a few days in Madrid, followed by a quick side trip to Toledo, just so I could say I'd been there, before ending in Barcelona by Christmas Eve. We were to meet Alex, Isaac and Dr. Anand again three days later. Arriving mid-morning to our Airbnb near Plaça de Cataluña, we dumped our bags and immediately set off to find food to sustain us over the next couple days when nothing would be open.

On Christmas Eve, we had a delectable meal of tortillas, serrano ham, and wine and sang carols and traded stories late into the night. I awoke Christmas Day to Rafi and Mary Ann cooking a feast for breakfast and strong coffee already brewed. We had picked up little gifts for each other on our travels, and we sat around in our pajamas to exchange them and savor our breakfast. By late morning, we were ready for a walk and set off to check out our surroundings. The streets were nearly empty, but a few blocks away, we heard bells toll and noticed a steady stream of people heading around the corner to a small cathedral for service. I hadn't been to a mass since I was young, and I felt pulled to join them. Though I wasn't fluent, I understood enough Spanish to grasp that the priest was focusing his sermon on love and kindness to others in the world. It filled me with peace and hope. Afterward, we headed back to the apartment to relax the day away with good books, card games, and more food. It was my favorite Christmas in many years.

The next day, we awoke to sunshine beating down. Since our friends weren't due to arrive until early the following morning, we set out to explore. Shops and markets that were closed yesterday were now bustling with merchants, and businessmen and women walked with purpose along the sidewalks. We got home just before lunch, and Mary Ann and I headed to a food market a few blocks away that we'd spied earlier that morning. Rafi happily chose to stay home and have a little nap. I was tired, too, but the lure of good food and Mary Ann's enthusiasm gave me energy. Forty-five minutes later, I was absolutely famished, so we made our purchases and headed back.

As we turned the corner, about two blocks from the apartment, Rafi exploded from the front door and looked frantically down the street. He waved his arms and yelled, but he was too far away to hear. Something was very wrong. He took off running towards us. In that moment, two black SUVs came to a screeching halt in front of us, blocking our way. Four men dressed in all black jumped out of the car. Two grabbed my arms on either side, sending the grocery bag exploding to the pavement. I struggled to loosen my arms as they pulled me toward one of the cars. Mary Ann screamed as the other two held her back. They wore black winter tuques, and yelled at each other in Spanish.

"Get her arm! Make her shut up!"

One with a mustache that twitched like a rat moved around in front of me and shoved his hand over my mouth. At the same moment, I saw Mary Ann get knocked to the ground hard and I cried out.

"Mary Ann! No! Leave her alone!" I gnashed my teeth at the hand, and the man made to strike me.

His partner dragged me backward just out of reach of the fist. "No! You idiot! She's to be unharmed!"

I was losing my balance being dragged backwards, and the other man, tattoos covering every inch of his scarred neck, moved around to my side in an effort to keep me off the ground. He had to let go a little bit of my arm to reposition himself, and I elbowed him hard in the temple as he bent to lift me. We both tumbled to the ground and the Mustache man loomed in front, grabbing at my arms to lift me up again. Just then, Rafi arrived out of nowhere and bulldozed his body into the Mustache man, sending them both into the road. They tousled as I fought harder to get to my feet. The man with the neck tattoos was fast, though, and grabbed my left hand at the wrist. I brought my right palm to his face just as a deafening bang rang out behind me. I whipped my head around toward the noise.

Rafi laid on the ground not six feet away from me, and Mustache man stood above him with a pointed gun. "Rafi! No! Rafi!" I yelled, and Mary Ann screamed again.

I tried to run towards him, but now there were three of the men on me, dragging and pushing me into the back seat, slamming the door in my face. I clawed at the handle, but it was locked and there was no way to unlock it from the inside. Mustache man and the one with neck tattoos got in the front seat of the car and screeched away just as I saw one of the men from the first car kick Mary Ann hard in the stomach. Rafi still hadn't moved, but now a pool of dark blood surrounded his body on the pavement.

"Stop! We have to go back! Rafi!" I began hitting the backs of the men frantically. "You have to go back! He'll die! Let me out! I need to save him! Please!" The tattoo man in the passenger seat took the back of his gun and struck my cheek hard with it. I ricocheted back to the window. The mustached driver yelled something to his partner, and they began arguing. I was dizzy and turned toward the window. The last thing I saw as we rounded the corner were people running over to Mary Ann and standing over Rafi. Then I blacked out.

I awoke to searing pain in my face and the taste of bile in my mouth. Fluttering my eyes open, it took me a minute to understand I was still in the backseat of the car. The men were quietly looking ahead to the road. The image of Rafi on the pavement came back to me in a wave of panic, and I jolted upright, then almost passed back out from the pain. Neck tattoo man noticed my movement and turned around.

"Please," I whispered. "I'll do what you want if you just take me back and let me heal them. I won't fight. I won't yell. Just please give me five minutes. That's all I'll need. Just five minutes to help them and then I'll do whatever you want." I tried to keep from crying but was starting to hyperventilate with fear.

Neck tattoo man gave a small laugh and sneered at me. In broken English he replied, "He is dead. They are nothing. You have more important job now. Worth more than them."

"What do you want?" I pleaded, though I could only imagine one thing my life was worth kidnapping me over. I decided to play dumb, maybe I could make them think they had the wrong person. "Why did you take me?"

Mustache man spoke this time. "No questions. Shut up and wait." He eyed me in the rearview mirror. "Fix your face," he said.

"I don't understand what you mean—fix my face," I answered.

"You think we are idiots?" Neck tattoo man asked. "You are the Healer. Heal your face now, or I will hit you again."

I suddenly remembered Mustache man yelling I was supposed to be unharmed. "No," I said. Neck tattoo man turned around more to raise his hand at me. "Go ahead," I said, though I know I flinched.

He backhanded the other side of my face just as mustache man yelled for him not to. The pain in my head was incredible, and I blacked out again. It must not have been for long, though, because when I came to, the two men were still yelling at each other.

"Now!" Neck tattoo man shouted at me. "You heal yourself now!"

"If you take me back and let me heal my friends, I'll heal myself!" I answered, my voice breaking.

He cursed me with a barrage of shouting and my head throbbed with the noise. Mustache man grabbed his shirt to get his attention and growled something at him before letting him loose again. He scowled at me.

"Not another word or we'll go back and kill the other one, too." Then he turned to face out the front.

I was in too much pain, physical and emotional, to fight anymore, and instead I silently looked out the window, with the hope of remembering some landmarks or possibly catching the attention of another car. But the windows were darkly tinted, and no one could see me from the outside. At some point, I must have passed out again, because suddenly we were parking in an underground garage. Even blinking hurt, but I looked around and readied myself for a possible escape. The men got out and Mustache man came and placed his hand on the handle of my door.

Through the window he said, "If you fight, if you try to escape, if you don't cooperate, I will drive back to Barcelona tonight and kill your aunt like we killed your boyfriend. Do not underestimate us."

At the mention of Mary Ann, all hope of getting away blew out of me. How had they known where to find us? I got out of the car and followed them up an elevator to the fifth and top floor. The elevator door opened to a long, dark hallway with worn red carpeting and fading wallpaper of red and gold paisley. On a door at the end of the hall, Mustache man knocked four times, paused and knocked three more, then waited. I heard the sound of locks being undone and the door opened a crack. Mustache man grunted something and the door was opened fully for us to pass in. What I thought would be a hotel room was actually a large apartment, and we entered into a living room space with two beat-up couches surrounding a low table. A large television sat in the corner, and the windows were covered with dark curtains. Three other black-clad men sat on the couches, in the middle of a card game, and a third stood at the door as we passed. I recognized one of the men on the couch as the one who kicked Mary Ann as we drove away, and my stomach turned. The air was thick with cigarette smoke and everyone was staring me down as we entered. I heard the one holding the door ask Mustache man about my face, and he replied implicating Neck tattoo man with a disgusted wave of his hand.

The man at the door, the only one not wearing his black tuque, gingerly took my chin and turned me up toward the light, inspecting my swollen face. He had light brown hair and freckles on his cheeks, and his breath stank of cigarettes and coffee. He carefully turned me this way and that, his eyes resting on mine for a moment in warning before moving me.

"She needs to heal herself. Heads will roll if he sees her like this." He spoke English with a British accent. He looked up at Mustache man. "She refused, so this bastard hit her again." He shook his head at the stupidity of his partner.

Freckles turned to me. "Why will you not heal yourself? Doesn't it hurt?" he asked, furrowing his brow. I just looked at him, not sure if I should say anything or not.

Neck tattoo man spoke up. "She's being a stubborn bitch. If we give her enough pain, I'm sure she'll do what she's told."

I looked back and forth nervously between them. Neck tattoo man was obviously the most dangerous in the room, and my skin crawled as he looked at me. I was finding it hard to breathe. A meaningful look passed between Freckles and Mustache man, and Freckles calmly walked over toward Neck tattoo man, then punched him so hard in the gut he doubled over coughing on the ground. He knelt down close to him.

"You're seeming to have a hard time following directions. Looks like it's you who needs some lessons in the order of things around here. You think you're not expendable? Don't be foolish. You'll have to answer to him when he sees her face. Then we'll see how tough you think you are." Then he stood and looked back at me. "Leah, right? Come on then, let me show you to your room."

He led me to the second door on the left of the hallway, just a few yards off the living room. The room was dark except for a small sconce lit over the bedside, like a reading lamp. The windows had been covered with plywood, letting in only slivers of light from where the wood wasn't quite flush with the window frame. Once my eyes adjusted, I saw the room was small but neatly furnished. The door to what looked like a bathroom sat off to the left. A chair was positioned next to the bed, and the bed itself was made up with a flowered bedspread and two towels folded on top. It was like I was a guest in an inn or something.

"Get yourself cleaned up. We'll bring food in a little while. There are books and things in the dresser. Don't be stupid. Just do what's asked of you and you might make it out of here."

With that, he closed the door, and I heard the lock turn from the outside. Now that I was finally alone, my body shook fiercely, and I fell to the floor as the fear and stress took hold of me. The image of Rafi lying on the pavement in a pool of his own blood flashed in my mind and I felt a wave of nausea. I got up and ran over, pushing open the door to the bathroom and swung the toilet seat up just in time to throw up. The intensity of vomiting made my face and head scream in pain, and I moaned with my hands over my head. Afraid I might lose consciousness again, I laid on the cold bathroom tile until the pain had lessened enough for me to regain my breath. The bathroom was lighter than the bedroom thanks to a small frosted window high on the wall, beyond my reach. I guess they decided it wasn't worth blocking since I was way too big to fit through it even if I could reach it. I stood up on shaky legs and looked in the mirror. My face was swollen and red mostly on the side where the gun hit me. The dark line of a scab about two inches long drew a line from my temple to my cheek, and my eye was only open a slit. I tenderly touched it and winced. I did not look good.

Just then I heard the key in the lock and a knocking on the door. I froze.

"Dinner is served, princess." The sickly syrupy voice of Neck tattoo man sent a shiver up my spine. "Come out of there, now."

I cautiously opened the bathroom door. He slit his eyes and looked me up and down, then walked to my side, leaning his head toward my ear. I stiffened and started crying, despite myself. "Enjoy this, princess. You make me look a fool? I do not forget." He gave a half-smile and left the room.

Once he was gone, I collapsed to the floor once more. A small, circular roller cart with a long white linen tablecloth was at the base of the bed. On top was a plate filled with food complete with a folded linen napkin. Gathering myself together, I walked over to see what they brought. The plate was filled with tortilla, ham, cheese, and bread, and a takeout ketchup bottle stood next to a water glass. At the sight of the food my stomach roiled again, and I turned away. *They took me from the street, shot Rafi, beat Mary Ann, and now were bringing me room service like I was a guest at some hotel? Why? What was the point of treating me well?*

A memory from the night before Alice's suicide struck me. The dream I'd had of Isis had been forgotten when Rafi charged in talking about his vision. Now, it came rushing back. I remembered being terrified that Set would capture me. That his plan was to hold me as a prisoner to keep him and his armies in health. That I would be his slave. Could that be what was happening? They killed Rafi and harmed Mary Ann—could I really expect to make it out of here? Despair threatened to take over my body. *No, Leah*, I told myself. *You have to keep it together for Mary Ann. You have to find a way out of this.*

I stood up and surveyed the room, my eyes searching for anything that might be useful. Going to the windows, I scratched at the plywood, but it was nailed into the frame and the edges were too narrow for my fingers to get through. I ran over to the food tray—maybe they were foolish enough to give me a knife with my dinner. Unfolding the napkin, plastic cutlery fell out. Damn—not so foolish. I moved to the dresser where Freckles said I would find books and other things. The top drawer had some old tattered Spanish fashion magazines and two books in English: one whodunit by an author I didn't recognize and the other had the telltale cover of a romance novel with a shirtless man whose long hair flowed in the breeze. The second drawer had ratty bath towels and two long, white shirtdresses, almost like nightgowns. Opening the third drawer I found nothing at all except dust and dirt.

I knelt down to look under the bed, but there were only dust bunnies. In the bathroom, I found extra rolls of toilet paper, one bar of soap, and a plastic travel set of toothpaste with the kind of toothbrush where the base and the head were separate. I put the toothbrush together and held it in my hand like a knife. I half-heartedly tested out stabbing it into my thigh and it broke apart with no effort—so much for that idea. My attention moved to the small frosted window. Maybe I could reach it if I stood on the toilet seat. I climbed up and my fingers were just close enough to meet the lowest part of the pane. I needed at least another twelve inches to reach the lock where it could open outward down from the top. I got down in frustration. What the hell would I use it for even if I *could* open it. It was only about a sixteen-inch square opening.

In the end, I had a flimsy toothbrush, plastic utensils, and old magazines to defend myself with. I supposed I could pull the curtains down if I yanked hard enough, and the small chair by the bed could be useful to hit someone with. I filed that information away just in case. Of course, there wasn't just one someone to deal with—there were at least five armed men in this apartment with me, including my mystery captor. I would need more.

A knock on the door snapped me to attention and the lock was opened. Freckles came in, looked at me with my still damaged face and my untouched plate and shrugged. "You're only hurting yourself by not eating. We don't give a shit. Come on. He's ready to see you now."

Freckles led me back through the living room to the door on the opposite end of the apartment to mine. Knocking gently, the door was opened by one of the men playing cards when I first arrived. His eyes widened at my still banged-up face and he looked fearfully at Freckles, who just shrugged again, and nudged me forward.

In the middle of the room was a large poster bed where a frail old man lay. His face was covered in liver spots and his hair was mostly gray with some streaks of the black betraying the color he once had. He wore a bushy mustache like mustache man, and an IV unit stood next to his bed, attached to his hand. His voice still showed strength, however, as he addressed me.

"Welcome, Leah, healer and savior! Please come closer. I'm so honored you have come to my aid," he said as though I was here by choice, as though I was an esteemed guest.

Freckles prodded me forward when he sensed my hesitation, and I inched toward the bed. A gasp came out of the old man and he sat up. "What has happened to your face? Who has done this to you?" His voice thundered in the otherwise silent room and I jumped, looking wide-eyed at Freckles who was now standing at my side.

"There was a slight misunderstanding when we picked her up, Padrino. She didn't realize we wouldn't harm her, and she fought back. Now she is refusing to heal herself." At the name "Padrino," a shiver of fear shot down my spine, and I looked more closely at the man on the bed. It was him. Older and frailer than the pictures from the news, but the same mustache, the same eyes that crinkled jovially when he smiled, disguising pure evil. El Padrino. His whereabouts had been a mystery for several months prior to the container ship being found, and the manhunt for him afterwards was unsuccessful. Now I knew why they couldn't find him. The understanding of what kind of person lay before me did not give me much hope. It was said that his organization extended throughout many countries and we'd only begun to scratch the surface of his illegal enterprises with the discovery of that ship. I was in a very dangerous situation.

Padrino squinted at me and asked, "Is this true? You received these wounds through your own fighting?" I hesitated to answer. If I told the truth, would I suffer the wrath of Neck tattoo man? Maybe going along with the lie would gain me an ally with the men? I gambled on that and nodded my head. "Why have you not healed yourself? Isn't it painful?" he asked.

I needed to come up with something fast and was feeling flustered. More than anything, I thought, I needed time. "It takes a lot of energy and time to heal myself. I haven't had a chance to do it yet," I answered.

This seemed acceptable to El Padrino and he gave a slight nod. "You will have time this evening to tend to yourself, see that you do." Then he relaxed back slightly into his pillows and appraised me. "You are even younger in person than you seemed on the news. I have been following your story very closely. A woman with the power to heal with her hands. It's beyond incredible, really. When my men reported you were coming to Spain, well—I knew we were destined to meet. That you were brought to me as a divine gift! I'm Manuel, but my friends call me Padrino. You may as well." He opened his arms. "I have brought you here because I have an affliction, you see. An affliction I know you have the power to heal. Because, as luck would have it, I have the same form of liver cancer that you cured for that man Winston Parker. The moment I learned that, I knew you would be my savior. Like Parker, I still have much to finish in this life. And now I have you to help make sure I live long enough to do it."

I was here to heal a monster. There was no way he would let me free.

He smiled at me expectantly. Clearly, I was supposed to speak now, but I had no idea what to say that wouldn't get me in trouble.

In a meek voice, I lied, "I need to be fully healed myself before I can heal anyone else—it won't work if I'm weakened."

"Of course, of course!" he responded, his tone conciliatory. "Now that you're here, we have nothing more to fear from this foul illness! You may have twenty-four hours to recover from your wounds. Go—rest up. Give her peace and quiet!" he said to the men around him. Then, to me in a voice laced with warning, he said, "Leah, you are, of course, here as my guest, so do not hesitate to ask if you need something. I'm afraid I cannot permit you to leave the apartment, you understand. I'm sure you will not worry now that you know we mean you no harm. And there is no need for fighting." He lowered his eyes to me, and I understood he was giving me a mandate: cooperate.

We were dismissed, and Freckles walked me back to my room. As we passed through the living room, my attention was drawn to the news playing on the large television. Suddenly, my picture flashed on the screen and I read the headline under the picture: "Healer: Missing in Spain." Freckles gave me a little shove and I was locked back in my room. The picture was one that Mary Ann took only just this morning as we were exploring Barcelona. I was wearing the same clothes even now. She must have given it to the police, which means she must be safe for now, thank God. It took extreme willpower not to think about Rafi in that moment, but now my focus had to be getting free. I had bought myself twenty-four hours. I needed to think of something.

I looked at the plate of food, still sitting untouched on the roller tray. Freckles was right, I needed to eat. It would not help me fight for my life if I was weak from hunger. The problem was, I wasn't sure I could swallow anything down with my stomach in knots like it was. I took the plastic ketchup bottle next to the plate and doused my cold tortilla with the red sauce, hoping it would help it slide down my throat. The bottle splattered a little on the napkin and tablecloth and my shirt as I squeezed it, and I swore. I hoped they wouldn't be mad that I made such a mess. Sitting down in front of the plate, I forced myself to choke everything down. Once the food was gone, I moved the tablecloth aside to see if anything was under the tray. I found nothing underneath but a stack of extra white linen napkins and a small container with more ketchup, mustard, salt and pepper, like you might find at a barbeque picnic table. I sat back up and looked again at the place setting. Suddenly, the splattered red ketchup on the white linen gave me an idea.

I grabbed the full ketchup and an extra white napkin from the bottom of the cart and brought them to the bathtub. Spreading out the napkin, I shook the ketchup and practiced writing a small letter on the top left corner. The red soaked in quickly and spread a little, but was still very visible against the white backdrop. Working with bigger strokes now I began writing. The napkin wasn't very big, but I managed to get three words big enough to be seen from the fifth floor:

HELP!

THE HEALER

Now I would just need to find a way to reach that bathroom window. I ran back into the bedroom and grabbed the chair next to the bed. I placed it on top of the toilet it, but was just a little too big and slipped when I tried to put weight on it. I put it back and ran to the dresser, grabbed all the towels, and stacked them on the toilet seat. Very carefully, I stepped onto the pile. Though I didn't fall, the towels caved under my weight enough that I was still too short. I needed about five or six more inches.

I ran back into the room and got the two towels from the bed and the books from the top drawer. I positioned the two extra towels on the stack already there, and the books side by side on the top. Placing one foot on each book I found that the roughness of the towels kept them from sliding around too much, but I was still a little short. Groaning in frustration, I got down once again. Finally, grabbing the magazines, I placed them between towels in the stack. Holding my napkin in my teeth, I gingerly climbed back up. With intense relief, I found I could just reach the top of the window. I opened it enough to slip the napkin through, words facing out, then held my breath that it wouldn't slip as I pulled the window closed again. Just as I latched it, one of the books slipped forward on the towel and my foot along with it. I grasped for the wall and my other foot found the sink just before I crashed to the ground. My heart was beating out of control, but I got myself down and looked at the window. A small corner of the napkin had moved slightly as I closed the window and was visible in the upper left corner, but there was no way I wanted to risk trying to fix it. I put all the props back where they belonged and prayed for no wind.

Now I knew I needed to heal myself. Sitting on the edge of the bathtub, I called forth the healing ribbons of light. It took five ribbons for the heat to come and by the sixth ribbon, I could feel it was done. Looking in the mirror, only a light pink line remained where the deep red scab had been, and the swelling was completely gone.

I went to the bed, but I knew I would not find sleep. I was afraid of letting down my guard even for a moment when I thought of the company just on the other side of the door. More than that, though, the sadness over Rafi consumed me. I must have drifted off for a bit, however, because the next moment I jolted awake to the sound of the key turning in my door. I had left the bathroom door open, hoping the small window would let me know when morning came, and darkness still surrounded me. Someone was coming in the middle of the night. I curled my fingers tighter around the plastic fork I'd brought to bed with me. As ineffective as I knew it was, holding it made me feel a little better.

The door slowly opened—whomever it was wanted to be quiet. In the darkness, I could only see the silhouette of a man backlit by the glow of the television. He stood in the entryway with the doorknob in his hand. I didn't dare move, hoping he'd believe me asleep. After a few more terrifying moments, he pulled the door closed again and relocked it. I exhaled and shivered with the terror of what might have happened.

Quail:
To recoil or shake from terror or dread.

CHAPTER 24

When the first light of dawn shifted in the bathroom, I was still awake to welcome it. I ran to check if the napkin was still in place. The little corner was still sticking a half inch into the room. Thank God it hadn't blown loose. I just needed someone to see it.

Not long after came the knock on the door and the turning of the key in the lock. The frightened man who let us into El Padrino's room the night before wheeled in a second cart fresh with breakfast. He paused wide-eyed when he saw my healed face, made the sign of the cross, and quickly retreated with last night's dinner cart. When I checked under this new cart, I found the bottom shelf empty. There would be no second chances at a sign, I just prayed the first one would work. I ate the breakfast, bread with jams and weak coffee. Just as I finished, a second knock came.

Freckles came in and inspected my face. "Good girl." He nodded, also noticing my clean breakfast plate. "You smartened up, I see." He handed me a plastic bag. "Here, Padrino wants you clean when you see him this afternoon. Have a bath and change your clothes to these. I'll be back later to check on you."

I took the fastest bath of my life, not wanting to spend a moment longer undressed than absolutely necessary. The bag held a pair of jeans and a hoodie, both just slightly too big, but warm. I folded my own blood and dirt-spackled shirt and pants into the bag and placed it at the end of the bed. With nothing but waiting to do, I shadowboxed around the small space in the room. If I needed to fight, I wanted to get my body ready to react. It gave me something that felt productive when everything else felt hopeless. Movement had always helped me think, and I needed a plan for when I would face Padrino again. The thought of healing such a horrible person made me sick. The questions surrounding Winston and Alice Parker returned to me, and I needed to make some decisions.

I now knew the past of the ill person before me. It was in my power to heal or let harm continue. If I healed, who knows how long his terror might continue, but I might keep myself, Mary Ann, and my friends safe. If I refused, I put us all in danger again, and some other monster in the organization would probably just come to take his place anyway. But he would suffer—and if ever someone deserved suffering, it was El Padrino. Hours passed before Freckles came to get me, and I was still not sure what the right decision was.

The TV was on as we walked past the living room, but the sound was off. I glanced over and the screen showed people marching for something. It seemed there was a protest of some kind happening. Then I stopped. The camera zoomed in on a section of the crowd and a woman held a placard that said Free The Healer in big, black letters.

Suddenly the screen went dark. I turned to see Freckles holding the remote. "That's no concern of yours. You have a job to do and you better do it right." He shoved me forward toward El Padrino's room.

Men lined the walls as we entered, just like the day before. This time, a chair was placed by the bedside.

"Leah! Come, sit. Let me look at you. Ah—wonderful! You are truly gifted," El Padrino said. "I believe it is now my turn, yes? I have given you the time you asked for—I have been patient. Now it is time for you to repay my kindness and rid me of this horrible disease." He sat up and positioned himself at the edge of the bed opposite the chair.

Summoning all my courage, I said, "I was hurt more than I realized yesterday. I…uh…I'm not ready to heal you yet. My power isn't fully restored." I forced myself to look in his eyes and he narrowed them at me.

"I see. I think that perhaps you should give it a try anyway. I believe this may bolster your strength a bit, hmmm?" He motioned to a man who slipped out, only to return a moment later dragging another man. When the second man was close enough, I let out a cry.

"Isaac!" I made to run to him but was held back. "What have you done to him?!" His head hung low and he shuffled forward, supported by the man who brought him. Isaac lifted his head enough to look me in the eye, and I could see he'd been beaten badly. His left eye was swollen shut and crusty blood stuck to his nose and cheek. His lip was split and there was blood all over his clothing. My heart broke to see him like this. "Why did you do this to him?!"

"Ah, you see? I thought perhaps having your friend here would strengthen you and make you happy. It does make you happy, does it not? To have your dear friend with you?" He sat so peacefully and unbothered in the bed while Isaac bled on his floor, I wanted to kill him right there. "Of course, he misunderstood our intentions as well and fought against us when we met him at the airport. It is a shame that he injured himself so, but I'm sure you will be able to help him—once you have healed me, of course." He smiled. "It was my wish that both he and the girl would be here to keep you company, but my men are not always as effective as I would hope." He sighed and shrugged his shoulders as if to say, "What can you do?"

My mind raced to find a new plan fast. I turned my back on Isaac and took a step toward the bed. "Thank you. I will heal you—and then may I have some time to tend to my friend?"

His grin broadened. "Of course, of course! I'm sure you have much catching up to do. Now, please." He gestured to the chair and I sat.

I took a deep breath and willed my hands not to shake. "May I place my hands on you?" He nodded, and I had to swallow my revulsion upon touching his arms. When I did, the blue lines appeared like I knew they would. *You are just doing what you need to survive, Leah*, I told myself. *For Mary Ann and Dr. Anand, Isaac and Alex*. If I thought about Rafi, there was no way I would get through this. Just then another thought occurred to me. "Please close your eyes," I instructed him. Then closing my own eyes, I whispered the dedication and the healing ribbons of light faithfully appeared. Moving one hand to El Padrino's right side where the diseased liver sat, I reached my other hand in the air to the ribbons. I made the movement like I was bringing ribbons down to his liver, but in truth I was not. I silently willed the ribbons not to latch on to me, and they seemed to listen. Only the very last one, the sixth, did I bring an actual ribbon down and let it enter his body, knowing he needed to feel something to believe I had done it. It killed me to give him even that much, but it wouldn't cure him—just make him feel a little better for a short while. And that's what I needed. I opened my eyes and removed my hands.

He looked at me wide-eyed. "I felt it! I felt the energy enter my body! It was incredible!" he looked around at the men in the room. "Did you see the light? The healing light where she touched?" Damn. I forgot that the whole world watched a healing on Isabel Hargraves' show, and he knew what to expect. The men all shook their heads no.

"The light doesn't happen every time!" I hurriedly said. "Don't you feel better?" I prayed he did—at least enough to believe I did what he asked.

He smiled and went to stand up. "Yes! I'm strong again!" he roared, ripping the IV off his arm. Taking my shoulders in his hands he said, "Thank you, Leah, Healer. Thank you!" Then he paraded around the room shaking hands or embracing each of the men. I said a silent thank you for the power of suggestion and stood up.

"Can Isaac and I return to my room, now?" I asked.

El Padrino looked around the room and settled on me. "Of course! Of course! You may enjoy the evening together.

I will have dinner brought shortly." I turned to go, and he added, "Oh, Leah—are you comfortable in your room? Is the food to your liking?" He walked so close to me that I could smell the decay of his body. I swallowed down the nausea. *Think, Leah, think*. In a day or two, he would realize he was still very sick, and something told me the food wouldn't be so nice then.

"The food has been wonderful, thank you. It's just that I'm very concerned about my aunt, and I think she must be worried about me. Could I at least try to call her? Let her know I'm alright?" *Please God, let her be all right.*

"I'm afraid outside calls are out of the question. You see, there are some unenlightened people who would be very interested in knowing where I am. I cannot give them any clues as to where to find me. I have a man or two who have need of your services as well. A small favor to me, please. Just a few more days—no more than a week. Then all will be right as rain and you can return happy and healthy to your aunt. You have the good fortune to be providing your services to my men in the meantime!" He spoke to me as though I was a member of the collective, his collective.

I simply nodded, unable to muster any other response. Isaac and I were returned to my room, the TV off as we passed through the living room. I'd bought at least another night with my sham healing—but tomorrow could be bad.

The minute the door was closed behind us, I rushed at Isaac. "Oh my God, Isaac. Let me look at you. They hurt you so badly!" I cried. "What's the worst? If you can't talk just point—do you think anything's broken?" He shook his head no and pointed at his face. "Come sit on the bed—I'm going to make it better, okay?" I pulled ribbons into everywhere that I could, and finally the warmth and light let me know it was enough. Isaac breathed fully and blinked at me, feeling his face with his hands, then gathered me into a fierce hug. Once he was sure I was okay, he told me what happened.

"They were waiting for us when we got out of the airport. No one was there to meet us or answering their phone. We figured we'd take a cab to the rental, but they jumped us as soon as we left the building. They had a car waiting—two guys came at me and a third went for Alex. I fought but couldn't get away before they shoved me into the car. I saw Alex get free as we drove away, though, and a swarm of bystanders came to help her." His breath became ragged. "I know she got away because they told me they needed to beat me twice—once for me and once for her." He pressed his palms to his eyes. "I've never been so scared in my life, Leah. Are Mary Ann and Rafi here, too?"

I swallowed hard and told him about my own capture and seeing Rafi on the pavement. I could barely say the words aloud. Then I let him know who our captor was.

"This can't really be happening!" Isaac moaned.

"I'm so sorry, Isaac. Everything is because of me!" I paced in front of the bed pulling at my hair. "I never imagined something like this—why the hell would anyone want a kid who never did anything in her life but cower and hide. I have this fucking curse, and now people hate me or want to use me—and the ones I love are being shot and beaten! I want it to go back the way it was. No one knew who I was. No one cared who I was. It was safe! It was simple! Not like this shitshow I've created!" I brought my fist down hard on the bed, then took a breath and lowered my voice. "I don't know how to get us out, Isaac. There are at least five armed men out there. I didn't heal him tonight, but I will have to heal him eventually. I don't believe he'd ever let me leave—why should he? I'd rather kill myself than resign to being a slave for him. But what if he goes after Mary Ann and Alex again? Rafi's gone. I'm trapped! And now you're trapped with me!" It felt hopeless, and I crumpled down beside him on the bed.

Isaac didn't speak for a long time. I could hear him take long, deep breaths. Finally, he shook his head. "No." He paused. "No, Leah, we can't spiral. You and I are here, but as far as we know, Mary Ann and Alex are safe. That means people will be looking for us, so we just have to hold out until they find us."

"The TV!" I jumped up in my seat. "When they walked me to Padrino, it was on and I saw people in the streets with signs that said, 'Free the Healer.' You're right, they're looking for us."

"We know we're only a couple hours from Barcelona because the car ride wasn't longer than that," Isaac continued. "I say we play nice for now. You do what they ask—keep yourself on his good side. I'm just here as motivation so that works for my safety, too."

We were interrupted by the knocking on the door and the same man who had brought breakfast brought our dinner tray in. He saw Isaac's healed face and crossed himself again before hurrying away. We ate dinner in relative silence, lost in our own thoughts and fears. I never knew terror before. It was shocking how it could hijack the brain and make even simple actions like bringing a fork to the mouth feel unfamiliar.

Finally, Isaac dropped his hands on the table and leaned into me. "Don't wish away what you've been through over the last year and a half. Don't regret it, either. We will find a way through this. I realize now how vulnerable having this gift makes you. But you know now that you're not the only one. Right now, the world only knows you, but that's why we need to keep going. We can't let one man derail the momentum of the last year. You decided months ago not to let fear stop you from seeing this through."

"But Isaac, I already lost Rafi because of what I can do. Do I have to lose you and Alex and Mary Ann and Dr. Anand because powerful people can just take me? I have healing power—not protecting power. I'm not willing to lose you guys because what is my life worth without you?"

"Your abilities, and the light you've shone on the potential abilities of others, will change the world. I know this. It's bigger than one life." He spoke about his life being worth less than my gifts with an eerie calm presence. I didn't like it.

"Isaac, I will not knowingly sacrifice anyone for this—I would die myself first!" I hissed.

"Then the world would be lesser for it, and it would have been for nothing."

I didn't have a chance to respond. The door opened and Freckles said it was time to take Isaac to his room for the night. We locked eyes as he backed out of the room and he gave me a small nod. I know it was meant to reassure me and I nodded back, but it was a small comfort being alone again.

I was sitting on the side of the bathtub staring at the window trying to come up with another plan when the door opened again.

"Hey!" I heard from the bedroom. It was Neck tattoo man and I stood up, alert. I had left my fork under the pillow and swore at my stupidity. "Come out here." I slowly opened the bathroom door without passing through it. He was smiling in a self-satisfied way that gave me goosebumps. "I know what you doing. I know you didn't heal El Padrino—I could see this." I started to panic. "You think he won't know? He is no fool." I said nothing, just stood still. "The men tell me you told Padrino you hurt your face when you fought back, and not from me." He cocked his head, considering me for a moment, then shrugged. "So I told Padrino he look better—all healed up." He grabbed the dirty cart to take away. "Enjoy your sleep, tomorrow may not be so easy." He left the room. At least I'd made one smart decision during this whole ordeal.

I went back to the bathroom and focused my eyes on the little corner of napkin in the window. I could see the shadow of the bottom edge blowing about. So much for calm weather. If no one could read it, then no one would pay attention to it. I needed a backup plan—but there were so many of them and only me and my plastic fork. The only one who didn't scare me completely was the wide-eyed card player from the first night. Crossing himself when he saw me healed made me think he was afraid of me. I wasn't sure how that could be of use—but I would try to find out more the next time I got out of this room. I took another lightning bath, the sound of the water drowning out my sobs, thinking about the night in Paris when Rafi and I promised our love to each other. It felt like a lifetime ago now. I boiled with hatred for all my captors, but especially Mustache man. My hatred toward him for pulling that trigger filled every cell in my body.

I sat in the bed and squeezed my eyes closed. *Was Isaac okay? Would I find him beaten again tomorrow?* These thoughts tortured me until exhaustion finally took over a few hours later.

***

"Horus! Where are you?" I shouted. My voice echoed back through the empty hall. We had lost each other in the chaos outside, and now I was frantic to locate him again. My sheath swished behind me as I ran around a corner. Horus appeared in front of me and I nearly ran into him.

"Mother! Come, we need to get you to safety. Set's army has nearly overpowered my own. Do you know a place to hide in the palace?"

I guided him to an adjoining room and slid aside a woven wall covering to reveal a hole and steps leading down. "Come quickly. Set knows of this passage but there are three places it leads. I will follow it north to the exit beside the acacia—you should take the western tunnel and find your sons. It is time! They need to leave Egypt now. Are they prepared?" I asked.

"Yes, but they resist, and their wives resist. They would rather stay and fight than flee their homeland." His voice

was thick with frustration. I grabbed his two hands in my own.

I implored him. "Horus, you must make them go. It is the only way! Tell them their queen demands it. They must spread their abilities throughout the world of men, or the powers of the healing stone will be lost forever, and mankind will be at the mercy of Set. Generations must pass so the numbers of healers are too vast to conquer. Do you understand? This is more important than my life or yours. They must continue what we've begun. For the sake of all!"

"I will make them understand, and I will see them escaped at any cost. It will be done." He nodded his head in resolve and took off running. I watched until he disappeared from view, then I turned and raced down the northern pass just as voices entered the room above.

***

I awoke in the dark and considered the dream. Isaac was right. We had to continue what we'd begun. This had become more than just me—one healer. We had brought light to the world about what was possible, and it couldn't stop here. We just had to make it out of here, and for that we needed time. I prayed we'd get it.

I passed the last hours of the night pacing the room and checking on the napkin in the window. Just as the blue light of dawn shone through the cracks around the plywood, I heard activity on the other side of the door. I ran back into the bathroom just as it was unlocked and opened. Standing out of sight in the bathroom, I heard someone come in and pause to look around, then quickly move toward the bathroom. The commotion from the hallway got louder with the open door, and men's voices in Spanish and English were shouting commands to one another rapidly. The bathroom door opened fully, obscuring me behind it, and the wide-eyed man moved in, gun drawn with a frightened look on his face. Scanning the room for me his eyes lingered for a moment at the window, jerked back to locate me and pull me roughly away from the door.

"We go now—get your things." Then his eyes went back to the little window and he walked closer to see what was sticking out. I panicked. If he found the note, there was no hope for me at all. I needed to act quickly. With him turned away from me, I threw the hardest side kick I could to his mid-back. His body flailed forward from the unexpected attack, his arms flying up above his head, and he crashed face-first into the wall. Before he got a chance to recover, I kicked him again in the head twice, then wrenched the gun from his fingers, and hit him across the temple with it. He sagged to the floor, unmoving.

Breathing hard and terrified what to do next, I heard another person run into the bedroom and slipped behind the bathroom door again.

"Marcus!" I heard the voice of Neck tattoo man yell before hitting the bathroom door open hard. The door slammed into me, but I held in my cry, and Neck tattoo man swore and knelt down by the other man's side. Holding the gun out in front of me, I moved from behind the door just as Neck tattoo man stood and swung around. He didn't have his gun out, but only hesitated for a split second before reaching for it. I squeezed the trigger as hard as I could. There was almost no noise from the gun, so I thought it didn't work, but his body flew back away from me and landed on top of his friend.

He moaned and clutched at his chest. "Ahhhh!" he yelled, and I quickly closed the bathroom door. I turned on him. "Ahh! Help me!" he pleaded.

"Why should I do anything but watch you die like you made me watch Rafi die! You deserve nothing!" He clutched his chest and moaned. "Please—you can heal me!" he whispered, his eyes wide with fear.

It sounded like fighting happening in the apartment beyond, and I realized I was not safe, not in any way. There were at least three other armed men and El Padrino in the apartment. Even with the gun in my hand, I would never get through all of them. I looked down at Neck tattoo man. The front of his shirt was wet with blood. If I let him die, then I would have killed someone. Self-defense or not, this thought terrified me. I was a healer. I was The Healer.

But they killed Rafi. Why should he get mercy when Rafi got nothing? These thoughts battled in my mind until the loudest thought broke through and made my decision for me. *Because you are not a murderer, Leah.*

I sank down next to him, my knee slipping on the bloody tile. "I hate you," I spit at him, then placed my hands to the air and called forth the ribbons. I pulled them one by one into the bullet wound…six…seven…it wasn't until the eighth ribbon that I felt the heat and knew it was enough. I opened my eyes. Neck tattoo man was breathing slowly and deeply, staring at me.

"I hope that bullet gives you a lifetime of pain," I said. Then I picked up his gun and hit him across the face like he'd hit me. He blacked out and I heard more people thunder past the bedroom. Armed with both guns now, I ducked into the tub and pulled the curtain closed in front of me. I heard the sounds of shots and yelling all throughout the apartment. There was no way that was only five people. What the hell was happening? Cowering in the tub, I said a silent apology to Mary Ann that I wasn't going to make it out of this—that she would have to suffer that loss. I was going to die here.

Suddenly, I heard something familiar out of the confused shouting. Over and over, it became clearer—someone was shouting my name.

"Leah! Leah!" came the male voice. "Leah, are you here?" he yelled. The shouting died down, but the man still yelled my name. "Leah!"

I moved out of the bathtub and threw open the door just as a man ran into the room. He was dressed differently and wore a uniform with a vest over it. As he turned toward the bathroom door, I saw the word *Policía* across the front of the vest. Oh my God—it was the police! I ran forward, throwing my arms around him in relief.

Misslieness:
(Scots dialect) The feeling of lonesomeness that comes from missing someone you love or care for.

CHAPTER 25

I jumped out of the car and ran up the steps to the police station, colliding with a body coming out. We both ricocheted back, and I looked up.

"Mary Ann!" I threw my arms around her, nearly toppling her down.

"Oh my God, Leah! My sweet girl!" We both cried hysterically, not wanting to let go of each other. "I thought I'd lost you—did they harm you? Are you hurt at all?" She held me at arm's length to look me over, and finding me okay, pulled me back in to her chest. "I'm so sorry this happened to you. I'm so, so sorry, sweet girl!" she cried.

"No, Mary Ann, I'm okay—look—I'm alright. But you! I saw them beat you!" Now it was my turn to inspect her. Her face was bruised on the left cheek and I felt murderous.

"Just bruises, just bruises, nothing serious," she assured me. I wiped my eyes with my sleeve and exhaled with relief. My thoughts turned to Rafi, but I couldn't bring myself to talk about him yet. I swallowed a sob and Mary Ann put her arm around me.

"Oh! Isaac! Thank God." Isaac had come up behind me, and Mary Ann got him in a quick embrace before Alex exploded out of the station with a shriek and tackled him. We all were crying now.

"Come on—let's go inside, it's gotten so cold out here," Mary Ann said.

In the ride from the apartment to the police station, Isaac and I had learned it was my napkin that alerted the police to our location. My kidnapping was all over the news, of course, and a young girl in a neighboring apartment building had looked out her window last night and seen my napkin. She didn't know who I was but saw the word HELP and went to grab her dad to show him. He immediately called the police, and the search and rescue operation was set in motion. They had no idea that they would also stumble upon El Padrino in their attack, and our successful rescue coupled with his capture was a positive outcome beyond hope. They said El Padrino, with his feeble body, had tried to fight the officers back using his IV stand. Unfortunately for him, he wasn't quite as strong as he believed himself to be. It was a good day for the Spanish police. At the first hint of my discovery, Mary Ann and Alex had been brought to the station in the small city of Reus, where it turned out Isaac and I had been taken. They had arrived only thirty minutes before we did.

A woman in a Policía uniform and broad smile brought us weak coffee in Styrofoam cups as we sat together in a small office at the station. We told Mary Ann what the last couple days had held for us as El Padrino's "guests." "You brilliant kids—I'm so grateful to have you back," she cried.

I couldn't hold the sobs in any longer. "I begged them to take me back to Rafi! To let me save him. I watched him dying and could do nothing!" Despair and anger flowed through me. "They killed him because of me—he had to die because of me!"

Mary Ann took my shoulders in her hands and lifted me up. "No, no, Leah. Oh, you poor girl. Rafi isn't dead!"

I whipped my head up, wide-eyed. "What? Are you sure? I saw the blood, he wasn't moving! I couldn't save him!"

Mary Ann was nodding along. "Yes, it was very serious, but there were so many witnesses that an ambulance arrived in just a couple minutes. He's still in the hospital, and he'd lost a lot of blood, but he's alive. He's alive, saved by good old modern medicine. I told him we found you—I called him right before I ran into you in the doorway. He has said nothing but 'Leah' since you were taken. Dr. Anand is with him."

"Let's go to him now, Mary Ann." I said.

Reus was an hour and a half from the hospital where Rafi lay, and it felt like the longest ninety minutes of my life. The moment the car stopped, I jumped out and ran into the hospital, the others following closely on my heels.

Alex kept shouting directions from behind. "Left here! Up these stairs! Right!" Finally, we reached his room and I busted through the door.

There was my love lying in a hospital bed surrounded by wires and Dr. Anand to the right. I ran over and fell to my knees by his bedside, covering him with kisses. He held my face in his hands and openly wept. Everyone else caught up and entered the room, and I was once again surrounded by the people I love.

Nikhedonia:
(Greek) The feeling you get when you realize you're going to succeed.
From Nike: Goddess of Victory and Hedone: Goddess of Pleasure.

CHAPTER 26

Though Rafi would not die, he still needed a lot of time to recover in the hospital. The bullet had lodged in his abdomen and required surgery to remove and repair some organ damage. I didn't leave his side that first night, getting special allowance to sleep in the room with him. My rescue had reached the news outlets, and a police presence was stationed just outside Rafi's room. The staff were all so nice, they wheeled a second bed for me and brought us food and tea. Rafi needed a lot of rest still, so we caught each other up slowly.

"I had a vision of them taking you, when I was napping on the couch. I'm so sorry I didn't get to you in time. I'm so, so sorry I couldn't stop them." His voice was heavy with sadness and guilt.

"Please don't, Rafi," I said. "You did all that you could, and we're here together now. Let's focus on that, okay?"

I saw him wince in pain and asked if he would let me heal him. He agreed, and we brought his surgeon in to make sure she believed he was ready. I remembered how Carlos' leg scar healed big and ropy because he hadn't sought stitches, and I didn't want that happening inside Rafi's body. After sitting down with the surgeon and discussing the healing process and what I thought I could do, she suggested we support his healing slowly for a few days, meaning one or two ribbons per day, so he didn't have a lot of internal scar tissue formed too quickly. The ribbons alleviated some of his pain, and he was able to sleep better. The next morning, everyone returned to Rafi's room. Mary Ann brought breakfast, and we set up a feast. I was so hungry, I thought I could eat forever and never stop.

"You wouldn't believe the response your kidnapping got, Leah," Alex said. "When I managed to get help and find Mary Ann and Rafi at the hospital, you had already been gone several hours. The hospital waiting room had a television and was playing the news. You know my Spanish is awful, and Mary Ann's is even worse," she teased, "but your name and face were there! That quickly!"

"I told the police who you were right away," Mary Ann added. "I figured this was one time to use your new celebrity status to your benefit. Then I contacted Charlotte to help us with communication on the Healer site and she posted a request for help in the forum, just in case anyone might know anything,"

Dr. Anand added, "It was by her urging that the initial groups of people took to the streets in protest, but already it was all over the news. Really the only thing on the news the last two days. Not just here either. Everywhere. Your kidnapping was internationally known almost immediately. By the next morning, even random people were gathering in support of your release, but because no one knew where you were, other than 'somewhere in Spain,', the protests just sprung up erratically all over the place," Dr. Anand added.

"It was wild," Alex chimed in. "I had to believe the same people who took you had also taken Isaac. It helped to imagine you together. But not knowing what was happening to you was driving us mad. We watched the news incessantly. There were prayer gatherings— hundreds strong in a handful of states—and at the Vatican even! The Pope held a special dedication papal audience for your safe return."

"I received personal calls—*personal*—from the president of the United States and the prime minister of Spain," Dr. Anand continued. "Not to mention Frida and Carlos, Karl Becker and Michael During from the Centre, the mayor of Chicago and, just this morning, Isabel Hargraves. They all expressed thanks and relief at your safe return." I was completely overwhelmed by the response to my kidnapping. "And the emails and posts on the forum are too numerous to count," he finished with a smile.

Ikigai:
(Japanese) One's purpose in life or reason for being.

CHAPTER 27

A week later, we were back home, gathered at the art studio. We left Spain the moment Rafi had been cleared by his surgeon, and all of us were craving familiar territory. Alex and Isaac's families were desperate to see for themselves that they were okay. Also, as details of our ordeal surfaced, we had been inundated with requests for interviews. No one was ready to relive the experience, so we put them off for as long as possible. But the time had come to face it. Just getting through the *now* had occupied the last several days, and we needed to discuss how to move forward—and if we would all be moving forward on the same path.

As the news of our epic tale unfolded, the madness surrounding us only increased. Everyone's house had a security detail. Isaac immediately began seeing a therapist to deal with the nightmares that plagued him after his attack, and Alex was by his side nonstop, terrified that he could be taken again. The same could be true for the rest of us. We were fragile with the remembrance of almost losing each other, and it made us cling tighter than usual. Even Dr. Anand, who had always coveted his alone time, barely left our sides. He confessed that Spain brought to light how much we had become his family, and he felt very protective. He even said he felt it was about time we started calling him Vihaan. I wasn't sure I could.

"So, what happens now?" Alex asked the group, and all heads swiveled in my direction. It was, in the end, my decision whether I felt I could go on as a known healer. How did I see the future of what we'd created together, and the future of all the other healers I'd met or communicated with? The kidnapping highlighted the dangers of having a gift that others covet—that others would kill to get their hands on.

"You don't have to continue, you know, Leah," Mary Ann said softly. "You've been through so much, everyone would understand if you needed to stop."

I looked around the room at these people I loved, every single one. The question of what came next had been on my mind since we'd returned home. I was ashamed to admit a big part of me wanted to walk away, move somewhere small and unknown, and live a simple life. The big part of me that was scared, that is. Scared of never being able to rest. Scared of being taken again, or of Mary Ann or any of them being hurt. Scared of running myself ragged so I was no longer myself. Scared that this might be the only thing to have for the rest of my life. I still wanted to continue college, wanted to learn about the world. When I'd sat with Rafi's surgeon in Spain, the thought that maybe I should go to medical school wafted around in my brain. Why couldn't I combine my innate healing talents with the ability to help in ways those talents can't, like with surgery? And now that the pope and the chief rabbi and other religious leaders had spoken out in favor of me, wouldn't that be huge for alleviating the tensions in the world? Dr. Anand had his grant to continue searching for healers among our prisons—I could only imagine what a positive impact his research could have for thousands of troubled souls.

Then I thought about Charlotte—and Jeorg and Magda and poor Max, and the hundreds of other healers who had come together over the last several months. I finally found a tribe of people like me, and I didn't want to lose that, did I? Now that I'd opened the eyes of the world to the extraordinary gifts that walked among them, did I want to be a part of the discussion of how the world moved forward? Yes. I needed to be here. I just desperately hoped everyone else felt the same.

"I can only speak for myself—I've dragged you all through hell and I will never not feel terrible about that. But I can't stop. I love you all so much, but I don't want to back down now. I was finally feeling like we were moving in the right direction before that asshole attacked us. I don't want to let him ruin everything we've worked for because I'm scared. And I am. I'm terrified. But when I think of what we could do, who we could help, I'm also determined. I got us into this mess, and I can't abandon ship now and leave the other healers to figure it out on their own. I could have never done it without all of you helping me, after all." Mary Ann smiled.

"Touring the Centre for Shamanic Studies last month made the idea of creating a place of our own tangible," I continued. "A place where people might be with others like themselves, and learn how to use their gifts. Why couldn't we work towards someplace like that? Where there's learning and healing and support and love for people with abilities that once seemed scary and dangerous? I mean, hell, we can change the world with a place like that, can't we?" I looked at everyone in turn and sighed. "That's how I feel about it, but you guys have to decide for yourselves what you want."

Rafi walked over and scooped me up in a giant hug. "Don't be stupid. We decided days ago that if you were game, we were game. We just didn't want you to feel pressured."

"What?" I cried, hitting his arm hard. "I've been in mental torment thinking you would all leave me after what happened! I mean, not leave me, but not want to be involved with the Healer anymore! How could you keep it from me?"

"You're the one most at risk here, Leah," Mary Ann said, her eyes glistening. "It had to be your decision to continue, not ours. So, yes, we went behind your back and made a pact that if you decided to continue, we'd still be right there with you every step of the way."

"We need each other," added Isaac. "It's going to take all of us to navigate what happens next."

"Well. I believe that's settled then," said Dr. Anand, positioning himself in the center of the room, putting his phone on speaker and dialing a number. It rang three times before the voice of Isabel Hargraves entered the room. "Hello, Dr. Anand! I've been waiting for your call!" she gushed.

"Everyone is gathered, Isabel. We're all here," he replied.

"Oh my God, I was worried beyond belief about you all! What a terrible experience, I'm so sorry it happened. But thankfully you're all safe and sound and back together now. I'm so happy!"

I looked quizzically at Dr. Anand. "Thank you so much, Isabel," I responded. "It was awful—but we are all okay. In fact, we were just sitting here discussing the future."

"Wonderful! That's exactly what I wanted to speak with you about," Isabel exclaimed. "I asked Dr. Anand to call me when you were gathered, because I have a proposal for you. A month or so ago, while you were in Germany, I believe, I called Dr. Anand hoping to connect with you, Leah. Just find out how you were holding up in the midst of all the protests. He mentioned the school in Germany you planned to tour—that you'd been thinking of starting a center yourselves. Once we hung up, I couldn't stop thinking about the idea. It would be an incredible opportunity for healers like you to be gathered together. Have each other, have a central place for a clinic where the ill could visit." She paused for effect. "I mean, without being overly dramatic, I believe the discovery of your abilities and others is going to change the world."

"We think so, too," I said. "It's what we were just talking about, actually."

"Excellent. Well, I would like to help you make it a reality. I have decided, if you accept my offer, to fund not only the building of the center, but the first five years' operating costs. You know I have plenty of money, and after you healed my friend, I have desperately wanted to repay you somehow. This is what I came up with. The healers of the world need to rise up, Leah! What do you think?" she finished.

We all stood there with our mouths agape. I looked over to Dr. Anand, but he seemed as surprised as the rest of us. The silence dragged on a little too long, and it was Isabel who spoke again next.

"I want to assure you I don't wish to control the process, that would be all your doing, though it would be an honor to be on the board if you decide to have a board. Please let me do this for you, Leah. With my heart and soul and mind, every fiber of my being, I believe it is what I'm meant to do." She spoke so earnestly, I believed her.

I broke the stunned silence. "Then it would appear we have some work to do."

THE END

Made in the USA
Monee, IL
23 April 2020